The Moon Maze Game

Tor Books by Larry Niven and Steven Barnes

The Descent of Anansi
Achilles' Choice
Saturn's Race

Dream Park
The Barsoom Project
The California Voodoo Game
The Moon Maze Game

With Jerry Pournelle

Beowulf's Children

Tor Books by Larry Niven

Destiny's Road
Ringworld's Children

Rainbow Mars
The Draco Tavern
N-Space
Playgrounds of the Mind
Scatterbrain
Stars and Gods

Tor Books by Steven Barnes

Streetlethal
The Kundalini Equation
Gorgon Child
Firedance
Blood Brothers
Iron Shadows
Charisma

The
Moon Maze Game

● ● ● ● ● ●

Larry Niven
and
Steven Barnes

A Tom Doherty Associates Book
New York

This is a work of fiction. All of the characters, organizations, and events portrayed in this novel are either products of the authors' imaginations or are used fictitiously.

THE MOON MAZE GAME

A Tor Book
Published by Tom Doherty Associates, LLC
175 Fifth Avenue
New York, NY 10010

www.tor-forge.com

Tor® is a registered trademark of Tom Doherty Associates, LLC.

Library of Congress Cataloging-in-Publication Data

Niven, Larry.
The moon maze game / Larry Niven and Steven Barnes.—1st ed.
    p. cm.
"A Tom Doherty Associates book."
ISBN 978-0-7653-2666-9
1. Role playing—Fiction. 2. Fantasy games—Fiction.
3. Fantasy gamers—Fiction. 4. Space colonies—Fiction. 5. Moon—Fiction.
I. Barnes, Steven, 1952–   II. Title.
PS3564.I9M66 2011
813'.54—dc22

                                                          2011013449

First Edition: August 2011

Printed in the United States of America

0 9 8 7 6 5 4 3 2 1

For the twelve who've walked there

Acknowledgments

Thanks are given to Dr. Tom McDonough, senior scientist for the Skeptic Society, and Dr. Joel Sercel of Caltech, for hours of informative conversation over an excellent lunch.

The Moon Maze Game

1

The Beehive

HEINLEIN STATION
May 12, 2085

Botanica was a medium-sized crater, recently sealed to hold an atmosphere of oxygen baked from lunar rock and nitrogen imported from Aeros asteroid. It was less than a kilometer across, and situated four klicks northwest of Heinlein station, five hundred klicks from the lunar South Pole.

Only in the last five months had the crater merited any special attention. In the beginning had come the standard exploration and mining teams, searching for He3 concentrations and fossil ice, but in the end Botanica was no more interesting than a thousand other craters of similar size, and nothing came of the initial efforts.

Its current condition would mock that first impression. The crater housed a dome now, the rock surfaces sealed, the weight of its water shield exquisitely calculated to balance the atmospheric pressure within and strength of the crust beneath.

At any given time a hundred men worked that dome, outside and inside and deep down. Lava tubes burrowed beneath Botanica, and drills had brushed pockets of fossil ice. On a day not too distant, hordes of tourists would walk and climb these modularly constructed halls and walls. Such a structure had never existed anywhere in the solar system, and despite a Luny's typically blasé seen-it-all-before attitude, the most recent modifications caused them to buzz with speculation. *What were they? What did it all mean?*

For days now, one man on the construction and painting crew had walked the hundred giant bubble-rooms that now filled the dome, spraying paint fixative along the connecting corridors. He was a tall, dark, thin fellow, with high cheekbones that cried out for tribal scars. Christened Douglas Frost, he had been born under another, more exotic name. Frost was currently three months from the end of a two-year lunar rotation.

So many times had Frost refilled his tank on his back that he'd stopped really looking at what he was lacquering. Today, for some reason, he'd begun observing more carefully, and soon his curiosity was piqued.

A political animal, during his lunar sojourn Frost had watched the Earthfeed for news of national and international power-jostling. The last six months had actually brought some of this electoral excitement to the moon, and he had watched with pleasure, enjoying the debates and friendly arguments, playing them over and over in his mind. Independence for Luna and the Belt? Or continued subservience to the national and corporate interests that had financed the original installations? They were a gaggle of privileged fools, pondering the stars while billions on Earth remained locked in eternal servitude.

Douglas Frost kept his opinions to himself. Lunar money was excellent, and his brother Thomas was the only friend he needed here. Beer-fueled political bull sessions were popular among these fools, but not for the Brothers Frost.

But something about this raised area had punched through his other thoughts, pulled at him, whispered urgently that there was something here, something elusive to the casual observer.

He was so busy staring at the frieze before him, that he never saw Hal Tessier drifting up behind him.

"So, Doug," Hal began. Even as he studied the lacquered wall, its gleaming wet sheen began to dull. Doug thought the man a pompous ass, whether debating politics or playing chess. "You're just about finished with your two-year. High marks across the board. Know McCauley over in Fabrication?"

Indeed he did. "Sure."

"Well, Toby authorized me to make you and your brother an offer to come back in a year. Interested?"

Doug hid his smile, pretending to be surprised.

Tessier was a short, forceless man with thinning brown hair and a gut that would have sagged like mud under Earth gravity. Doug wondered if his supervisor had rigged his compulsory PT points. In theory, everyone took their exercise time seriously. In reality, there was a gap between the official tally and the actual amount of healthy physical stress.

Weak muscles, brittle bones . . . some of these *makaku* were never going home.

"You know? If you'd asked me last month, I might have said no. But . . ." Doug shrugged.

"But?" Hal asked.

"It grows on you, doesn't it?"

"Sure does," Hal nodded. "I feel like I'm part of something . . . I don't know. The future? Does that make sense? This is about more than just us, you know?"

Moving down the hall, looking more carefully at the images so recently sealed, Doug was splitting his attention between Hal and a visceral sense of excitement, something that he had not experienced in far too long. Life in Heinlein base was unbelievably involving, but this new possibility was something else.

"I do," he replied.

"Look," Hal said. "There are a lot of people who'd like to come up here, but you two have the experience, the skills, and you can handle close spaces just great. What do you think?"

Doug tore his eyes away from . . . glossy creatures that looked like a cross between a merman and a centipede. Strange. Very alien. But . . . somehow familiar. Hadn't he seen this before, somewhere?

"Is the first month back as hard as they say?"

"First six weeks on Earth are murder. How are your points?"

Hal sucked his gut in as he said it, as if suddenly aware that he was asking questions he himself would prefer not to answer.

"Hundred a week minimum, straight up. Bone density's great. DPA has me at 105 percent of normal." *Dual Photon Absorptiometry,* the standard measuring technique in medical. "Upper body strength 10 percent greater than when I left New York, lower body about 2 percent greater. Top two percentile on all counts."

Hal blinked, impressed. "Watch your joints, though. Listen. When you make a decision, let me know, and we'll put you on the schedule."

Hal walked away. Despite his ample gut, he moved with a sort of springy bounce-step virtually impossible to train out of the Earth-born.

Doug chuckled, dropped his safety mask back into place, and continued spraying. He'd worked on several different aspects of this new construction job. This included working with prefab structures dropped from orbit, and extruding lunar aluminum there at the surface. All had had their challenges and rewards.

None was even remotely as rewarding as this new, incredible possibility.

After his shift, Doug spent an hour researching his suspicions. Then Doug took the Heinlein tram, closed his eyes and leaned back against the seat as it zipped to the main crater under its reflective awning. Eighteen months ago, he and Thomas had actually welded panels in the cooling tunnel. Trapped in eternal lunar night, the rails easily maintained the frigid temperatures required for superconductivity.

During the four-minute ride, he thought about the Beehive. Some wag had christened the dome "Beehive" after they'd started honeycombing it with Liquid Wall bubbles. They'd had no clue of its eventual usage. Then, when Cowles Industries applied for special tourist licenses, sponsored a major expansion of the guest lodging facilities, and implemented special-purpose construction similar to buildings already standing on a few very special locations on Earth . . .

Cowles Industries. Tourism. Modular construction, similar to that used at a certain California tourist attraction.

Rumors leaked out. Immediately, Cowles stock rose by 17 percent.

Doug was so deep in his thoughts that he barely noticed his car sighing to a halt. The pressure seals hissed as the doors opened, and Doug was in one of the connecting nodes spaced around Heinlein's rim. From here, he could take a tram about the rim, or simply Moonwalk. He Moonwalked, bouncing through the springy, athletic strides that challenged balance and got the heart pumping.

A rover teleoperator named Willis Chan cycled up next to him, puffing as he pedaled with arms and legs. "Dougie!" he cawed. "We need a fourth for squash. Up for a few backflips?"

Normally, the idea of an hour or two of pinwheeling athleticism appealed to Doug. His body was flexible and enduring, with a hunter's coiled strength. He enjoyed taking Willis' money. Not today. He could barely wrench his focus away from his private thoughts to make time for a polite answer. "Thank you, but no thank you. Job things."

Willis nodded and wove off, huffing through the traffic, working the arm and leg pedals of his bike until sweat-blossoms darkened his armpits. Then he was gone around the rim's gentle curve.

Workers lived in a variety of housing, some on the surface, some far beneath the regolith. Many craters were linked by subterranean shuttles. Give Heinlein another ten years and the dome would sit atop a thriving underground city.

But all the living spaces were resistant to the basic lunar problems: seismic instability, solar radiation, thermal fluctuation, and meteoroids.

Doug rode the elevator down and then Moonwalked the next stretch, bouncing through the halls on the balls of his feet. Excitement bubbled up inside him like jolly lava.

The door marked *Suite Five* slid open. Doug stepped into an antechamber just wide enough for three people to stand abreast.

The door slid closed behind him. The inner door opened, and suddenly the air swirled with fecal dust and animal stench. Doug kerchewed! and swung his hand as a feathery football-sized projectile sailed toward his face. The Rhode Island Red flapped its coppery wings and looped through the air with an aplomb beyond Earthly poultry's wildest dreams.

Suite Five was one of Heinlein's seven farms. Dozens of dedicated farming pods were scattered across the lunar grid, but most large craters also had their own, smaller facilities, where residents could fatten their own meals in advance, like restaurant patrons selecting lobsters from the tank.

Rabbits bounced around like little helicopters, every furry leap a world record. Hornless goats grazed on hybrid lunar grass, hydroponically grown and bundled as hay. Their meat was a treasured delicacy, far more tender than their Earth-grown cousins.

All seemed supremely unaware of their cook-pot destinies. Even though raised from embryos here at Heinlein, they seemed to relish their lunar agility, as if consciously rebelling against genetic limits.

Fist-sized bots whisked chicken and rabbit droppings from the glossy floor.

Doug reared back as a dark red Buckeye flapped its wings clumsily, spiraling directly toward his chest as if it couldn't control its flight path. He had frozen in place when a slender pair of pale arms yanked the bird out of the air. A smiling, densely freckled woman with shaggy blond hair stuffed the squawking poultry under her right arm.

"Getting slow, Dougie? Looking for Thomas?"

He didn't recognize her, and glanced at her breast pocket. A very nice swelling there, beneath the name *LINDA*. "I'm sure you know Tommy?"

"Better all the time," she winked, and jerked a thumb upward. "Up top."

Doug looked up. A scaffold stretched across the domed ceiling, holding three workers. Sparks spiraled down, singeing the occasional high-flying chicken. Doug thanked the tech, selected the nearest ladder and began to climb.

He had reached the scaffold, and was heading across when the man closest to him killed his torch, turned, and slipped off his mask. The man could easily have been mistaken for a Senegalese or Jamaican, with the same lean cheeks, bright, inquisitive eyes and close-cropped tightly-curled hair that Doug saw in every mirror.

"Dougie," Thomas said. "What's up?"

"Take a dinner break," Doug said, maintaining a tight, neutral smile. "I'll make it worth your time."

I'll make it worth your time. Code words since childhood. Never misused, never ignored. Thomas raised his eyebrows, but nodded and turned to the other men. "I'm clocking out. See you tomorrow."

They waved at him. All work hours and progress went into central processing. No slacker could hide in a community as small and regimented as Heinlein.

Thomas cooled his torch, doffed his hat, and the two slid down the ladder past the deliriously spiraling chickens. His heel squished in goat droppings. A whiskbot arrived the next instant, and Thomas held up his foot, so that its little vacuum could suck him clean while Doug tried not to let his smile bloom into open laughter.

Doug refused to talk as they bounced around the hub to the cafeteria nearest their sleep quarters, although twice Thomas attempted to initiate questions. Thomas was five minutes the younger of the two, but Doug often acted as if they were years apart.

So. "Big" brother had a secret, one capable of generating a bit of suspense. Well, Thomas enjoyed games as much as anyone. . . .

The cafeteria's hologram ceiling and walls were tuned to a Polynesian channel, something pleasing to their General Manager's sensibilities. All about them blue skies framed tropical palms, blindingly white beach and crashing waves. Workers generally ate here, enjoying the happy cacophony, or carried their food off to their private quarters. The twins ordered tai fish and fresh hydroponic fruit (Thomas chose mango, while Doug selected a mixed salad) and walked it around to the worker quarters.

The hall door sealed behind them. Six doors down, the scanner read their eyes and biochips, and opened the door.

The cabin was narrow, spare, with two beds (nets with elastic sheets stretched over them) and a toilet and sink. Metered bathing facilities were just down the hall. They were too far below the surface for windows, but a vid wall would display any vista in the library. The current shimmering design was New York's crowded, Christmas-parade skyline.

Thomas watched patiently as Doug sat on the bunk opposite, opened his container of food with meticulous, almost mechanical precision, and ate the first three sporkfuls in silence. He closed his eyes as if gathering thoughts, and then spoke.

"When was the last time you worked on Botanica?"

Thomas squinted, counting backward. "Maybe a month ago, blowing bubbles." "Bubbles" were the pressurized globes blown from tanks labeled *Liquid Walls*. A hundred bubbles in varying sizes, arrayed in nine rows, A through I. Once dried, the plastic spheres made perfect foundations for storage, work, and living spaces. Some were the size of a broom closet, others the size of auditoriums. "Why?"

"Because the furnishings are starting to go in." Doug began to enumerate the things that had most recently come to his attention.

Thomas listened, searching for the punch line. *Yes, yes,* he thought impatiently. Doug passed Thomas a flexible viewer the size of his hand. Thomas flipped through page after page of friezes featuring vast swollen grub-like creatures, insectoid herdsmen and odd aquatic creatures with many legs.

"I don't understand," Thomas said. "What's this about?"

"Now look at this article from a gossipmonger in our capital," Doug said. He touched the screen, and the image of a thin young black man in a Japanese samurai robe, standing at a podium appeared. In Central African Kikongo, the caption read: "The Prince Takes a Bow." It dealt with rumor that the only son of the President of the Republic of Kikaya was, to the mortification of his father, a web-strip superhero artist. He had won a first-place finish for drawings of his *Swahili Samurai,* a webzine with thousands of fans.

Thomas' brow wrinkled. Doug could almost read his mind: *Disgraceful, of course, but . . . ?*

Before he could speak, Doug went on. "Our Prince, the future of our country, is obsessed with this mindless trash. He does this. He also attends 'science fiction' meetings for which he flies to America and appears under a false name, cloaked in asinine costumes. Few have any idea that the artist known as 'Ali' is our Prince. Now, look at this creature." He called up the webzine, and the month's adventure appeared. He did a quick search, and pulled up an image of a creature with the upper body of a man, and the lower body of a centipede.

It was identical to the image on the wall.

"So . . . ? The artist for the Beehive is a fan of our Prince's work. Perhaps we should be proud." The last word was laden with irony.

"*Think,*" his brother whispered. "We know that the Beehive is built by Cowles, and what bastard has money in that company? Whose son wastes our nation's wealth on such indulgences, games in which he pretends to be a wizard or warrior or monster?" No names were needed. "The Bastard" meant only one man, one powerful, dangerous man. "We know that in just months, Botanica is set to open. Think about it. With an image from our Prince's work woven into the story? I researched. And the player list has been published. And there is an 'Ali Shannar' listed as a player. Nationality? Republic of Kikaya.

"Then . . . let us say that this live role-playing game everyone's talking about has been tampered with. Say that it is filled with imagery that the Prince has created.

"Say that the guest list is classified. Say that our sources in the republic can verify that the Prince is on the move . . . or even that I am right, and that he is planning to make the trip. Planning to take part in this foolishness. Coming here, to the Moon. To *us*. Think about it."

Thomas cocked his head to the side. Doug was laying out the bones of a situation without fully making the argument. But where was he going?

Doug leaned forward. "For years we've dreamed of driving

the dogs from the palace, taking back our country. *We could go home!* The Prince was one of only three things we ever believed might pry the Bastard from his throne. My brother . . . if I am wrong and I am merely fantasizing, I hope you will forgive me. But if I am right . . ."

Thomas reared back, the implications suddenly hitting him like the full strength of the unfiltered lunar sun. Doug had hesitated to speak directly, had danced around rather than speak his mind. Now it was out of the bag. Could a thing so nearly unspeakable be possible at all? Were the logistics feasible? The funding? Theoretically, they had access to adequate resources . . . but talk had always been a cheap commodity. Would their Earthbound, cocktail-party radical friends actually come through? Would they dare even try?

And they had another resource, someone right here on Luna, who owed them a debt best repaid from the shadow.

Dared they even try?

Gaming. Cowles Industries. Webzine monsters. Yes, yes, yes. The more he thought about it, the more the whole thing smelled of the Captain, the royal Bastard's only son, another indulgent adventure to drain the republic's coffers.

There was a problem with raising a question, one that became clearer as the night went on. Some questions, once asked, could not be ignored.

If Doug's suspicions were true, and the twins acted boldly, and their radical friends were patriots with deep pockets, then a great deal of good might be accomplished by bold and determined men.

In truth, if the operation could actually be mounted, what in the world was there to stop them . . . ?

2

Cocoa Angel

GENEVA, SWITZERLAND
June 22, 2085

For five hundred years, the world's finest timepieces had been designed and assembled in Geneva, Switzerland. After centuries of conservative tradition, the twenty-first century saw a flowering of mechanical engineering and micro-electronics, as well as telecommunications, information technology and artificial intelligence.

Geneva had become Europe's Silicon Valley, with all the money, power and glamour that that implied. According to *Zagat,* four of the world's top one hundred hotels were located in this one ancient city, and the very best of these was the Geneva Arms.

Tonight, the Arms swarmed with luminaries and paparazzi, the streets lined with fans hoping to glimpse the wealthy and famous at play. The street and sky were crammed with traffic. Lightly drifting snowflakes dusted the street, lending the cobblestones an almost ethereal elegance.

Scotty Griffin stood near the doorway, eyes on the crowd. "Station One, Starburst is leaving the ballroom. Do you have visual?"

From his observation position two hundred feet away, Scotty's partner Foley Mason answered. *"Affirmative, Moonman. All clear."*

Moonman. If he hadn't been on duty, Scotty would have either laughed or winced. He could hear his father's voice in his head: *You're there for the client, Scotty. Stay focused on the job . . .*

"Entering limo," he said, and cleared the way for his primary, a seventeen-year-old Belgian chocolate heiress. Her snow-white hair and pouting ruby lips had graced a thousand magazine covers, especially those adhering to the Fit/Fat standard of beauty currently in vogue. Her body had the kind of effortlessly sensual plumpness that no teenager could appreciate, and any woman— and most men—over forty would die for. Adriana "Cocoa Angel" Vokker.

The girl favored the videographers with a slow-motion wave, a practiced regal gesture. She flipped her blond hair back and thrust out one ample hip, canted that beautiful rounded jaw into an angle no tabloid could resist, and smiled. It seemed to Scotty that she spread that charm equally thick across the entire crowd . . . but seemed to linger on a rather severe, powerfully built blond man, who smiled and nodded in return. Scotty turned slightly toward him, the video feed on his sunglasses automatically recording the man's image.

Scotty remembered the blond man: The big fellow had danced with Adriana twice during the evening's ball, and there had been much merry whispering between them.

Might be nothing at all. At seventeen, she was of legal age in either Belgium or Switzerland, and technically able to make her own decisions, but her father—who was paying the bills—seemed to have a tight grip.

The limo door closed, and it lifted from the ground and into traffic.

Adriana Vokker sighed massively and tossed her head. "That was . . . boring," she said, in deeply accented English.

Scotty smiled without laughing. He rarely laughed in front of clients. "Boring? You never sat out a dance, miss. I wouldn't have thought you were bored."

She closed her eyes and leaned back against the seat. The night skyline glittered outside the car as they melded into the traffic flow, heading back to the hotel. "Scotty," she said, as if speaking to a child. "It's all image. Sparkle, sparkle, sparkle. Believe me, it wearies." English was her third language, but while thickly accented, her speech was skilled. Some emotional undercurrent in her voice caught his attention, then vanished before he could decipher it. Ah well. It wasn't really his job to read the little minx's mind, just to keep her safe.

"I'm turning in early tonight," she said, face still turned away.

"Your call, Miss Vokker." He clicked his tongue against his back teeth, switching on his necklace mike. "Station One, Starburst is returning to roost. Let's make it an early night."

At the moment, there was nothing more to say. Their human chauffeur was for window-dressing and emergencies: All aircars rode the city grid. Still, the man went about his job's minimal obligations soberly, scanning the instrument panel as if he might have to take control at any moment. Good man.

Well, so far nothing out of the ordinary. So, then . . . the day after tomorrow Adriana would return home, and Scotty's assignment would be over.

The snow-sprinkled streets sped by beneath him, and as long as Scotty refused to look up at the naked stars overhead, he was just fine.

Some things change with dizzying rapidity, but certain aspects of the security trade had not changed in centuries. Clients often rested in high-end public hotels, but the average guests never saw celebrity guests coming or going. For men in Griffin's peculiar profession there would always be staff to vet and guests to watch. There were always back doors, side entrances, underground garages and guest rooms to sweep.

The man meeting them at the private roof pad was Foley Mason, a former Dream Park employee who had worked with Scotty's dad, Alex, before the old man retired, and now took gigs primarily to keep the rust off. He had served with distinction in the Second Canadian war, and was twenty years older than Scotty.

Foley had grown a little soft around the middle, but still had the eyes, the ears, the instinct for the work. He preferred to stay back from the action, coordinating and integrating.

"Everything tight?"

"Airtight," Foley said. "Pretty much a milk run."

Adriana seemed a bit distant. Scotty was curious about the little chatterbox's uncharacteristic silence, but kept his questions to himself. It was none of his business what the girl was thinking. Men? Fashions? Money? Traveling home? He knew little and cared less.

They rode the tube down, and Scotty remained in the hall as Foley swept the suite. When he returned, nodding, Adriana sashayed in, damned near curtsyed to them, and closed the door.

Scotty shrugged. He glanced at his wristwatch. Swiss, of course. It read 1:15 A.M. "That's it, I guess. She'll call if there's anything."

"Slipped a tracer in her hair," Foley said casually. "Nape of the neck."

Scotty raised an eyebrow. Adriana had refused to carry one. When had Foley pulled off this minor miracle?

As if reading Scotty's mind, Foley said, "In the tube. Listen, youngster: You're ultimately responsible to your calling. Not to the father. Not even the daughter. You have to do what *works*, not necessarily what's popular."

"No wonder Dad fired you."

"The Griffin canned me so we could ferret out the son of a bitch selling the Liquid Walls formula, and you damned well know it."

They chuckled, shook hands, and headed to their own rooms: one on either side of Adriana's. Silk sheets and gold-plated toilets. The very definition of a good gig.

Scotty stripped down, doffing shirt and pants, examining his naked body in the full-length mirror. He had broad shoulders, a compact waist and thick upper arms, and while "fit" he didn't feel *animal*. He'd need to hit the Flow class when he got back to L.A. Nothing like twisting and torquing, tensing and relaxing your body to neural feedback–generated music cues.

Had he changed much since coming back from Luna? Emotionally, perhaps. After his near-fatal accident the once-pleasurable lunar experience had become clammy and claustrophobic. He suffered weeks of night sweats, waking up unable to breathe or move until his eyes focused. Kendra might have been the love of his life, but living like that was no life at all. There was no question of her leaving, no chance of him staying.

It wasn't until coasting home on that long, long loop to Earth that he fully understood what he had done to himself.

But Mom and Dad had been great. Without missing a beat, Alex Griffin had networked a dozen old security contacts and found Scotty work. As soon as Scotty had rested and rehabbed, gotten his leg and core strength up to snuff and managed to survive a decent judo *randori* (about four months of sweaty work), he was ready for duty.

He brushed his teeth, trying to focus his mind. Something niggled at him, and he couldn't find it. And that *something* still chewed away like a muskrat in a trap as he slipped into bed, and wound his weary way toward dream.

An alphanumeric 1:58 A.M. flickered on the ceiling as Scotty rolled over and opened his eyes. The security alarm had beeped, and within two seconds of opening his eyes, he was sitting up, the fretful dreams evaporating like frost on a spring morning.

The motion detector bleeped plaintively. "What the hell . . . ?" he muttered, and rolled out of bed. Before his feet hit the ground, the beeping stopped.

And that worried him most of all.

Scotty was half dressed and at the connecting door in five seconds. He pressed his ear against the cool wood paneling. Nothing, no sound. If anyone was moving, it was on little cat feet.

Stunner in hand he tapped on the door. Nothing. He clucked, activating the throat link. "Exeter hotel, main switchboard. Suite 1108, please."

A brief pause, followed by a ringing tone. He heard nothing, but that was hardly surprising: Adriana probably had the com switched to light or vibration. Of course, that was his more optimistic self speaking. The grim truth was that he heard nothing at all.

Heart hammering, he punched the override on the keypad. The biopad read the nine-digit sequence, his fingerprints and capillary patterns. The door opened.

Scotty slid in, stunner at the ready.

The suite was old luxury, fading colors and softly rounded furniture, more her daddy's style than Adriana's.

The bedroom and bathroom were empty. No one in the spacious dining or living rooms. The drapes opened onto a panoramic view of nighttime Geneva's spiraled skyline.

The Cocoa Angel was gone.

He raised his cuff link. "Wakey wakey. We have a shit-storm."

"Here, Scotty," Mason said.

"Adriana's gone."

"What the hell?"

"My very thought. Get the manager. We have to sweep the hotel . . ."

He spotted something on the glass table in front of the window: A black speck the size of a pinhead. Had it fallen onto the rug, he might never have seen it at all.

A knock at the door, and then Mason was across the threshold, tucking in his shirt and sealing his pants. "How could she . . . ?" He saw what Scotty was holding up to the light. "Is that . . . ?"

He nodded. "Apparently, she took it off, and crushed it. That implies that she was pissed. Wanted us to know we couldn't stop her. Probably a nasty little message to Daddy."

So Adriana had spaced her tracer, and disappeared from her suite. Scotty remembered the blond man in the crowd, and the secretive look he and Adriana had exchanged. An assignation? That fit the little twerp, and god*damn* him for not being more suspicious of her early-to-bed nonsense.

Security had swept the Exeter hotel door to door, awakening enraged clients, a few of whom were almost as influential as Adriana's father. Thermal body counts suggested that she was no longer in the building. Suite 1108 was belly-to-butt with managers and bellhops and, just now, arriving police.

Scotty saw the Federal Security men in the corner of his eye, and postponed an inevitable and unpleasant conversation for a few more moments. "She *what?*" he asked the aging bellhop.

"Sir, the lady asked me not to see her, and tipped well for the blindness. I couldn't, I mean really *couldn't* go against a guest's direct request, unless, well . . ."

Scotty steadied his breathing in an attempt to keep himself from ramming the man's head through the nearest wall. "All right," he said, and turned toward the approaching Swiss security man.

The short, rounded man extended a broad flat hand, but the shake lacked warmth or enthusiasm. "Inspector Gemmon, Federal Office of Police."

"We spoke on the issue of concealed weaponry," Scotty said.

The Inspector ignored the attempted pleasantry. "Ordinarily," he said, "the FOP is responsible for the safety and security of visiting dignitaries. And, if I might say, if we had been in charge from the beginning, the young lady would in all likelihood still be asleep in her room."

Scotty ignored the heat building beneath his collar. The Inspector's carefully worded rebuke would not be the worst thing he heard today. All that mattered now was Adriana's safe recovery.

A harried-looking Germanic blonde entered the room. The Exeter hotel's night manager. "Sir!" she said. "We have *this*!" She held up a slip of paper. For a moment she seemed uncertain whom to hand it to, then decided upon the Inspector.

There it was. Just that swiftly, Scotty and Mason had become nonpersons. Even worse, they were embarrassments.

The Inspector read it to himself. With childish satisfaction, Scotty noted that his lips were moving. "It is a note . . . ," the Inspector said. "Where did you find it?"

"It was delivered to the front desk just minutes ago by courier."

The Inspector read aloud: "*'We have the girl. Do not try to find her, or heaven gains another Angel. We will communicate our demands within ten hours.'*"

The Inspector turned to Scotty, radiating contempt. "Have you anything to add?"

"That's a stall," he said. "They don't need ten hours to communicate their demands. They need that time to move the girl to a more secure location."

Inspector Gemmon regarded him pleasantly, rather as if he were a myna bird that might, if prompted, say something quotable but ultimately mindless.

"There was a man," Scotty continued. "Long blond hair, athletic. Flat hard face. Adriana seemed to be sharing secrets with him. It's possible that there was an assignation that turned into a kidnap. I have images of this man."

The Inspector nodded, unimpressed. "We will take those images. After debriefing," he said, "I believe your services will no longer be required."

Without another word, Gemmon turned to his men, speaking in rapid-fire Italian. Then he left, leaving behind two men who immediately began scanning the room.

"So," Scotty said quietly to Mason. "What was he saying?"

Mason laughed bitterly. "All employees to be debriefed, and concentrate efforts on air traffic around the hotel. And that the two Americans no longer have authority of any kind."

Lovely.

Debriefing had taken a half hour, at the hands of a junior inspector who seemed focused and intelligent, if abrupt and somewhat condescending. By the time the clock read 3:30 A.M., they were back in Scotty's room. Mason poured himself a bourbon. Scotty would have joined him, but knew his limitations. Mason could stop at the one drink, regardless of the stress. And right now, if Scotty started drinking, he was afraid he'd drown.

Scotty lowered his head into his hands, thinking hard, trying to sink past the shock and personal insult, to the place that was calm enough to crunch data.

Mason laid a sympathetic hand on Scotty's shoulder, perhaps mistaking his younger friend's posture for one of depression. "Scott . . . everyone makes mistakes. The trick is bouncing back from them. Your dad would expect you to bounce high."

Scotty looked up at him, eyes clear, even if his heart was

thumping too loud. "So . . . what is it that we're thinking right now? Some golden-haired playboy flirts with her, and lures the silly twit into a kidnap? The ten-hour stall is to make time to slip her out of Switzerland to someplace without an extradition treaty."

"Let's say that's right."

"Everything's happening too quickly," Scotty whispered. "We have a diplomatic snarl . . . confusion of jurisdictions. You'd better believe the Belgian ambassador's linked in, and Daddy is having a coronary. Shit." He shook his head. Behind his words lurked a wellspring of bitter self-recrimination. *If the baby climbs out the window, it isn't the baby's fault.*

So they could trust the FOP to cover the fast-moving escape route. The only useful thing for him to do was to think in exactly the *opposite* fashion, to look at what the Swiss might be missing. There was a notion there, but when he tried to lay hold of it, all traces vanished into mental darkness.

And then he had it.

"I don't buy this crap." He called up the desktop visual display, generated a simple map, and used his finger to trace a line in the floating web. "Look at the route: aircar to private airport, some suborbital hop to a country with no extradition. Hefty ransom, ten-day wonder. Over and done."

Mason shook his head in disgust, then cocked his head. "You don't think so?"

"No," Scotty said. "Look. Air traffic is faster and more convenient, but it's also more tightly monitored. Lot more satellite power looking over your shoulder."

"And your conclusion? Is she still in the hotel?"

"I think that the FOP is searching all the usual channels. Why duplicate that effort? If she's here, they have the manpower to find her. We don't. More useful for us to assume that she's not in the hotel . . . but wasn't spirited off in an aircar either. Get me all of the imagery for the hotel between eleven and one."

A glowing translucent communications field appeared at Mason's chest level. Mason poked at it with his forefinger. A web of tiny laser lines blossomed, linking data points like constellations. In a hundred seconds Mason had accessed a sky-eye view, focusing and adjusting until Scotty was peering down at the Exeter hotel's roof and surrounding block. Then he ran it backward four hours: cars flew and rolled up to the hotel, vans and limos pulled away, and foot traffic streamed in and out of the front doors.

Scotty's eyes narrowed. "What's that?" he asked, poking a finger into the shimmering web. A blocky truck, larger than a limo or passenger vehicle.

"A garbage van?"

"At one in the morning? Do you know what the usual pickup time might be?"

"On it," Mason said, and pulled away to speak quietly into his communicator.

Scotty gazed at the grid, dreaming.

When Mason returned to him, his round face was grave. "The usual pickup is a garbage chute leading down to a disposal tunnel. The garbage van services other, smaller hotels, and occasionally drops by for an emergency pickup."

"So . . . who called the emergency?"

"We don't know. It could have been one of a dozen people. So far, nothing. They'll get back to me."

"Now, look," Scotty said. "Whatever happens, we're taking the heat. I say that we jump on this. Tap into the EU security satellite, backtrack and lock on to the garbage truck. Let's see where it went."

Mason wagged his head sorrowfully. "We can't tap into it. We've lost our courtesy pass."

Damn. "I doubt we can get her father to help us . . . so let's ask another question: What's the route? Where's the terminal, or wherever the truck goes? That might do it."

Mason rolled his eyes up toward the ceiling. "But even if they didn't diverge from their route . . . they might have stopped two dozen times. She could be anywhere."

"Let's feel optimistic. Let's take the answer with the fewest moving parts. So . . . they need a garbage truck. That's available at their central motor pool. Contacts there could provide a

vehicle and a safe hiding space, as opposed to hijacking a truck—
any police reports of vehicle theft?"

A minute of searching dispatches on the Web. "None that I
can find."

"And then dropping her off at another secure location before
finishing the route . . ."

"Or just coordinating with a ground or aircar . . ." Scotty could
see that Mason was getting a headache. Couldn't blame him.
"I don't know. It's pretty thin."

Mason shrugged. "Had my drink. Got nothing better to do.
Let's go do something stupid."

3

Skeleton Crew

They had arrived from the east, slipping over the horizon before dawn brushed the darkness from the eastern sky.

For twenty minutes, Scotty Griffin and Foley Mason had camped on a grassy picnic area a thousand meters from the outer fence of the Cheneviers waste treatment plant. While Scotty studied the T-shaped building with binoculars, Mason fiddled and fussed over his briefcase-sized deep-scan equipment. The hundreds of windows on the broad head were mostly darkened, the parking lot with its rows of charging posts only one-tenth filled.

Scotty and Mason didn't have extensive apparatus. They'd have preferred police-level hardware, or, better, military quality. But all they had was the standard kit Scotty carried on any job, anywhere in the world: first aid, communications and tracking gear, scanning equipment.

"Standard waste treatment plant. Early-morning staff. Skeleton staff."

"So?"

Mason rolled over onto his back on the grass, staring up at the dark, early-morning sky. "If you have a tiny crew of bad guys, and can get 'em all scheduled for the same graveyard shift, you could lock down a place like this, yeah."

Scotty nodded. "Hear anything?"

Mason had switched from thermal to optical zoom, and had triggered the voice scan software. He was using a sample of Adriana's voice to search for a match.

His partner was so fully engaged that for a moment Scotty thought he hadn't heard. Then Mason answered him. "Not yet . . . but it doesn't mean she's not there."

"Doesn't mean she is, either. I'm going in."

"Figured you would, kid. I'll keep scanning."

Scotty donned a black knit thermal isolation suit, goggles and a throat mike.

"Wish you had a real piece," Mason said, as Scotty checked his stun gun.

"Makes two of us." Twenty-eight bee-sized capacitor darts loaded into a pistol grip with a five-inch barrel. He hadn't tested the unit on a real, live bad guy, but the specs said it kicked like a mule. "That said, if they're innocent, I'm not expecting much security. Who breaks into a garbage plant?"

"Scavengers. The Sewage Diet. Ten billion sewer rats can't be wrong. That's if they're innocent. What if they've got her?"

"Well, I'll just have to be clever, won't I?"

"I wasn't aware miracles were an option . . . Wait! I think I have something."

Scotty hunched down. "Where?"

Mason pointed. "Northwest corner. Three thermal images. One seated. I think I caught something a second ago. *'Est-ce que je peux aller à la salle de bains?'*"

"That I recognize. 'May I go to the bathroom.' Adriana's voice?"

"Fifty-two percent certainty. Woman, under twenty-five. That's all I'm sure of. It's a chance."

"I hope so." He sniffed the predawn air. "Hope so. This place smells like armpits."

Scotty headed for the building's rear, circling to avoid pools of yellowish light. If this was a wild-goose chase, he prayed that the Swiss security forces were as hot as their reputation, would find and secure Adriana on their own. If she was here . . . well, he had an equally urgent prayer that he could pull this off. Adriana was arrogant, petulant, willful and no doubt partially responsible for her current plight, but she was a child, for God's sake. Even more importantly, under these circumstances she was *his* child, his baby. *His* client, and that made the Cocoa Angel his very personal problem.

Slipping into the building was less trouble than he'd thought. At the base of the T's upright, far to the rear, stood the dome-shaped incinerator and microwave dish array. From time to time the dome's doors slid wide, and the glare was as bright as the desert sun. The wind shifted, wafted gusts like the breath of an aged wino. The two men supervising the burnings turned their heads away whenever the incinerator mouth opened.

It was right after one of those moments, knowing that they would turn back toward the incinerator, that Scotty slipped behind them into the slender main building.

Quiet within.

No gun-toting thugs, no excessive, guilty security presence. The cavernous interior was four stories high and lined with offices, the concrete-floored interior filled with red and green barrels and automated forklifts. The conveyer belt ran outside the building. Six squidlike steel tentacles descended from the ceiling, snatched up red thousand-liter barrels and carried them to the conveyer belt. Stacks of green barrels were stenciled with a bright silver recycling emblem, and were evidently to be processed in some other fashion.

Scotty spotted a first-floor doorway reading *Stanza di Preparazione* and slipped in. *Dressing room.* He dove behind a locker as two employees exited. His brow wrinkled as he heard their voices.

"*Kiam are oni coming?*" the first one said.

"*Baldaux.*" The second man replied, as they passed Scotty's hiding place.

Scotty wanted to slap himself on the side of the head. "Did you hear that?" he whispered. "What the hell language is that?"

"*Damned if I know,*" Mason said in his ear. "*Pigeon Italian or something. Are you ready?*"

"Talk me through it."

Relaxed and unsuspecting, the two men opened the door. "*Did vi auxdi la oni cxirkaux la farmer's daughter?*"

Scotty felt like he was in some kind of odd dream, fought to keep his focus from wavering as he rifled a locker, finding a set of gray overalls. As he climbed into them he clicked his throat. "Farmer's daughter?"

"*Keep your mind on the job!*" Mason barked. "*There should be stairs to your left. I'm merging your tracker with my blueprints and the thermal map. It's pretty fast and dirty, but I see you . . . and maybe her, too.*" Scotty eased out of the dressing room into the main hall. "*Duck back, someone coming.*"

"Got it."

He leaned back into shadow.

"*Virino estas a iom bitch . . . ,*" the taller one said as they disappeared back into the hall.

"What the hell are they saying?"

"*Stay on point, kid. Go now.*"

He exited, and scurried up the stairs. "I'm here," he said as he reached the first landing.

"*I see you. Two in the room. One seated.*"

"Hold on," Scotty said, and pressed his ear to the first door. This wasn't low-tech. This was *naked,* and he felt ridiculous.

"Your transport is coming. You will be in a more secure and comfortable location by *tagmezo.*" A woman's voice.

"What?" a second woman. His heartbeat raced. That was Adriana.

"I am sorry. Noon."

Adriana made a chuffing sound. Fear? Laughter? He couldn't tell. "Must you speak that mongrel nonsense?" Even through the door, Scotty could hear the fear mingled with Ms. Vokker's imperious tones.

Now it was the other woman's turn to muffle emotion. "I wouldn't expect a Corporatist brat like you to understand."

He had no idea what all of this raving might be about. What

he did know was that the floor was clear, and that this might be his only chance. "I'm going in."

Carefully, he tested the doorknob, then flung the door open. Flashshot appreciation: bare office, standard desk, two file cabinets. Adriana sat cuffed to her chair, looking very small despite her brave words.

Then the other woman.

Blond hair. A square jaw, so strong that for a moment he thought he was dealing with a man. Broad shoulders and eyes that were bright, alive, taking him in in an instant and reacting with eye-baffling speed. Her hand blurred, heading for her waist. Scotty fired just as she was bringing a black automatic level with his chest. The dart hit directly over her breastbone. Instantly the blond's arms and legs exploded out, as if she were an epileptic starfish. Her teeth clicked together hard enough to crack enamel, and she collapsed.

Whoa! Nonlethal or not, that looked nasty as hell. Blondie would be dreaming for an hour, and probably wake up with a headache the size of Clavius. Scotty realized he was shaking, and knew why. That woman was deadly, at least a fifth of a second faster than him, and alert as a cobra. If his weapon hadn't already been leveled, she would have killed him. Easily.

Jesus Christ. Who *was* she?

For an instant he thought Adriana was going to cry. Then her old, confident expression returned. She squared her shoulders and said, "What kept you?" Her voice cracked on the last word. A tough kid, but still a kid.

"Had to wade through a klick of your bullshit," he said, deliberately brusque. Tenderness might trigger emotional collapse, and he hadn't time for tears. He examined the cuffs. Standard civilian-issue restraint system, and Scotty had no key. He did have a pocket torch, and within seconds had burned through the plastic links. "Let's get out of here," he said.

He dragged her out of the office and down the stairs. So far, no sign of alarm.

But almost immediately after they reached the ground floor someone above them screamed bloody murder.

"Damn!" Scotty could hear the feet, didn't need to look, or ask Mason. "I can't get you out of here yet," he said.

Now her stunned expression flattened with fear. "What are you going to do?"

"Find a place to sit tight, call in the marines. Mason?"

A voice in his ear. *"Here, kid."*

"I've got her. Get help *now*."

Adriana tugged at his arm. "What do I do until then?"

Scotty scanned the floor, looking for an exit. There was nothing save boxes, and those endless rows of red and green barrels.

And he got an idea. "Listen," he said. "Those red barrels are garbage . . . these green ones are recycling bins. I'm betting the green ones are processed during the day."

She looked so wan and desperate that the sudden flash of hope in her blue eyes almost made him laugh. She understood, thank God.

"So . . . this is the idea. You're climbing in. If anything goes wrong, get *out,* you wait until you hear the police arrive, understand?"

Before she had the chance to protest, he had Adriana stuffed halfway into a green barrel. In her current, vulnerable state, she finally looked her seventeen years. For a moment, that moment, he felt so protective of the girl that he hugged her.

She melted against him. There was nothing sexual about it. It felt as if he were sheltering a little sister from the rain. "What are you going to do?" she whispered.

"Draw fire." He cupped her cheek in his palm, then slid the top into place.

Scotty crouched down in a corner against the south wall, avoiding the pattering feet and increasing sounds of worry and anger, some of them still in that odd language. "Mason," he whispered. "Warm bodies?"

"Two, headed right for you."

"And the other side of the wall?"

"Nobody."

"Finally, a piece of good news."

He put his back to the wall and set his feet against a two-tiered row of red barrels. Pushed until he felt it give a bit. At the last moment, he realized that kicking out a lower barrel just might collapse the second row right on top of him. *Whoops!* Back wedged against the wall, feet braced against the barrels, he crab-walked up, wiggling along with his shoulders and butt providing most of the locomotion. Still concealed by the line of barrels, Scotty inhaled, tensed his leg muscles and *pushed* just as the angry voices approached his hiding place.

For a moment the barrels felt as solid as steel, then he found his leverage. They trembled, tilted and fell. He lost his place and tumbled to the ground, but landed on hands and feet as crashes and screams rang out from the floor.

Before his pursuers could organize, he had found a door and disappeared into an office cubbyhole. Would they follow? A bullet spanged into the wall over his head, answering his silent question.

"How long 'til the cavalry?"

"Ten minutes? Less?"

Scotty ran, leading his pursuers farther away from Adriana, through a warren of supply boxes. At first the pursuing footsteps were frighteningly close behind him . . . but then someone took a wrong turn, and they fell back.

He heard more shouting, another shot. A curse.

He couldn't be certain, but guessed that the kidnappers had just collided with the noncriminal element working the night shift. Scotty hoped no innocents would be killed or injured, but *something* was certainly happening out there. Feet running. A grinding sound from the conveyer belt, followed by an odd whine from the overhead tentacles. They paused, and then lashed wildly, like a nest of angry boas.

Scotty moved through the office's side door, exiting into an observation room of some kind. A glass wall separated him from the loading area.

All he had to do was wait for the cavalry, and that he could do. The deep shadows swallowed him. Scotty laid low and kept his eye on the door while the plant's employees, fair and foul, duked it out. If Adriana just stayed put, they were halfway home.

Running feet. More shots, although he saw no police yet. A muffled explosion, followed by some kind of detonation down the hall. He tried the office door: locked. He pressed his face against the glass. A tendril of smoke drifted from the direction of the T's crossbar. What exactly had he started?

Then, through the growing haze, a glimpse of something that almost stopped his heart. The overhead steel tentacles seemed to be thrashing about randomly, plucking up red and green barrels without distinction. A red barrel, a green barrel, another two reds, a green. And then . . . Adriana's barrel.

There was no mistake about it. It was her barrel, the one resting under the red *cautela* sign, that had just been plucked up. And now, it was trundling toward the conveyor belt.

"What the hell? They aren't supposed to burn those barrels!"

"What are you talking about?" Mason's voice.

"They're going to burn the recycling barrels."

"Must be old barrels."

"Idiot! Adriana is in one of them!"

"Who's the idiot? Get her the hell out!"

Scotty tried the door again. Locked. He smashed his shoulder against it twice, to no effect. The mechanism probably needed a magnetic key, but he had the next best thing. He shot the mechanism with his stunner, heard a sizzling *zap-click* as the circuits fried. He slammed the door with his shoulder again. One hell of a racket, but it flew open, and he rushed out.

Directly into an ambush. Scotty shot the man in front with a shock dart as a second jumped him from behind. He collapsed to one knee beneath the momentum, but had the presence of mind to reach back and grab a handful of hair as he did, pulling his attacker forward, face-first onto the concrete floor with a bone-splintering *crack*.

But then at least two others piled on. Scotty tried to tell them to stop, that Adriana was in danger. *Stop those barrels!* But he couldn't inhale deeply enough to speak as he was kicked and clubbed until the room spun.

His cheek was pressed against the floor, eyes turned to face the door leading to the loading area. He watched through blurry eyes as the barrel disappeared toward the conveyer belt . . . and then was gone.

Suddenly, there were no more blows. Distantly, and then more closely, he heard the *whoop-whoop-whoop* of Swiss Air Police. His attackers fled.

Scotty forced himself up, and staggered toward the unmanned conveyer belt. He watched the incinerator door slide shut. The barrels were gone.

Flashes of light. A few curls of stinking smoke.

Then nothing.

"God . . . Adriana . . ."

"Yes," she said, a soft, pensive voice suddenly beside him. "It smells terrible, doesn't it?"

He couldn't breathe. Slowly, Scotty turned around. She stood beside him, apparently unaware of his panicked thoughts.

"Wha . . . what are you . . . why aren't you in the barrel?"

She shrugged. "I cannot abide tiny spaces. I got out and hid in a storeroom. I suppose that once again I have angered you."

He stared at her in disbelief. Then relief washed through him like a cool tide. He picked her up and swung her in a circle as the Swiss police closed in, weapons at the ready, their faces relieved but professionally quizzical.

4

An Offer

Sleep-deprived, bruised and emotionally drained, Scotty stood in the middle of the Imperial suite on the eleventh floor of the Exeter hotel, the very last place in the world he wanted to be. He was in absolutely no mood to be abused by an enraged father who was relieved, but not mollified, by his daughter's rescue.

Christian Vokker was a short, stocky man, dwarfed by his three bodyguards, who encircled little Adriana like alps sheltering a hillock. The girl sat with her legs folded primly, fingers folded in her lap and face blank, the unwilling focus of the current conversation.

No, that was wrong. It wasn't a conversation. In a conversation, one person speaks and another answers. This was a monologue. Mr. Vokker had been speaking nonstop at Scotty and Mason for five minutes, and very little of it had been easy to hear.

"Yes, I am grateful," he said. Something in his tone made Scotty hope he was winding down. "And I understand that you placed your life at risk. It is only for those reasons that I simply suggest you find other employment, rather than purchasing advertising in English, Chinese and Spanish, etching your colossal ineptitude on every Web and across the sky, for all with eyes to see."

Scotty managed to smile. "Sounds grateful to me."

Vokker made a dismissive gesture, and turned his back. Adriana peered between the enormous bodyguards, face pinched. *I'm sorry . . .*, she seemed to be saying.

"Son of a bitch . . . ," Scotty muttered as they left.

Older and wiser, Mason merely shook his head.

An hour later Scotty lay alone in his room, staring up at the ceiling. He rotated the glass in his right hand, listening to the ice clink. Now was *definitely* the time for a drink. Long past time, he figured. And if he didn't stop until Wednesday, well . . .

"Well, that's two careers and a marriage down . . . ," he muttered.

Quite unexpectedly, a com field blossomed above his briefcase, on the desk across from the bed. At the edge of the field blinked a man-in-the moon icon.

"What the hell." So. Vokker wasn't done with him. Part of him wanted to roll over and sleep until dinnertime, or until they kicked him out of his room, whichever came first. Another part urged him to freshen his drink. Another wanted to hear what the chocolate king's lawyers wanted to say. "Open," he said, triggering the icon.

The face of a very dark black man appeared. Triple vertical scars on his cheeks proclaimed him African with strong tribal affiliations. A remarkably relaxed intensity suggested that he was accustomed to command.

"Welcome to my home," he said. "I am Abdul Kikaya the Second, President for Life of the Republic of Kikaya. I have a proposition I would like to present face-to-face. If you are amenable to travel, my shuttle will arrive for you at noon, your time. In exchange for traveling here, and merely hearing me out, I promise you ten thousand dollars, against a much larger possibility. Then, if you are not interested, my shuttle will take you anywhere your passport will allow. If you accept, I promise you an adventure unlike any other, one you are uniquely equipped to enjoy. Please respond, but the shuttle will be there, on the roof of your hotel, at twelve noon your time. I will await you . . . or your answer. Thank you."

Well I'll be damned, Scotty thought, and smiled as he took a sip. *One door closes, another opens.*

Maybe his career hadn't bled out quite just yet. He looked at the time again: 4:15 A.M. Just time for a good nap, and packing. And then, what the hell? Maybe a little trip.

Just maybe the trip of a lifetime.

••• **5** •••

Vegas Odds

An anemic sun hung low on the horizon, casting baleful shadows across a glittering field of bloodstained ice. The plain was littered with the honored dead, their sprawled corpses mangled into arcane siguls, redolent of valor, and skill, and death. Thousands lay split-skulled, their brains cooling and drying beneath a pale, cool sun. A few dozen of their stronger, more fortunate companions battled on, armor bent and bloodied, swords notched and gore-crusted.

From time to time the warriors paused, wiping sweaty arms against their helms, leaning on their swords like exhausted amputees on bloody crutches, gasping and glowering at their opponents before they hoisted swords and began the slaughter anew. Action swirled around an oversized human shape: Loki, writhing in the grip of a snake thrice his size.

The tableau shifted: The darkening sky bled red, then split. Clouds parted as a flock of winged wolves appeared. At first they appeared as faint specks against the pitiless clouds. Now they resolved into sharper focus.

A brassy wail drowned out the ring of metal on metal, and the moans of the wounded and dying. Combatants raised their weary eyes to the heavens, and laid down their swords, stretching their arms up as if calling to the beautiful Valkyries whose crimson or golden hair flagged out in the wind, placid faces surveying the carnage with infinite compassion and calm.

The wind seemed to shape itself into a controlled whistle. A cynical ear might have suggested that it sounded much like Wagner's "Ride of the Valkyries." Played through a kazoo.

Now even the dead rose from their places, and held their arms up to the sky. The Norse angels plucked up first one, and then another . . . and carried them off to the skies. A parade of Valkyries carried off more and more of the dead and dying. Each survivor was spirited away, along with about half of the dead. In less than two minutes, it was over.

The winged wolves wheeled and returned to the heavens. Clouds roiled as the sky closed. The remaining corpses moaned and cursed in a manner unbefitting the dead.

"Shit! I *never* get chosen—"

Lights snapped on and the frozen plain, the cold mountains and the bleak sky all disappeared, leaving behind eight frustrated people in a domed room fifty meters in diameter, just large enough for three times that number to swing padded swords without thumping one another.

Amid a chorus of disappointed curses, they unbuckled their light armor. The losers trudged off the combat stage toward the dressing rooms and showers, and, thought a thoroughly bored Wayne Gibson, probably the slot machines and gambling pits, to drown their disappointment in more disappointment.

"That's a wrap," he said to his one-woman crew. Buffy Childress applauded ritually, as if it had truly been a job well done.

Eighteen months past he would have agreed with Buffy. Two years ago he had landed this job at the Fantasy Park Escalade, a tenth-rate Dream Park rip-off a half mile off the Vegas strip. Three times daily he coordinated the Escalade's big games, the motifs generally rotated on a monthly basis. This month was The Ragnarök Experience™. Fifty minutes ago, twenty bright-eyed players had entered the arena. Judging by the body language, adrenaline and exertion had toasted them all.

The side door opened and the winners, who had been quietly asked to leave the stage—only a fool argues with a Valkyrie—emerged. One of the survivors was a woman most would have thought too skinny these days, but Wayne liked just fine. He had recognized her superior coordination and conditioning the instant she had stepped onto the platform. There was something familiar about her, but she was using an assumed gaming name, wearing a mask, and had declined to use a gaming profile. So . . . whatever happened here wouldn't affect her IFGS points (not that she could pick up many from a place like the Escalade). She was just enjoying a little anonymous slaughtering of her inferiors. Not especially admirable, but he'd done as much himself, in bad moods on bad days.

"What now?" Childress said. She had the body of a showgirl and the bored manner of a blackjack dealer on a midnight shift. Just Wayne and Buffy were needed to run the game. The Escalade's management weren't the kind to spend pinchable pennies.

"Now, we take a break, and do it all over again in two hours."

She nodded and began her standard checklist of the computer systems while Wayne stripped himself out of the control suit and his shell-shaped chair.

"Time to make an appearance," he muttered. He walked the narrow corridor to the door of the combat stage. He fixed a smile to his face and opened the door, holding his hands high.

"Welcome!" Wayne said, forcing cheer through his waxy smile. "And congratulations to those stalwarts who have survived, and been chosen to receive the Escalade medal of honor!"

The top 50 percent of the players applauded, commending themselves more than him. They were tired and battered to a pleasant soreness and not one iota more. Armor absorbed 90 percent of the impact of the padded swords. Only a hemophiliac with glass bones would sustain any real damage.

The Ragnarök Experience™ was actually a pretty sweet deal for the guests. Half of them "won" on any given game, thereby accruing points to play more sophisticated contests elsewhere. Some of them even went on to play low-level IFGS games, but he imagined most were satisfied with the illusion that they were real rootin' tootin' gamers. They would return to their mundane lives, and remember the time they strapped on armor and wailed the crap out of a Tuskegee stockbroker for fifty minutes without garnering either a coronary or a criminal record.

But he kept those thoughts to himself, smiling and nodding and bowing . . .

And noticing that one woman in the back, the one with the killer body, was clapping without letting her palms touch. Pure symbol. Her half-face mask shadowed a sardonic smile.

He completed the rest of his pitch encouraging them to come back any time, and every time, and compete for more points and prizes, and to go out and spend the rest of their vacation money at the gaming tables.

After a few weary claps, they trudged back to their changing cubicles.

But the mystery woman walked up to him and said with perfect diction, "Good to see you haven't altogether abandoned bullshit."

If she had hit him in the chest with a Mitsubishi shocksword, it couldn't have been a bigger jolt.

"Angelique," he said, struggling to find something clever to say. "Angelique Chan. As always, your consonants are remarkable. Since when do you play with the kindergarten?"

"I wanted to find out how much of your talent remains unsquandered," she said bluntly. "It's been a long time."

Was that a reference to their prior relationship, or his current level of skill? There was something lurking behind her words, and he just couldn't imagine what it was. One dark, hot spark of hope flared for a moment, and Wayne tamped it down. Hope killed.

Angelique was five foot ten, just one inch shorter than Wayne, and taller in her heels. She was dressed as Hela, the death goddess from Marvel Comics: black shadings and a spiky headdress. She was leaner than a Valkyrie, a meld of Chinese and Filipina blood that promised both sensuality and fierce intelligence, and delivered on the promise.

No good could come of those memories, and he shut them down. He said, "So . . . you've seen."

"Your subroutines?"

"Yeah. The hotel bought some standard games, but I get to tweak and then I get to operate."

"Not bad, really. You need to tighten up the automated response loops, but really I have no major complaints." She cut her eyes sideways at him. She was playing a game. Angelique was always playing a game. "Time for a bite?"

He managed a grin. "Schmoozing the customers is part of the job. The Escalade has a great buffet."

"We can do better than that," she said, twinkling at him. "Give me ten to get showered, and meet me at the eastern slots."

*"**There is** nothing like a dame, nothing in the world . . ."*
The naval-white clad waiters and menus sang in unison. The walls exploded in a riot of tropical color, the ceilings opened up into a Busby Berkeley fantasy of clockwork dancers . . . the White Way restaurant had everything, Wayne figured, with the possible exception of memorable cuisine.

But at the moment, even the finest food would have done little for his numbed tongue. Wayne sat on his side of the table, nibbling at a five-bean salad, watching Angelique wolf down a massive chef salad, wondering where she tucked it all. Her body should have filled out until she resembled one of the Fit/Fat models parading their chubby perfection in every vidzine and holo ad. He wondered faintly if his rather retro taste in slender females was just a rebellious nature prolonged beyond adolescence.

"So," she said between bites. "What do you know about me?"

"You mean since you dumped me?"

"Yes," she nodded. "Since then."

"I've followed your career," he admitted. "Hard not to. You're probably the most successful female gamer in the world. I saw that ceremony where Acacia Garcia passed the baton. She still looks pretty good, actually."

"Better in person," she said. "I'm guessing pineal transplant, but who knows?"

"Anyway, you play at the highest levels, and win more than you lose. The others are chasing you, but can't catch up. I think you're about eight thousand points above your closest competitor."

"I'm impressed," she said. "I didn't think you'd keep such close tabs."

"You're hard to forget." He'd actually researched that last bit while she was showering, but why tell her? He rolled the next question around in his head, wondering if he'd really ask it. "All right, we've established that I know what you've been up to. So what do you know about me?"

"I know you LARP around town," she said. *Live-Action Role-Playing.* "You run some games—I really wouldn't call it a Game Master role, would you?"

Those slanted green eyes dared him to contradict her. He couldn't find the moxie to do it, and finally had to grin. "It's a living."

"Not a really good one," she said. "I did a credit check. You've got markers all over town, Wayne, and some of them are in unfriendly hands. A little gambling problem?"

He winced. Anyone working for the casinos or hotels was vulnerable to credit checking, exposing patterns of . . . er . . . entertainment investment? Spontaneous analysis of cumulative distribution functions? Oh, what the hell: call it gambling. He wanted to curse at her for invading his privacy.

But reconsidered. Why would she look into his financial affairs? This was sounding less and less like idle curiosity, more and more like a serious inquiry of some kind. Angelique Chan was dangling bait there, but where was the hook? Was she testing his temper? Why did she want to know how he behaved under pressure?

You know why.

"So you've been helping bookies adjust odds on LARP action. And some of that gambling paid off. I know that two years ago you won a weeklong orbital vacation. How was that?"

As she nursed a forkful of ham and greens, there seemed something studiedly neutral, *calm,* about the way she asked that question. Calm enough to set off alarm bells.

"It was fun," he said, more mystified than ever. "I took Buffy Childress, one of my coworkers. We had the honeymoon suite. You should try it." There—another little dig. Was this a come-on? And if she was interested, would the Buffy story get under her skin a bit?

Rather than becoming upset, her lips curled in a smile. "I'm glad to hear that," she said. "My friend didn't have such a great time. Developed inner-ear problems. If he hadn't come back down he would have upchucked his belly button."

"There are drugs for that."

"Everyone has a special talent. Eddie's seems to be resisting massive doses of antiemetics. I got a little tired of breathing barf."

Two waiters warbled arias from some musical play that Wayne couldn't name.

"—land of the Free and the Brave
We caught the Second Wave
After two hundred years of sweat and toil
We told the Arabs to drink their oil—"

Hmm. Probably something about the Second Canadian War. Their voices were actually quite good. *Talent isn't enough,* he reminded himself. You need luck, too.

For a moment, he forgot himself, and his problems, and concentrated on the lovely, slender black-haired woman before him. He even began to wonder if she simply needed a friend to talk to, perhaps a broad perspective from someone who wasn't in the game anymore. Could he handle that? Could he remember that sometimes, you just gave because it was needed, not because of what you might or might not get in return?

He sighed. *All right. Let's just do this right. If this is the last time you ever see her, how do you want her to remember this conversation? That you were a good guy, in her moment of need, and agile of mind. Try that one.*

"You seem stressed," he said.

Her smile was wan. "And you're probably wondering why, and what this is all about."

"Well, you've gone to some trouble."

She put another forkful in her mouth, chewed thoughtfully, and then spoke. "Why am I stressed? I've won my way into the greatest game of my life, and there's a part of me that doesn't want it."

"That does *not* sound like the girl I knew," Wayne said.

"I think that people are kind of like trees," she said. "Cut down a tree, and you see all these rings, like the younger tree is still in there, just covered up with new bark. We're like that, Wayne. That girl is still there, but there's been a lot of mileage along the way. It's hard to reach her sometime."

"I tell you what. Just tell me what's going on. Maybe I can help. And if I can, I will." Even though she was the one who had come to him, he could see that she had a hard time trusting or believing. "You're not sure that you want the gig you've nailed. Why? Isn't it everything you've been working for?"

Her smile was a bit haggard. "Oh, yeah. And one thing I hadn't counted on. The Game Master."

Her voice clearly implied the capital letters, and in his experience, that could only mean one thing. "Xavier?"

She nodded. "He'll grind my bones to make his bread."

"I thought it was only giants that did that."

"Close enough."

And dammit, she was right. So . . . the rest of the situation was starting to drop into place. It was the Moon game, the game people had been dreaming of since the first lunar tourist touched down in '37.

That, and Xavier. Brilliant, reclusive. Sometimes wealthy, sometimes dead broke. A gambler, the kind of high roller the casino sent drop-jets to fetch. He'd pretty much created modern LARP gaming theory, the entire mathematical basis for the interactions of Lore Masters and Game Masters, formalizing the entire culture.

Live-Action Role-Playing took root in the 1970s, when a

subculture of mad folk created an organization called the International Fantasy Gaming Society, based on a series of popular novels. The IFGS governed the interactions of "gamers" and "Lore Masters" as they posed each other intellectual puzzles and physical challenges in the midst of one fantasy game or other.

But in 2060 or so, Xavier, then a brilliant teenager who had been gaming since the age of eight, published the first formal gaming theory papers ("LARP Simulation and the Syntax of Combative Improvisation"), and modern gaming was born.

LARPing, which first leapt to world prominence when industrialist Arthur Cowles opened his Dream Park in 2020, was no longer exclusively a Dream Park experience. Still, the parks were considered the supreme expressions of the art, providing mental and physical challenges of the highest order.

Games were still competitions between Lore Masters who were players within the games, and Game Masters who designed and controlled the events from afar, deciding life and death with godlike power. In addition to these competitions, there were also power struggles between different teams within the games themselves.

Xavier, Angelique and Wayne had met at UCLA, and bonded over their love of gaming. Xavier had been six years their senior, a graduate student when Angelique and Wayne were mere freshmen. He was already an expert mime with ten years of ballet on his résumé. But the campus IFGS club was a great leveler. Game points were redeemable in real-world status.

And the three of them, separately or together, were brilliant.

Wayne and Xavier had competed for Angelique. She'd been a tall, raven-haired tomboy in jeans and T-shirts, her huge dark eyes perpetually cast downward as if no one had ever told her she was beautiful. Wayne and Xavier had zoned in on her instantly, competing as they had at everything else. They'd suspected that nestled beneath her ice slept blazing coals. Wayne had been first to fan them into flame.

That was damned near the only contest with Xavier Wayne had ever won, and Xavier had never forgiven either of them. While still perfectly friendly on the surface, beneath that exterior the genius seethed with resentment. And as time went on, more and more often it seemed Xavier found reasons to play against, rather than with them.

And while it wasn't easy for a Game Master to single out specific players for ire, Xavier knew their psychology, game play and character preferences. At times it seemed the games had become more complex and lethal for them, but not for others. Some of the fun had gone out of the play, and if it hadn't been for their competitive natures, Wayne and Angelique might have dropped out altogether.

And then . . . scandal. Xavier left UCLA under a cloud of suspicion, accused of plagiarizing part of his doctoral dissertation from an obscure twentieth-century Bulgarian mathematician. Following this event, he voluntarily submitted himself to an institution for "rest" several times. His relationship with his Nobel Laureate father became painfully strained.

And that was the story as he knew it to this point. Because Xavier had been a graduate student, actually teaching some of Angelique's and Wayne's classes, there had always been a bit of the student-teacher dynamic about them. At this point, Xavier was . . . what . . . forty? While Wayne was thirty-five, and Angelique thirty-four. And that gave Xavier a psychological edge that might prove damned hard to beat.

In the backs of their minds, they might *always* see him as the teacher.

Wayne understood the problem now. Moon Maze was the game of a lifetime. Xavier was the Game Master. Xavier frightened Angelique.

The public disgrace of losing the Tsatsouline Math Fellowship, the accusations of intellectual theft, had nearly broken the man. But . . . Wayne remembered the last time he had seen Xavier. His old frenemy had radiated pure hate. *You did this, damn you. I don't know how . . . I swear to God, I'll get you . . .*

Wayne still felt chills when he thought about that last meeting. He wasn't certain he'd ever seen hatred twist a man's face like that. Deep inside, he'd suspected that Xavier was just posturing for Angelique. That under pressure, Xavier had actually plagarized data, and was blaming anyone, everyone for his problem except himself.

From Wayne's point of view, Xavier had been gaming when he should have been working on his papers. The man had simply run out of time and tried to cut corners. . . .

He didn't know for certain, and doubted he ever would. He'd never encountered Xavier again. A year before, Xavier had come to Vegas for a high-stakes poker tournament, and Wayne had watched him walk the red carpet. For a fraction of a second Wayne had considered catching Xavier's eye. Ultimately, nerve had failed.

A question niggled at the back of his mind, and Wayne sensed that on one level, he already knew the answer. "So . . . Angelique, you aren't here to talk about old times. And you don't need my advice. It's been a long time since I could tell myself I belonged in your league. You've been in the game continuously while I've been out making a living. You're current on things I'd have to research. What do you need?"

Now, for the first time, she seemed unable to meet his eyes. "I want you to be my partner," she said.

"In . . . what?" he couldn't quite believe his ears, even though one part of him had anticipated just such an invitation.

"Eddie can't do the thing. If he can't control his nausea, he can't do the trip. You could. I want you for my partner."

He pushed back, away from Angelique, squinting, head suddenly pounding with a nascent headache. Gaming again, *real* gaming, after all these years? And with Angelique Chan?

He had fallen out of formal gaming when his win percentage was circling the drain, and he was offered a job running games for paunchy tourists. *Nothing wrong with a little income security,* Wayne thought. A health plan. Retirement.

Those voices in his head belonged to his smallest, most fearful aspects. He remembered the way his friends had looked when he'd made the choice. His relationship with Angelique was long over. He'd wondered: If she hadn't existed, wasn't still a gaming force to be reckoned with, wouldn't he have left the field long ago?

And now . . . the carousel had swung around again. Even worse—or better, depending on how you looked at it—it was the Big Game. The biggest game ever. The first *lunar* game. No matter what happened, no matter who won, everyone involved was headed for the record books.

But . . . why him? "Does he still blame me?"

Angelique leaned across the table, her fingers folded. "What do you think? He's never forgiven you for ratting on him."

His heartbeat accelerated. "I didn't!" Even to Wayne, the protestation of innocence felt a bit too automatic.

Angelique smiled. It was a nasty smile.

"Riiight," she said. "And he never forgave me for sleeping with you. I suppose that never happened, either?"

The discomfort vanished, replaced by another, equally powerful sensation. "Touch makes better memories than sight. How about a little reminder?"

"Hah," she replied, but her smile was warm. So. She remembered their previous relationship with a certain fondness, just as he had. "Business. *Only.*"

"Then I take it my evenings are my own?"

Her lips remained pursed into the same smile, but a tiny furrow had appeared between her eyebrows. Still a bit of possessiveness there? "I need your attention on work."

This time, he grinned right back to her. "Stress relief is part of the package, dear heart."

They both knew exactly what he was talking about. Gaming was a highly intense experience . . . emotionally, intellectually and physically. And the evenings were often filled with intense stress relief. Gaming relationships were as intense as those in Olympic villages. Yum.

"I'll trust your professionalism," she said.

"Why me?" he asked. "This isn't just a game to you, and you're playing OTG."

That was another gaming term. "Playing Off the Grid" meant using tactics and strategies designed to upset or unbalance the other players, rather than to concentrate on the game itself.

Just like poker: *Play the player, not the cards.*

"I need the truth," he said, "or I can't even think about this."

She drummed her fingers against the table. She'd known this moment would come, and probably wondered exactly how he would react when it did.

"Six years ago," she said. "It was the Tesseract game. Xavier was the Game Master, but I'd thought that enough time had gone by that maybe bygones were bygones."

"And they weren't."

She shook her head. "No. They weren't. He humiliated me publicly, made me look like an idiot. He's good enough to do that, to entertain himself privately and still function professionally."

"What was your estimation of his skill?"

"Aren't you listening?" Irritation was creeping into her voice. "I was at the top of my game, and he tore me to pieces."

He thought about that for a minute. "So you don't want me for my gaming experience."

A short shake of the head.

"But for the fact that he hates me."

A brief nod. She wanted Wayne Gibson *because* Xavier hated him, not in spite of it. Because he'd taken the woman that both of them loved. Dear God—she wanted to rattle Xavier's cage. He'd respond by trying to destroy them both. The other gamers would take advantage of his distraction, and leap ahead. His professional pride would force him to spread his attention thin. They could predict some of his responses, and in those predictions might lie a momentary, fractional advantage . . .

She was playing a desperate, chancy game. But it just might pay off.

"This is either a brilliant move," she said, reading his thoughts, "or the biggest mistake of my life. If you're not an asset, you'll be a lightning rod. So tell me: Want to find out which it is?"

After all these years, a path back into triple-A gaming? A chance to undo some of the mistakes that he had made? And dear God—a chance to go head-to-head with Xavier, with Angelique at his side? In front of the biggest audience in history?

"Asset," he muttered. "Definitely asset."

She nodded. They were back on the same page again. "And speaking of asses, mine is off limits. This is strictly business. Can you handle that?"

"I'm tougher than I look," he said.

"You'd better be. Do we have a deal?"

"I'll need more information. Wheres and whens. I've got a job. Not much in terms of ties, but . . ." His mind was wheeling. His bosses would bend over backward to give him this opportunity. For their resident Game Master to participate in a major IFGS event would give the Escalade a credibility it sorely needed, and could translate into a major draw. And given that, whether he won or lost, he'd be able to renegotiate his contract.

So he was in and he knew it, and she knew it. Damn her, Angelique had known that even before she'd ever sat down with him.

"How much time do I have to think about it?" he asked.

She seemed a little startled. Surely, she had expected him to jump at the chance and he could understand why.

She gave him until noon the next day to decide.

Midnight was hours gone, but Vegas never sleeps. Walking the streets, you passed from one casino zone into another. Seen from a distance of miles, the desert city was a complex of spires and theme attractions designed to convince Dad to leave his wedding ring on the dresser, and Mama into emptying the college fund. But on street level, only one casino existed at a time. Walk from one zone to another and each business manipulated the visual fields so that their casino, their restaurant, seemed to be the only one. Each establishment was a self-contained world, complete with food, rest, money and sex. Everything that a tourist needed to survive.

One world, multiplying endlessly into many worlds. It was so easy to get lost. Which he had, willingly.

Wayne had come here ten years ago, a minor gaming star, and become fixed in the firmament. He was just another of the has-beens who signed long-term contracts to sing or dance or tell smutty jokes or make tigers disappear on the casino stages.

How had it happened? How had he been caught in a life that brought him so little satisfaction, playing a game that he had once mastered, that had then proceeded to master him?

The truth was simple: *He couldn't do it.* He just couldn't engage with the game deeply enough anymore. It was like a line from one of his favorite old movies.

I've been to the puppet show. I've seen the strings.

Gamers had to believe. Gamers marched arm-in-arm with the faithful.

Didn't they?

He had passed from the Azteca casino, with its hourly human sacrifices, to the edge of the Da Vinci, with its ornate bridges and flight stunts. Real people in those winged machines, even if the engine designs would have baffled the legendary inventor. He'd heard some of them had actually trained on Luna. No holograms here, except the visual field that transformed the entire world into fifteenth-century Milan.

"Listen to me carefully, for I tell you this from the bottom of my heart," he said. "Get a life." Half a dozen passersby didn't even glance at the apparent madman. He must be talking on a phone. Wayne stepped onto a bench as an ersatz soapbox and continued William Shatner's classic "Get a life!" speech for the City of Illusions.

He was going to the Moon. He was going with Angelique. He didn't even have to win to come out ahead. How could any man resist?

There had to be a way to deal with Xavier.

Did Wayne still have the mental agility to play it by ear? Xavier was a monomaniac. Tunnel vision. There would be *something* he'd overlooked. Go to the Moon, and see.

6

Kikaya

1523, Congo Brazzaville Time, June 23, 2085

The flight from Switzerland to the Republic of Kikaya had taken three hours, most of it with autopilot locked securely into a diplomatic flight grid. While they referred to their time zones differently, the Republic of Kikaya and Switzerland utilized the same time zone, so his body felt no oddness.

The shuttle was first class, the hostess who kept the champagne flowing even more so. The alcohol, in combination with his fatigue, encouraged Scotty to recline his seat and close his eyes for a blessed catnap.

When he regained his senses, his glass had been balanced carefully on the serving table and the pilot had taken control for the landing.

The girl was lovely, dark as eggplant, hair woven into tight rows that exposed a scrubbed scalp. Her epicanthic folds were so pronounced her eyes were almost Asiatic. When she spoke, her accent suggested that her English teachers might have actually been English. "Did you have a pleasant nap, sir?"

"Very," he said. They were at about three thousand feet. Spokes of golden light radiated through the eastern clouds. His

body still felt heavy, but his spirits were light. He had been offered work, an opportunity to blot out the memory of the last
seventy-two hours.

Excellent.

The shuttle descended through the clouds, over a patchwork
of cultivated land and crisscrossing roads. The agricultural lands
slowly transformed into residential spirals nestled within urban
squares, housing arranged in circular patterns subtly different
from comparable European or Asian housing tracts. This was
followed by an industrial region. That gave way to another urban sprawl, this one with tighter, more carefully designed spirals
and circles, evidence of greater organization and wealth.

Ahead, just touched by the first rays of sunlight, lay Marozi,
the capital of Kikaya. The business district, and at the center of
it, the royal palace itself.

He'd done a bit of Internet research on the republic before
boarding the plane. The country had been carved out of the Republic of the Congo in 2034 by a bloody coup. Kikaya I had
been a Congolese general with ties to royalty, the family connections sufficiently impressive to entice allies at home and investors
abroad. Seizing power had been the easy part. Crafting the RK
into a prosperous and healthy country was another matter. He'd
look more deeply into that later, but now, at least he had a basic
idea what he was dealing with.

With a barely perceptible shush, the shuttle landed. The hostess smiled. "We are home."

The grit of fatigue and irritation still grinding under his eyelids, Scotty grabbed his hastily packed overnight bag and followed the lady. If this turned into an actual assignment, he
would call the hotel in Geneva and have them send the rest of his
luggage, including his equipment. For right now, this was enough.

As he ducked his head and stepped down from the sleek shuttle, he wondered if a band was going to play the local version of
"Hail to the Guest," and was slightly disappointed when it didn't
happen.

There was, however, a spiffy officer whose blue-black skin

gleamed brightly as the gold braid on his shoulders. His spine was so erect he might have been smuggling bamboo.

"Mr. Griffin," he said in perfect English. "I trust your flight was pleasant?"

"Fine, thank you," repeating his automatic reply.

"I am Mboui Otama. At your service, sir. May I take your luggage?"

Scotty offered the bag, but held on to one of the straps, so that both of them were holding it at the same time. "My understanding was that if I didn't like the proposition, this shuttle will take me wherever I want to go. Does that offer still hold?"

"Of course."

"Then let's just leave my things here on the shuttle, and if I need them, I'll send for them." A symbolic gesture. He was watching carefully gauging the reaction.

Otama didn't flinch. "Fine. This way, please."

He hated to admit it, but he enjoyed this to an absurd degree. It seemed a throwback to some older, more elegant time. "Does everyone get this treatment?"

Otama's lips turned up in a slight grin. "Almost everyone."

Ah. *Deflate the American.* Scotty squashed a flash of disappointment. "Oh," was all he said.

Otama grinned now, a mouth filled with gold teeth. "I joke. Only guests of the royal house are treated in such a manner."

Scotty grinned. He doubted that Otama joked like that with everyone. Was he being tested because of his own dark skin? "And that's me?"

"That, I believe, is you."

The airpad was at the center of a young hedge maze, and the honor guard followed at a walk as Scotty and Otama were shuttled through it, to the steps of a three-story, white colonial mansion with eight porch columns and at least a hundred windows. The filigree looked handwrought, knobs and handrails inset with ivory and gold.

Again, Scotty was impressed. "This is . . . amazing."

Otama nodded. "Built for King Leopold in 1879. At one time,

it was thought that the King himself might come to visit his rubber-tree holdings."

"It never happened?"

A warm, friendly smile. "A good thing for him. His plantation workers were sharpening their knives."

Scotty had been many places in his career and travels, but never in a palace. Its high, arching ceilings and ornately carved abstracts were almost overwhelming. Striding toward them was an imposing white-haired black man in regal dress, effusively extending his hand. Scotty recognized him from the computer images. This would be Kikaya II, the son of the country's first leader. Scotty didn't know whether to kiss the hand or bow, and settled for a warm, dry shake. Calluses crusted that broad flat hand like barnacles on an old battleship. "Mr. Griffin. So kind of you to come."

He nodded. Kikaya clasped his hand affectionately. Scotty sensed that he was being thoroughly measured. What was this man looking for? In all likelihood men of this nature were used to indirect approaches by petitioners currying favor. Scotty was in the odd position of being the one sought, and decided to use that. "Your highness," he said. "It's been a long trip. I'd appreciate knowing what this is about."

Kikaya tilted his round head. One of his eyes, Scotty noticed, was slightly offset. "Ah. You have no idea at all?"

"None," he admitted, "but the retainer was large enough to catch my interest."

"Take my arm, please."

Scotty did, and as if they were old friends, they began to walk now, toward an unspecified destination. Probably a tea or meeting room of some kind, but first a stroll past paintings and statues and images of the ancestors.

"Is money all that motivates you?"

Scotty shrugged. "I like to travel."

The Kikayan monarch brightened. "Do you indeed? In my younger days, I enjoyed travel as well. My responsibilities currently prevent me from enjoying such freedoms."

Scotty decided to head off the slight sense of irritation he was beginning to feel. "Mr. President, I don't mean to be rude, but I

haven't slept in twenty hours, and I'd love to find out what it is
that seems so urgent. And . . . ah . . . there was mention of ten
thousand New dollars?"

Kikaya II grinned. Money, it seemed, was a universal language. He touched his thumb to a bracelet on his left wrist, and
a computer screen hovered in the air before them. "Your bank
account. Please note the recent deposit."

Very nice. Efficient. Even better, his request had triggered no
offense or indignation. These were all good signs. "Cool. All right,
what can I do for you, sir?"

"What do you know about me?" President Kikaya asked.

There is simply no substitute for research. "I know that you
ascended to the throne at the age of seventeen—your bloodline
was the only one that all factions could agree upon after the Independence War in 2034. For the first thirteen years some called
you a bloody tyrant, but you are currently thought a progressive
leader."

"And if I was still thought a tyrant?"

The answer came to him at once, but he took his time speaking it. "We wouldn't be having this conversation."

Kikaya stared at him, and then roared with laughter. Scotty
allowed himself a polite chuckle, but was careful to rein it back
in before Kikaya's explosion ceased.

"You speak your mind," Kikaya said. "I like that. Next time,
don't wait so long after you have decided what to say."

"Fair enough," Scotty said. "So . . . why am I here, sir?"

Kikaya's round face split with a quieter, more private amusement. "A moment ago I was 'your highness.' And now I am merely
'sir'?"

Scotty shrugged and took a chance. Kikaya had invited a certain informality. *All right, let's see if he really wants it.* "I'm not
saying that familiarity breeds contempt, but it certainly encour-
ages a certain informality."

Kikaya's smile seemed genuine. "Indeed it does." He lowered
his voice and arched his eyebrows, one man sharing delicious
speculation with another. "In fact, without a certain amount of
familiarity, it is almost impossible to breed anything at all."

Apparently, Kikaya liked his guests to laugh with him, and Scotty obliged heartily as a four-man honor guard parted, and the door to a spacious office was opened. Kikaya saw him to his seat as a male assistant inquired into his desire for nutrition and fluids. After arrangements were made, Kikaya folded his hands and spoke as if they were old friends.

"You are the son of Alex Griffin, retired vice president of security for Cowles International. And your mother was a vice president of guest relations for Cowles Entertainment, which controls, among other things, the Dream Park franchise. Is that correct?"

"Yes . . ." Where was this going? He hoped to God Kikaya didn't want him to squire some grandnephews around an amusement park.

"You served in the American Union's National Corps at the age of seventeen, and quite distinguished yourself. Your future wife Ms. Tuinukuafe won an academic work-study slot at Heinlein station when she was twenty-four, worked her way up to comanager in two years. She recruited you at that time. You spent four years at Heinlein base, and then for reasons unclear to my sources, you returned to Earth. Without, apparently, seeking a formal divorce."

He arched an eyebrow at Scotty.

"Personal," Scotty said. "Personal reasons."

"I see. I hope that you can understand how a prospective employer might wish details. If you would be so kind . . ."

Scotty sighed. "There was an accident. I was trapped in a landslide in a leaking suit for an hour, and it . . . twisted my mind a bit. I thought it would be safest for me to return to Earth."

"Because you were no longer suitable for advanced lunar maneuvers?"

"Yes."

"And basic maneuvers?"

"For tourists. Boring."

"I'd hoped you'd say that. Well. There is certainly no negative reflection in any of your personnel files . . . Although one suspects that a kindly ex-spouse might have had something to do with that."

The skin on the back of his neck flamed. Why would this man say something like that? Another test? "If you brought me here to insult me, please keep your money, and have your shuttle take me home, your majesty."

For another full minute the two men studied each other, then Kikaya nodded approval. "You are strong. Although your most recent assignment ended on a less than glorious note, you have an excellent reputation in the personal security community."

Without allowing his ire to cool, Scotty answered: "Cowles has the best training simulators in the world."

"I believe you. And I believe that your résumé and pedigree make you perfect for my purpose."

Another long pause. This time, Scotty decided not to speak, to put the burden of communication on the man on the other side of the desk.

"My only son," Kikaya said, "has been chosen to compete in the first lunar Dream Park game. There will be training and travel and risk. I wish Ali to have a professional companion, one knowledgeable in security matters. Such a man must pass muster with Cowles Industries, and is preferably a space hand. You, young Griffin, qualify with flying colors."

The Moon? This man wanted him to return to the Moon. Dear God. A chance to get back on the horse. But . . . he hadn't been to the Moon in three years. The accident had left him with a mix of phobic responses: claustrophobia, fear of asphyxiation and variations on astrophobia or kenophobia: a fear of stars and empty spaces that might create problems during space travel. And a broken marriage. Yes, let's not forget that little thing.

Quotes from sessions with Dr. Brenner felt harmless enough, but the stars glared, baleful in his mind. Windows were scarce on the Moon. He was not used to staring at stars. The fear of death was overwhelming and humiliating. Anchored to his field of vision, it all created a powerful phobic response.

When he'd been a kid, some feared that moving an asteroid into lunar orbit could end the world. A mile-wide chunk of rock called Aeros ghosted across a remembered starfield. His fingers gripped at the seat of his chair. He didn't want Kikaya to see his emotions, but didn't the man have the right, in fact the *responsibility* to know everything about the man to whom he entrusted his son?

No. My shame is my own. If I turn this down, I'll do it for my own reasons.

He felt the weight of Kikaya's stare. He *could* say yes, dependent on research and discussion . . .

"What exactly is called for?" he asked.

"There is a period of training and evaluation. Follow this with travel time, and the game itself. We can provide you with what information we have, but I've little doubt that your own sources are better than mine."

He felt as if he'd inhaled a gust of minty wind. *You'd see her again.* "I assume you understand that any connections I do or do not have with Cowles Industries, or Dream Park, cannot be used to your son's advantage during the playing of a game. In fact, if I am to accompany him, I see no way to do that save by actually *participating* in the game. That further limits the information that I can ask from those contacts."

Thoughts, images and impressions flew more rapidly. "In fact, seeing that that is the case, you might want me to accompany him, but not participate in the game itself." He shook his head. "In fact, I'm not sure I understand. Your son earned his place in the game . . . but that's not a double ticket. How would *I* get into the game?"

Kikaya smiled. "You have to understand that this is more than just another game. It is also an opportunity to promote lunar tourism to the entire world. I have substantial investments on the Moon, sir. If wealth did not encourage accommodation, men would not seek it. For the son of a national ruler to have legitimately earned his place in the competition is unprecedented. Because you have no gaming experience—"

"I wouldn't exactly say that. I grew up around Dream Park."

That cool wind blew again, this time carrying memories before it like dried leaves. Not tourist memories: behind the scenes. In the caverns beneath the park, in the engineering alcoves, working the rides and refreshment stands to earn pocket money as a teenager. Good memories.

"But you have no standing within the IFGS. I'm told we can admit you; you would have no unfair advantage. You might even be seen as a handicap."

"Now wait a minute . . ."

STOP.

Dammit! Kikaya had manipulated him, pinched his competitive nerve. Damn. He could get back to the moon, see if all the hours of therapy had made a difference. His problem wouldn't be a hindrance to his performance, so there was little downside there. He could see Kendra again . . .

But could he work with Prince Ali? He noted that the young man was not in the room with them.

He'd done a bit of preliminary research. Prince Ali was a brat who had cowed his father's subordinates and even the teachers at the Foxcrest Academy, the English military school he'd haphazardly attended.

A comment made by one of his comrades, very off the cuff: The Prince lived in a cocoon, a carefully maintained illusion of superior mental and physical skills. No one dared tell him no, or defeat him at anything. He could guess that Ali might have convinced his father to invest heavily in the Moon, perceived by many of his countrymen to be a waste of precious resources.

A spoiled brat. He'd danced that dance before, and too recently. "The numbers discussed for full participation. Is that amount still on the table?"

"Yes."

"I would need an additional 20 percent applied to the principal, and the per diem. In essence, I'm off the market for almost a year."

"That can be accommodated."

Damn! Well . . .

"Sir, I would like to provisionally agree, depending on completion of research and interaction. But . . . I have to admit it sounds interesting."

"I thought that you would."

"And I would like to meet your son."

7

The Prince

Most of the palace was a mixture of styles ranging from European colonial to traditional Congolese and Pan-African, celebrating the lives and accomplishments of Kikaya's ancestors and people. The west wing was Kikaya III's wing. It seemed to Scotty that the decor celebrated, more than anything, an exhaustive addiction to science fiction, fantasy and gaming. He noticed that Kikaya II, walking at his side, grew tight-lipped with disapproval as they moved deeper into the fannish abyss.

Complete sets of original Heinlein, Bradbury, Clarke, Le Guin, Butler, Kanazawa. Scotty recognized signatures on wall paintings from Kelly Freas, Frank Frazetta, Michael Whelan and Sue Tong.

Sculptures crowded every nook and cranny. "Your son is quite the collector."

"Yes," Kikaya said. "Some even have value. Purchased through agents, or by traveling to these science fiction conventions. Have you been to such a 'convention'? The people seem . . . quite strange."

"One or two. And the fans are actually pretty normal people in outside life. They just like to cut loose from time to time."

"He is actually an artist. He has had the best teachers. These drawings are his." Framed images of mutant sea horses, tool-using insectile creatures and strange robotic devices graced the hall opposite the Prince's door. The King sighed, and entered without knocking.

Every wall of the room was covered with video chips, capable of slicing the wall into a hundred separate screens, or submerging the occupants into a completely immersive environment. Right now, stepping into that room was like stepping onto an Antarctic plain, even down to the blast of cold wind blowing from the ventilation system. This was a full-service gaming room, custom built by Cowles Industries or a close competitor.

"Ali," King Kikaya said.

There was no reply. His sole heir gazed intensely into the game room's control field, using his eyes and hands and feet to manipulate the image of a sled-dog team apparently attempting to outrun a herd of ravenous Yetis. The boy was of moderate height, whip-slender, his hair braided into rows and nodes so tight his head resembled an ear of corn. His facial features were almost excessively fine, as if carved in chocolate by a woman's hand.

Kikaya raised his voice. "Ali!"

"In a minute, Father."

The Prince was given his sixty seconds, and when there was still no answer forthcoming, the King clicked a "kill" code with tongue and teeth. The images froze.

Ali rattled off a string of rapid-fire Congolese, and his father replied in the same language. Then, for the first time, the boy looked directly at Scotty. "My father considers it discourteous to speak in a language a guest does not understand. I do not wish to be rude." He said this in a voice that implied *You are not needed.*

"Father," Ali said. "I was approaching the seventh level!"

Kikaya seemed to struggle to control himself, perhaps not wishing to lose his temper in front of an outsider.

"Ali," he said. "Here is someone I want you to meet. He will travel with you on this lunar adventure."

"The bodyguard," Ali said, mocking. "The Moon is an assassin's paradise, I am sure."

King Kikaya shook his head. "How will you control this nation?" he asked. "You have sworn to me that you will be ready to accept the mantle of leader, but I do not see it, Ali."

Ali looked up, earlier irritation giving way to a far more conciliatory tone. "Father. I swear to you that I will fulfill my duties. Until then, I don't understand why you criticize my little entertainments."

"And your past follies?

Scotty had an odd feeling, almost as if he, as a commoner, was too unimportant for these two to edit themselves.

"Like England's Henry," Ali smiled. When his father did not reply, Ali turned again to Scotty. "Do you know your Shakespeare?"

"Henry set a trap for his father's enemies by pretending dissipation." He paused. "Just call me Falstaff. We'll get along fine."

Ali raised a royal eyebrow. "Indeed?"

Kikaya wagged his leonine head. "My son, the time for kings is past in this world. Our people want democracy."

With a last regretful look at the screens before him, Kikaya III slipped off his mesh cap and goggles, and stood to face his father. The boy was slender, whipcord strong and straight. It seemed to Scotty that the monarch was struggling to maintain a stern demeanor.

Did Kikaya remind his father of his own youthful dreams, his own efforts to measure up to paternal demands?

Scotty had read up. Kikaya II's life had been filled with war and intense political action. His son, in comparison, had been given the world. There had been rumors of tension between father and son . . . and now he understood. Nineteen-year-old Ali was a spoiled brat, and Daddy was afraid that, when his time came to take power, the boy would be eaten alive.

Every father wants his son to have the advantages he himself was denied. But then, if you provide those advantages, you risk producing a weakling. The core parental paradox.

Ali was speaking to his father, but in another way, he seemed to be talking to himself. "Father . . . all my life I have awaited the moment when you felt I was ready to serve my people. I hope you live to be two hundred, but I know that when the time comes, I will be a good king. The last king of Kikaya."

"And what of your own firstborn?"

"He will be raised to wealth, power and privilege . . . but not a throne. Our family has vast holdings. That will have to be enough."

It was the right answer, but felt rehearsed. So the grandson wouldn't be king. Scotty silently bet himself that the kid would go for "President for Life." What the hell—every other dictator did.

Kikaya II sighed. "You see what concerns me, Mr. Griffin. My son does not appreciate the truth of power. It is all a game to him. I hope that this trip will be the end of one phase of his life, and the beginning of another."

"Sir," Scotty said. "I'm sure the Prince will be everything you wish, and more." He tried to detect a change in expression on Ali's part. Any hint of his attitudes and emotions. Not much: The kid was a cipher.

Kikaya spoke first. "You need to get to know this man," he said. "He has agreed to accompany you during your training, transportation and during the game itself."

Finally, that caught Ali's intention. "So? You would use your influence to put an anchor around my neck? You bring this American thug here, ram him down the—" Ali lapsed into Congolese again, and his father did the same.

Scotty held up his hand. "Pardon? May the American thug interject a few words?"

Ali whipped his head around, squinting with anger. "By all means."

"Well, where I come from, 'American thug' is a compliment, and I'll take it as such." There, that should confuse him. "The truth is that I grew up at Dream Park. My father was head of security, my mother chief of guest relations."

"Really?" Ali seemed intrigued in spite of himself.

"Have you been to California Dream Park?"

"Of course. In disguise, four times."

"And did you go to the Santa's Workshop Adventure?"

"Yes, a minor game, but entertaining."

"Well, I was the third elf, the one who says: 'Who kidnapped Santa?' I was only eight years old at the time, and the kid who was supposed to play the role got the flu. Mom got me in."

Ali stared at Scotty, and then laughed uproariously. "You are an elf! And a bodyguard as well?"

"Yes, and a Luny. I've been around."

Ali's eyes widened. "You've been to the Moon? And you know gaming?" Scotty watched the kid's gears spin. "Perhaps . . . perhaps you are not an anchor after all. Father," he said, "I would like to have breakfast with this man. Will you leave us together to talk?"

Kikaya smiled approval at Scotty. *I think you will do fine,* that expression said. He shook Scotty's hand, and said in a low voice, "Please. He is my only son. Convince him. Protect him. Please."

They locked eyes for a moment, not monarch and commoner, but two men with a common interest: the health and safety of a boy. "If I take the job," Scotty said, "he's safe. I promise."

"Take the job, Mr. Griffin," Kikaya said. Then nodded to his son, and left the room

Ali and Scotty faced each other without speaking for a moment, then the boy said: "Have you ever had an ostrich omelet?"

"Never."

"Our chef makes them with little fish from Lake Victoria, garnished with a local onion found nowhere else in the world, and forbidden to export. Will you join me, Mr. Griffin?"

Scotty smiled. "Only if you'll call me Scotty."

"Yes," the boy said. "Scotty. And you may call me . . . Prince Ali."

A pause, and then Ali broke into laughter, and Scotty followed. And at that moment, he decided he liked the kid, and would take the job.

8

Neutral Moresnot

October 10, 2085

In any modern society, privacy is one of the most prized commodities. This was as true on Luna as anywhere else. More so, perhaps, as every spoonful of water or breath of air was produced or managed by a central processor, and every human being was tracked at all times.

As a result, the ability to promise secure communications between Earth and Moon was a lucrative business, birthing a half-dozen communication streams boasting high-level encryption and guarantees of hack-free voice- and facemail.

Doug Frost sat in his cubical, enjoying the fruits of such privacy. But even with guarantees, the current communication was conducted with coded language and careful tones.

The face on the screen was a man's. Then it shifted and became a woman's. The skin tone shifted to black, and then Asian. As it did, the vocal tones shifted as well. There was simply no telling who or what a "Shotz" actually was. Frost's sources speculated that he was a man, but there was no way to be certain. All they knew beyond question was that a person known as "Shotz" was Shotz, leader of a group called Neutral Moresnot, the most successful practitioners of a very specialized criminal profession.

Kidnapping had been big business for hundreds of years, and the Moresnot group was reliable, conducting twenty high-profile extractions a year, usually leaving little trace, and always demanding high fees.

"You have received all data?" Doug said.

The Chinese woman on screen smiled. Was that a real interpretation of Shotz's mood? He had no idea at all. "Yes."

"And were there any last-minute concerns? I'm not certain why you requested this unscheduled conversation."

"It has to do with a passenger list," Shotz said. "Of course, we would be interested in anyone traveling with our . . . person of interest."

"Of course."

"And we see that he is traveling with a man named Scott Griffin. Are you familiar with this person?"

"No," Doug said. "Should I be?"

"Our records show that he was married to the current Chief of Operations, Kendra Griffin." The Asian woman was morphing, melting into a dark-skinned Latina.

"Was? She still wears his name?" Many western women could not wait to shed their former husband's names, once the divorce was concluded. "Is that a problem?"

"It is a matter of some interest. His path crossed ours several months ago. He interfered in an operation of substantial value. He harmed a valued associate."

"Will that cause a problem? I was assured that you were professional. Surely revenge—"

Shotz cut him off. "Not at all. But he is competent. And therefore dangerous. On the other hand, a personal connection between this man Griffin and his ex-wife might help us to maintain control. She has kept his name. Perhaps there are still feelings."

The voice was certainly synthesized, as was the visual image, but something about the conversation was chilling. "We want no unneccessary violence," Doug said. "Everything is in place, and the situation will be volatile enough as things stand. We need no complications."

"There will be none," Shotz said. "In fact, I think that this man Griffin's presence might actually work to our advantage. To tell you truthfully, my . . . associates and I would enjoy the chance to deal with this man."

"Is there anything else?"

"No. Everything is on track. The remainder of the monies are to be paid into our accounts by the end of the month. You have arranged for our equipment?"

"Yes." Fabrication of gear that could not be brought through lunar customs. Acquisition of funds through expatriot groups on Earth. Identification of an effective organization capable of carrying out a bizarre and demanding plan. Contact with revolutionary forces within the Republic of Kikaya itself . . .

Yes, they had accomplished miracles over the last months. Exactly what was required if they were to have any chance of achieving the miracle to come.

Freedom for his people.

A thin mist of perspiration blossomed on the back of Doug's neck as the reality of their situation finally descended upon him.

"Is there . . . something wrong?" Shotz asked. "Her" face was shifting again. Morphing into a more masculine form.

Doug felt it: He had paused too long. "Everything is fine. I am just eager for it to begin."

The screen image smiled. "Soon, my friend. All that is required is for both of us to perform as agreed. If we do this thing, then in a few short weeks, we change the world."

The image faded away, the connection broken. Yes, indeed. In a few short weeks, the world would be changed.

Now, it was either succeed, or . . .

Or what? Death? Dishonor? Incarceration? He was not even certain of the laws they would be violating.

Well, if they did not proceed, he was certain that there would be hard, serious men and women from around the world and across the solar system who would be more than happy to inform him. At painful length.

The thing, then, was not to fail.

··· **9** ···

Kendra

October 25, 2085

The former Kendra Tuinukuafe, now Kendra Griffin, opened her eyes. She nestled naked in the midst of a wide, wide hammock, peering up through her wavering water shield to the half-Earth visible above. The walls were more than four meters high, decorated from floor to ceiling with little ledges and picture frames. Her home looked a bit like a hobbit house, crammed with books and mementos, some shipped up from Earth, others fabricated or acquired in the intervening years. It was, of course, a hole in the ground. Radiation was a problem on the Moon.

Her alarm trilled again, pulling her to full wakefulness just as the wake-up lights began to rise.

"Right on time." She yawned heartily and rolled out of the hammock, landing lightly. Now the hammock cleared her head by nearly a meter. Her broad shoulders and upper back, webbed with flyer's muscle, flared almost like wings, narrowing her waist.

She tocked her tongue, and spoke.

"Audio live," she said.

Her assistant's hologram appeared. Chris Foxworthy was tall, prematurely balding, muscularly self-assured, and carried himself with an air most interpreted as "distant." He was staring right through her, understandable since she hadn't engaged the live feed. People were always a little stiff when speaking to avatars.

"Boss," Chris said.

"Chris. I have time for coffee?" Gram for gram, her Colombian was Luna's most expensive legal luxury.

"Always," Chris said.

Kendra yawned wider as she approached the coffeemaker. Judging by the control lights and fragrant cloud of steam, it was already preparing a cup.

She sniffed deeply; even the smell of the coffee cleared cobwebs from her mind. "Mmmm. Yummy."

"Has anyone ever told you that you have a cruel streak?"

"On the hour." Steaming dark fluid poured sluggishly into the cup. Even at lowest pressure, some still slopped up over the edge. She waited for it to stop, then lifted the cup and sipped. Heaven. "So . . . how are the polls runnning?"

"You're up ten points on McCauley, but that still makes me nervous with a month 'til the election."

"Me, too. What's on the dock today?"

"Tons. We've got a load of oranges and finger bananas in from Clavius."

"We're trading . . . ?"

"Spare gigawatts from the Bullwinkle array and the Tsiolkovsky power plant. Fifty gigs over the next month. Falling Angels is dropping a load of foamed steel to complete the dorms," Chris said.

Kendra frowned. "Isn't that cutting it a little close?"

Chris shook his head. "Temporary shelters—steel skeleton, spray-foam skin, webbed furniture . . . We'll make our dates. Might be a little spare, but short-timers only log sleep and shower time in their rooms. Too busy seeing the sights." Chris waited patiently for his boss as she threw some clothes on, prepping as she went. She bounced through each step.

Kendra looked in the mirror. "Suitable," she said, then tocked her tongue again and raised her voice. "Video live."

"Ah, there you are," Chris said. "Nice slacks."

Tck. "Call the car," she said, summoning a shuttle. "Stack my calls, Chris. I'll have to fit them in around my duties."

"No problem."

The living room's front door opened into a sealed tunnel. Neither Kendra nor anyone else at Heinlein owned a private vehicle. She wasn't certain such a thing really existed on all of Luna.

The tunnel was actually the connecting node for the base shuttle system. As she watched, one of the golden tube-cars flashed to the rail outside her house, then decelerated toward the branch line. Her outer door slid open, the car entered, the door shut. The pressure coupling sealed itself to the pod, and her inner door opened.

Kendra seated herself, strapped in, and waited for the door to seal. Once all three safety lights went green, she murmured "Landing pad," and the pod rolled out of her garage. Accelerated by magnetic pulses, it circled her home twice. After reaching full speed, it joined the traffic flow on the main line.

Her thoughts ranged to plant management, and political connections to other colonies. She looked up at the Earth's misty blue disk. There was one very particular Earthling heading her way. Soon. *And what will that do to your life, Kendra?*

Why didn't you change your name? Because nobody can pronounce Tuinukuafe?

"So . . . what's on the docket today?"

"Talos asteroid. We're bartering hybrid seeds for ore. Then we have a bottleneck at Fabrication."

That was Toby McCauley's work. On the surface, it was just a disagreement about apportionment of the floating labor pool. In reality, it was an attempt to make Kendra look bad. And it could work.

"I want you to look into their energy usage. Someone's been getting a load of overtime there. We should be able to make the point that just because McCauley has trade rights with anyone willing to negotiate, that hardly guarantees priority access to manpower."

If McCauley could make her the bad guy, make it look as if

she was stifling free trade and entrepreneurship, even if he never raised the subject in open debate, conversation in the blue-collar lounges would be ugly, and affect voting. On the other hand, if she allowed him to dominate the labor pool, it would seem she was siding with him against Heinlein's major investors, who wanted a tighter rein on all financial activity.

A nice bind. *Well done, Toby.*

"Look," Kendra said. "There's nothing we can do about that. Everyone's fighting over the same resources. Nothing special here . . ."

Her phone began to beep. "I have to take this," she said.

The view bubble above her flickered into a screen. Scenery whizzed past at a kilometer per second. Any faster and the little pods would rise into orbit.

"Mom! Dad!" she said.

Millicent was a tall black woman just past sixty. Smiling hollowed her cheekbones. Despite the separation, Kendra still called her "Mom."

"Sweetie. Glad we could get you. Alex, is Scotty online?"

The image divided. One at a time, the faces of her former family: Millicent, Alex and Scotty. Kendra had little blood family. It was one of the reasons living on the Moon didn't sting. Meeting Scotty, and marrying into his clan, had been wonderful. Even after the divorce his folks had made it clear they still loved her. That was part of the reason the next month was going to be stressful.

No matter what anyone said, they had to be hoping.

Was *she*?

"Have him right here," Alex Griffin said. His hair was gray, his face long, edging toward jowls.

"Hey, Kendra." Scotty seemed a little stressed. None of their conversations since the split had been easy, but this was something different.

"So," Kendra said. "How's the training going?" She raised her voice. "*Tck.* Audio out."

The hologram went mute. Chris canted his head sideways, pretended to pout.

There was a perceptible lag, and then Scotty answered. "Craziness, but winding down. We lost a couple to the first days of zero gee. They're on drugs. I've been demonstrating the exercise routines. I've figured out that funny yoga that keeps your core muscles hard, but my client is having trouble with that. He can't learn the lunar shuffle until we're actually on the Moon."

Alex Griffin laughed knowingly. Kendra missed that warm laughter. Her own father had been austere and demanding, descended from a line of Tongan war chiefs. "You knew the job was dangerous when you took it."

"Not exactly danger . . ." Scotty drifted for a moment, and then focused on them again. "Listen, this is going to be great. We'll all be together for the first time in what . . . seven years?"

"You're sure your client is good with that?" Alex asked.

Scotty said, "I'll see him through the game. Afterward, Foley Mason's meeting us. He'll escort my client back to Earth."

"He's a good man," Alex said. "Did I ever tell you about the time in Cairo . . . ?"

"This is expensive, Alex," Millicent chided gently. "Old war stories later, please."

"We can listen to all of them again when I see you," Scotty said. "I can find plenty to do aboard ship to keep me busy for two weeks until you two can get up . . ."

"And then it's party time," Kendra said.

Once upon a time, there had been plans to get Scotty's folks to the Moon. One big happy family, with the low gee offering another decade of life. But things kept getting in the way, and now there seemed little hope. "How are things there, Mom?" Her voice might have been just a little too careful.

"Fine, dear," Millicent said. "Just some more tests, and I'll be through the first round of chemo. There's a new . . . I'm not sure, some kind of nanotech, exploiting genetic instability in the cancer cells." Despite her optimistic tone Millicent's voice stumbled, just a bit, on the word "cancer."

Alex finally interrupted the uneasy silence that followed. "The doctor's not worried, so I'm not going to be. We'll be there."

"All right," Kendra said, then squinted through the window. "I'm coming up on the dock. Good talking to you—can we try again in a couple of days?"

Millicent squinted at her. "Everything all right, darling?"

Kendra sighed. "I just . . . miss you all." She forced herself to smile, and focused on her adopted parents. "Mom, Dad—let me have a minute with Scotty, would you?"

"Sure, hon," Millicent said.

Alex nodded. "We'll talk next week."

The two older folks winked off. Scotty alone remained.

"So . . . how are you, really?" she asked. "Are you ready for this?"

"I'm heading up," he said. "I wouldn't if I had any doubts."

"Nightmares?"

"Got them under control. How about you, hon?"

That question caught her off guard. "What?"

"How are the nightmares?"

She felt as if he'd knocked the air out of her chest. "That's not fair, Scotty."

"Why not? You've certainly spent enough time worried about my welfare."

"You ran away, Scotty." Almost before the words crossed her lips, she regretted them.

Scotty laughed without humor. "I wasn't going to be much good to anyone up there, least of all you. I didn't need to be a quarter-million miles from Earth to work a desk job."

After the accident, that would have been about all he was qualified for, too. No more surface travel. No vast, razor-like moonscapes and pinpoint stars for Scotty. Life here was hard enough without stress-induced phobias. All the headshrinks agreed that he should go home. Even if it cost a damned fine marriage.

"Are people still talking? If so, I'm sorry." A pause. "I miss you. And that's the truth."

"Me, too. There really hasn't been anyone much . . ." She trailed off. Dammit, she didn't have to explain herself. Lunar relationships were a lot like the ones that formed in Antarctic stations: intense and temporary. Human beings did the best they could.

But even given the circumstances, Kendra had always thought they had something special. Something that might have endured, even if they'd had to go to Earth to nurture it.

She felt her eyes mist, and wanted off the line before she wiped them in front of him. "I don't have time for this right now. Let's back off before we start fighting."

He nodded. "I'll be up there soon. We'll get it all worked out. Promise."

She sighed, and managed to smile. "We'd better. I can still kick your butt in thumb-wrestling."

"Only if you cheat."

They shared a time-delayed laugh, and the mood genuinely lightened. A good point to end things, while they were still smiling. "Bye, Earthman."

"Bye, Moonmaid."

The line winked off.

10

Arrival

November 5, 2085

The lander arrived precisely on time: a spiderlegged caterpillar settling in a fountain of dust on a wide red double-spiral target pad. The shuttlecar rolled up against its side. Automated flanges locked into place. The doors opened in sequence, three sets, sealing behind the passengers as they boarded a car that looked like a silver sausage. The car ran them to the base airlock and another triple airlock.

At first Kendra saw only two exceptionally statuesque women striding down the ramp, one Asian with straight black shoulder-length hair, the other European with brilliant red hair of similar length and texture. Both were conspicuously muscular with fashionable fat padding. Then they stepped apart, revealing a tiny man—no more than five foot two—walking just behind them as if they were a royal guard.

Even in rumpled travel clothes, Xavier radiated theatricality. Somehow he transformed his typical newbie's lunar clumsiness into performance art, bouncing and then awkwardly catching his balance with every other step. His escorts were better at it.

Still, she could tell that he struggled to remain unimpressed by his surroundings.

"Mr. Xavier?" Kendra asked.

"Just Xavier, please." He was beautiful for a man, shaven-headed, with blond eyebrows capping a delicate face. His eyes were a brilliant blue, intense and intelligent. He was small-boned, barely rising to her shoulder, but already flirting with her. "My assistants are Wu Lin and Magique. Magique does not speak."

"Welcome to Heinlein base," Kendra said.

Xavier's angelic little face split in a smile. "I have to admit I thought I'd been everywhere and seen everything. These last weeks have opened my eyes."

Kendra and her holographic assistant exchanged an expression of surprise.

Kendra said, "We have a pretty tight schedule today, but we want to get you to the game center, and then to your rooms."

He nodded. "That would be fine."

They waited for the luggage pods to be loaded onto their vehicle, and then boarded a tube-car for the gaming center.

"I understand that we'll have privacy?"

"Yes. Much nicer than the dormitories," Kendra said. "Your own private crater."

His answering smile was pornographic. "Perhaps you'd care to show it to me."

"One crater's pretty much like another," she kept her voice light and pleasant. "Not luxurious, but hopefully adequate."

He was staring out through the glass partition at glare-white and coal-black scenery. "Luxury is not imperative. My requirement is seclusion."

"I've heard that gaming parties tend to run wild . . ."

He shook his small, perfectly formed head. "Not what you think. I can become . . . intensely emotional when I game. Lamps and chairs and waitrons and cleaner mechs can be at great risk. There is often . . . a bit of breakage. *To create you must first destroy.* I believe Picasso said that."

"*'Think left and think right and think low and think high. Oh, the thinks you can think up if only you try!'*" She paused, then when Wu Lin seemed puzzled, added, "Dr. Seuss said that."

Magique choked on a silent giggle. Xavier's thin lips curled up in a smile.

"At any rate," Kendra said, "if space is what you need, we have plenty of it."

"So . . . Dr. Seuss," Xavier said, nodding as if she had confirmed something. "Have you children?"

"No."

"Married?"

Kendra said, "Once upon a time."

The red-haired Magique smirked. She was gorgeous, and muscular with a fatty sheath, in the current European Union Fit/Fat style. The goal was to maintain a perfect blood pressure and immune profile, with the roundest curves possible. She signed to Wu Lin with her plump hands. Wu Lin giggled.

"How long have you been up here?" Xavier asked.

"Seven years."

"And the ratio of women to men . . . ?"

"We're outnumbered. As you must know." Kendra sighed. "I'm fine, thanks. No help needed on that front. While we're at it, may I ask . . . ? Magique said something that triggered merriment."

Wu Lin nodded. "She said you look like a twentieth-century fitness model." The redhead nodded happy agreement.

The trio radiated a cozy, slightly predatory sensuality. Kendra couldn't resist visualizing a zero-gee anaconda ball, and suppressed a chill of revulsion. Maybe they just thought they were being polite, assuming she'd feel rejected without an invitation to the fun and games. Fortunately, they had reached their destination, and she was able to change the subject.

The Game Center was a dome, of course, the ceiling five meters high. The last few workers were still nipping and tucking, and the smell of fresh paint still tinged the air. Xavier bounced onto the central stage, stopped and looked around himself. He said, "Very similar to the Euro Dream Park unit."

He waved his hands in an input field, and it calibrated. She'd thought she'd be edging her way out the door, but Xavier's manner had become more professional the instant he began manipulating alien forms like stringless marionettes. His annoying, smarmy persona faded, and in its place appeared a virtuoso performer. Despite her irritation, she found the transformation fascinating.

A circular metal stage in the center of the room glowed, and a ball of yellow light levitated above it. Xavier bounced up the two steps to the platform. As he did, an insectoid alien bounded into the floating light field. When the little man shifted position, the insect followed his motions precisely. It wore a bandolier hung with weapons shaped to its big padded hands. It moved with an oddly disjointed grace. When Kendra glanced over at Xavier, he was performing the same odd dance.

Wu Lin doffed her shawl and joined him on the stage. In immediate response, a second creature appeared in the hovering light beside him.

Magique manipulated the controls, and suddenly six aliens crowded the field. She joined them onstage, and now there were nine. Somehow they interacted with each other as if they were actually manipulated by nine different puppeteers: talking, rolling, jumping . . . Xavier and his assistants lending eccentric mimelike precision to their roles, populating an entire imaginary hive with a succession of simple shrugs and shoulder hunches.

Kendra was open mouthed with amazement. These were masters at play. No . . . at *work*. They were calibrating the equipment, accustoming themselves to the reduced gravity. She felt honored to witness such a masterful display.

Xavier stopped, and stepped down from the platform. For all the exertion, she noted that his breathing was barely elevated. His eyes seemed distant. "Tomorrow, we'll start looping the movement for the holos, the virt, and the bots. We'll need to meet with the local players by day after. The gamers arrive in eight days."

"Yes. Six P.M. adjusted local time."

He mused. "NPCs arrive thirty hours earlier. We'll need to be ready. I want a sleep cycle adjusted for Montreal winters."

"Polarized dome, or artificial lighting? Whichever you prefer."

She couldn't help it—she was actually quite impressed by the little man's artistic focus. Subtract the egotism, and despite his height she might have found him appealing.

He yawned. "I'd like to see where I'm sleeping now."

"May I ask a personal question?"

"I did," Xavier laughed. "Proceed."

"Your father is still alive, isn't he?"

He pressed his lips together tightly. "Yes."

She paused, trying to work out the right way to ask the next question.

"Was he . . . worried about his calculations? The Aeros asteroid?"

His face tightened as well. "That's one thing he never doubted. Did you? You had to have been . . . what . . . seven years old?"

"I still remember," she said. "Everyone frightened. Your dad bounced this asteroid out of its course. It came within ten thousand miles of Earth. Something could have gone wrong. We can't survive without Earth—"

"Not Dad. Not ever." His smile was entirely too bright.

"I remember," she said. "Yes. Well . . . shall we take a look at the maze itself?"

"Give us a few moments first, would you?"

Kendra nodded, and left them.

Wu Lin and Magique mimed their way through phrases of human and insectile body language, as well as a few that defied simple categorization. Then Xavier froze the images.

Panting, Magique flipped her red hair and waited for approval. Her hands babbled at Xavier.

"Good as anything I've ever worked on," he replied. "First rate. Kinesthetics are a little better in California, but the auditory is spot on, and I think the visual might be superior. Feels *lighter,* somehow. Better depth and color correction at oblique angles. I think they modified some of the French waldo gear."

"But is it good enough?" Wu Lin asked.

He nodded enthusiastically. "Oh, sweetheart. I'm going to give them the time of their lives, and Angelique . . ." His smile went dreamy. "Oh, she and I have old matters to resolve. And

Wayne Gibson . . . never in the history of the world has anyone traveled so far to be crushed so badly. My children . . . this is going to be fun."

The Beehive dome was deceptive. Two hundred meters in diameter, it was smaller than the first major gaming dome, still active in California. Not large enough for a major event. Ages before, a meteor had plowed deep into an ancient maze of lava tunnels above a pool of dirty ice. Digging had not been the tricky part. Sealing the tunnel walls, making connections and barriers, creating an airtight lacework under a simple water shield, and *knowing* it was airtight, enough to bet lives . . . that was the hard part.

And now it was filled with a hundred major and countless minor bubbles of various sizes, distorted spheres of woven aluminum alloy. Doors and tubes linked the bubbles, but they would seal in case of a leak or blowout.

Five or six tall Lunies still worked scaffolding around the walls of a cavernous sphere. They paused to observe the visitors. Xavier ignored them.

"Of course," Kendra said, "you'll have a more complete tour later, and will be supervising the final work, but we wanted you to inspect the interior."

He nodded. "We had a mock-up in Calgary, but the gravity . . . my, it really does make a difference."

He jumped to the top of a huge, frilly mushroom and then up again. He scampered hand-over-hand up the wall, a performance that would have impressed the greatest rock climber who ever lived. Xavier's gorgeous posse followed him up, climbing over frost that crumbled under their hands and rained down at Kendra. Again and despite herself, Kendra was impressed.

This was like playtime at the gifted weird kids class.

It was time to move on. Kendra said, "Your rooms are ready, and your luggage has already been deposited. Shall we go?" She led them away.

When hundreds of human beings breathe each other's recycled air for months at a time, the opportunities for chemical or biological contagion are endless. Someone was checking the system at all times, and no one paid a bit of attention to the men in the blue suits.

Doug and Thomas Frost had watched everything, pretending to check wall conduits for the dome's trace contaminant control system. They remained silent until after the little man and his assistants retreated to privacy.

"So . . . that was Xavier," Doug said.

Thomas suppressed a nasty, quiet chuckle. "I wonder," he said, "what he'd say if he knew how strange this game was *really* going to be?"

11

Shotz

The twins were in the main Arrivals lounge a half hour prior to the shuttle's drop from orbit. The silver and red capsule flexed its crab-like legs and blew a cloud of lunar dust against the view windows, then settled down as the pressure tunnel wriggled out like a metal snake and locked to its side. Five minutes later, the passengers disembarked and passed through the pressure locks into customs, where they were given opportunities to declare valuables. There were thirty-two passengers on this flight, six members of the press, twenty tourists, and six Lunies returning from mandatory Earth furlough.

The press declared their vid gear, Lunies declared luxury items ferried back from L5 or planet Earth, and most of the tourists declared only enough to deflect curiosity. On the way home, they'd have moon rocks and other mementos, but few carried anything worthy of note.

This was particularly true of the men and one cold-eyed woman who all wore *Eddington Crater Tour* buttons.

"Welcome," Thomas said to the largest of them, a man he knew only as Shotz. "I hope the trip was pleasant."

"All but the last few minutes," Shotz said. His voice sounded like metal against metal. "The captain seemed to find it amusing to postpone deceleration until the last moment."

If you didn't do that, you ran out of fuel. Thomas didn't say so.

The woman, a beefy redhead with piercing blue eyes, flexed her full red lips into a smile. "It would be interesting to have words with him." Shotz turned his head slowly, gave her a disapproving glare. "Later," she amended.

Another eleven quiet, cool-eyed men were clustered around these two. Thirteen in all. Thomas waited to see if any of them would initiate a conversation. It only took ten seconds to remind himself that these people were not here for words.

"Well. It is good to see you. Before your tour, we've arranged the interview you requested."

"Mr. McCauley?" Shotz asked. Nothing wrong with using the name. Little remained a secret for long on the Moon. Anyone who cared to look would know that these people had visited the Fabrication hutch.

The *why* and the *how much* of their visit, on the other hand, could remain mysterious.

The Brothers Frost led their very special guests to luggage claim, and from there to the maglev system. A car was just pulling out as they arrived at the platform, but there was nothing to worry about: Another would be along within ten minutes.

Tick-tock. Tick-tock.

··· **12** ···

Gamers

November 13, 2085

Considering everything that happened, and what the events of the Moon Maze Game came to symbolize, it is surprising that more lies aren't told about how and when it all began.

In one sense, it all began on November 12, 2085, when the first load of gamers and tourists appeared at Heinlein pad number 8, on the shuttle from Lagrange Two.

The popular lie would be that it arrived with no fanfare, that nonessential tasks from Clavius to Mount Bullwinkle had not ground to a halt as Lunatics paused to watch the shuttle sink into a bloom of moondust.

The lie would be that the gamers and Non-Player Characters were not completely awed by their reception, reduced to appreciative murmurs even after transit in the shuttle. And chiefest among those attempting to remain nonchalant was Wayne Gibson.

Gibson had been unable to sleep at all for the last thirty-six hours, even knowing how desperately valuable dream time would be over the coming days.

He *should* have cocooned himself in his cabin. He should have wired himself into a d-web and let the ship computer coax him down into healing slumber. But then he couldn't have watched the screens and haunted the shuttle's narrow corridors and annoyed the pilots.

If he'd slept, he couldn't have hung out with the other gamers and NPCs in the undersized lounge—and protocol be damned! There would be plenty of time to play prima donna once they touched down.

And what a group they were! The midsized Spider-class shuttle was snug, but up at the L2 point, they'd had a little time to just party and relax together.

As soon as the juddering had stopped, the captain's voice sounded over the ship intercom, and his face appeared floating in the air above their webbed cots.

"And that little pull you're feeling is all the gravity we've got in this neck of the woods. I want to welcome you all to Luna, Heinlein base, named for the twentieth-century science fiction author. If this is your final destination, I invite you to pick up your luggage at the immigration station. Hey! That kinda rhymes."

Wayne grinned to himself, wondering how many times the captain had retreaded that lame little joke. It didn't matter. All he wanted was a chance to get up and actually put his feet on . . . well, if not lunar soil, at least lunar concrete.

"And if you're continuing on to one of the other bases . . . well, you still need to go through immigration. Your luggage will be examined separately, and taken to your transportation, whatever that may be. Welcome to Luna!"

The *Fasten Your Web* sign dimmed. All over the shuttle air seals audibly popped. The walls vibrated with cheers, his own louder than most.

You're on the friggin' Moon! The voice in his head boomed, still amazed.

Even after the invitation, after grueling weeks of training, after liftoff from Earth in the orbiter craft and the intervening stay at the L2 Hilton . . . some part of him still couldn't believe it, had been holding his emotions in check.

You're on the Moon.

He was almost afraid to stand up, so powerful was the unexpected wave of emotion. Why? Why did he feel so gut-slammed by all of this?

Angelique Chan, his beautiful room-if-not-bunkmate peered down over the edge of the upper berth and grinned at him. "Because you've looked at it all your life, silly."

"How do you *do* that?" he asked, shaking his head.

Her smile became even more mysterious. Even upside down, her lustrous hair had taken its own sweet time descending to fringe her face. "Trade secrets. I tell you, and you tell two friends, and pretty soon no one needs me anymore."

She performed a flipping roll-over only a Cirque du Soleil contortionist could ever have managed on Earth. She landed bouncing on her heels, taking a moment to catch her balance.

"Whoa!" She crouched, settled and then spun to face him. "Are we ready for this?"

"We've come an awful long way if we're not," he said.

"No . . . you don't understand. You really don't."

"Then teach me," he said.

"Everything until this moment? Just preparation." She came near enough that he could feel her breath on his face, and smell its sweetness. "Everything we say, everything we do is about to be judged. Everyone is watching for advantage. The training is over—"

"But the game doesn't start until tomorrow—"

"*No!*" she said fiercely, and grabbed his shoulders. "The game starts *now,* do you understand? Everything you see and hear that comes from another gamer, or a bribed NPC—"

"What?"

She scrunched up her face. "You've got to be kidding me. An NPC who takes a 'suggestion' from an associate of this gamer or that Game Master might be fined, or blackballed, but the game's still *lost.* There is only one first lunar game, and I wouldn't put anything past any of them."

"You brought me here to distract the Man," he said. "But you're going to take my advice, too. I've come too far to shut my mouth."

Her jaw worked, then tightened. She was listening.

"Too much emotion. Too much old history. Xavier will want to know that he beat us clean. Above board. I'd bet my socks on it."

They'd had this conversation before. And until or unless there was definite evidence either way, they'd have it again. "Maybe," she finally conceded. "Perhaps. We'll see."

During the last sleep cycle, a bundled parcel had been left before every door. Wayne unwrapped his. A tall black hat, with a golden cluster and feathered top. A red cloak with two vertical rows of silver buttons, gold chevrons and tasseled shoulders. An officer's uniform. British, he reckoned.

It took him only three minutes to strip off his clothes and fit into the new garb, which was, despite its appearance, of some light and stretchy material that conformed to his body like spray paint.

Angelique had stripped her package open as well, but her costume was a well-tailored tan explorer's costume, like something some proper Englishman might have worn on an expedition up the Congo. He doubted Dr. Livingstone had ever looked so edible. The fabric accentuated her form without exaggerating it.

She slipped on her pith helmet and gave it a jaunty slant. "What in the world is that little bastard up to?" she wondered, but he heard the excitement in her voice, in a way he had not in years. *Just like the old days.*

Hell. Win, lose or draw, this was going to be fun.

It only took Angelique and Wayne a combined total of twelve minutes to pack up their cabin possessions and stuff them into the scan-bags for pickup. Clothing was bundled to be scanned, and everyone wore similarly lightweight pseudo-period clothing. Most seemed British, or referenced some part of the British Empire. India. China. And . . . Africa? The sun never set, so they said.

When the next bell rang and their room door opened, Wayne and Angelique joined a line of thirty passengers in the hall outside.

Wayne fought excitement and a newly blossoming sense of claustrophobia. He'd bottled it up just fine for the past week, but now, so close to disembarking . . .

The explosion of relief and anticipation was almost overwhelming.

Angelique's bound club of lustrous dark hair bounced and settled beneath her helmet's rim with every step.

He became aware that the man behind him was chanting "The Moon, the Moon, the Moon . . ." in little breathless exhalations.

Wayne looked back. The guy's name was Roger something. An NPC, he thought, wearing a white sailor uniform that would have seemed in place on a British frigate.

Roger stood about four inches shorter than Wayne, and had the kind of loose skin around his neck that suggested recent weight loss. The guy was bright-eyed and carrot-topped, radiated "gaming" from every pore. He sighed in exasperated joy as they locked eyes.

"Can you believe this? Everything automated and slick for the last two weeks, but the last two minutes just goes all to hell."

"Way of the world, old boy." Wayne grinned at himself. Unbidden, a creaky British accent had crept into his voice.

British Empire. Nineteenth century. Pay attention to the clues.

To his credit, Roger adjusted almost as quickly. "Never better," he said.

The corridor was lined with costumed well-wishers. Some played their roles impeccably, but others seemed vaguely uncomfortable. He suspected this last group had little gaming experience. They'd be Lunies recruited as extras, playing their parts as best they could for unseen cameras.

Angelique was keeping her smile bright, but she whispered out of the side of her mouth. "Damn. I'd hoped we'd have a little time before the"—a swift shift in tones as a brightly lipsticked woman of middle years materialized—"Junie Bug! How *are* you?"

The two women exchanged bobble-headed air kisses. Even Wayne recognized June Simmons, the publisher and head reporter for the Web's largest gaming zine, *Fan-Tasm*. So Earth

was sending up the A-team, not just leaving it to the local string-
ers to file workable stories.

Oddly, that thought pepped Wayne up. He found himself strut-
ting through the doorway into the main hall, where they were
hustled into elevators as guides chattered greeting.

A woman who looked as if she might have been Samoan, with
beautiful strong curves and a good smile, greeted them in the
foyer. "My name is Kendra Griffin, Chief of Operations of Heinlein base," she said. "It is my honor to welcome you to our home."
She wore a lovely lace-frilled gown that reminded him of a water
lily. It offset her golden skin beautifully, and would have been
right in place on the lady accompanying a British officer to a
regimental ball. "You are on the surface level, only one of seven
floors, each disk-shaped and sunk into the lunar regolith to a
total depth of four hundred feet. We're going down to the third
level. Your gear is going down to level five, and you'll rejoin it
later. Right now, we want to invite you to look at the chart right
here—"

As they proceeded down the corridor, wisps of chamber music
rose up to meet them.

The folks lining the hall seemed more . . . comfortable in their
roles, and he suspected that more of these were genuine actors,
Non-Player Characters, a few of them even imported up from
Earth itself for the event.

Mickey and Maud Abernathy wore vaguely Middle Eastern
garb. Did the British Empire have holdings in the Arabian penin-
sula in the nineteenth century? Their Aladdin-esque pantaloons
and flaring blouses certainly suggested as much.

"Excuse me," he asked. "I'm not certain we've been intro-
duced."

Mickey smiled graciously. "The Abernathys," she said. "We've
just returned from a research expedition in Egypt, uncovering
the lost temple of Solomon."

Ah. Backstory right there. So, Xavier was letting them keep
their names, but changing their histories. The Abernathys were
an academic couple from Brighton (Mickey taught history, and
Maud was a published fantasy novelist) who usually played as

paired psychic sensitives. Saying they were recently returned from Egypt on a dig suggested that their IFGS points would manifest as a combination of human psi-ability and Oriental mysticism.

Marching at Wayne's side was a plump woman in . . . what was that? The female version of a nineteenth-century British Raj military uniform? The actual insignias had been removed, but the style was right. He guessed a female soldier of fortune. The woman's name was Sharmela Tamil, a Gold Ticket winner from Sri Lanka. Not an IFGS kingpin, but a loyal fan who had dropped her hundred bucks—or the local equivilent—in the lottery.

They entered a bank of elevators (oops! lifts) in which he was polite enough not to notice the anachronisms. There was a limit to what the IFGS could modify on the moon without infringing upon safety or utility.

The door slid shut. The elevator fell with a recorded rattle.

The most interesting personage packed in the little room with him traveled not on her feet, but in a capsule with twin five-inch treads. This would be Asako Tabata, the TechWitch herself, the girl who was probably the best pure gamer in the world. Five years ago she would have dominated the entire proceedings. In the intervening time, muscular dystrophy had finally caught up with Asako. It was a miracle she was there at all.

She couldn't walk. Most certainly she could no longer climb, and that was a real pity, because Asako had been one of the IFGS' finest wall crawlers. But by fan request and special dispensation, she was attending the first lunar game as an actual player, not merely an NPC. He wondered at the negotiations for that, and guessed that many of them had been commercial in nature. But how in the world did they justify such technology in a nineteenth-century game?

Time to find out.

"Excuse me," he asked. "Do I know you?"

Her answering voice was partially synthesized, but you would have to listen very carefully to detect it. She played behind the shield of her isolation bubble. No longer able to breathe without mechanical assistance, she had invested over a million dollars of her lifetime winnings into the damnedest gaming costume imaginable. It was her life support unit, but the gleaming silver and gold capsule had both arms and wheels.

"Asako Tabata," the speaker said. Behind her shield, she smiled as her lips moved. He had never met her, but had seen her in interviews and gaming vids, and the computer voice matched her own very closely. "Step-niece to the esteemed Prince Dakkar Nemo," she said. "He himself fashioned my capsule, that I might join him exploring beneath the waves, despite my physical infirmities."

Captain Nemo. Of course. A man of sufficient genius to develop an electrical submarine by the time of America's civil war. Who could doubt that, if he had survived, he might not create something along the line of Asako's life-support bubble? In all likelihood, she had only been given a bare outline. It would be her job to improvise in the days ahead, creating all the backstory she wished.

Asako was in her late fifties now, her face sharp-edged and pale. The wrinkles of time and woe had stolen much of her appealing waifishness, but when she smiled, he felt an almost absurd urge to bow.

And did so. "M'lady Tabata," he said.

She couldn't raise a hand—the disease had progressed too far for that. With a barely audible *hum,* the machine nodded her head for her. As the lecture progressed he scanned her treaded cocoon.

"You may not know me, but I know you," she said.

"Do you?"

"Yes." Her lips moved, but her voice sounded a bit augmented. "You are Lieutenant Wayne Gibson." A pause for breath. "They say that in India, you saved an entire regiment during the late unpleasantness."

She was feeding him. *Late unpleasantness.* He wondered what that referred to? So . . . he was British, and a war hero? "People exaggerate," he murmured.

The elevator doors opened, and his claustrophobia vanished in a single sigh.

The room yawned, surely the most cavernous on the Moon. Its domed ceiling stretched high above them.

The walls were draped with gigantic red-white-and-blue Union Jack starbursts. A standing-room only crowd burst into applause as they entered. If he'd been nonplussed by the NPC-lined halls up top, what happened next was an absolute assault.

A banner stretching from one side of the room to another read: *The Adventurer's Club Welcomes Our Daring Crew!*

Only then did Wayne look down. The floor was composed of some transparent material, plastic or glass or something else, set over a swimming pool or reservoir. The water was clear enough to see golden coral growing thirty feet beneath them . . . and even as he watched, a squadron of merfolk swam into view, a wedge of bronzed skin, emerald flippers and for the females, discretely positioned chest shells. He estimated about fifteen of them, but it was difficult to be certain because other guests obscured his view. The pyramid of swimmers fractured into smaller groups, then pairs. They scooted and somersaulted through the water, then reformed into a wedge and swam out of view.

All but one. One mermaid remained behind, a pug nose with blazing red hair and a fleshy, muscular body. Fit/Fat again. Looked good on her. She gazed up at him, and winked one emerald eye. Bubbles gushed from her lips as she mouthed the word: *Later.*

She swam away.

"Quite amazing," a rotund fellow in Beefeater garb said. His handlebar mustache was slightly askew. "I believe Professor Challenger brought them back from Fiji."

The room was filled with bejeweled and gowned celebrants, perhaps two hundred of them in a room that had probably never held more than a hundred and fifty. They displayed an array of costumes that must have occupied every amateur or freelance seamstress and tailor on the Moon for months. What a show!

"Hallo." A tall, broad man in another red Beefeater uniform approached. His British accent was phony-thick, but dammit, at least he was trying. He looked like a fleshy John Wayne, with a receding hairline and strong laugh lines. The Duke approached with his hand extended, and Wayne automatically reached out in return. The very vaguest of recollections danced at the edge of memory.

"Good seeing you, sir!" the guy said. "Name's Chris Foxworthy. Met you two years ago in the desert." *Ah. Vegas?*

"Had a good run with you there, and actually took honors." So . . . he might have come through the low-level game there, and won a few points.

"Good man," Wayne said. He lowered his voice to a conspiratorial whisper. "I came when called, of course. But it was all so hush-hush. Do you know what the boffins are up to? They certainly have enough to work with, after . . . well, you know. The unpleasantness."

Foxworthy wagged his head solemnly. "Sorry old boy. Not for me to say."

A string quartet seated in the room's corner began a Straus waltz and four pairs of NPCs danced with clockwork precision.

This was all just lovely. Clearly, they were already on camera. Performing a waltz in one-sixth gravity while pretending to be under Earth Normal was quite a trick. Not all of them succeeded, despite obvious practice. Sharmela Tamil had grabbed a female partner and joined the fun, but a too-enthusiastic spin launched them both into the air, to drift like autumn leaves. They looked just wonderful, as if they were floating.

He was certain that the broadcast and the inevitable edited video streams would be great hits.

An oddness presented itself: In the last five years he'd grown accustomed to the *pop* his knee made when he stood. Here, it didn't. Less weight stress perhaps? He damned near pushed himself off the floor when he straightened, and noted that several of the others had the same tendency to bounce up when they moved.

"Have you met everyone?" Wayne asked, and steered Foxworthy over to Mickey and Maud Abernathy. Like Asako Tabata they were fiftyish now, and the last time he'd seen them before today had been in their Pushmi-Pullyu costume at a Dream Park New Year's soiree. There was something different about them now, more than just the Middle Eastern costuming, and he couldn't put his finger on it.

"Mickey? Maud?" Mickey raised a haughty eyebrow. Right. Too much informality for nineteenth-century Britain. "Pardon.

Mr. and Mrs. Abernathy? I would like to present Mr. Christopher Foxworthy—"

"Pleased to meet you," Maud said.

"Charmed," Mickey said. His accent was Cambridge layered over Cockney. Wayne suspected he'd been a scholarship kid. Maud, on the other hand, seemed veddy upper class.

"I suspect we'll be seeing more of each other in the future," Foxworthy said. In other words, despite his present costume, the guy was almost certainly an NPC who would be making their lives miserable in the coming days.

As they started their chitchat, he looked around the room, wondering where Angelique had gone. He became aware of a disturbance on the other side of the room, people cheering. He saw two tall, superbly vital women, one Asian, one quite Nordic. And a full foot shorter, but walking as if he were riding an elephant, a tiny man with a gleaming, shaven scalp.

Oh, God, he thought. *Here it comes.*

Like a miniature icebreaker carving its way through a glacier field, Xavier plowed toward the middle of the room. He nodded here, shook a hand there, as he stopped to hear a joke, question or compliment, laughing politely in turn. His every word or nod of a shaven head an act of noblesse oblige.

Then his forward progress stopped, and he mounted a small stage at the back of the room. "Your attention please!" he called, voice booming from hidden speakers. Instantly, all conversation ceased.

"I, Lord Xavier, am honored to welcome you to the Adventurer's Club." A hot current rippled through the room. Whatever he said next would shape the next seventy-two hours of their lives.

"Many of you have no doubt read the sensational newspaper accounts of the disappearance of Professor Cavor, and his adventures upon the Moon. Perhaps you have even read the fictionalized accounts of this fantastic journey as written by Herbert George Wells, which ended in a disrupted radio call, with no further communications to come. We all believed that this was the end of this great man. Then just two months ago our dear

American friend Nicola Tesla received an almost unbelievable radio message. Cavor was *alive,* and after years in captivity, had somehow created a radio powerful enough to send a signal to Earth. He not only gave us details of his captivity, but sent the formula for the amazing Cavorite, which allowed him to break gravity's shackles and fly to the Moon. The Queen's top scientists have been able to re-create his invention, and with it build a device capable of taking ten stout souls on a mission of rescue.

"I warn you: Not all are expected to survive. You have accepted our commission without fanfare or promise of reward . . . except for that of serving our gracious Queen, and the ability to proclaim, now and for all time, that they are the very best and bravest. That, and the right to plant the Union Jack on the Moon itself. Who is with me?"

A moment of stunned silence, as Wayne's mind whirled. They were on the Moon, pretending to be on the Earth, about to travel to the Moon. But not the *real* Moon, but the fantasy Moon envisioned by H. G. Wells.

The sheer poetic madness of it all fairly took his breath away.

That sentiment seemed shared, because there was a long, incredulous pause, then Angelique stepped forward, fetching in her tan jungle explorer regalia.

"I, Angelique Chan, accept your commission. My compatriots have come from the four corners of the Empire not merely to rescue the great Professor Cavor, but to claim the Moon itself for our beloved Queen."

Choruses of "Hear, Hear!" arose from around the room, and Xavier nodded in satisfaction, his shaven head shining.

"Then I ask only that you enjoy the hospitality of the Adventurer's Club, that you may carry our respect and admiration with you across the cold stellar void. That you enjoy libations aplenty, that they may stimulate your courage, that you not quail regardless of the challenge ahead. That you live this night, and every day from now on, as if it is not your last, but your very first."

As the room exploded with applause, Xavier hopped down from the stage.

Xavier passed through the crowd, flanked by his Valkyries, smiling and nodding and shaking hands as he went.

Then his forward progress stopped, and he was talking to . . . Angelique. He nodded politely, then turned and looked directly at Wayne. And headed his way, the crowd parting before him, Angelique close behind. As they approached, Wayne could almost hear dramatic showdown music blaring, maybe some of that classic Ennio Morricone wail from *The Good, The Bad and the Ugly*. Many of the crowd had the threadlike flexcams woven into their costumes. These images all flowed into a central bank and synchronized so that distant viewers would ultimately be able to swoop, dart and hover like hummingbirds through a virtual party.

This was the beginning of the game, and Xavier knew it. The munchkin had been here for a week. If there were any psychological or physical adjustments needed by lunar tourists, Wayne and his companions would be right in the middle of those changes, while Xavier had already adapted.

"Well played," Wayne said as Xavier reached him, and they shook hands. *My, my, aren't we all polite when the cameras are on?*

"To what exactly are you referring, Sir Wayne?"

Oh? He was a knight now? Damn, this was more fun all the time!

"Well, if I'm not mistaken, our day begins in just over ten hours. Should we really partake of libation until the early hours?" Wayne winced at his faux Britishisms.

"The journey is long, Sir Wayne. You will have time to recover, I promise you."

Wayne could see it in Xavier's icy blue eyes. His first guess had been correct: Xavier hadn't forgotten or forgiven, but he wasn't going to cheat. When he crushed Angelique, it would be completely aboveboard, leaving her no grounds for appeal.

Xavier smiled. "You look well. The desert air must agree with you."

There it was, the poisoned needle hidden in the haystack, a coded reference to his current status in Vegas. *Couldn't let it alone, could you?* "I take the billet assigned," he said. "For Queen and country."

For a moment, the tension between the three of them dropped, and they just looked at the disk-shaped room, the hundreds of fans dressed as nineteenth-century Englishmen and -women. This was it, the greatest entertainment event in human history. Perhaps, just perhaps, that was enough to temper the antagonism.

A waiter passed, carrying a tray of brandy snifters filled with champagne. Angelique plucked one from the tray, and they did the same. She raised her glass. "To a fine adventure."

Xavier raised his glass. "To old friends, old memories, and a fine adventure," he said. Then Xavier and his coterie glided away.

"Not . . . quite what I would have expected from Lord Xavier," Angelique said thoughtfully. "One wonders if he has fully revealed his intent."

Well, it was probably safer to be too cautious than too trusting.

"Ah well. If we knew everything, would it really be as much of an adventure, Sir Wayne?"

"Nicely observed, Lady Angelique," he said, and they raised their glasses in toast.

Kendra had seen Scotty at the other side of the room, and knew that he would make his way over to see her in his own time. Every broken marriage is broken in its own way.

In the meantime, she watched the crowd. The gamers, the tourists, the Heinlein staff and those who had come in from around Luna and the L2 to be a part of this . . . everyone who had been given costumes and instructions on playing their parts.

Her heart was starting to trip-hammer. She'd wondered how she would feel, seeing Scotty again after three years. Now she knew.

"Well, Ms. Griffin, don't start counting your chickens before they cross the road."

She turned to look up at Toby McCauley, well over six feet of broad shoulders and narrow hips, dashing in his vermilion tailcoat with double vertical rows of silver buttons. His gut had spread a bit, but the Fabrication shop steward she'd dated for a month three years ago was still imposing, a fact he was putting to good use in his campaign against her. He was quite good at smiling while he slipped the knife in, and was perfectly aware that he was responsible for the nickname "Sheila Monster." Unfortunately, the moniker had stuck. And the "Ms. Griffin" part. She'd kept the name because it was easier for people to pronounce than Tuinukuafe had ever been. And she still liked the way it sounded. The way it felt to say it.

"I'll find other entertainment, then," she said.

He grinned at her lazily, and she wondered what odd and perhaps embarrassing memories he was hauling out of mental storage. Dammit, she didn't know why she reacted that way, but she didn't like it.

"Well," when McCauley was making a point, and wanted to seem all folksy, his Outback accent tended to rise to the top. You'd hardly know he'd taught engineering at Monash University, before winning his berth at New Melbourne. "Are we having fun yet?" He smiled, but she detected a certain tautness there.

"Isn't fun a good thing?"

"Everyone has a lot at stake here. Especially you."

"You, too."

"I know. This whole game thing . . . could make us look silly, you know. It better run as smooth as glass."

His eyes flickered away from her for a moment. That was interesting. She'd played poker with Toby, and seen that twitch and glance when he didn't like the cards he'd been dealt. Maybe he wasn't quite as confident about election as he wanted her to believe.

Or maybe something else. Jealous that Scotty was coming, perhaps? His smile brightened, and the odd expression was gone. "I just don't want us looking like clowns, love. I'm not the only one worried about this gaming rubbish. And worries equal votes."

Three weeks until the election, and there was little doubt that Mac's polling was pulling even with her own. She still had a margin . . . but he'd cut it in half in the last week. But the Moon Maze Game could work in her favor.

"Hope you haven't made a blue, love," he whispered, circling behind her like a shark nosing an unguarded limb. *Made a mistake*. Aussie slang. "Then there's always hubby dear."

"What about my Scotty?" she said, already knowing the answer.

"Here comes drongo ex as we speak," Mac said, and smiling politely, wove his way away. Modern Australian slang didn't quite mesh with nineteenth-century Britain, but she doubted their conversation would make any of the game-vids. There were limits to the amount of fantasy she was willing to tolerate.

Counting to ten controlled her temper, forced a smile back to her face as Scotty and his partner arrived at her table.

Kendra stood for a chaste hug, and a small, dry kiss. "You look good, Scotty."

"Back at you." His hug was warm but unpresumptuous, his arms as strong as a flyer's. He said, "Kendra. I would like to present my friend Ali. Ali, my ex-wife, Kendra Tuinukuafe."

"I usually use Griffin," she said, smiling her warmest welcome. She shook hands with the little man.

His palms were moist and warm, but pleasant. Ali was quite dark, and lithe in a wispy way. He wore golden pantaloons and a buccaneer shirt that felt more *Arabian Nights* than nineteenth-century sub-Saharan, but he seemed entirely unconcerned. Ali bowed deeply. *"As-Salamu Alaykum"*

"Alaykum As-Salaam," she replied.

"Even in my far and humble land, I have heard of Kendra Griffin," he said. "I believe you keep an eye on some of my father's treasures."

"I do my level best," she said. "But be not so humble. Your name has traveled far, as well." She refrained from speaking further details aloud: Doubtless many in the room already knew of Ali, but she had no intention of broadcasting his identity to anyone who hadn't made the connection. Privacy is a precious commodity. A prince masquerading as a prince was a delicious conceit.

Ali surveyed a knot of gamers congregating around a glittering, meticulously detailed ice sculpture of Buckingham Palace. "I think I'll join my new friends," he said. Then to Scotty: "You can see me from here, yes?" The sarcasm was unmistakable.

Scotty pretended not to notice. "Sure. Go ahead."

Kendra sipped at her drink for a few moments, and then sighed. "I won't lie. I wondered how it would feel to see you."

"And?"

"Feels good. But a tad worrisome."

"What's to worry?"

She took a long sip. "You remember McCauley?"

"Think so. Big Figjam? Heard you dated for a while." "Figjam" was an Aussie acronym: *Fuck, I'm Good. Just Ask Me.*

Kendra chuckled, but wondered who'd had the big mouth. "That's the one. Well, he's the face on the anti-Independence movement."

"How serious is that? I have to admit I've been all gaming and training, the last few months."

"Very serious, Scotty. Luna needs a seat at the table. We're the ones who've made the change."

"What change is that?"

The string quartet had begun playing again, very stately. Out on the dance floor, a pale balding gentleman in top hat and tails was leading a dozen couples through a graceful series of twirls.

She paused. "Back at the end of the twentieth century, there was a guy named Frank White who wrote about something called the 'Overview Effect.' Hear of it?"

"Sort of a long view on Earth because you're seeing it from space?"

Kendra nodded enthusiastically. "High marks. Look. On Earth, you can actually see only fifty miles or so, up to the curve of the horizon. Psychologically, it's very easy for corporations, churches or governments to convince you that your little corner of the world is the best place, the only 'real' place, and that people off somewhere else are somehow less . . . human."

"Wars work that way."

"And pollution, and economic exploitation, and land grabs. The human race suffered through that for a long time."

"So? What's wrong now?"

"Complacency. Earth was headed for trouble—energy and raw materials—before we caught the Second Wave back in 2020." Efficient fusion, and just in time, too. "And I think that people don't realize the degree to which every move, every dollar invested, every orchestration of every resource is still guided by our old way of looking at the world. But up here . . . looking at the Earth, it's hard not to think of it as an egg, fragile, but destined to give birth to something . . . else. Something better."

"Better than *Homo sapiens?*"

"*Homo interstellar,* perhaps." She winced. Even to her own ears, she sounded a bit evangelical. "I know, I know. But whether I'm right about that or not, it serves Earth just fine for her colonies to stay colonies. To remain children, in effect. But what would have happened to Europe if America had never grown beyond a patchwork of colonies? The United States generated an entirely new vision of human potential, and changed the world. I think that Luna, and the L5s, and the Belt can do the same for Earth, but we have to speak with one voice."

"Hear, hear," Scotty said, and raised his glass.

"But things aren't that simple."

"They never are."

"McCauley is backed by a half-dozen concerns—including Cowles Industries, as if you didn't know. The tendency has been to keep all of the negotiations case-by-case, rather than leveraging everything into a single package. If we stand together, we can change the world. The solar system." She leaned forward. "The galaxy."

Scotty felt his right eyebrow tense. "The galaxy? Ain't that a little grandiose?"

"You've read the SETI reports. We still have zero real evidence of nonhuman intelligent life anywhere in the universe. A few amino acids here and there, and something that might have been some kind of fungoid fossil. What if we're all there is? What if it's our job to take this green plague and spread it across the stars?"

"The Green Plague." He laughed, but under the mirth was a touch of unease. "Most people mellow with age. You sound more like a true believer now than when I met you."

She laughed, and then laid her warm hand on his. Love had never been the problem between them. There had been hurt, but not betrayal or accusation in their parting. "Scotty, the timing of your return either couldn't have been better, or couldn't have been worse. I'm really not sure which." She laughed. "When Mac attacks me, I can deal with it. But these are highly independent, alpha-plus psychological types we're dealing with. They'd have to be to survive up here. I'm asking them to pull together in ways many of them fled Earth to escape. And their self-image is pure testosterone, believe me. Figjam to say the least."

"I remember."

"Then remember how you left."

He didn't want to. Once upon a time, the fear and pain had lashed him on a daily basis. To this day he could not simply lie on his back and peer up at the stars as might any schoolboy. They threatened to suck him up into the blackness. And then he knew why Kendra's eyes were both narrow and moist.

"They're saying I'm a coward," he said. "They're using my accident against you."

She nodded without speaking. He sighed. "And what do you think, Kendra?"

"I know how you make a living," she said. "I know you put your life on the line every day that you work."

He nodded. "But then, that's not exactly what we're talking about, is it?"

Her face didn't move, but he saw reflected in her eyes all the answer he needed. There was a particular variety of nerve necessary to make it up here. And Kendra's ex-husband, whose name she still carried, didn't have it. And if the husband lacks courage, what of the wife? *Why else would she want to bind us into some singular group, of one will and one word . . . "Freedom" from people a quarter-million miles distant means tyranny here at home.*

Then again, the argument could have been made the other way: *Does Kendra secretly want us to keep our apron strings? Does her husband's cowardice infect her? Will she sell us out to Earth, once we give her power . . . ?*

McCauley could attack her two ways with a single premise.

"God." He squinted, hard. "I hate politics."

"Me, too," she said. "But its all we've got. Listen, love. Play your game. There will be time for personal talk later. Right now, I'm just glad to see you."

And it was to her credit, and the strength of the relationship they'd always had, that he actually believed her.

"I should win," he decided.

"That would be good," she said. Then grinned wickedly. "I'll make it worth your while."

13

Downtime

Two hours later the music and merriment came to an end. The bald little man called Lord Xavier herded Scotty and the other gamers down a gleaming narrow hallway into a neighboring room. It was another cavernous chamber, lightly decorated, and Scotty had the sense that it was a storage unit of some kind, hastily reconfigured to resemble a hangar.

A thirty-foot grayish metal sphere balanced on four telescoping legs. The surface was covered with little flaps, and at the lowest edge a six-foot door opened onto a ramp.

At the base of the ramp, Xavier turned and faced them. "I present the Cavorite sphere, built to the professor's specifications. This is the beginning of your adventure. It will take you ten days to make the lunar passage. We will be in contact with you during that time, thanks to our great friend Mr. Tesla. I wish you Godspeed, and good luck."

He soberly shook each of their hands as they walked the ramp. The small hand within the white glove was soft and warm. Lord Xavier's eyes were very clear, bright blue and twinkled with mirth. He paused for a moment with Scotty. "Commander Griffin," he said gravely. "You are not known to me, but your father was. A mighty warrior, and I believe he was simply known as 'The Griffin,' was he not? In fact, I know that he distinguished himself highly on missions for my department, and I expect no less from his son."

Scotty bowed. "He set a very high standard indeed. I will endeavor not to shame him." And then passed up the ramp.

What was *that* about? Certainly giving Scotty more reinforcement about his role . . . the Non-Player Characters had circulated the room, casually mentioning aspects of the players' backstory, allowing them to springboard their role-playing off the NPCs. A general framework for improvisation, their names and personal histories worked into their new identities.

Interesting. He'd been told to expect that. But the reference to his father "The Griffin" implied that Xavier knew exactly who he was. Did he know the Prince's true identity as well?

The question was answered a moment later. "Prince Ali," he said to Scotty's charge. "You have traveled far, all the way from the Republic of Kikaya, to partake in our adventure. Now you travel farther still. *Salaam Alaykum.*"

"*Wa Alaykum As-Salaam,*" Ali replied courteously. But when Scotty met his eyes, it was clear that the young man was worried. Later, Scotty would reassure him. Surely, there was no safer place for Prince Kikaya than Heinlein base.

They marched through the door . . . and into a maze of plastic struts. Assistants hustled them off to the side, so that they would not obstruct the doorway. From this position, he saw that the great curving wall was a hologram-assisted facade. When the last gamer and NPC was aboard, the door was closed, and the assistants gave a collective sigh of relief.

"We're off!" quoth a plump, charming redhead. Scotty noticed that she seemed rather attached to Wayne, who himself was linked to Angelique Chan. "Game time is over, you are all off-duty until nine tomorrow morning. Please follow your escorts to your lodgings, where you will find your personal gear already stowed. If you have any needs, please let us know. Game starts at ten tomorrow morning, and until that time no cameras or recording devices will invade your privacy." Again, she glanced significantly at Wayne. Her eyes were liquid heat.

A lunar hookup. Sweet.

"So . . . ," Angelique said. "What is happening now? I mean in game time?"

"Look for yourself," the redhead said.

She clapped her hands and the bare wall blossomed. In the void, a crowd waving British flags cheered as a Cavorite sphere lifted off from the middle of Piccadilly Circus. Like a feather caught in an updraft it drifted into the sky, accelerating until it was swallowed by clouds.

"Ten days of game time will be condensed into ten hours of real time. A clock on the screen will give viewers on Earth and even here on the Moon a countdown to tomorrow's game. We had to make a choice: either reduce the number of hours it takes for a sphere to reach the Moon, or use time-lapse. We chose time-lapse. Any other questions?"

She was so bright and perky, and it all seemed so reasonable, that he relaxed. Fine. The game aspect of all of this was well in hand.

The redheaded mermaid's name was Darla, and her two-legged incarnation had attached herself to Wayne during the party, all twinkling eyes and smiles and warm soft promise. Her voice hinted at north Texas, or Oklahoma. She wasn't exactly pretty, and her Fit/Fat curves were fuller and rounder than Wayne's usual flirtations. But her energy was irresistible, her obvious interest in a tryst provocative as hell. His fingers tingled when they touched hers.

Angelique had raised an eyebrow at their connection, but after all, she was the one who had insisted that their partnership was all business and no yum-yum.

"I'll be ready," he said. "Trust me." Muscles and joints still ached from the months of training, and he knew that there was no way he would waste all that he had done, all that he'd been through.

Darla walked him to a rim elevator, taking him up to the surface, where shuttles waited to hustle them out to a clutch of dorms set in minor craters around Heinlein's rim. At every step, they'd each had to thumbprint the reader to pass to the next station.

The shuttle sped over its levitation track and deposited them in the dorm in about thirty seconds, barely enough time to accelerate and decelerate. The windows were deeply polarized, but the sun still blistered the white sandy ridges and meteor pockets. Hypnotic. He'd seen this territory countless times in films and vids, but to actually *be* here . . . !

The dome rose before them, and the shuttle slowed. Darla had leaned into him more fully. He could feel her body heat even through his dress uniform.

"Ask me in, darlin'?" she asked.

"I'm not sure I could find my way without you."

She giggled as the door opened. The hall outside was sealed to the side of the shuttle, the extending walkway firmly in place. "I assume my luggage is already here?"

"You assume correctly," she said. "Twenty-one, and twenty-two. Here you are. Your thumb?"

He extended it, and she took hold of it, and pressed her lips against the pad. They were pillow soft, and quite warm.

Wayne's throat felt thick. "I'm actually not sure I'm supposed to have anyone in the room with me . . . technically speaking, I'm on game time."

Her smile was gamine, her bright green eyes twinkling at him. "These pods need permission for overnight guests," she said. Then she pushed her thumb against the card. It flashed green. "See? I'm already clear."

Questions instantly raced through his mind. When had she inserted her name in his file? Had she been so certain of herself? Or . . .

"Are you . . . ?"

"Shhh," she whispered, and shushed his words with a kiss. Her breath was peppermint and brandy. Then she pulled back. "I asked for you. That's all you need to know."

An NPC? On a mission of seduction? Was Xavier operating Off the Grid?

She shook her head. "We're on our own time until morning," she said.

"Is that the truth?" He came close enough to brush noses with her. She never blinked. "Are you friend . . . or foe?"

Her eyes were hot enough to melt glass. "Search me."

Chris Foxworthy was floating on air. The halls of level four were almost deserted: It was between shift changes, and most people on the Moon drifted toward the time zones of their youth, all else being equal. Chris had grown up in California, and on the West Coast it was now two o'clock in the morning. In a little more than five hours, he'd be on the clock!

Gaming had been a part of his life long before he reached Luna and took a position as Kendra Griffin's personal assistant. In California, either in commercial venues or hooked into the 'net wearing reality gear, he'd loved the international community of loons who would forgo a weekend's sleep to be part of the latest Middle Earth or Berserker campaign. They were his folk, and in fact it was in the beginning of the Oort Cloud Game back in '68, which began in a secret alien ship buried beneath the lunar surface, that he first fell in love with Earth's Moon.

His first years on Luna had been as exciting as anyone could have hoped, but anything eventually becomes just another twenty-four hours, as the daily grind transforms the extraordinary into the commonplace. He'd thought about putting in for a billet on Ceres, when the first rumors about the Moon Maze Game filtered down through the ranks.

Flash forward two years, and Chris was pulling every string, calling in every favor, and cutting every corner to get on the NPC short list. Even then, he'd had to tap-dance his ass off. There was nothing easy about it, and even in a community as seen-it-all as the Lunies, a chance to participate in the first major off-planet game in history was intoxicating. Sure, there'd been some minor zero-gee LARPs on some of the stations and L5s, and there'd been brouhaha and global coverage, but this was different: a real gaming environment, top-notch players . . . This was for the history books, and Mrs. Foxworthy's little boy Chris was in the middle of it.

The door to his sleep capsule sighed open, and Chris stepped in, having to slide sideways to slip past his costume, which hung next to the little bathroom stall.

He fingered it appreciatively, laughing to himself. All the NPCs had received their Victorian costumes days before, and attended a four-hour workshop on carriage and dance. Of course, they had received far more training than that for the days ahead, and he chortled at the thought.

Most of them would ride the shuttles to the gaming area fully masked. It was going to be Halloween tomorrow, and even the most sober Joes would have to work hard to keep the grins off their sorry faces.

The gamers would walk the halls, getting into mischief and then escaping into their anonymity. He could hardly wait.

Chris brushed his teeth and sealed himself into the shower stall. The hot water bounced back at him from angles highly unlikely under full gravity, and he happily scrubbed and scrubbed. For the next three days, a good bath would be hard to come by. The water clung like a sheath of jelly, but Chris was used to that. He used his hands like blades to scrape water off his limbs into the suction grills. He finished by letting the cyclone whip the moisture back into the vents, air drying.

He stood to look at himself in the mirror. Fit enough, thin, bit of a paunch but nothing to be ashamed of: abdominal muscles just didn't work as hard up here, whether for breathing or posture, and it was common to see people with toned arms and great, low heart rates, and little potbellies. He was going to be fine.

Chris programmed his bed to start cooling a half hour before wakeup, and asked his clock to monitor his sleep rhythms to find the best time to awaken him within fifteen minutes of 8:00 A.M. lunar standard time. He was sliding into a mild dream state when his door chimed.

"Yes?" he asked as a sleepy-eyed man's face appeared in his mirror.

"Costume change," the man said. "You are chosen for an up-grade. It will only take a minute."

The guy's voice was vaguely accented, like middle European . . . Bulgaria or something. He hadn't seen the guy before, but he figured the Dream Park people had to be sending up all kinds of new talent. No surprise there.

He opened his door. The guy stood maybe a centimeter shorter than Chris, but broader across the shoulders. The ready smile seemed a little *too* ready, as if he was trying to stay polite and focused after a long, long day.

Hell, he could empathize with *that*.

The man held a square box in his left hand, and a metal slip with his right. "Thumb here," he said, and Chris stepped back as he stepped in, lowered his head as the door sighed shut. There was a brief, very brief moment when something in Chris' mind said *This doesn't feel right*—

Then he felt the arm slip around his neck, and knew he was in trouble.

But then, so was his attacker.

There were many favorite sports Lunies used to keep them-selves fit, and one of the most popular was nullboxing. Actually, *real* nullboxing was performed in zero gravity, a combination of grappling and striking performed in a chaotic cluster of jabbing elbows, gripping hands and frantic head-butts. On the Moon, there was so little gravity that most boxing or karate-type foot-work went to hell pretty fast, but the resistance of another live body made wrestling, and nullboxing training, a pretty intense way to get your PT points. And Chris had been there from the begin-ning, sweating and snarling through his workouts three times a week for the last three years.

And one thing he knew was that newbies, even those with grap-pling experience on Earth, took time to adjust to the change in gravity. An Earth-bound combat man would have to be ungodly strong and agile to turn a front somersault with a full-grown op-ponent on his back. Chris was neither. He simply knew that the move was possible, and the man who attacked him did not.

The effect was startling. When they went off their feet, his assailant was taken completely by surprise, and loosened his grip long enough for Chris to slam elbows back into his face.

Only the first one landed, but it was enough. In an adrenaline-crazed frenzy at a sixth of earth gravity, the two men exerted enough energy to send them flying into the walls at jarring speed.

They literally bounced off the far wall, and then . . .

The back of his attacker's head precisely struck the corner of a table, and his body spasmed, eyes snapping open and shut again like a marionette with tangled strings. He made a few wet rattling sounds, and then sprawled limp. Bloody spittle drifted toward the floor.

Chris bounced off the ceiling, frantic to grapple before the attacker got his bearings. As the man drifted upward, Chris slammed into him, swarmed around onto his back and got him in a headlock. The man was limp as a codfish. It only gradually dawned on Chris that the man might be—

His eyes were half open. His muscles were limp. He wasn't breathing. His head was dented.

Foxworthy made a rapid check of the body, and cursed to himself. He was shaking so hard that his teeth threatened to click.

Dead. A dead man in his apartment. He touched the phone pad. That was the move, to get Security here as soon as possible.

Nothing. The screen wouldn't respond. What in the hell?

Chris fished his shirt out of the laundry and spoke into the collar. Nothing.

Well, he would run down the hall, call from the first node. "Door, open," he said.

Nothing. Panic fluttered at the edge of his mind, but he managed to tamp it down. "Door, open." Nothing. No ready lights. Well, that was all right. There was a manual override . . .

He wrenched open the panel to the right of his door, and turned the little dial. That should have done it, should make the door pop right open . . .

Nothing.

Panic was beginning to look like a better and better idea. What the hell was going on here?

Foxworthy turned his attacker over, searched him and found

a communications device of unfamiliar design, fist-sized, like an old cellphone. Little green lights oscillated around a three-centimeter color screen with the words *Security Override* flashing once per second. And beneath that: *Enter Code*.

This device . . . this thing had somehow blocked his communications and sealed his door, using some security feature he had never even heard of. And now it wanted him to enter a code to turn it off? There was an alphanumeric pad, and also a microphone for voice entry. "Open?" Nothing. "One, two, three . . ."

Damn. There could be millions of codes. He was stuck here for the duration, until someone came looking for him. Stuck in a tiny room with a cooling corpse. Had he been the target? Or . . . something to do with the game? What in the hell was going on?

Foxworthy pounded on the door, screaming for help. Finally, when his hands were sore, he slid down the door and sat, arms wrapped around his knees, staring at his attacker's body. The dead eyes staring back.

···14···

In for Good

Scotty Griffin checked himself and Ali into guest dorm 312, the third floor of a prefab hutch set in a small crater a klick south of Heinlein station's central bubble. The main facility had good accommodations, and frankly he would have preferred that. Security felt better there. On the other hand, on the Moon the harsh external conditions were a security shield all in themselves. Trekking from dome to dome without proper training was like tap-dancing on a tightrope. Paparazzi would be at a minimum, and frankly there hadn't been a lot of attention for Ali at the party, which had annoyed his primary no end.

Scotty had to laugh. So far, even considering the training and preparation, this had been pretty easy, and in fact, a lot of fun. He had completed basic space training years before, but old Kikaya paid very well for him to do the kiddie version again from scratch. When this was all over he'd have enough money to take two years off. Do almost anything he wanted . . .

What he wanted right now was to disappear into makeup, or other anonymity. It was inevitable that silly things would happen during the game, and those silly things would be used against

Kendra in the election. Well, she was right about one thing: The miners and construction hands loved their "last of the old-time pioneer" personas. They liked loners, sure, but they liked winners even more.

He was going to give them one. That would be the way to do it. He was going to win the damned game. At the very least, he wasn't coming in last. That would be fine for a first-time gamer playing at this level. *Just don't come in last.*

Burdened by the first sense of unease he'd had since landing, Scotty went through his mental checklist in preparation for sleep.

"Moonman," Ali said.

Scotty didn't turn. "Here."

"We have arrived," Ali said. "All throughout our training, I sensed that you could not take things with complete seriousness."

"Your safety I take seriously. The game . . . well, it's a game."

"Not to me," Ali said. "You promised that once we arrived, you would, as you said, 'get into it.' Well. We are here. Have you?"

"Have I what?"

" 'Gotten into it.' "

"I'm doing fine," Scotty said. "My primary job is protection. My secondary is to see that the client enjoys himself. We'll be fine."

"And how will you protect me if you are killed out?" His voice was challenging. "And that is what will happen, if you are not completely present."

There it was again, a touch of imperious presumption that had begun creeping back in on the way to Luna, a reminder that Ali was a prince, and Scotty a pauper. While he suspected that this was just a way of dealing with a nervous stomach, Scotty fought to avoid irritation. "I always, under all circumstances, do my level best to avoid dying."

Ali held his eyes for a beat, and then nodded. "Good. Please do that." Something in the Prince's face said he'd be relieved if Scotty was killed out of the game. After all, bodyguards were his father's idea. With Scotty dead, Ali could concentrate on winning.

By 2:00 A.M. Lunar Standard Time, most of the guests had sunk into exhaustion. Counting travel from the L5 station and the arrival party, most of them had not slept for at least twenty hours. Some had grumbled that Xavier had deliberately arranged the times to confuse and fatigue them. Others just shook their heads wryly, knowing that they were in for a serious tail-wringing in only eight short hours. So sleep pills and delta-wave units were in heavy use, nightcaps were swallowed or smoked, and experiments with low-gravity sex conducted.

And now, the vid calls had stopped, and talking dropped to a soft burr.

By 3:00 A.M., silence had descended upon the dorm. The rooms sealed themselves into emergency mode: The doors would not open. Whoever was in there was simply in for good.

15

"Have a Good Game"

0730 hours, November 14, 2085

Wayne awakened slowly, eeling over in his mesh to find the previous evening's chubby and improbably agile entertainment already awake, her face hovering just inches above his.

She leaned forward, red hair dangling. She rubbed his pointy nose with her stubby one, and kissed him lightly. "Hey there, sweet stuff," Darla said. He placed his hands against her hips and pressed her against him, wiggling experimentally. It was a nice fit.

"Not now," she said, then closed her mouth and chewed at the corner of her lip.

He knew that expression. *And not later, either. Playtime was over. Maybe after the game. If you still want me.* He believed that she had enjoyed their evening together. She had certainly displayed all the appropriate signs.

But . . . that little flash of insecurity in her smile. Gaming relationships could be brief and intense. He was a celebrity, and despite the current fashion for healthy padding, she might have a bit of unprocessed fear of rejection. She was used to being appreciated . . . once or twice.

Of course, he could be wrong. Their play had been intense . . . maybe too intense for a purely casual liaison. And anyway, win, lose or draw, in a few days he was heading back to Earth. No time to get all dewy-eyed.

"Playtime," he said, hiding his disappointment even as he felt it dissolve. There was greater sport here, and he felt his gaming gland begin to pulse. Wayne was almost mechanical in the way he rolled out of the mesh and headed for the shower. When Darla joined him in the little spray cabinet, he was only perfunctorily welcoming.

But the water clung to them like jelly, and they needed each other to scrape it off and into the drains. He was completely new to lunar gravity. That was first frustrating, then fun, then—well, they were in haste. By the time he dried and began to dress, it was her turn to watch him with a smattering of disappointment. How could a man have forgotten her presence so easily?

But Wayne heard the thrumming beneath his feet, the distant *bing-bong* awakening the sleepers, felt if not heard the sound of water pumping through the walls, imagined that he could hear a dozen voices as dreams became reality, shortly to turn to dream once more. In five minutes they were dressed, and had eaten the tube breakfasts pushed through the door slot.

He hit the intercom button. "Fifteen," he said, calling the room next door, where Angelique had turned in last night. She responded quickly.

"Wakey wakey," she said. "Busy night?"

"Slept like a baby," he said. Darla curled her tongue at him suggestively. *Say hello to my little friend.* She was definitely in character. Her behavior told him that something was going to happen, and it was going to be fast. Instinct warned him that, game-wise, Darla wasn't going to live long. She was overplaying her hand, trying hard to make an impression.

"Meet you in the corridor in five?" he asked.

"Make it three," Angelique said, and clicked off.

Fair enough. He slipped in his gamelink contact lenses (capable of receiving personalized signals from gaming central) and packed his bag. He was wearing tan Brit explorer regalia with mesh shocksuit underwear. Darla, dressed in a curve-accentuating feminine version, watched approvingly, and then stood. He grinned at her. "Let's have a good game," he said.

"Game?" she asked, too damned innocently, and stood out of his way as the door to the outer corridor slid to the side. She kissed her fingertips, then pressed them to his lips. "You go ahead," she said. "Maybe I'll see you later."

So. This was where their paths parted. Had she been sent to spy on him? Was this supposed to set him off balance? Was . . . ?

He stepped out gingerly, not quite certain what to expect.

Nothing. Just a hallway, with Angelique entering a moment later, dressed similarly, carrying a pistol and a saber in a scabbard.

"What do we know?" he asked her.

"Look for anything Wells."

Asako rolled out into the corridor: The bubble girl, looking alert despite last night's revels. Wayne saluted with his sword. She smiled.

Another door in the hallway slid open, and Mickey and Maud Abernathy entered the corridor. He hadn't known them before departing Earth, but knew their track record, of course, and a tiny bit of their personal history. They would be the oldest among the gamers, close to sixty if memory served him right. They had once been married, but then one of them had lost interest in gaming, and the relationship had drifted apart. If memory served, it was Maud who had gafiated. Mickey continued to play, but his solo characters weren't as successful as their double-team. Their team personae were paired psychics. In a magical game, that might manifest as full-blown Dr. Strange–style abilities. Here, the effects would be more subtle, but no less powerful.

Mickey looked just a bit hungover, and Wayne didn't blame him at all. Last night's party had been massive.

Mickey and Maud extended hands to Angelique. "We're not completely familiar with your portfolio, Lady Chan."

"Perhaps you could refresh our memory?"

"I've studied many traditions of the sword," she said. "And not merely the sword that kills. Also, the sword that gives life."

Ah. A reference to sword techniques designed to take captives rather than slay. In this context, then, perhaps some of her healing points would still apply. The IFGS watched out for their players.

Whether the game was fantasy or science fiction, her powers tended to be the same: a swordswoman whose blade could suck or restore life force. Whether "steel" or glowing energy blade, she was an odd and spectacular meld of killer and healer. In a game with no fantasy or SF element, she would have great skills as a medic or doctor.

Mickey and Maud bowed as if they were joined at the cerebellum. "We are honored to meet you," they said as one.

Sharmela Tamil appeared next, still dressed in a feminized nineteenth-century Raj uniform: a white turban, a uniform of thick blue fabric with draped cords across the chest. Medals Wayne did not recognize, and a military bearing—but also bangles and gemstones on fingers and ears. He sensed a complex and fascinating backstory, and promised himself to inquire at first opportunity.

Suddenly, a red light began to flash in the corridor. "Shuttle arrival in ninety seconds. Please make your way to the central departure gate."

A series of bright arrows ushered them toward the previous night's entry doors. Just as the last of the group arrived, the safety lights began to flash from red to green, and the door sighed open. They walked through a short coupling tunnel and took seats in a twelve-person shuttle with side windows and a bright central viewscreen.

"Buckle in, please," a woman's voice asked. Wayne recognized Darla's mild Oakie twang. As soon as the last buckle was fastened, internal lights flashed from green to red, the door sealed.

Scotty heard a *click* as the external coupling was disconnected, and the shuttle began to coast.

If Scotty kept his eyes toward the ground, he could look out of the windows and feel no flash of panic. The same gray-white dust, the same cratered surface, rolling past in a surreal tableau.

He could hear the *ooh*s and *aah*s around him and appreciate their reactions, while keeping his own reactions muted.

Ali kept his face glued to the window, fingers spread against the glass like a kid at a candy store. The gaming dome loomed up in front of them, ten stories high, wide as a football field, built within an impact crater older than the Coliseum. Their shuttle slowed, then crawled up a graded track to the side of the dome. He felt it shudder as it mated with the dome's external wall-track, and after a series of little jolts it began to climb vertically.

*Ooh*s and *aah*s again, as the perspective began to shift, and their view of the crags, cracks and valleys, the craters and unweathered jutting spires of lunar landscape expanded. It took them two minutes to climb ten stories, at which point the shuttle rattled again as the track beneath them shifted, and they were pulled to a coupling at the very top of the dome. The shuttle sighed to a halt, and there was a nervous moment waiting for the safety lights to change. Scotty only realized he'd been holding his breath when green flashed, and the door opened.

A woman in explorer's gear crawled out of the vehicle's cockpit. "Ms. Tabata will exit last, please," she said. This didn't feel very genteel to Scotty, but he didn't complain. Red hair: He thought he recognized last night's mermaid.

The tunnel connected to a revolving escaladder. One at a time the gamers took hold of the rungs and descended into the top of the dome. Nice option for a puzzle, Wayne thought, but he saw nothing.

The mechanism went through some kind of clanking shift, and Scotty peered up the escaladder well, watching Asako maneuver her pod into position for the mechanism to take hold and lower her capsule to the floor.

When she had fully descended, the gamers all applauded. They followed their guide—Darla, Wayne noted, entering the game early—as she led them twenty meters away under a curved ceiling, to a ramp in the flooring. They descended again, and found themselves in a mock-up of the original Cavorite sphere, complete with plush seats and pewter-colored "Cavorite" scrolls, a few rolled up to make square windows. They buckled themselves in, Asako purred down and anchored her capsule. The ramp folded into the ceiling, and they were ready to go.

A countdown clock appeared on the screen, showing that they had ninety seconds until the game began once again. Wayne strapped himself in, and gave a hard exhalation. This was starting at a rush.

"Her name was Darla," he murmured.

Angelique didn't look around. "Did Xavier send her?"

"She didn't say. I didn't ask. But that's her." Wayne pointed with his nose. "The guide."

"Dr. Darla McGuinness. Her backstory is she's an astronomer. Studied the Moon. Xavier will kill her out as soon as he thinks we're depending on her."

"Right."

"What did he think you'd do when you saw her in the game? Flinch?"

"Yeah. Or kill her. Or *you're* supposed to kill her." Or he was supposed to hesitate and let her kill *him*. Or be preoccupied with the possibility of some mid-game nookie, and miss a clue . . .

"Or he's just messing with our heads." Angelique scowled. "We wait."

Only the lack of weightlessness told Scotty that what he saw was not completely real.

When the last of them were seated in the mock-up sphere, the light suddenly vanished from the room, plunging them into darkness. Scotty heard a soft *clunk* that might be Asako's wheel grips locking against the floor.

Light came in patches: Screens rolled up one at a time to reveal a curved glass surface, and a glare like yellow-white bone cratered with acne. It was the Moon, and it was growing, hurtling toward them at reckless speed.

He looked for Ali first. His charge was seated and belted in. Then Asako: Her bubble chair locked against the floor. The gamers all seemed to be belted down and waiting. Then the blocky shape of a big man rolling up metallic-looking screens, exposing more of the Moon and a terrifying glare of stars. "Landing might be rough." A marked Scottish accent burred his words. The big man's naval uniform gleamed in the reflected lunar light. Their Captain.

The big man straightened like a soldier standing at parade rest. Moonglare lit a bristly haircut and a luxurious handlebar mustache. "Ladies and gentlemen, we are approaching the lunar surface. You—"

"Excuse me, Captain," Maud and Mickey said.

"A poor time to disturb me, madam. Best remain seated and wait." The big man began manipulating the blinds again.

Despite the knowledge that it was all illusion, Scotty's fingers crushed the armrests as the dappled surface approached. And then . . . he was confused. Xavier had made clear references to H. G. Wells' Moon. Scotty hadn't ever read the book, but had a vague memory of the CliffsNotes version. Wasn't Wells' Moon a living planet? He saw nothing but rock and shadow.

Wait . . . there were dapplings of pale green below, visible only as they approached more closely. That wasn't right. At least, it wasn't the Moon he knew.

He heard the intake of amazed breath around him, and Ali whispered: "Wells' Moon."

Then the last thousand meters passed in a blink, they were plummeting, and their Captain was frantically pulling levers. The *click* of opening and closing Cavorite shutters rattled through the room, and at the very last instant, their descent slowed.

With a mammoth *crunch* they slammed into the surface. The air outside clouded with dust. Their vehicle yawed side to side crazily, flipping almost upside down at one point, so that he felt dizzy and sick, as if he had swallowed a dozen raw eggs.

Then a smooth skid, dirt piling up against the outside of the sphere, and then stillness.

"Is everyone all right?" the Captain asked.

"All parts seem in working order," Angelique said, and then checked with her crew. All seemed to agree that they had survived.

"I will wait here with the ship," the Captain said. "I wish you Godspeed in your rescue attempt."

The gamers gathered their gear, and, unable to conceal their eagerness, crowded against the curved transparent hull.

Scotty peered out. They were in a vast circular plain, on the floor of a giant crater. High walls closed them in on every side. Sunlight was just cresting above a jagged gray cliff.

Pale summits and rocky protuberances were pretty much what he would have expected. But there was more. Much more.

The entire plain was covered with a curling, coiled profusion of plants and vines and grasses.

The other gamers and NPCs had gathered around the windows, gazing out on the display.

So far, he saw nothing that looked like a tree, or the beginnings of one. But there were cactus-like plants, and young bushes, and the infancy of a grassland.

The ship's Captain had completed a series of movements near the door. Scotty now saw a rectangular gate in the middle of their inner door, because the Captain had screwed it open. Into the rectangle he inserted a cage containing two white mice, extending them by means of some apparatus a foot or two beyond the door, into the central air chamber.

The Captain closed his eyes, seemed to offer a prayer, and pulled a lever. With a series of clanks and groans, the outer door opened (*poof!*) and lunar sunlight flooded into the airlock.

The window was wide enough for four gamers to peer down into the chamber, and Scotty made sure he was one of them. The mice were eating seeds at the bottom of their cage, completely unaware of the fact that they were the first Earth creatures in many years to breathe lunar air.

After a minute, the Captain closed the external door. Then gingerly, he opened the internal one.

The air had a sterile, grassy smell, like the first spring after a cleansing frost, and just a whiff of spent gunpowder. "Volunteers?" he asked, and a forest of hands sprang up.

Mickey and Maud Abernathy, Angelique Chan, Wayne and

Ali hustled themselves to the front of the line, and the others applauded their courage. Scotty thought about it for a moment, decided that Xavier wouldn't dare pull a lethal *Gotcha!* at the beginning of the game, and went to stand beside his charge. The six of them were ushered into the airlock. The Captain handed Angelique a furled Union Jack. "Do us proud!" he said. And the door closed behind him.

This isn't real . . . this isn't real . . ., he licked his lips, and found both tongue and lips to be dry. He had spent too long on the Moon to be able to take anything that looked and sounded like an airlock with anything save complete sobriety.

The outer door slid open.

Wayne took a deep sniff and said: "Good, there's air here." Angelique rammed a discreet elbow into his ribs, and stepped past him down the ramp. Scotty's feet touched "lunar" soil for the first time.

And now the confusion was total. Scotty knew his eyes could be fooled, but not his proprioception. And every muscle in his body, and all of his joints, said that he was under one-sixth gravity. He was on the Moon. The general contour of the ground was lunar. He had seen it for himself. But plants? Grass? A whorl of leaves and blossoms, covering the slopes as far as his eyes could see?

Impossible.

His eyes said it couldn't be the Moon. His body said differently. He fought to keep his equilibrium. He looked up. The sky was pale, filled with clouds. Thank God. If there had been a night sky up above him, blackness and stars, he might have dropped down a deep, dizzy hole.

But the impossible tableau both disoriented and steadied him.

He reached out to touch. Certainly, this was all visual field manipulation . . . ?

No, it wasn't. He touched a nearby plant, half thinking that his fingers would pass right through the leaf, and was pleased to feel the pebbled texture. He bent, and sniffed: a hint of mint. Marvelous.

Behind them, the Cavorite sphere was buried to its equator in greenery. The door opened again, and another clutch of gamers and NPCs exited. Asako Tabata rolled out last, although he supposed that she could have emerged first, considering that she had her own independent air supply.

Angelique Chan threw her shoulders back, posing for invisible cameras beneath the deep blue of a lunar sky. She planted her Union Jack into the ground. "I claim the Moon for Great Britain," she said, to unanimous applause.

"All of this," Ali said. "It has to grow, and feed, and mate—whatever it is going to do, in fourteen days."

Wayne examined the soil, then stood and gazed out at the horizon. "I have a suspicion that our sense of time might be distorted here."

Mickey and Maud Abernathy exchanged a brief glance. "Yes, that would make sense. We need to be careful not to let night fall before we return to the ship," Maud said.

"And I can see just how an accident like that could happen," Mickey said.

So could Scotty. If they couldn't trust their subjective sense of time passage, they could end up breathing vacuum.

"What now?" Scotty asked.

Ali grinned at him. "What now?" he asked. "And now . . . this!"

And without another word, Ali crouched and exploded up into the air. He went up ten, fifteen . . . twenty feet, sailing in a stupendous arc before he glided back down once again.

Scotty stared. In all his time on the Moon, he had never really *done* that. He had been so worried about not looking like a stupid tourist or a greenhorn in front of his wife or their coworkers. Where was the simple joy!

How had he cheated himself?

When hyper-competitive, all-business Angelique Chan leaped into the air, sailing like a ballet dancer in slow motion, higher and farther than any Bolshoi prima ballerina had ever dreamed of . . .

Scotty threw caution to the wind, gathered himself and jumped.

The ground receded below him, a half-dozen gamers staring up at him in stunned surprise . . . and then suddenly the air was filled with bouncing, bounding gamers, sheer joy in stupendously magnified motion.

Lunies didn't do this because there was never enough room. Somersaults, handsprings, flying kicks and jumps that made world-class martial artists out of neophytes, Olympic gymnasts from couch potatoes.

Even Asako was gunning her capsule around like a little go-cart, tearing up plants and dirt as she spun and raced about.

The redheaded guide was airborne, too.

And then Angelique screamed: "Where the hell is our sphere?"

In a moment, Scotty's joy bled out through his fingers and toes, and a sick sinking feeling hit him like a fist in the belly.

It took him three bounces to slow himself down to a walk, and then stand still. All about him, up to his knees, were the red and pink flowers, covering a plain as far as the eye could see.

No sphere. The other gamers were bouncing to a halt as well, and now the nine of them stood in a rough circle, scratching their heads.

"Damn," Wayne said. "I'd swear it was right over there, to the left. South?"

"I have no idea. What in the world . . . ?"

Angelique closed her eyes, her expression tight with disgust. "We were so busy jumping for joy that we lost track of where we were," she said. "We lost the sphere. Just like in the original story. Dammit!" She smacked her fist into her palm. "I should have known."

"What do we do?" Ali asked. "Spread out? Search?"

She shook her head. "We won't find it. They didn't."

Scotty searched his memory, trying to find a wisp of the Wells book, but couldn't. He unearthed a vague memory of a BBC production, and one of an old herky-jerky stop-motion movie—not one of Harryhausen's best—but those traces couldn't be trusted. Could anything? Dammit, why hadn't he kept up his reading more faithfully?

"What do we do?" Scotty asked.

Angelique held up her hand. "Wait. What's that sound?"

For a moment he wasn't sure what the Lore Master was talking about. Her slender, aristocratic Chinese face was intense, momentarily resembled a painting he once saw in the Louvre of a Buddhist nun in prayer.

The air was thin, and slightly cool. There, faintly, the sound of a weak wind fluttering its way through the flowers. What was that? The ground shook . . . not a single thump like something heavy tumbling down, but almost like a drum stroke.

What?

"I hear it," Mickey said, and Maud nodded in synchrony.

And now there was more than that thump. A very distant insectile sound, like bees buzzing, or crickets chirping.

Growing closer by the moment. "It might be best," Angelique said, "if we hide."

That suggestion required no show of hands. They dove into the flowers, Scotty making sure that Ali got down safely before he hid himself. Chin in the lunar soil, he had to chuckle to himself: Whatever came next, they were in just about the safest place in the entire solar system. If ever he had been paid good money to take a vacation, this was it.

Whatever came next, he was determined to enjoy it.

16

The Mooncow

0827 hours

BOOM. BOOM. BOOM.

The ground beneath Wayne shook as with the strokes of a giant hammer, as regularly as clockwork.

The sun was nearing the western horizon. How could they not have noticed that before? The sound seemed to originate not merely beneath them, but off to what Wayne took to be the north. There were jagged mountains in that direction, and he thought that they would be easy to recognize, and that was as good a reason to choose an orientation as any.

They'd already lost the sphere . . . he could imagine that Xavier had just waited until they were busy bounding, and then distorted the visual field to "disappear" the sphere, a simple magician's trick aided by their dizziness and disorientation.

Damn. It had happened in the BBC version, as well as the Harryhausen film. Take it as part of the script.

Now the ground itself seemed to be protesting their presence.

Angelique Chan raised her arm, poking it up from under the tangled flowers to Wayne's left. "Head toward the sound," she said, and they started to crawl.

Mickey whispered, "I haven't been able to get down on all

fours like this for donkey's years. This lunar gravity is great for my back!"

Maud chuckled, and then went back to serious crawling.

Mickey was right, of course. Wayne barely felt any pressure on his palms or wrists at all. The slightest flexion of his wrist sent his hands and knees springing up off the ground, thumping back down so lightly it was a joke.

The plants were waxy to the touch. A closer inspection revealed that they had little or no scent, and rooted into some kind of web just beneath the dirt. Were they all part of one life-form, like the mycelial mass beneath a clutch of mushrooms?

Or were they perhaps just manufactured en masse and rolled out like an artificial lawn by the wizards of Dream Park?

He giggled to himself, and concentrated on what he was doing.

Boom . . . boom . . . boom . . .

The ground beneath them trembled. The gigantic circular plate beneath their feet first revolved, then began to slide away.

Gamers crawled backward away from the opening as fast as they could, as the lid retracted like the lens of a crocodile's eye.

They could peer down into the depths, from which a deeper *boom . . . boom . . . boom* rang hollowly, like Mjöllnir striking the anvil of heaven.

All right. Dammit, he should have read the original book. Were they supposed to go down? Was something coming up after them? In the movie the Moon was *hollow,* all caverns. Was it in the book? And if so, would Xavier confine himself to canon?

He crawled up to the edge and looked down. The tunnel dropped away shallowly, not sharply, a ramp leading up to the surface rather than a vertical mineshaft. The edge of the doorway was about three feet thick, with a series of dull glowing lights pulsing and moaning around the edge. Their low, bone-rattling intensity made his fillings ache.

"What is that sound?" Angelique asked. She was squinting, but seemed to be thinking hard. "Alarm? Alert?"

Before he could answer her, they both received an answer, in the form of a lowing groan behind them.

Something was coming. And whatever that something was, it wss groaning in sync with the sound coming from the rim of the flat circular door.

"It's a homing call," she said. "They're telling the cows to come in."

She raised herself up onto her elbows and called to the others. "Keep an alert! Something is coming. It's big, and you don't want to be seen, or stepped on. Look sharp!"

Boom. Boom. Boom.

The sound from below and the shaking ground behind them seemed to meld, and so suddenly that he felt adrenaline jolt up his spine, as the first sign of lunar animal life appeared.

It was *enormous,* like a segmented caterpillar half the length of a city block. Its flesh was white, and dappled, and with every laborious breath those sides rose and fell. Wayne could see no feet, and from the way it rose up and inched forward like the greatest worm that ever lived, it was more lizard than snake.

"Mooncow," Maud said quietly. "That's what it was called. A mooncow."

All he knew was that he didn't want to try to fight something this size. Its six eyes were relatively tiny, clustered around what he thought of as its nose. The caterpillar's neck was fatter than the main section of its body. It opened its mouth and emitted a bleating noise that rolled over the crater rim and resounded from the clouds themselves.

Six, no *seven* man-sized creatures appeared around the mooncows. Their eyes were faceted, and their thin arms were covered with some kind of horny carapace, a substance that reflected the sharp light with a faint blue sheen.

One of the insectile creatures (Selenites? Was that the word?) looked in his direction, and Wayne ducked down. He felt something . . . a vague creeping sensation rippling up his back, at the same time that the earth itself seemed to tremble. The spit dried in Wayne's mouth. Despite his best attempt to stay steady, a sour sensation that he recognized as fear began to boil in his stomach. He wiped his hands on his pants, and tried to slow his breathing.

Couldn't let himself get spooked. Not so soon, anyway.

When he looked back up, the mooncows were halfway down the hole, humping along. At the right angles, their bodies were partially translucent. He thought he could see the contents of their stomachs, vast clots of vegetable matter churning their way through the beasts' digestive systems.

Then finally the last of the mooncows was down the hole. The Selenites kept watch until the last minute, but he had the sense that they weren't specifically looking for intruders, just keeping a mindful presence. Then they entered the hole, and a moment later the clanging sound began anew, and the lid slid shut.

Angelique held up her hand, palm flattened, and they rose from hiding.

Wayne jumped down onto the circular door with a *thump*. "Well," he said slowly. "I suppose it would be too much to hope that they just left a door open for us."

Asako Tabata's pod speakers were normally indistinguishable from a human voice, but now they were amplified. "There may be a problem," she said. "I note that the temperature is dropping."

Wayne looked to the west, where the shadows were stretching toward them. To the east he saw something that made his skin creep: There where the sky was darkening, the clouds had blackened as well.

Even as he watched, the very first snowflake touched his upturned face.

"Oh, *shit*," Scotty Griffin said, and he looked not the slightest bit happy. "Nightfall. The air is freezing."

"We've got minutes," Angelique said. "We'll freeze to death out here."

Asako zipped her pod around the metal door's circumference, stopping here and there to probe with little metal arms. Wayne got down on his hands and knees to inspect more closely. Arcane symbols, things that looked like dancing worms and burning leaves, were etched around the edge, but these might be just Moon-speak, and not necessarily gaming clues.

"How much time do we have?" Angelique whispered.

"Not much," he said. The sky above them was scarred now,

ripped by a silent storm. Pinpoint stars burned through the thinning air, bright enough to sear his eyes. What would happen as the night fell? First, the temperature would drop drastically. Then . . . the gases would start freezing. What would freeze first? Free oxygen? Nitrogen? CO_2? He didn't know, but figured they'd be dead long before they knew.

It was snowing now, and the air was starting to feel like the middle of winter. He shivered, teeth clattering. The other gamers must be wishing they'd brought parkas. The plants around them were shriveling, browning and curling up. So . . . they were seasonal . . . if the Moon had twelve seasons a year. Or did every month have four seasons, which made a total of forty-eight seasons . . .

His mind was drifting. The cold was getting to him. Jesus! Was this Dream Park's doing?

"I've got it!" Asako called out, and they ran to her side as her pod emitted an ear-shredding squeal, a higher-pitched version of . . .

"The mooncow sound," Angelique said.

"Brilliant," Wayne said, shivering.

The sound wavered then swooped low. The instant it hit the same tone that the mooncow had used, the door beneath them shivered and began to slide open. They had to scramble for safety, but the slab slid only a third of the way open, perhaps awaiting another mooncow call.

"Let's get in there," Angelique said.

And not a moment too soon. The sky above them was filled with snow, and blackening as they watched. Nothing would survive on the surface for more than another few minutes. The gamers jumped down into the darkness.

··· 17 ···

First Fen in the Moon

0837 hours

Angelique landed in a crouch, alert and silent. The ramp ran all the way to the lip, so she supposed she could have just walked down, but it was more satisfying, and certainly more theatrical, to jump.

The tunnel stretched down into the lunar depths for what looked like miles, with side tunnels branching off. Its brassy ridged sides reverberated with faint echoes. Selenites and mooncows, humping away into the distance? Possibly . . . but that implied that sounds carried well down here. Not necessarily a good thing. She held up a flat hand, signaling for silence.

One at a time, the others gathered around her, and as they did, the circular lid slid shut. *BOOM.*

So. They were in the meat grinder again. No way back. They had two assignments now: To find their ship, and to find Cavor. One might lead to the other.

"Quietly," she said. "I'll take lead. Wayne, you take the rear. Asako . . . stay with me."

The woman in the bubble nodded, and off they went. Angelique noticed that the bubble's treads compensated for the terrain effortlessly, lurching up and then back down as they passed the first tunnel ridge. The tunnel looked as if it might have been constructed from preformed sections.

"What's this?" Mickey Abernathy called from up ahead.

"You're the psychic. You tell me," Sharmela said, but when she squinted into the dark to see more clearly, her voice fell silent.

There in the middle of the tunnel was a pile of brownish muck half as tall as a human being. Broad coarse tufts of moon grass jutted out of it, and the consistency was a lot like peanut butter. *Warm* peanut butter. And it stank.

Wayne howled and wiped his hand on the tunnel floor. "It's mooncow sh— dung!" he said, correcting his language for a family audience. That bald-headed son of a bitch! Some kind of joke? Hoping to bump them out of character?

If audiences back home were enjoying Wayne's discomfort as much as his companions, this game was going through the roof.

Just as he finished wiping his hands on the ground, the walls around them began to hiss. Steam gouted forth, three streams from each side and the ceiling, focusing on the pile of mooncow excrement. The gamers scrambled away as the pile melted, shrank, finally sluiced away into grates in the floor.

The vapor hung in the air, dissipating so slowly that it might have been smoke. Ali, the skinny African magic user, backed up with one hand on his sword. "There's something in the mist," he said.

Angelique stopped laughing instantly, and dropped into a crouch. "Alert!" she called. "Ali. Sharmela. Can you dispel?"

Sharmela ran up to stand at Ali's side. She was a little shorter than the kid, twice his thickness, with a forceful bearing that led Wayne to suspect she could break him into pieces.

The pair might have been practicing for a month. In tandem, they raised their arms as they stood before the growing, billowing cloud. Not steam now, but some kind of smoke.

"By the bones of my ancestors—" Ali said.

"By my mother's blood—" Sharmela chanted at the same time.

"Dispel!" they both called. A wind swept down the tunnel,

punching into the mist like a fist into a cotton cloud. For a moment, they could see clearly. Perhaps two dozen Selenites stalked toward them, their carapaces vaguely warlike, as if they had been born in armor and battle helms. Each of them gripped a staff with a crooked head. Their faceted eyes glowed red as the mist dissipated. They howled, and charged.

"Ali, Sharmela. Back to second position! Wayne, front and center!" Angelique drew her sword and charged.

Regardless of his years in gaming, all his experience and skills, for the first hours of a new game it was impossible for Wayne to totally turn his mind off, to stop noticing the glitches, stop trying to second-guess the Game Master.

But . . . there was a moment, there came a time. When the illusion of the game, the effects and the scenario and the players all melded together and overwhelmed the part of his mind that knew he was Wayne Gibson, nobody, current address Las Vegas. When the adrenaline started to run, he became *Wayne Gibson, thief and warrior.*

The slithery whisper of steel on leather as sword left sheath was music to his ears. The sword balanced like a willow wand in his hand.

His sword was a Mitsubishi FlexMax 80, designed for close-quarters impact work. Eyepieces recommended. (And he noted the faceted goggle-eyes of the Selenite masks. Protection for NPCs.) No sharp edge, and a telescoping point. While not suggested for use against bare skin, the soft plastic surface above a foamed metal core would generally produce about as much damage as a willow wand while simulating the deadly appearance of any sword imaginable. To all but the most discerning eye, the FlexMax resembled a British army officer's sword with a brass handle and snakeskin grip.

Dream Park's computer system would eventually augment the localized holograms, improving the images for discriminating Earth-bound consumers. Wayne couldn't care less: In his mind, he was fighting for his life against an entirely convincing alien horde, and a moment's hesitation meant death.

For Queen and country! Wayne Gibson was out for alien blood.

Angelique stood to his right, guarding his flank as he defended hers. From the corner of his eye he caught Griffin backing them up. He was a thief, yes, but a thief with a sword. And he looked as if he knew how to use it.

Game fencing was different from competition saber or foil. You could be an Olympic saber champion, and without IFGS points your thrusts and parries simply wouldn't register. Meanwhile, a relatively unskilled opponent with gaming experience would cut you to ribbons. So the fact that Griffin appeared to have a bit of genuine sword skill was irrelevant. What were his *points*? In some games you knew everything there was to know about your teammates. In others, like this one, you learned as you went along.

But as the gamer part of his mind took over from the logic, all he thought was *My sides and back are covered. Let's get it on.*

The first Selenite stepped into range. Sword crossed staff. A blue light at the tip of the staff glowed violently, and a brief, sharp tingle ran up his arm. Damn! He slid his head to the side, and a flare of blue fire boiled out of the tip, missing him by an inch. Those behind him would just have to fend for themselves.

Wayne ducked under the stream, disengaged his blade and thrust. The Selenite's scream was more like a teakettle's whistle than the anguished howl of a living being.

The blade slid in, and a thin stream of greenish ichor flowed in return. Wayne kicked the Selenite away and turned back to the fight in bare time to avoid the touch of a staff.

"Stun staffs!" he screamed.

Angelique swayed to the side and thrust at a Selenite's segmented chest. "Can we neutralize them?"

"Better hope so," Mickey said. He and Maud had linked hands, and then raised them, and a shrill squealing sound rang through the tunnel.

The insects howled in pain. Instead of clapping their hands to the sides of their heads, several of them dropped their staffs and hugged their sides, twisting and dancing in apparent pain.

Angelique grinned. This was going to be a slaughter. At first she had worried that Xavier was playing some kind of really ugly game. Would he really kill them in the game's first hour?

No. Any entertainer knows that an audience can be angry with a short show, especially if they have paid premium prices. Xavier knew that an excessively dangerous game would actually diminish the profit of his *next* event. She could be fairly certain that his early challenges would be irritating but not lethal.

Of course, that was assuming that he was playing for posterity, and not personal vengeance. . . .

Her team had made a tight knot, and moved forward in formation, hacking and slashing. Thieves used swords and knives, but lacked the lethality of the warrior class. That was fine: They made up for it with stealth.

Griffin and his little friend Ali were having a grand time, slaughtering Selenites by the bunch. Darla was hanging back, sword raised, ready for attack from the rear.

Wayne killed an insect man and scooped up the energy spear it had been carrying. He blasted another Selenite, then slid the weapons down his shirt front, catching Angelique's eye.

The insect folk kept arms and elbows tucked to their sides and were unable to defend themselves effectively, so that even Asako Tabata was able to score kills. Her pod's stubby little arms spouted threads of fire, perhaps a laser of some kind, cutting through their enemies so that the tunnel was heaped with smoking corpses. Mickey and Maud kept their arms raised, chanting and concentrating. The air around them rippled with energy, distorting the view of the tunnel so that the entire visual field flexed and shimmied.

The Selenites finally broke and ran, screaming for their lives. Or . . . so Angelique thought.

Then the walls, as if they were actually in some kind of immense speaker system, began to vibrate with a tone similar to the one Mickey and Maud were broadcasting.

Pain!

An electric crackle crawled up her shocksuit, and she cursed. In game reality, that meant they were being hit with a pain or immobilization ray of some kind, and the shocksuit's buzz would cause genuine discomfort if a gamer didn't get the hint.

She dropped her sword, and clapped her hands over her ears, dropping to her knees. Around her, her team was collapsing, as the Selenites reflected the psychic wave right back at the intruders.

Angelique collapsed. *Paralyzed.*

They were caught.

They hadn't long to wait. Within a minute, a hollow clanking in the walls presaged the sliding of doors, circular openings in the metal walls so cunningly designed that they had been neither seen nor suspected. A small horde of bulky Selenites emerged: not the skeletal soldiers, but more like fat beetles with six arms and legs.

These creatures were designed for work. Longshoremen Selenites, perhaps. Two of them addressed each of the downed gamers, lifting by hands and feet, hoisting them up and then hauling them toward one of the circular doors.

Angelique ground her teeth. For a moment she came closer to Griffin's face, and almost laughed at his frustrated expression. *Nice eyes,* she decided.

No, IFGS had approved this paralysis. In her mind, that meant that this was just a transition. They were being taken somewhere that related to their game. There, the gamers would receive information, and begin to orient.

If they were lucky, they might even get lunch.

The tunnels were cold and dark, and echoed with distant, vaguely *crawly* sounds. She heard what she might have expected to hear in a beehive or ant nest: burrings, buzzings, chewing and crawling sounds. But there was something else she noted as the longshoremen carried their limp human burdens along.

Out there in the cloaking darkness, some of the insect sounds had a disturbingly *human* quality to them. What in the hell was that? An insect imitating the sound of a human voice? Humans trying to imitate insect sounds? She liked the first answer more, and wondered what Wayne thought. She couldn't turn her head to try to find him. But without moving, she could see just behind her, to where two insect hulks were lugging Griffin down the narrow tunnel. She'd noticed the nice shoulders on the way down. That, and his soft, clear voice and warm hands. She giggled to herself. Was she getting a crush?

The game was getting more interesting every minute.

She estimated that they spent about four minutes being lugged about, until they went through a second door and out into a larger chamber. The translucent surfaces glowed with a pinkish bioluminescence. If she squinted, Angelique could just make out larval shapes curled in octagonal chambers on the far side. Breeding chamber?

The wall slid up a meter, and a delicate golden wormlike creature crawled forth, moving one segmented portion of its body at a time. It had what she was tempted to call a feminine face, with twin feathery antennae and two hose-like protrusions below at the corners of its mouth. The bulky stevedore creatures stepped aside for her, and she approached Angelique with grace that such a creature could never have equaled in full Earth gravity.

It was about six feet long, and half again as thick as a human body. The room's pale glow actually illumined the insides of her body. She was filled with floating organelles, and sacks filled with some kind of orange fluid.

The creature canted her head sideways, coming very close to Angelique's head. Her faceted eyes reflected the gamer's face back a hundred times, and it seemed on the verge of speaking . . . then the twin nozzles at the sides of her mouth gushed a stream of pinkish froth, splashing up and down her frame in a silken web.

The web gullivered Angelique to the spongy rock floor from ankles to shoulders. The froth dried within moments, and as it did, the tingling paralysis promptly ended. Paralysis was no longer required—they were well and truly caught.

The golden worm turned around, doubling herself in a way impossible to any creature with a spine. Then it was through the door and gone.

Angelique turned her head to the side and saw Wayne tied there, straining against the bonds. Fine. If the shocksuit paralysis had ended, then it was fair for them to attempt escape. As she expected, his struggles (and hers) accomplished nothing. She had enough wiggle room to turn her head to the other side. Asako Tabata's pod was anchored to the ground: They must have paralyzed her electronics. Mickey and Maud were trying to lean their foreheads against each other, boosting the psychic signal. Couldn't quite reach. The redheaded guide was writhing without effect . . . probably wasn't supposed to get loose at this point.

Ali was wiggling around, floundering. Seemed to her then he was a little green for this game, but a good Game Master went with the team she had. But now she saw that he had somehow kicked or cut his left foot free.

Griffin . . . again, she found herself engaged in pleasurable speculation. His broad shoulders were relaxed, but as she watched, he inhaled, flexed so that his uniform swelled . . . and then contracted. He didn't look stressed out at all. In fact, he seemed admirably relaxed. She liked that.

The door opened again. Several things that resembled the golden slug emerged, carrying a bench made of some silvery bright metal. Seated on the bench was a creature thinner and probably more frail than anything she had seen so far.

It was perhaps five feet tall, and its fully fleshed limbs weren't much thicker than the bones of a human adult. It reminded her of a mantis, again with the faceted eyes, and delicate insectile movement.

The carrier slugs brought her into the middle of the circle in which the gamers were arrayed. The bench settled, and then began to turn, as if the slugs were spinning like schoolchildren trying to get dizzy and throw up.

Slowly at first, then a complete revolution every two seconds, the greenish creature spun to survey its captives.

The chamber was awash with a dull, mourning buzz. A whispering voice filled her ear:

"Who are you? What do you want? Why have you come?"

The voice repeated once, twice, and then again.

The other gamers had begun to speak, but when they heard Angelique's voice rise, they quieted. "We come to rescue Professor Cavor. Give him to us, and we leave in peace."

"And if we do not?"

"Then our two great civilizations will be in conflict, a thing I dearly wish to prevent."

"You will regret coming here. We know of your violent ways. Cavor told us, long ago." Its glittering eyes shifted color from greenish to red. Anger? Fear?

"We dealt with him then. We will deal with you now. You will regret ever coming here."

The shrill whine spiked again, and with it came a prompting tickle. *Pain.* The Earthlings were deep in torment, and were expected to act that way for the hidden cameras. Worse, they were confined, and obviously intended to just lie there and take it.

She hated this, hated the sense of powerlessness in being whiplashed by psychic or magical forces, unable to fight. Suddenly, a well of old emotions filled and brimmed over: anger and frustration and even a bit of fear. Suddenly, she was the nine-year-old girl who had crawled into Lewis Carroll and J. K. Rowling to find refuge from a house filled with screaming adults. A girl who had found the world of fantasy far more pleasant than—

Wait. Wait. Angelique realized that her breathing had shifted up into her chest, become rapid and shallow. Her blood felt like it was boiling, and the world tasted oddly sour.

Fear. She was filled with it, and even with the emotion clawing at her, she knew that something was wrong. *Wait. This thing is trying to get to me, trying to make me even more terrified than I already am.*

Wait. That last thought had been from the position of the character, not the player. The fantasy wall was breaking down a bit. She imagined Xavier performing an act only a perverted yogi could love. The little skinhead was cheating somehow. He had set some kind of trap for her. She didn't know how he was doing it, but he had just used his knowledge of her personal history to attack her. Legal, but nasty.

The gamers all around her were arching their backs and screaming, those sounds peaking to some kind of crescendo when—

The wall exploded.

18

Rescue

Smoke and dust choked the air. Juice from shattered insect cocoons slicked the floor. Several embryos were dead and still, but others curled and crawled blindly, seeking shadows.

Ali wriggled out from under his sticky bonds. He'd left some outer clothing, but he had his sword. He swept it around him and slashed along Wayne's left side, Wayne being the nearest.

A dozen insect soldiers stepped through the wall, climbing with a segmented angularity no human being could manage. Angelique had the bizarre impression that they were holding their power-spears in the same fashion a British soldier might have held his rifle in bayonet-ready position. As disciplined as any corps of Beefeaters, they advanced in a line. The one behind them might have been an officer: larger, scarier, four arms ending in metal claws, and a demon mask with teeth like a saber-toothed cat's.

The emerald creature shrieked, and a dozen guards appeared in the room, positioning themselves between the green interrogator and the sudden incoming threat.

Ali was trying to cut other gamers free, but it was slow work.

Wayne was still half tethered. Only his arm and the Selenite blasting spear were free.

The guards scrambled, thrusting with stun-staffs and sharp objects that looked as if they might have been snapped off a praying mantis' foreleg.

The newcomers thrust and parried in a manner reminiscent of classical European swordplay. The parries, ripostes and dégagés might have seemed perfectly at home in a French saber *salle*. The green one had retreated against the wall. It opened to receive her just as the newcomers pushed the guards back and formed a line between Selenites and gamers.

Wayne aimed his blasting spear at the newcomers' officer. Its weapon swung toward Wayne—as Ali knocked his weapon aside.

What?

"Ally," he said. A beat. The officer could have killed Wayne, but didn't. How the hell did Ali figure *that* one? Wayne gaped, then nodded.

Angelique gasped as several of the newcomers lifted her up like a sack of potatoes and carried her out of the room.

And from that point, aside from the sound of insectile screams and metal-on-metal, she knew no more of what happened in that chamber.

The gamers were swiftly spirited through a maze of darkened tunnels, until she lost track of all the twists and turns. Perhaps ten minutes later, they were in a chamber with softly glowing golden walls, with shining cushioned floors, and a shining ceiling.

Their rescuers deposited them on the ground gingerly, with a degree of respect and consideration that their previous hosts had entirely lacked. Ali was being led; though armed, he remained docile. As for the rest, their bonds were slashed, and the gamers rolled to their feet—except for Asako, whose pod treads finally activated again, so that she was able to roll around the room, exploring.

Wayne asked Ali, "How did you know that thing—"

"Sir, I know my Wells. And I believe he described such a creature, and gave it a friendly disposition."

What? Where? But . . . well, damn, Wells had a gigantic oeuvre, and it made sense that the kid might know something he didn't. Still, it irked him. "Fine." Exasperated. "It *didn't* kill anyone. Now it's taken us to this hive—"

Ali said, "What do you think is going on?"

"Civil war?" Wayne asked.

"Is this a cell? What are we supposed to do now?"

"*Save us.*"

The voice came from everywhere and nowhere. Angelique turned this way and that, hoping to catch a glimpse of her benefactors, but the shadows defeated her.

"In the walls," Maud said, and pressed her hands against a golden surface. Did she see something? Mickey wore virtual gear, contact lenses capable of receiving images from the central gaming computer: magic users and psychics who wore such lenses could literally see things the other gamers could not.

She and Mickey joined hands, and Ali came to stand beside them, lending his magic to their efforts. And . . .

The walls dissolved. At least, that was the visual effect. Became translucent, perhaps. Arm-sized, glowing grubs appeared in the hexagonal wall chambers. Dozens of them. Perhaps hundreds. Unborn, but moving slowly, like restless, sleeping infants.

"Who are you?" she asked.

"*We are the future of our nest, and we need your help.*"

"Where is Professor Cavor?" Wayne asked.

"*The great one is lost to us. He showed our people a new way, and then was taken from us. But we remember him, and follow his teachings.*"

"His teachings?" Angelique said.

"*He told us that we have the right to decide what our lives will be, that we are not only to toil unto death in the darkness, at the pleasure of our Queen. And for these teachings, he was sentenced to death.*"

There it was, the word that they had hoped not to hear.

"Then . . . Cavor is dead?" she whispered.

"*No. He lives.*"

"I don't understand."

"*We rescued him. The guards assigned to protect us were mind-locked to follow our commands. They rescued him from the executioners, and took him to the caverns, where the colony dares not go.*"

"The caverns?"

"*The deep darkness, where the Old Ones live, the ones who could not be bent to the hive ways. There the Queen has no authority. There, Cavor lives . . . or did until last lunar day when he sent us a message.*

"*Even though he hides, he still inspires and teaches us. We need him. We dare not enter the caves, for such transgression might birth war. But you are outsiders, as he was. You can go, and find him, and bring him back. If you do, then the hive might rise up and take its freedom. Overthrow the Queen.*"

"And then . . . if we do this . . . we would be able to leave? I will tell you honestly: We come to take Professor Cavor back to Earth."

"*That would be perfection. He would return to Earth our emissary, capable of brokering a peace between our peoples.*

"*Will you help us?*"

Well, that was more like it. A rescue mission. And perhaps then a battle to win the Moon. With their retreat Angelique's spirits soared.

"We accept," she said.

There was a trilling *burr* from the walls, as if an entire forest of cicadas had awakened from their slumber at once.

"*We are so grateful to you. May we show you appreciation?*"

"What do you have in mind?" she asked.

The walls parted and insectile creatures appeared, carrying platters of steaming meat and vegetables. "*Professor Cavor showed us how to make the food he loved. Our fungus can be trained to produce flesh of any flavor and texture. Please accept this offering.*"

Scotty Griffin snagged a chunk of meat from the platter, and took a healthy bite. The rest of them looked at him, as if their growling stomachs were suddenly awakening from slumber.

Angelique sat beside him, and he noticed that Sharmela had arranged to sit closely next to her. Their knees brushed. Sharmela took a healthy bite and grinned at the Lore Master. "Tastes like chicken," she said. "As long as your chickens taste like tofu."

19

Overnight Sensation

From Heinlein base to Hanzo crater and the Pan-Asian group, to the European Union spray on Luna's dark side . . . to Falling Angels, the industrial complex orbiting in geosync, to the L5s and the surface of Earth a quarter-million miles away, the adventures of the first lunar expedition into nineteenth-century fantasy dominated the entertainment news.

They crowded in bars watching the vidscreens, they hosted home parties with overflowing bowls of popcorn served to couches filled with engineers and tram-jockeys hypnotized by wall screens, they programmed their watches and glasses and the corners of their transport windows to display the streaming live or edited feeds from the gaming dome.

And that was hardly the extent of it. With seconds or minutes of delay, the feeds flew out as far as the asteroid belt, to the other L5s, and crossed the quarter-million-mile gap to Earth. And there, if the reaction on the Moon had been in any way restrained, all pretense of dispassion dissolved as soon as the images hit the thousand million screens.

From Rangoon to Portland, from Tunisia to Tel Aviv, it was estimated that 12 percent of all the viewers available were tuned

in to what the IFGS called the Moon Maze Game. Legal and illegal gambling had already placed a half-billion New dollars;
that amount growing by the second. And the network had yet to
edit much of the footage at all: This was raw, real and unfiltered.
The secondary market for more polished versions was enormous. While the initial viewers were treated to the occasional
glitch or imperfect effect, those willing to wait for a day received
visual perfection. In forty-eight hours they got supplemental nar-
ration, and a week after the game the gamers themselves would
have laid down their own commentary.

Games were always popular. But unusual games, with unusual stakes or locales, could become cultural phenomena. The
Moon Maze Game was arguably the most expensive game ever
mounted (the final details wouldn't be available until the in-
sanely complex web of subsidizers, exchanged labor and energy,
and all construction work was combed through by an army of
lawyers and accountants) so a half-billion Earthviews was not a
particularly impressive number. In fact, it was assumed that the
IFGS was still chewing its collective fingernails.

And would, until the game was over.

"Chris? Pick up, dammit." Wu Lin was fighting a rising wave of
irritation, trying to keep it out of her voice, and losing the struggle.

*"Hello! I am currently evolving into something unrecogniz-
able. Leave your message at the sound of the beep."*

"Chris, this is Wu Lin. I have tried everything sane to get to
you. Xavier says you're on *now*. Get your hideously modified
arse into the game." Pause. "Oh, wait, the word is you've already
entered. Why aren't you at your post? I think I have to call Security, Chris."

Wu Lin drummed her elaborately tapered fingernails on the
desk, lips puckered into an angry O. Something was wrong,
she could feel it. Something always went wrong, which was why
redundancy was built into all games. First things first: She sig-
naled her assistants in the dome to slip an alternate into Foxworthy's role.

Second, she called Piering in Security and told him to send

someone to Chris Foxworthy's pod. Find him. Break the door down and wake him up. Whatever it took.

Five minutes later, Max Piering had arrived at Foxworthy's door. An attempt to establish electronic communication had failed, suggesting some kind of glitch. It happened. He remembered back in '76 when a computer error had sealed a pair of newlyweds into their pod for two days, and they'd barely noticed—

Piering banged on the door, heard a faint, muffled shout from inside, followed by the dull, repeated *thump* of a fist. He clicked his tongue. "Maintenance? I need door 88-C opened right now. Jammed, I think. Send someone up?"

He had barely finished replaying the delicious scene presented when the newlyweds' door opened, when Mike Berke, one of the Maintenance techs, whisked around the corner on a go-bike, hopped off and immediately opened a tool pouch on his belt.

"A jam?" he asked.

"You tell me."

Mike whistled a bit as he slipped a pronged tool into the door jamb, pulled, and the door popped open.

Chris Foxworthy had been leaning against the door. He tumbled out into the corridor, hyperventilating.

"What the hell, Chris! You all right?"

Foxworthy couldn't speak. He braced himself against the far wall and pointed a finger into the room. The finger shook.

Piering took one step into the room, inhaled, and stepped back out. He clicked his tongue. "Kendra Griffin," he said. Then when she came online, he said: "Boss, we've got an excessively big problem . . ."

The corpse was rapidly identified as a "Victor Sinjin" who had recently arrived from Earth. Foxworthy knew less than that. He said that the box Sinjin had been carrying was supposed to be a change of costume. It held only tissue paper and a pair of slippers with gooey-looking soles.

By the time Kendra arrived at Foxworthy's apartment, the

first U.N. cops had already been summoned, and would be no more than five minutes behind her.

Chief of Security Max Piering had been the first one on the scene. She hadn't ever known the guy well. After the disaster that almost killed him and Scotty, the big man had put in for an indoor gig, and she had been impressed: Too many men and women, after a major mishap on the Moon, packed their bags and fled home to Earth. Too many Moon marriages gone. She could hardly blame Scotty for making tracks.

On the contrary, she was impressed with both of them: Scotty had returned, and Piering had never left at all.

The attacker was turned at an odd and ugly angle; the expression on his face one of terminal ease. He was dressed in a classic green microfiber business suit, a little loose, and even so the fight had ripped it down the back. "He jumped you? Did he try to kill you?"

Foxworthy was inclined to babble. "I wasn't minded to negotiate! How would I know what he wanted?"

"You had some luck," Piering said. "Unless you aimed his head to hit just there? No. We'll look into his background, Chris."

"There's something else," Kendra said.

"What?"

"Chris was slated to be an NPC in the game." She tapped her epaulet, and it beeped in response. "Macy?"

"Here."

"Patch me through to gaming central."

"But they're still in the middle of a scene."

Kendra grimaced. No point in asking how Macy knew that.

"Emergency. Get one of Xavier's assistants on the link. Now, or I shut the game down."

The line wasn't clear for more than a minute before her epaulet beeped again. "Griffin."

"Xavier," a voice said, high and irritated. "You've got a hundred and twenty seconds."

"Then don't waste it with attitude," she said. "You have an NPC named Chris Foxworthy in the game?"

A pause. "Yes."

"Why didn't you report him missing?"

A snort. "Because he's not."

"Not an NPC? He's listed—"

"He's not *missing*. Look, what is this?"

Not missing? She shot Piering a glance. "Listen. Hang here for the U.N. guys. I'm going over to game central. We have a problem."

It took three minutes to reach the western control room, now given over to gaming. While only Xavier and his two associates were the official Game Masters, in the hours since arrival at Heinlein base, a gaggle of groupies and sycophants had clogged the west quadrant.

Everyone wanted to catch a glimpse of the little man, or to ferry in food or supplies, or help Xavier and his exotic assistants in any way possible. Kendra had to thread her way through them to the sealed and guarded door. The guard was a big guy named Trainor from Food Services. He had no real authority, but as a member of Xavier's fan club, had apparently plucked a plum assignment.

"Ms. Griffin," he said, and saluted. He wasn't one of the ones who kept his exercise points up. His gut bulged above his belt, but didn't sag as it would have on Earth.

"Let me in, Sammy." He stood aside, and the door slid open.

The control center's basic structure, including the holostage that had been modified from a mining waldo, remained much the same. In the four days since Xavier had arrived, the walls had been covered with posters and maps of the gaming dome, pictures of alien critters of every imaginable stripe, drawings of costumes and strange alien equipment, as well as other equipment that seemed a hybrid of alien and what had once been labeled "steam punk."

What in the world?

"Cavor has been busy," Xavier said at her elbow. She turned to look down at the little man, who grinned up at her as if he was standing in a hole. She caught no whiff of insecurity about their relative size, and she knew that he was already calculating how he would manage *this* or *that* if he ever managed to get her in bed.

"We figure that in the years since his capture, he's shared some aspects of Earth technology with the Selenites, resulting in some really nifty hybrid tech. Angelique will have a kitten trying to figure it out."

Dammit, she felt a smile wanting to tug at the corner of her mouth. Even under the current circumstances, she could appreciate the work and care and creativity, let alone the resources, that had gone into the game.

She hoped to God she wasn't about to blow it all up.

"We have a problem," she said.

Xavier frowned. "A problem? In my game? What exactly are you talking about?"

"You have an NPC named Chris Foxworthy?"

Xavier blinked. Without turning his head, he said: "Wu Lin?"

Both his assistants were up on the platform, twisting and turning their bodies like contortionists while the computer transformed them into alien worms. "Hold," Wu Lin said. "Yes, Xavier?"

"We have an NPC named Foxworthy?"

"Yes. Local, won a lottery, I believe. Playing a minor Selenite during a melee, but he's out of place. I called Security twenty-five minutes ago."

"Let's find him."

Magique stepped down from the stage, narrowing her eyes at Kendra as she approached the wall console. "NPC holding area personnel list please."

The wall displayed a series of faces, some of them familiar, most not. Twenty in all. And one of them was . . . Chris Foxworthy. His avatar blinked in the dome's third level restroom.

"Give me video in that toilet area," Kendra said. A chord, and they were looking in the restroom. The cubicals glowed emerald. *Empty.* The hair on the back of her neck tingled.

Magique's plump hands fluttered, and Wu Lin watched carefully. When she had finished, the Asian girl said: "Magique thinks he ditched his tracer. Show me all the NPCs." The screen divided into rectangles, each rectangle filled with a costumed gamer.

"That's not live, is it?" The background behind each of them was a uniform blue, and she noted that their smiles and grimaces were repeating. This was some kind of a looped program.

"Ah . . . no. These are just the CAD models for each of them. But they show in the holding area."

"Do you have a live feed into that area?"

Xavier was curious now. He chorded in the next set of directions personally. The wall shifted, showing a room with a couple of couches, lots of chairs, and a table stocked with cold cuts and pouches of juice and soda. A dozen or so people lounged around the room, talking and watching monitors. Some were in Selenite garb, others dressed as even stranger creatures, although their headpieces were off, giving them a damned strange aspect.

"Do all of these people match your records?"

Wu Lin hopped down and joined them. "What's going on?"

"We have a missing NPC," Xavier said.

"I know. He entered the gaming dome, then—poof."

"Actually," Kendra said, fighting to keep her voice calm, "I'll be rather surprised if he turns up."

"And why is that?" Xavier said. It wasn't quite a snarl, but it would do.

"He's in my office right now. Someone attacked him last night, maybe trying to keep him out of the game. He's been locked in his room. Whatever the intent was, the question remains: Who the hell checked in to your game as Chris Foxworthy, and where is he now, and why?"

... 20 ...

The Aquifer

1013 hours

Initially a volcanic bubble created by the geological activity
that had marked Luna's ancient volcanism phase, Heinlein base's
main aquifer had been blasted and sealed until it could hold a
hundred million gallons of melted lunar ice.

It had taken decades to build up enough lunar water for the
subject of recreational swimming to be seriously broached, but
at last it had. And with the specter of tourism and the income
that such tourism promised, the possibility of using the aquifers
for water sports on the moon was delicious.

In one-sixth gravity, scuba and snorkle and swimming took
on a completely different feeling than it did on Earth.

There were three entrances to the aquifer within the main
dome: one in the main rec room, one in the water recycling facility and one in central maintenance. Because the sealed cavern
was irregularly shaped, some of its pseudopods extended outside the main dome, and one reached under the dome now designated as "Gaming A." In fact, the underground lagoon had
been co-opted as a part of the game.

Thomas Frost considered these things as he made his way down
through the dome's service corridors, careful to deactivate or scram-

ble any security cameras along the way. It was quiet and cool here, down where the main bubble's support struts were sunk in bedrock.

Quiet, too, now that he had closed the vacuum safety doors behind him, sealing them and moving on. It was much like descending into a tomb. There were other paths, wider and better lit paths, descending into this darkness, but this one seemed not merely adequate, but appropriate.

Nothing that Thomas had planned or had done in training on Earth had quite prepared him for this. This was not theory or plot or dream. This was deliberate, and real. Their primary believed that anyone whose visa included off-Earth low- or zero-gravity experience or travel would be flagged and given special attention as a security risk.

Had that happened to Victor Sinjin? The man assigned to trade places with Chris Foxworthy had failed to check in. They couldn't reach him. They'd had to use a backup plan.

Or . . . perhaps trained spacemen would pose a different kind of security risk. Certainly, if Kikaya III was in any danger from Earth, said danger would come in the form of operators experienced in the ways of vacuum.

Thomas and Doug had gone another route. Every man they'd hired was used to deep-water operations, with all that that implied about pressure and oxygen and the dangers of a single unguarded moment.

What had happened to Sinjin, in an unguarded moment? Were they blown? Was it too late to call this off? Yes, infinitely too late. They could only go forward.

It felt as if his heart were pumping ice water. He didn't want to consider what would happen when Shotz learned of this mistake. This all had to be timed properly. He'd heard that was the secret to any military operation. Surprise, courage, force and timing. When they worked in your favor, you won.

At this moment, all of them were working in the favor of their plans. If that continued, Shotz would be in a good mood, and if he was in a good mood when he learned about Sinjin . . .

Then the men of Neutral Moresnot might just fulfill their contract, after all.

The stairwell descended through a steel framework anchored deep in lunar rock, three stories down before terminating at another pressure door. Their hack had deactivated the surveillance cameras, giving instructions to play back a previous hour's video and thermal scans, leaving security with nothing to concern themselves. Soon enough Piering would panic, but by then they'd be able to crash the entire grid with no fear. For now? It was little cat feet. Pure stealth, until Shotz gave the word.

Thomas unsealed the pressure door with the scan card provided by their primary. He admitted to a moment of unease while he waited for the little green and red lights to stop dancing.

No problems: The lights went green. A *hiss* and a *sigh,* and the door opened.

The chamber within was more unfinished than others he had seen in the dome: mostly a pocket of natural lava bubble, partially spray-foam sealed at the edges. On the far side of the bubble a second door opened into the room. The middle of the floor was an open pool, blue-green, with lights wavering up from the depths.

He was early, but not by more than sixty seconds. Everything was on a tight leash now, and unless he was very mistaken, or Shotz and his crew were not the product as advertised . . .

No. He saw the first of them now, a human form rising up through the murky depths, into the lights. A golem of a man emerged, climbing up along the safety rails built into the side of the pool, up the steps carved in lunar rock. One, two, three . . . finally six men in recreational lunar wetsuits with standard rebreather gear. That was the ticket: Use as much local equipment as possible. It was not just a matter of saving luggage weight: Everything traveling from Earth to Luna carried a huge risk of inspection.

The first man out of the pool was the tallest. Wide across the shoulders and thick through the chest, with a round head and short strong legs, Shotz peeled off his face mask and ran his fingers through his shoulder-length blond hair, squeezing out water.

"Towel," he growled, and held out a hand to Frost. Thomas opened the small bag he brought with him and extracted a fluffy yellow cloth. Shotz took it with a grunt of thanks, and ruffled his hair.

He threw the towel back just as the last of his men emerged from the pool. "Cold," he said.

"Yes, it is."

"Why are you dressed as a giant bug? And where is Victor?"

"He didn't report this morning," Thomas said. "I had to take his place. I had to dress as an NPC and didn't have time to change."

Something ugly glittered behind Shotz' eyes, and then was gone. "Status."

"The gamers are eating right now. This is a programmed rest break, and they'll be starting the game again in . . ." He checked his watch. "Ten minutes."

"Have you been monitoring the security channels? Any word about Sinjin?"

"None." He had, and there had been no obvious fluttering of panic among their targets, or the local administration. "I don't know what happened, but that was why I was inserted into the game, as backup. We're still on the planned timetable."

"Good. It is your responsibility to keep it that way for the next hour."

"And then?"

Shotz hadn't heard him. He had already turned to the others: solid, strong men . . . and one frightening woman, Celeste. Celeste was all breasts and hips and full lips and a cascade of blond hair. It wasn't until you looked closely in her green eyes that you realized that the promise of sexual warmth was as toxic as the sweet kernel at the heart of a flesh-eating plant. Pure lure. Instinct said she was as dangerous as Shotz. Celeste was in this business because from time to time she got to hurt people. She smiled at Frost, allowing him a flash of those heavenly breasts, and his stomach recoiled. A powerful sexual response combined with a deep sense of rot, a stench without a scent.

"Celeste." He nodded carefully. With this one, it was best to stay neutral. The others were from, he believed, Greece, the United States, somewhere in the Middle East, and perhaps Britain. By agreement if not dictate, members of Neutral Moresnot spent little time discussing their backgrounds. The extreme nature of this commission had called for the team to spend more time than usual in training and preparation. A bit of information leak was normal. All names were assumed, but he believed that clues based on vocal inflections and casual conversation could reveal national origin. At the very least, it was a good game. Yes. He and Doug were playing a much better game than the stupid Earthers.

With far higher stakes.

Eight Europeans, two black, three Asians. Twelve men and one woman. The thirteen stripped off their dive gear and checked the equipment inside the sealed plastic bags. Quick verification that the seals had held, and then slipping on dry black pants and long-sleeve shirts, and black composition-soled shoes. They broke into pairs: Celeste and Shotz checking each other's equipment, then handing them back.

"Are vi prata?" Shotz asked.

"Jes."

Only English or that damned esperanto on the job, Frost thought. Shotz was crazy, but it was his show.

Thomas Frost led the way, climbing out of the dome's depths into the shadowed main level. Lights were low, but only a thin wall separated them from some kind of staging area. Low voices, a few creaks as equipment was moved into place or last-minute adjustment was made. He understood little about this gaming thing, other than a few vids Shotz had acquired for them, and some speculations on how the gaming environment had been laid over the basic dome interior.

That information had been exhaustive, as well as the power systems, entrances and exits. Once they gained control in (he checked his watch) fifty-six minutes, there would be little anyone on the outside could do to stop them.

For now, it was a matter of avoiding the Non-Player Characters as they prepared to add a little excitement to their lives. He had to shake his head: Moon-people playing science fiction for a jolt. Well, get ready: There was a pretty big jolt about to land on them like a mountain, and it would be no game at all.

21

Arbitration

1033 hours

"So . . . what in the hell is going on?"

Kendra and Xavier sat in a com room not fifty feet down the corridor from gaming central. Xavier's eyes glittered like little acetylene flames. He swung his feet from the edge of his chair like a petulant gnome who considered a human's death to be little more than a personal inconvenience.

"What's going on is that my game is in suspension," Xavier said.

"Excuse me," Kendra interjected, fighting to keep her voice level. "A man is dead, apparently during an attempted assault. Chris Foxworthy was sealed incommunicado in his room by some kind of override device. Despite this, he apparently checked into your game."

Leonard Cowles III was the on-site arbiter for the International Fantasy Gaming Society. He had been here for over a month now overseeing the final construction, recruiting gamers, coordinating travel, publicity and expenses. Happily, this was *his* headache. "Please," he said. "Slow down. Ms. Griffin, you said that this man Victor Sinjin was found dead . . . but that some time between the time of death and the discovery of the body, someone using Foxworthy's identification checked into the gaming area?"

"Yes."

Cowles' mouth flattened into a thin line. "And what do you conclude?"

"I don't know. I just know that we have to stop the game so we can search the gaming area."

"Wait just a minute," Xavier said. "So one of my NPCs was assaulted, and killed his assailant. And someone still used his ID to get into the game, somehow. I can understand your concern. But we can't just shut the whole thing down right now. Four hours and we quit for the night. Then you can tear the whole thing apart: We're off the clock."

"I'm not sure that you understand. This is a murder investigation."

"And that dome is private property, by the terms of our lease with Cowles Industries," Xavier said. "I want this cleared up as much as anyone, but we have a worldwide audience exceeding a billion people. Are you aware of the web of finances necessary to connect a billion people? The obligations I've incurred? Do you have any idea of the lawsuits I will be exposed to, if this game is delayed by more than a few seconds?"

"I'll take personal responsibility," Kendra said.

"It's not that easy," Cowles said. "The liability negotiations were especially intense from my family's side of the table. The only way the board of supervisors would ratify the deal is if the IFGS assumed all responsibility for what happened in the dome from the time the doors locked until the conclusion of the game. The dome has its own battery bank and communications, the gaming system is on a separate link from everything else. This was your choice, please remember."

Kendra thought she was going to scream. She saw where this was headed, and didn't like it at all.

"You're telling me you think I have no authority to search the dome?"

"I'm telling you that the repercussions are huge. My family has made a large chunk of its name in the entertainment industry, which is why I've taken personal responsibility in this matter. What you propose to do now could risk its relationship with the IFGS, and gaming worldwide. Do you want to make that decision?"

"I do. My husband is in that dome," she said.

"All the more reason to assume that things are secure," Cowles said. "All we're asking for is four hours."

"Four hours," she said. "A lot can happen in four hours."

"I'm afraid that I insist on the right to appeal to my board of directors."

"As on-site chief, I have the ability to make decisions—"

"And if the dome actually belonged to Cowles at this moment, that might make a difference," Leonard Cowles said.

"Four hours." Kendra drummed her fingers against the table. "In all good conscience, I cannot allow this."

"It is not your decision to make."

Kendra felt a burning sensation on the left side of her head, deep behind her ear. Dammit. The air in front of her rippled. "Ms. Griffin?" Stan Linberg said urgently. "There is a news bulletin that you might want to see. Now."

Something was very very wrong, even worse than she currently dreamed, but she couldn't detect the shape of it. It crawled her scalp. Bad times coming.

The air rippled, and a newsfeed appeared, an Asian newsman reading from a teleprompter as images of explosions in some tropical country played in the background.

"—death in the Republic of Kikaya, where rebel forces hold both international airports and the major communications facilities after a lightning raid in the early morning hours. King Abdul Kikaya, the last remaining monarch in sub-Saharan Africa, has responded swiftly. Paralysis among his troops suggests that there has been a deep penetration of his military chain of command, and—"

"Cut," she said, and the image froze. "All right, Stan, this is bad news for someone. Why me?"

"Because . . . at least one of the gamers is playing under an assumed name, and his point of origin is the Republic of Kikaya. We have investment capital from the republic, and . . . we actually have two workers from the republic here at Heinlein."

"Really?" That raised her eyebrows. She knew of several Central African workers among her people, but didn't remember any from Kikaya.

"Yes. They're naturalized American citizens, but I remember some conversation about them. They stand out because they're twins."

"Twins?" That raised a memory. "Thomas, maybe?"

"Yes, and Doug. They were supposed to cycle back to Earth, but both extended their tours. Anyway, because of those connections, when I was going through the gamer list I saw the red flag and looked closer. There was a secret of some kind there, and I admit I dug into it."

She felt like a cold lump of rotten cottage cheese was sitting in the pit of her stomach. Something bad was coming. "And?"

"And the participant traveling as 'Ali Shannar' is actually Prince Ali of Kikaya, heir to the throne."

"Shit," she said. She looked up at Xavier and Cowles. "And what do you make of that?"

"Ms. Griffin. I am sorry to hear of instability in the Republic of Kikaya, but that is an unstable region, I believe. What possible connection can it have with events a quarter-million miles away?" Spreading his hands in supplication, Cowles seemed the very soul of reason.

"Xavier?" she asked. "You are Game Master, and if you gave permission, we could elongate the break time, and do a sweep of the dome—"

"Let's not," he said. "Most of the dome is already under observation. Patch in the security cameras to the gaming units, and create a full dome image. I'm sure our missing player will turn up."

"And with a perfectly reasonable explanation," she said. She sighed, and stood. "Well, I'm afraid that you're right: The IFGS controls that dome for the next three days. But when I can get

that board meeting, our lawyers are going to look at that contract." Kendra placed her hands flat on the table and locked eyes
first with Cowles, and then Xavier. "But you'd better pray that
there's nothing wrong in there."

∙∙∙ **22** ∙∙∙

Interruption

1056 hours

Asako Tabata's capsule buzzed up to the edge of the abyss. A slender camera probe extended from the tip and bent down to peer into the darkness.

"What do we have?" Sharmela asked.

"A *looong* drop," Asako said. They had finished their meal, and, after reiteration of their mission (to travel into the forbidden lunar depths to rescue Professor Cavor), had been ushered into a gloomy rock tunnel by an insectoid guardian and sent on their way.

The nine gamers and their guide proceeded with greater caution now. While Xavier would never have killed one of them off in the first hour of the game, now that they had been fed and rested, he might very well consider it all in good fun to slaughter a couple while they were digesting their food.

Ho ho ho.

Wayne watched Asako there at the edge of the drop, a four-foot fissure slicing the narrow tunnel in two. Perfectly easy for most of them to make a jump like that, especially on the Moon. But Asako, in her bubble?

Her withered hands manipulated several controls, and a little rail extrusion grew out of her front bumper, three feet long . . . and then four. It anchored to the far side, making its own bridge, and her pod began to hitch itself across. When she made it to the far side, they broke into appreciative applause. Then the others just jumped across one at a time. Only Mickey Abernathy had any difficulty at all, and that wasn't from the length of the gap. He misjudged his angle and hit the wall a meter up, almost bouncing back into the gap. Maud grabbed his tunic and pulled him to safety.

More applause as Mickey pretended to be even more off balance than he really was, wheeling his arms and making a great show of being terrified.

The show must go on.

The bioluminescent fungus glowed just enough to make an effectively creepy passage. Somewhere up ahead of them, water dripped against rock. Angelique held up her hand, and they stopped, listening.

Somewhere up ahead of them, someone or something screamed. The sound was low, so full of echo it was barely discernible as anything originating in a living throat. But it was enough that swords and guns emerged from sheaths and holsters.

Angelique motioned Wayne up to the front, but as he passed Scotty he whispered, "Take the rear. Something's coming and you move as if you recognize the sharp end of a sword."

The big black guy grinned like a shark. "Kept me breathing a time or two."

Why did he have the feeling that that extended outside the gaming world? And was he Ali's friend? Relative? Lover? Something else? No time now. That echoing sound was closer . . . and then gone. Silence as they walked through the tunnel.

His skin started creeping again. Dammit! Why was he experiencing that? He'd heard that Dream Park had some trade secrets they refused to discuss publicly. A former DP tech had appeared on a vid special discussing something called "neutral scent" and various subliminal sound cues designed to freak players out.

His teeth were starting to feel as if he was licking a battery, but he refused to let the creepy feeling shut his head down.

Generations of alien feet seemed to have worn the stone smooth. The walls were cool and damp to the touch.

Sharmela held up her hand. "Wait. I sense a vibration from ahead."

Wayne couldn't see anything, but his lenses were coded differently. "What?" Angelique asked.

"Near." Sharmela closed her eyes. Now Mickey and Maud had pulled up even with them, locking hands and rolling their eyes convincingly.

"What is it?"

"Ambush," they said. "We see . . . ladders. And stones. And enemies." Mickey lowered his voice to a portentous growl. "We must face them."

Dum da dum dum.

"Alert. We have warriors front and rear. Watch every step. They'll hit us hard, if they can."

If he had allowed himself to think outside the tunnel of his concentration, Xavier would have gone stone-cold berserk. He was confident in Wu Lin and her silent partner Magique, but that wasn't the point: He needed *focus* as he sank into the control board's master chair. From here, he could watch the layout of the entire dome, monitor the network running the live game, the simulation screens debugging the coming scenarios, and the holostage where his assistants were still modifying the body language for the video overlays.

Everything was in place and running, including all the Earthfeeds. The commercial contracts were long past executed. It was running, dammit. Everything was in place for a great game and Angelique's savage humiliation if she stepped just one tiny toe over the line. And he knew she would. That would give him all the excuse he needed to kill her nine kinds of dead. Wayne Gibson he would torture more slowly. Kill him out? Hardly. Wayne would live every minute of the game, thrust into a leadership position and completely neutered, incompetence splashed across the solar system until he begged for a death that would not come. He would be the last surviving member of the team, a laughing stock until the day he died.

The world's biggest audience, for the world's biggest sporting event, and the world's greatest revenge. And now *this* lame nonsense. So a player had had an accident, and someone had grabbed his ID to sneak into the game. Wouldn't be the first time that had happened.

And there was another factor: Wasn't the woman Kendra the ex-wife of one of the gamers? In which case, wasn't it entirely possible that she was trying to manipulate the situation for her ex? What could their play be? Moving information or equipment into the dome? Breaking Xavier's rhythm and concentration with some kind of trumped-up excuse? This "Foxworthy" guy was probably sitting back smoking a cigar. He might have actually entered the game, and the whole attempted murder was a distraction. *"Oh, sorry,"* they'd say later. *"There was a misunderstanding . . ."*

And there would go his game.

"Xavier?" Wu Lin said. "We're about to start the obstacle course. Any last-second changes?"

He broke out of his self-induced coma and ran a checklist in his mind. "Everything's fine. Let's see if we can't kill someone, shall we?"

Wu Lin smiled.

He knew there was only one thing she liked better than killing gamers, and that particular pleasure would wait for their post-game celebration. "Let's do it."

"Here we go. Climbing wall active. NPCs coded and standing by?"

"All at the ready," Wu Lin said.

"Then three . . . two . . . one . . . and *go.*"

But in the moment before he dropped back down into tunnel vision, he noted that the computer caught, just for a moment, a flash of unregistered body heat. Almost as if there were other people in the gaming dome, someone neither a technician nor an

NPC. But it was only for an instant. Was there someone there, and had they cloaked? Or was it an artifact, just a ghost in their machine?

No time to hunt it down now. The game was afoot.

"Never, ever ever would I try to take a team up something like this," Angelique said. She was staring up an airwell, a vertical rock tube leading up toward a wavering light. It was about five meters in diameter, studded with rocky nubs up as far as the eye could see. She held something like a polished crystal rock, the size of a hen's egg. A little guidance device the Selenites had given her. The little flashing red light said it was time to climb.

"But the rules are different here?"

"It's the Moon. Gravity is low enough that Asako can get her pod up the walls." In fact, Xavier's engineers would have to have allowed for Asako. Her pod was a political sop to disabled gamers, and an odd advantage: Once Asako had the go-ahead to enter the game, the layout had to be modified to allow her to play. That gave her a fractional Off the Grid advantage.

Asako's little pod was already humming around the walls. "There seem to be grips here. The rock is soft enough for my claws, but too wide for the legs to hold me horizontal. I'll have to climb vertically, but that puts me out of action until I can get back on horizontal. I'll need coverage."

Good news and bad news. So Asako's bubble could climb, but while climbing, she'd be useless in a fight. So Mickey and Maud were right: They were about to get hammered.

"We'll need two climbers to get up to the top. Drop a safety line to Asako. Then we can leave someone down here with her, climb, and work the line as her pod climbs."

"Sounds like a plan," Scotty Griffin said. "I could get up there, secure the line."

"Then take point," Angelique said.

For the first time since beginning the game, Scotty Griffin felt at home. Climbing was something he understood. The vertical shaft was about twenty meters high, with irregular boulder-shaped protrusions jutting from the sides. Asako Tabata's pod would make it, but only just. It would require a gamer at each end, top and bottom, managing a line the entire time.

Why? As he began his climb, that question ticked at his mind. Yeah, maybe the Selenites just happen to have made it this way . . . but Angelique and Wayne both seemed to think that this guy Xavier had something ugly up his sleeve. If that was true, then if it took two people to control the pod, that functionally removed three people from the fight.

He could have made the climb under Earth Normal gravity, gripping with fingers, bracing feet, twisting this way and that to inch up a foot or so at a time. But here upper-body strength alone launched him up the tube to the next rock. His hand strength was more than sufficient to support his weight easily. This all would have been more fun if he didn't expect an ambush at any moment.

Just before he reached the top, Scotty looked back down to see the faces tilted up at him, almost lost in the shadows. Showing off by hanging from one arm, he made an "okay" sign with a circled thumb and forefinger, and then scrambled up over the lip.

He had to crouch a little, because the rock ceiling was only six feet high and he didn't want to bump his head. Glowing fungus lit the front of the chamber, which seemed only a dozen feet wide, but long enough to vanish into shadow. He paused, barely able to discern a scratching sound, something distant, but close enough to unnerve him. Oh, yes, there was something out there.

Scotty yelled down the hole for two more fighters to climb up, producing fast action from Wayne and Kikaya. The kid seemed to be having the time of his life, which was good: God knows it was costing him enough.

As soon as his backups arrived, Scotty unspooled a length of line and dropped it down the well. Angelique attached it to a tether point at the front of the pod, then a second line to the rear.

"What . . . maybe three hundred pounds Earth Normal?" he said. "About fifty pounds here. Only takes one of us to pull her up, if the other two are keeping guard."

"I think you're the strongest," Wayne said. "Two thieves and a magic user. What say Ali and I take guard while you pull."

His two companions took position on either side of the well, Ali making arcane hand gestures and torquing his body into strange, spiderlike positions. *Have a ball, kid.*

Now then. Only about fifty pounds to lift, but he wanted to give Asako a smooth ride. He set his heels, wound the line around his wrist to anchor it and began to pull. Smooth and steady did the trick. He almost *wanted* it to be harder.

"We've got company . . . ," Wayne whispered.

"I know. Ali?"

Ali hummed to himself, squatting to look into the shadows beyond the pale glow. "Many," was all he said, voice just a little tense.

"How many is 'many'?"

"Perhaps twenty. Or more. Hard to say."

"How far?" Wayne asked.

Ali touched his temples. "We've got about a minute."

Scotty pulled faster, and between pulls yelled down the hole. "As soon as Asako is up, get your butts up here!" Now he suddenly remembered his character and added: "The infidels are upon us!" feeling just a bit asinine.

Scrape, scrape. He looked over his right shoulder at Ali, who knelt, peering into the gloom. Scotty couldn't see a thing. Then . . . he realized that he was looking in the wrong place. He was looking at the tunnel floor. Wrong. The ceiling *swarmed* with enemy.

Selenite locomotion was a bizarre cross between termites and human beings, and the only thing that had saved Scotty and his companions was that the enemy was moving gradually, carefully, and not at full swarm. Curious? Fearful?

Wayne couldn't help himself. "Have you tried: 'We come in peace'?"

The pod was almost up, the nose rising above the lip, and one more pull and Asako was up.

At the instant the pod's treads bit into the lunar rock to right itself and take control, the Selenite warriors shrieked and swarmed.

"Get up here!" he screamed, pulled his sword, and the battle was on.

The Selenites bore no weapons, but their claws and jaws were threatening enough, and the humans were outnumbered six to one. When the first jumped, Ali spread his arms and screamed. Light flared from his chest. Scotty noted now, in the fullness of the light, that varicolored, hairy ringlets surrounded their necks. Blue, red and yellow, if the glimpse was accurate. The yellow-fringed Selenites screamed and shriveled before Ali's onslaught, and three of them fell at once. But the others directly targeted Ali, came right at him. One grabbed his leg, which was instantly bathed in red light.

Ali yelled and kicked it away as Wayne leaped in, sword at the ready. By the time he got there, two more Selenites had grabbed hold of Ali, and Wayne had his hands full.

"Go!" Asako said through her loudspeakers. "I can guard this side."

He didn't waste time doubting her, but did snatch a glimpse down the well: The other gamers were coming up. He turned back around just in time for one of the Selenites to jump onto his chest. In lunar gravity, it didn't weigh what he would have expected. In point of fact . . . it weighed nothing at all. A brief moment of surprise, then Scotty remembered that he was on camera, and stumbled back, screaming, "grabbed" the creature and threw it to the side.

It made a particularly satisfying *splat* against the wall, as if the thing was just a bag of green blood. He pivoted, pulling his antique pistol and firing point-blank at a spider Selenite as it dropped from the roof to the floor, catching it in midair. It squished, squealed and flopped back.

From the corner of his eye he caught Asako Tabata's pod as it righted itself and went on the attack. Twin shotguns poked out of the nose of her craft, doing serious damage to what seemed an endless flood of Selenite bug critters. He saw some of them dropping down the hole, and heard cursing from below as the climbing gamers suddenly found themselves under attack. He saw the red-haired guide speared on a bolt of lightning, thrashing, her hair standing on end.

That must have been great fun. He almost wished he hadn't volunteered to climb first.

Angelique Chan grimaced as her back slid against the pipe's side. She lost some of her footing and fell two feet before managing to brace herself again. Damn that Xavier! You *never* attack gamers while they are climbing without safety lines . . . but considering the reduced lunar gravity, who really cared? Must have been a special dispensation from the IFGS. No more time to think, because Mickey and Maud and Sharmela, coming up behind her, were shrieking:

"They're coming from down here, too!"

Angelique had managed to draw her sword, hardly her favorite weapon in such a confined space. The Selenite spiders snapped at her, scratched at her, and when she stabbed one, the yellowish ichor dripped down onto her face. Damn! It was real, and warm, and stank, but tasted like liquorice. Game-toxic, not real-toxic.

A little present from Xavier. She was going to murder that dwarf. Angelique spat out the gunk, and forced her way another few feet up the pipe, stabbed another Selenite and was relieved to find that this one was a hologram.

"Rule Britannia!" Mickey said, right beneath her, and the tube was suddenly filled with bright blue light. Selenites screamed and burst into flame, and ash fluttered down the tube, even as the afterimage from the flare partially blinded her. Angelique slid, but her foot hit Mickey's head and he howled protest.

"Sorry!" she said and forced her way back up, charging now, stabbing if not slashing, and got one hand over the top. One arm was strong enough to pitch her entire body up, with the *flare* of an Olympic gymnast if not the balance. She wobbled on her toes and almost fell back down. At the last instant, Griffin stopped eviscerating Selenites and lent her a steadying hand.

Now there were four of them up top, two on each side of the

pipe, and the entire tunnel was a sword-swinging, gun-blasting, Selenite-spider-splashing cacophony.

By the time Mickey and Maud made it up top, the battle was almost won. Below them in the pipe, curls of stinking blue smoke suggested that there was little left alive to hound them.

When the last Selenite fell, Angelique was horrified to see Sharmela leaning back against the wall, her hands clutched to a gaping wound in her midsection.

"Maud!" Angelique called. Maud was a primary psychic, with secondary healing powers.

Maud knelt by the wounded girl and ran her hands over the gash. "I don't know, I truly fear, that Sharmela's damage is severe."

"There are healing forces here," Sharmela gasped. "My powers tell me that"—she paused, probably listening to prompts in her earpiece—"a glowing fungus in the next airwell might . . . might help."

She reached out with a bloody hand and gripped Angelique's arm. "Please, don't. I think it's a trap."

"I—"

And then the lights went out. The glowing fungus in the tunnel just died. The darkness that had been a mere inconvenience was now deep enough to swallow them. This wasn't the game, it was a major power failure of some kind.

"I'll be damned," Angelique laughed. "Never seen this happen to Xavier before. He must be hopping."

Their laughter had an odd, nervous edge. This was an occasion for genuine amusement. In a few minutes the backups would probably kick in, and then—

"Angelique," Wayne said. "Someone's coming."

She stood and looked down the tunnel to her left. The darkness was parting now, and three . . . four flashlight-sized lamps were bobbling as the newcomers approached. What in the world was this? God, sounded like a major breakdown if they were inserting repairmen into the game.

"What a bleedin' botch," Mickey said under his breath. "Seen nothing like this since Bizarro World back in 'sixty-eight."

"Well," Maud said. "Considering the venue, I suppose you have to make allowances."

"Stay where you are," a male voice said. "And listen closely to what we say. If you follow our orders to the letter, no one will be hurt."

She couldn't quite place the accent, but understood the message instantly. "What's wrong? Is there a breach?"

"You might say that," the man said, and now, finally, she could see him. A huge man with flowing blond hair and a flat hard face. A fan of scars creased the left side of his throat. "All you need to know"—he said. His voice was pure gravel—"Is that your little game is over, and a new one has begun. The stakes are quite a bit higher." He smiled, and by some unfathomable transformation became handsome. Dashing. The sudden change was quite disturbing. "In this game you win by not dying."

23

Hostages

1125 hours

"What is this?" Ali asked. "Are you . . ." He searched for words. In the intense, bleaching light he looked young and lost. "Did Professor Cavor . . ." He was trying to work it out, make sense of it all in the framework of the game. "Who are you?"

Scotty Griffin's nerves were burning. He put a hand on Ali's shoulder and pulled him back, warned him to silence with a shake of his head.

"Very good," the leader said. "I don't mind you knowing my name. Before this is all over, everyone on Earth will, and I'll never be able to use it again anyway. I am Shotz."

Confusion, not panic, was Scotty's dominant emotion as their attackers herded the gamers into a room perhaps twenty meters across. This bubble had no Wellsian motif, just a domed space littered with boxes, equipment and costumes.

Prince Ali tensed as the intruders ordered them about, seemed about to swell up like a frog. The wrong damned time to be imperious. Scotty gripped his arm until Ali winced, gave him a quick, warning shake. *Not now.*

"Move! Move!" The blond woman who looked like a biker

angel said the words calmly, but there was a kind of frenzy under the surface, well-leashed. For now. She held some kind of jerry-rigged air gun, and Scotty didn't want to test her speed or accuracy.

He thought he heard this "Shotz" character call her Celeste.

Even though the gamers, NPCs and techs were herded efficiently, their captors missed one. Just one.

Darla Kowsnofski, killed out right on schedule, had been creeping through back passages, avoiding gamers on her way to an NPC holding area, when the intruders showed up. Now she crouched in a shadow, prying at the edge of a hidden hatch. Muttering a prayer.

Darla cursed herself for a coward. Should she try to help someone else escape? Or just take care of herself, and consider that victory enough? Even as an awkward honor student at Oklahoma State, Darla had always thought of herself as a good person. She had always had more confidence in her mind than in her generous, well-cushioned body . . . and that mind had taken her all the way to Heinlein. But at this moment all she wanted was to be somewhere dark, and alone, and away from the people with guns. And God help her, there was no part of her that felt guilty about it.

"Please, please, please," she whispered, prying at the panel. Just before she gave up hope it slid open an inch. She got her finger under it, levered it up, slipped in and was gone.

In Heinlein base's nerve center, Kendra found herself juggling a dozen conversations with two dozen different people. Her assistant buzzed her. "Ms. Griffin? We have a call on two-nine-nine." A pause. "It's from inside the dome."

For a moment Kendra was taken aback, but then she jumped on the communication. "Hello?"

She was looking at a mask: not a game mask, a diver's mask. The voice on the other side was gravelly, almost as if it had emerged from a machine, or a damaged voice box. "Ms. Griffin?"

"Yes. Who is this?'

"Call us Neutral Moresnot."

She blinked. "I can't pronounce that without being rude. Who are you?"

"We are the very serious people who control this dome, and every human being within it."

That she accepted without another thought. "What do you want?"

"At the moment, what I want is to put your mind at ease. I have no wish to kill our hostages. In fact, if my demands are met, they will all be released unharmed."

"Does that include Chris Foxworthy, my assistant?"

"I trust so. I seem to have lost contact with my man. Would he be in custody at this time?"

"No. There was an accident. Your man is dead."

"Dead?" She couldn't read that damaged voice, but her best guess was that his response was one of surprise. And not mild surprise, either. Anger?

"Oh, my," he said. The mild words and flat vocal quality concealed hidden emotional currents. "I wasn't aware of that. Well, that is regrettable, and unexpected. But he can be the last, if you follow my directions."

"And what directions are those?"

"You will send over a Scorpion transport vehicle. Twenty-eight seats, if it matches spec. There will be no weapons on board, and no one in the transport. We will be scanning."

But of course he would. By this time, the intruders were probably tied into every communication line they had. "And you are using this transport to . . . ?"

"Evacuate twenty members of the gaming staff, professional and volunteer."

"From the kindness of your heart?"

"Madam, under the current conditions, do you truly consider antagonism the wisest course? Until you can demonstrate such restraint, I suggest you listen more than you speak. And please have the Scorpion here in ten minutes."

"If I don't?"

"We'll send them out walking . . . without suits."

And with that, the visual field dissolved.

Foxworthy drummed his fingers against the console. "What do you think?"

"I think that he wants to reduce the number of people he has to manage. Most of the NPCs are Lunies . . . locals who know more about the Moon than he does. This way, he's mostly got gamers. As ignorant of the Moon as he is. Easier to control. And most of them are Earthers. That means off-planet political pressure on us. They want to muddy the water, Chris."

Foxworthy nodded agreement, as if he had already come to that conclusion. "What do we do?"

"Send him a transport. No tricks." Pause. "Yet."

Foxworthy was on it instantly. "Give me the garage. I need a transport for twenty people delivered to the gaming dome. No one on board. No tricks. A Scorpion if you've got it."

The garage manager's voice was both professional and curious. "What in the hell is going on over there? I've heard rumors . . ."

Kendra interjected. "Keep them to yourself. We'll have an announcement within the hour."

24

No Resistance

1150 hours

Fear hung in the room like a curtain of hot, wet air. It was like trying to breathe steam. Scotty Griffin examined the plastic bands cuffing his wrists in front. Given time he could find a way to sever them . . . but would he have time? He couldn't guess when or even if such an action might be advisable. And even if he managed to free himself and his companions, where could they go?

The captives were sequestered in a storage bubble. Ali had been separated a few feet from the other gamers. The implication was perfectly clear: This was all about the Prince.

Judging by the degree of deference displayed by the others, the lead kidnapper was the one named "Shotz." A golden-locked golem, as solid as a granite spur. His face could look flat and hard or masculinely attractive, depending on his expression. Shotz radiated a sense of disconnected amusement about everything, and Scotty wondered where the man had picked up the scars on the right side of his throat. His second-in-command seemed to be the red-haired Viking goddess they called Celeste. He had the ugly suspicion he had seen her before, briefly, in Switzerland. And wondered if she had recognized him in turn.

She and a couple of the others had entered and exited the

room repeatedly. She was now looking down at them with a low flame in her eyes, as if she enjoyed their helplessness and hungered for the opportunity to exploit it. He reminded himself not to give her an excuse.

"These names: Michael Abernathy, Maud Abernathy, Angelique Chan, Sharmela Tamil, Wayne Gibson, Scott Griffin . . . move to this side of the room," she said. "On your knees, hands behind your heads."

Ali looked as if he wanted to faint. Scotty wanted to say something, but was cautious about announcing their relationship to these people. Why give them information they had, as yet, shown no sign of possessing? "What about me?" Ali said weakly.

"Ali Shannar? Excuse me: Ali Kikaya the Third. You will come with me."

Time to forget caution. "I'd like to go with him."

"And you would be . . . ?" The blonde said, smiling pleasantly. Her eyes roamed over him.

"His friend."

She chuckled. "Well, 'friend,' I think not." She leaned close. "I think I know you, my friend." So much for Switzerland. "We may have playtime later. But now, I think you had better get back on your knees. Shotz?"

Behind her, Shotz seemed to come out of his internal trance, almost like popping in and out of a separate reality. "Here is the situation: We have business with Ali Kikaya the Third. In fact, it is this business that brought us here. We have no interest in any of the rest of you, which may be to your advantage, assuming you cooperate. If you cooperate, you will remain unmolested. You will be reasonably comfortable, and will have all the amenities we can offer in exchange for your cooperation. Because we don't care about you."

A pause. "But . . . if you cause us difficulty of any kind, that will be an entirely different matter. Because we do not care about you. Do not care whether you live or die. It is marginally easier for us to keep you alive than it is to shoot you, or march you naked into the sunlight. I would suggest that you remember the word 'marginally.' "

Behind Scotty's shoulder, Angelique snarled. "You can't get away with this. There are security forces."

The woman looked at Angelique as if she were something in a petri dish. "If the dome is attacked, you die."

Their bonds were checked carefully. Shotz left the room, and Celeste turned to face them. "There is nowhere for you to go. If you cooperate, you will be reasonably comfortable. If not . . ." She shrugged, but again, Scotty saw the little light go on in her eyes. *This one wants to make an example of one of us,* he thought.

As lightly as if he were a baby, she picked Ali up by the arm, and carried him from the room.

The door had just closed behind the kidnappers, and Wayne could no longer constrain himself. "Who the hell is Ali? I mean, I figured he was some kind of rich kid, but . . ."

Mickey picked up the topic swiftly. "But these bastards went to a hell of a lot of trouble to get their 'ands on him. People are going to *die* as a result of this." He wiped his mouth against his shoulder. "Yeah, they've been polite enough so far, but this isn't going to end well. I think that we deserve to know what the 'ell is going on." Stress made his Cockney more pronounced.

For a long moment Scotty debated lying or stonewalling. But dammit, now they were all in this mess together, and they deserved better. He sighed. "His name is Ali Kikaya the Third. He's heir to the throne of the Republic of Kikaya. His father thought that he might be at risk, but nobody could have anticipated *this*."

Angelique looked like she wanted to skin him and roll him in salt. "So what do they want? What do they think they're going to do? There's no way out of here!"

"I don't know. But I do know that they seem to know what they're doing. And they haven't made a mistake yet."

Not yet, Scotty thought. But the day was young.

The room on the far side of the door was just more undecorated storage beneath a curved, unpainted gray ceiling. It wouldn't have been a part of the game at all. Shotz was sitting on a corrugated cardboard box that probably would have folded under his weight on Earth.

"Frost," Shotz said. "They said that Victor was dead. Why is this news to me?"

Thomas tried to meet Shotz's eyes, failed, and then tried again. "It's news to me, too. I knew nothing of it. He was alive when last I saw him."

Shotz's eyes glittered in the dim light, and for a moment he seemed almost buoyant, as if the two of them held a great and mysterious secret. "Was he? There will be more about this later."

Kendra Griffin sat at her main conference table. The men and women around her, trained and experienced administrators, blinked and frowned furiously, as if trying to awaken themselves from a nightmare. She thought that they used to call the condition shell-shocked. "There are twelve people who checked into Heinlein base who are, at present, unaccounted for. All of them are tourists."

Foxworthy bent his head, one hand cupping his left ear. "Kendra, Alex Griffin on line two."

A ray of sunshine on a foggy, moonless night. Kendra clicked her tongue, triggering her com link.

The air in front of her cleared, and Scotty's father appeared. "Kendra. What is happening up there?"

"I'm betting you've heard. Dad, you still have fingers everywhere. Who are these people? Who or what is a 'Neutral Moresnot'?" Her pronunciation was perfect.

A quarter-million miles put a short but perceptible pause in every conversation, about a second and a half per comment. "Kendra, I'm linking with some of my people. Just bits and pieces right now, but 'Neutral Moresnot' is the code name for a kidnapping ring."

"What nationality?"

Alex wagged his head. "I'm not sure. I remember hearing about this group before I retired. But nothing since. I'll call Foley Mason. He keeps his hand in."

"Please."

There was a long, awkward pause. Then Alex spoke in a very quiet voice. "Kendra. Have you heard anything from Scotty?"

"Not a word," she said. "And I have to assume that we won't, until this thing is resolved."

"Dear?" Millicent Griffin came online. Her expression was all business. "I've been researching while Alex was talking, and here's what I've come up with. 'Neutral Moresnot' is the code name of an international kidnapping ring. Kidnapping is big business. Officially speaking in Esperanto to hide their nationalities, they take their name from the country Esperanto devotees once wanted to create. They have no politics. Current speculation is that they are there to kidnap Ali and put pressure on his father in the Republic of Kikaya: Abdicate, or lose a son."

"Are they willing to kill?"

"Yes. And have. But only if their demands aren't met."

Neutral Moresnot had set up primary communications in bubble 37-C, twenty meters in diameter with a parquet floor and glow panels for windows. Their commander held up a hand, pointing to their observation screen. "We have a Scorpion inbound this way from Heinlein. No one on board. Automatic, riding the rails. Arrival in three minutes?"

"And nothing else approaching from any direction."

"Excellent," Shotz said.

Lunies and Earthers who had until quite recently believed they were in for a jolly adventure were clustered in bubble 35-C, supervised by McCartney and Gallop, two very professional, very unsympathetic men. Gallop was a heavyweight bodybuilder, huge, twice McCartney's size, but was notably cautious and deferential to the smaller man, and for good reason. Shotz entered and surveyed the lot for a moment, finally nodding in approval. "All individuals designated Non-Player Characters will shed their costumes and prepare to enter the transport," the blond man said in his dead, fractured voice. Without a smile, the face beneath the brilliant hair resembled a slab of raw rock. "There will be no talking, no resistance, or I promise you that there will be screaming and dying."

Nineteen NPCs and techs were escorted from 35-C down through the infrastructure to bubble 137-H on the ground level, out an airlock and to the Scorpion transport. The kidnappers watched until the doors sealed, then the transport broke dock, and headed back toward Heinlein base.

"*Mi ami gxi kiam a plano veni kune,*" McCartney said.

The blond shrugged. "Might as well lose that. We're finished after this. Might just as well speak Spanish."

Inside the Scorpion transport, the nineteen NPCs and techs sat strapped in their seats, marveling at their narrow escape, hugging each other and celebrating as the treaded vehicle chugged back toward Heinlein. "We're safe!" cried a sheet-metal worker who had, until recently, hoped to spend a few playful hours as an insect.

Then he looked around, and a curtain of concern fell across his face. "Where's Darla?"

Inside the dome, Darla gasped for breath. Not that the quality of air had actually diminished, but she found that, under stress, she was experiencing her very first bout of claustrophobia.

She was crawling in the spaces between the bubbles used to create the main room systems. It was so dark she was forced to navigate primarily by feel and memory, but from time to time a pinhole of light showed her the way. That was enough to give her hope. And sometimes, as her mother had told her all through a childhood darkened by a succession of grabby stepfathers and drunken "uncles," hope was all you had.

In the break room, now a makeshift communications room, Ali sat leaning against the wall of bubble 37-C, squinting at the beige walls, wrists bound in the front with plastic cuffs. "What do you want from me?"

"Not you," Shotz said. "Your father."

Ali sat up so straight his head banged against the wall. "What?"

"For him to step down from the throne of Kikaya. The people who fund me would like that very much."

"Who are these people?"

A man entered the room who looked like a Congolese to Ali. A countryman. He held his breath. Danger had entered the room. "I, for one. Look in my eyes. I wish you were your father." Ali held his breath. The other men were professionals. This Kikayan was a true believer, a far more dangerous thing.

"What did my father do to you?"

The man knelt down to Ali's level. His breath was sharp. "He crushed the dream of a true democracy. Just the fact of his existence, his belief that he is entitled to a throne others died to protect . . . is an affront."

"Who are you?" Ali breathed.

The man's nostrils flared. "They call me Douglas Frost. I am the son of Kweisi Otoni. Thirty years ago, my father was driven from Kikaya. I have never even seen my country."

"What do you want?" Ali asked. He tried to keep the fear from his voice, but did not entirely succeed.

"I want your father to die. Or, if that is too much to ask, that he leave, and allow our poor country to heal itself."

Ali's head swam. "Kweisi Otoni. I don't know that name."

Douglas Frost spat. "Of course you don't. You know nothing of the true history of your country, and yet you probably think that you are worthy to inherit the throne. You are what people say."

"Was Kweisi Otoni an important man?"

Frost's eyes narrowed, and Ali instantly knew he'd said the wrong thing.

"He was to me," Frost replied.

··· **25** ···

"This Door Has Been Mined"

1215 hours

Despite the attempts to keep things quiet, Heinlein dome buzzed with speculation. Kendra had made a brief announcement, asking for calm and noninterference. In such a frontier community, it was easy to imagine someone trying something heroic and suicidal.

Right now, her offices were crowded with engineers and experts of various kinds. It hit her that security was understaffed. But who could have anticipated such a thing?

"We're pretty much shut out," Toby McCauley said. "Scans suggest welds at all entry points, and the doors electronically sealed. They only open from the inside." He paused. "But there is just one possibility I see."

"I'm almost afraid to ask," Kendra said.

"Well, all of the primary power was cut. They pretty much ran a perfect game there."

A Japanese engineer raised his hand. "But they missed something."

"What?" Kendra asked.

"Well . . ." The engineer's communicator bleeped. "Pardon." He tapped his chest tag. "Ishikura."

The lower levels of the Heinlein dome connected with the aquifer that served as both reservoir and recreational pool. Part natural cavern and part blasted and sealed by very serious men.

One of those very men was Pete Hamm, a round little man who was one of the oldest Moon hands still active on the base. He had led a crew down through cold moistureless air. There, through paths cut through unweathered Moon rock, they finally reached the aquifer's pressurized door. He wasn't certain how the kidnappers had gained access. Had someone betrayed Heinlein? The question was pushing Pete's blood pressure into a dangerous spiral.

Through the glass portal, they could see a blinking device attached to the far side of the door. A note on the door read: *THIS DOOR HAS BEEN MINED. IF YOU ATTEMPT TO OPEN IT, YOU WILL DIE.* Big square letters.

Hamm tsked twice to activate his com link. "Communications," he said. "Kendra. Boss, we've got a problem here . . ."

Ishikura's plump, slightly crooked little mouth drew into a tight, thin line as he listened to the communicator. He looked up at Kendra. "We have a problem. There seems to be a bomb wired to the door, from the other side. We'd need to put someone in from the aquifer side to see what we're dealing with."

"And for obvious reasons, that presents a difficulty," Kendra said.

Gaming central, the domain of Xavier and his crew, was only minimally less panicked than the rest of Heinlein base. Kendra and her people entered it in a phalanx.

Xavier's fury gave him subjective height. "I demand to know what exactly is going on."

"We need to talk," she said.

His smile was pale and humorless. "You go first."

The gaming stage was deserted now, and all of the Lunies and Earthers who had gathered to participate in the adventure of a lifetime were sitting with expressions ranging from anger to impatience to fear.

"As you can see," Kendra was saying, "all of the primary power and communications conduits have been cut. But the negotiations with the IFGS included some new redundant systems designed to protect their investment during the broadcast event."

Xavier blinked, and for the very first time, confusion rather than arrogance shaped his face. "Are you saying that I can conduct the game? I would think that a dozen kidnappers in there might have an opinion about that."

Kendra sighed. "You aren't hearing me. Look. This is a map of the dome. These people sealed all the external exits, but they apparently came in through the aquifer, and sealed that exit behind them. We believe it can be reopened. On our side, the door has apparently been mined, but could be disarmed—from their side. If we can get our gamers to the aquifer, I believe we can get them home."

The little man's eyes narrowed. "And just how, exactly . . . ?"

Kendra pointed to the lights. "Kill those, please."

The lights came down, and an expanded map of the gaming dome appeared, a grid of lines and pipes and glowing conduits.

"This," she said, "is a map of the dome as it was originally configured. These plans were filed during initial construction. But in the last three weeks, partially as a result of your petition to the IFGS, Xavier," she nodded to him, "some additional systems were added."

"Just power systems for the illusions, and communications . . ."

Wu Lin chimed in. "And the backup video system."

"What are you trying to say?" Xavier asked.

"The gaming system is less compromised than the main communications and environment systems. We think the kidnappers might not have neutralized all of it."

The air swirled with dome schematics. Xavier walked into the middle of it, absorbing, sniffing deeply, as if able to sense the information directly, much as he did the gaming data. He grinned, and laughed. And once he started laughing, couldn't seem to stop.

At last Kendra couldn't hold her irritation any longer. "May I ask what you find so amusing?"

Xavier couldn't answer, he was doubled over, holding his sides. Kendra looked at Wu Lin. "Do you mind letting me in on this?"

The Chinese girl smiled. "It is very simple."

"Elucidate."

"Xavier feared that the game was over. Instead, it seems that things have just begun."

Xavier wiped the back of his hand across his eyes. "Yes, if they have the wits to take the first move. I know her. Angelique's idea of a curveball is dragging an old boyfriend to the party. She will fold under pressure." He laughed again.

"She needs a miracle."

Navigating a narrow space between two egg-like structures, Darla crawled, so frightened she had to struggle to remember what the hell she was doing. "Think, think."

She scooted around, squeezing between the bubbles, feeling with her fingers. There was virtually no light, except a few threads where someone had drilled holes in the bubble, then sealed them with translucent epoxy. She glimpsed people moving, talking. Planning. Moving.

She pressed her ear to the side of the bubble, and could hear muffled voices, followed by silence. Then babble, softer now.

She felt around until she found the edge of a rounded trap door, and pushed against it. She pulled a Swiss Army–style multitool from her side pocket. One of the blades was a knife. She sliced through a layer of sprayed plastic.

All right, Mama. Let's just see what hope gets me.

The air reeked of fear, as thick as oily rain. Scotty Griffin wrenched at his plastic cuffs again and again, and when he rested the torn skin for a minute before his next effort, spent the time weighing his options. None of them was very good.

"These cuffs are pretty standard law-enforcement plastic. We could probably—" He stopped as he heard the floor open. "What the hell?"

A chubby, redheaded vision appeared, her game makeup smeared.

"Darla?" Wayne asked. She wiggled her way up into the room.

"Wayne?" she said. "Is everyone all right?"

"Compared to what?"

"Can you cut us loose?" Sharmela asked, dark round face anxious.

Mickey cleared his throat. "I'm not so sure about that. We don't want to antagonize these people. Those air guns look like they'd blow a hole right through you."

Maud winced. "Michael, you are such a *coward*. Sometimes I can't believe Papa let me marry you."

"Probably couldn't wait to get you out of the bleedin' 'ouse."

"Young lady. Darla? If you can cut my cuffs and leave his attached, there's a fiver in it for you."

Darla managed to smile. "Can't do that."

"One does one's best. Ah, well . . . tell me. Is there anywhere to go?"

"Yes. So let's see about the cuffs." She examined one, then took her multitool and selected a soldiering torch. "Plastic," she said.

"You're a tech."

"Bet your baby blues," Darla said. "Built this dome. Thought it would be fun to play here." She shook the tool and grinned ruefully. "Don't leave home without it," she said.

Darla melted through the first cuff. The stench was sharp, acrid.

"This will take too long," Scotty said. "We need to get out of here before they come back. They'll smell burnt plastic. Where can we go?"

"When we built the dome," Darla said, "there were spaces between the bubbles. Interstitials. We put trap doors in some of them. Just places to squirrel away to without anyone seein'. Real privacy. Not much of that up here."

Scotty blinked. "Make me understand."

"Imagine a bowl filled with . . . I don't know, darlin'. Cherries.

Cherries and oranges and limes. That's the way the domes were when we filled them with bubbles."

He could visualize that. "So if we crawl *between* the bubbles . . ."

"I can get us to another bubble, maybe one where we can hunker down."

"Then jam the door," Scotty said. "Start getting them out the hatch while I work on . . . Wayne's handcuffs. You up to it?"

Wayne nodded. "Let's move before I come to my senses."

Mickey shook Maud's hand off his arm. "Wait just a minute."

"Asako?" Sharmela said, suddenly grasping.

"Exactly."

"She can't exactly prowl around in the spaces between bubbles, can she?"

Asako's mechanized voice cut through their babble. "Don't talk about me as if I'm not here," she said. "Don't worry about me. They won't see me as a threat. I should be all right. Don't tell me your plans, and don't you dare wait."

Angelique raised her fingers over the glass dome sheltering the woman. "Asako. Are you *sure* . . . ?"

"Go," she said.

In the "green room" bubble 37-C, things seemed to have begun to stabilize.

Shotz regarded Ali, who stood leaning against the wall, cuffed hands at his belly. "Are you comfortable?"

Ali ignored the question. "When will you release us?"

Shotz' expression never changed. Perhaps he had never expected this question to be answered. "I'm afraid that you cannot be freed until . . . this entire matter is complete."

"How do you intend to escape? Surely you don't believe that you can sneak out of here and all the way back to Earth?"

"Are you comfortable?" Shotz' head inclined slightly to the left, so that, momentarily, he was peeking out from under blond bangs. "Whether you believe it or not, I harbor no animosity toward you. You would be best served by courtesy and cooperation."

A pause. Then Ali hung his head, the moment of defiance passed. "I am fine. Thank you for asking. I will require water, food, air and a toilet. And if at all possible, I would prefer to be with my friends."

"The last, I cannot provide. The other requests I allow."

In various locations around the dome on levels A through D, members of Neutral Moresnot linked into various networks, snipped wires, set up com field disruptors, severed computer connections. Took readings. Then, their assigned tasks completed, they nodded with satisfaction, and headed back to bubble 37-C.

Celeste, Shotz and a bodybuilder called Gallop entered the green room. Ali watched them, fantasizing about bloody murder. Despite all efforts to protect him, he'd heard rumors of his grandfather's early days.

"We've got everything under control," Celeste said. "Time to send the first message." Shotz nodded, and Celeste clicked her teeth, then spoke into a throat mike.

"Phase one complete," she said.

While the threat level was raised to red around Heinlein base, Douglas Frost remained on duty in the poultry area. When a light blinked on his wrist communicator, he sighed. The air rushing out tasted foul. "I need to take a break," he said.

His boss' face twisted in an expression that, on another day, might have been thought a smile. Everyone seemed stretched thin that day. "Sure, Thomas."

Doug grinned. No, no one could tell them apart.

The main communications node was only five minute's Moonwalk from the farm. He sat, slid a data clip into the input slot, and waited as it called an interplanetary prefix and access number. Doug knew it was sending a photograph across a quarter-million miles of space to a satellite circling Earth. And from there to a certain General Motabu, currently commanding the rebel forces storming a certain Central African palace.

The game was going very well indeed.

Scotty and the gamers crawled through the sterile, micro-dust coated spaces between the bubbles. The air in those dark curved spaces felt cold and confining. Above and between the bubbles, tunnels had been grafted like vines in a tropical forest.

"How far does this passage go?"

"They kept changing as we reinforced and added the safety baffles," Darla said. "But even though we weren't finished, it was up to code, and we could authorize Cowles to run this game."

Scotty mopped sweat from his face. "The short answer?"

"I can get us about halfway down. Hopefully, we can figure it out from there."

She felt around the walls until she found her trap door. She cut through the plastic inner lining. Then they climbed up into the bubble.

The walls within were broken bubbles. A few of them still had grubs curled within. The floor was inscribed with a variety of curlicue patterns.

"What is this place?" Scotty asked.

Darla shook her head. "Don't really know."

Angelique frowned. "What do you mean, you don't know?"

"Xavier didn't tell us everythin', just what we needed to play our parts. My part's already over."

Sharmela was crouching down near the floor. "This is very strange. The power is off, but . . . do you see this?"

"See what?" Angelique asked.

"The indicators. The gaming indicators are still on."

"That's strange. They must be on a different circuit."

"Or even independently powered," Scotty said. "Angelique. What do you know about this?"

"Standard procedure," the Lore Master said. "Backups in case of failure."

"Is that some kind of safety arrangement?"

Wayne managed a chuckle. "It's a gambling thing. A lot of

money rides on these games, and that means that everything has to be recorded. If the signal fails, and there aren't backups, a lot of bets will forfeit. Is that important?"

"Maybe. It depends. I'm thinking that we can't communicate directly with Heinlein . . . but there might be a way to talk with Xavier. And . . ."

"Cameras," Wayne said.

Scotty frowned. "What?"

Angelique pointed to the ceiling, to the corners of the room. "There are cameras everywhere, not just the security stuff. Resolution of the three-dimensional images requires . . . well, I don't know the tech on it, but my guess is that they are on independent power. Low-power pinpoint cameras all wired into the central com field. Probably some hardwired backup as well. We're probably guessing in the right direction if we assume that Xavier can see us."

"Which means that they can help us, even if they can't talk to us," Scotty said.

"We might be able to fix that," Darla said. "But first things first. We have to get out of the dome."

"Not without Ali," Scotty said.

Angelique squinted. "What is it with you two? Is he your boyfriend, or . . . ?"

"I'm his bodyguard."

"This one's gonna look great on your résumé," Wayne said.

Scotty repressed an urge to remove Wayne's front teeth.

"Griffin," Angelique said. "I know that you have obligations to your client. But I have obligations to my ass. We have a little miracle here: Darla can get us the hell out. The kidnappers got what they want. We can skedaddle on out of here. Or you can stay behind, and rescue him. But I'm getting my people out of here."

"Not to mention your ass."

"Not to mention."

"I completely understand your position," Scotty said. "Just help me figure this place out. Where I am relative to where we were? And if there is a way out, how do I get to it?"

"There are at least two emergency suits," Darla said. "Know how to use them?"

"Spent two years up here. Where are the lockers?"

"Down on D level. Look."

She bent, wet her finger and drew on the floor in dust. "This is the dome. It's been divided into eight levels, with about a hundred bubbles distributed between them. Seven of the levels are above ground: A through G. H is underground, in the foundation just above the aquifer level. We were on level C . . . in fact, we still are. Most of the gaming was going to be on C, with some lesser action on D through H, and the climax down in the aquifer. That's where we were supposed to exit, and I'm hoping we can still get out. But there are emergency exits here—and here." Again, she dabbed at the ground with a moist finger.

"All right. I'll take my chances."

"Alone?" Wayne asked.

"Alone." Scotty stood up. "I have to go after Ali."

Angelique cocked her head. "I don't hear anything. I don't think they know we're gone yet. You've got a narrow window until they check on us again."

"What are you thinking?"

"I'm thinking that Ali deserves a chance."

"I'm thinking about him," Sharmela said. "And about Asako."

"We had to leave her." She paused. "Didn't we?"

"Maybe she doesn't have to stay left," Scotty said. "Does anyone here read . . . Morse?"

"I was a Girl Scout," Angelique said. "I can. What do you have in mind?"

"I want to talk to Xavier. But first we have to see if he's watching us."

26

Breach?

In gaming central, the light from the central monitor washed over Wu Lin's face, making it appear even longer and paler than usual.

"So they made it out," Kendra said. "Where are they?"

"Scans shows human bodies in a bubble two rooms away from the kidnappers," Wu Lin replied.

"Can they get out from there?"

"Perhaps," Xavier said. "Perhaps. If you look at these earlier vids, you can see this woman—"

"I know her. Wu Lin? Face rec."

"Darla Kowsnofski, structural engineer."

"Thank you, Wu Lin. That's a very good thing. She seems to know her way around the dome. She might be able to get them out. I wish we could talk to them."

"It's a miracle we can—"

"Xavier?" Wu Lin said. "We've been watching the gamers, and I think something is going on. They're trying to make contact."

Kendra was at her side in an instant. "Have we got sound?"

"We can," Xavier said. "Pipe gaming auditory auxillary 'A' into the main channel."

There was a moment of silent anxiety, and then Angelique appeared in the air, waving her hands at the camera. Her hands gestured: palm-palm-palm, fist-fist-fist, palm-palm-palm.

"What is she doing?" Xavier asked.

"Morse code," Kendra said. "Scotty and I met through an aviation club, and we both loved the twentieth-century stuff. Pilots used Morse for their VHF omnidirectional range navigation systems. Let me have the switch."

In response to Kendra's urging, the light in the gaming dome began to pulse.

In the crèche bubble, lights flashed on and off in what first seemed a random sequence, and then settled into a recognizable pattern of dots and dashes.

Scotty grinned. "That's Kendra's fist. Great. We've got contact."

In the bubble where Ali was being held, the Kikayan heir watched Gallop and a thin man named Miller wedge explosives charges against the wall. "I hope your people know what they're doing," he said.

Celeste smiled at him mildly. "We knew the doors would stop working. And your Security teams might be stupid enough to try something. We're changing the map."

"Fire in the hole!" Miller yelled, and the wall exploded. Light streamed in from the next room.

Celeste looked through the hole, and her expression was unreadable. "What the hell. Wow. It seems you people prefer very strange entertainment. Well, shall we?"

With one arm she lifted Ali until his feet dangled from the ground. He squinted at her. "That would be impressive if we weren't on the Moon."

"Funny man," she said. "I like funny little men. They make me laugh. Especially when they scream. Move."

The next room was piled with dead Selenites. Their staring, faceted eyes gazed out at eternity.

In another life, at another time, Ali would have been de-lighted. "Some kind of alien morgue, perhaps. I don't know how the game was planned." The woman and her partners were so curious about their surroundings that for the first time they seemed to have forgotten about Ali. "There are two tunnels in, so one might be the entrance, and the other the exit. Look—" He pointed at an alien who had been half shucked out of his shell.

"They're using the shells for something," Miller said.

"Some kind of sculpture, perhaps," Ali said. "All I can tell you is that it's a puzzle."

"Puzzle?" Miller asked. "This whole thing is a game, yes?"

"A game," Ali said. "I came all the way to the Moon to play a game. All the way to the Moon to avoid the politics of my father."

"That's the thing about politics," the man said. "It follows us everywhere."

Ali grabbed a handful of fake alien guts and smashed the goop into Miller's face. He sprinted for the open tunnel. Before he could reach it, Celeste stepped out of the hallway directly in front of him, her open palm smashing him in the face. Ali's head snapped back, his feet flying out in front of him, and he hit the floor. Celeste thumped her foot down on his chest.

She smiled down at him. "Little man, we were told to protect you. Not to hurt you. But make no mistake: If you try to escape again, I will blind one of your friends."

"No. Please."

"Very good," she said. And then to the others: "Barricade that door. We have to settle in for a while."

"Are my friends . . . all right?"

"Should be. Perhaps they have to urinate. I assume that there are restrooms in this dome?"

"Yes. They'll be marked with the usual crescent moons. I'm sure everyone would appreciate some relief."

"I'll organize that," Celeste said. "We're almost finished here. But remember that if you try anything else, you won't pay for it alone."

In the crèche, Scotty was impressed, but disappointed. "Xavier can't help us?"

"Not here," Angelique said. "Independent power for the game. He can't open the door, but we can."

"And the door leads . . . ?"

"Straight to bubble 38-C," Angelique said. "And Asako is in . . . 35-C."

"Then we have to move fast. What are our clues here?"

Wayne, Angelique, Sharmela and Scotty got down on all fours to look at the floor. Sharmela spoke first. "It looks as if the floor is divided into panels and pressure switches."

Angelique next. "Must be recalibrated for one-sixth gravity. What do you think?"

"A drop," Wayne said. "Maybe an alarm."

"The alarm on the same circuit?" Angelique said.

"Good thought," Wayne said. "It might not be working."

Scotty frowned. "Do you really want to risk that?"

"Not in the slightest," Angelique said. "I'll go." She stripped off her gear. She was built like a dancer. Without glancing at them, she began posing for invisible cameras. The floor was divided into hexagons, like the walls. When she stepped on one, a soft light glowed in the crèche wall, and a larva was momentarily highlighted. A sound like a sigh before it settled back down.

Another step, followed by a higher-pitched sound. A larva squealed, and Angelique backed down.

"Auditory-based," Wayne said. "I think this thing is some kind of lullaby machine. We need to make a song that keeps them asleep, or they'll wake up. That's the alarm. We need to work this together. We need balance and sensitivity for this. Who's had dance training? Gymnastics? We can't be sure the main computer is compensating for gaming points."

"Eighteen years of jujitsu," Scotty said. "No dance."

"Twelve years of *kathak*. Indian dance," Sharmela said, and wiggled her ample hips.

Wayne nodded. "That'll just have to do."

Scotty, Sharmela and Angelique walked carefully across the floor, the grubs singing in their sleep, now more responsive, now less. A discordant note, and Wayne backed up, trying another hexagon. Then the grubs all glowed in sequence, and hummed, blended and harmonized . . . and the door opened.

"That answers that question," Scotty said. "Main power, down. Localized power, reverted to backups. How long will the backup batteries last?"

"Maybe four hours," Darla said.

"Let's not waste them."

They entered bubble 38-C, stacked to the ceiling with pale ovoids. An egg chamber?

Angelique whistled. "I have no idea what we were supposed to do here."

"I don't think it matters," Scotty said

Together, they ran across the dome to the far side.

"There's another security hatch built in here," Darla said. "Lift it up, and we'll be in the superstructure again, next to the dome where Ali should be hiding." She fiddled with the hatch, slid the door out. Poked her head out. The dim light revealed a welter of support struts, darkness. It looked like a long way down.

One by one they moved out, weaving their way through the struts carefully, until they reached the next bubble.

"Now what?" Scotty asked.

"Now we hope that Xavier is punctual," Angelique glanced at her watch. "And that our Morse is up to snuff."

Sitting and waiting, miserable, Ali felt something. His feet sensed a slight rumble, so low it was at the very edge of his awareness.

Celeste's eyes shifted back and forth. Beside her, the man said, "I sure hope this structure will tolerate the explosives."

For the first time the blond woman seemed a little uneasy. "Shotz has the specifications. He knows."

"He knows," Miller said, picking the last of the Selenite guts out of his hair. Ali didn't quite believe him.

In the gaming center, Xavier was gesturing into a three-dimensional map of the gaming dome. "We have simulated charges designed to fake explosions *here* and *here*." He pointed at spots on the B and D levels. "We can pump up the subsonics, maybe even play with the environmentals a little."

"Heat?" Kendra asked.

"We've been raising the heat over the last ten minutes. In a few seconds, a blast of cold air will have an interesting effect." His smile was vicious.

"Sixty seconds . . . fifty-nine." Xavier said. "Wu Lin—bring up the rumble, please."

Ali's heartbeat was starting to soar. The floor trembled. Around him, the kidnappers were confused, sweating. "Subsonics," he whispered, unaware that he had spoken aloud.

"What?" Celeste said.

"I said that these cuffs are hurting my wrists. Can you—"

"Not on your life. Damn!" She wiped at a film of sweat on her forehead. "Is there no way to—" Celeste began.

Suddenly, the dome rocked with dull, thudding explosions, followed by a sharp *crack*.

The kidnappers lurched, even though the floor hadn't really moved that much.

"What the hell?" Celeste said.

"The dome!" the kidnapper said. "We must have damaged it when we blew the wall."

The kidnappers shouted orders back and forth, panicked, Ali momentarily forgotten. Wind howled, and the lights died. Within moments, their flashlight beams probed the darkness.

"Damn! That air's *cold*." Gallop's growling voice. "Is that a vacuum breech? Is that what it feels like?"

Ali's eyes shifted to the side as a disguised security hatch popped open. Tiny gaming safety lights gave just enough illumination to see a shape crawling across the floor.

Then Scotty's voice: "Shhhh."

"I don't know what this is." Shotz' voice now. "But there is no pressure drop. Repeat: no pressure drop—"

"Screw this!" A panicked opinion, shrill in the darkness.

Scotty dragged Ali back through the hatch, across the struts.

"Let's go," Scotty whispered.

Hands bound before him, Ali crawled down through the floor, into the spaces between the bubbles, then into the crèche. As he arrived, Mickey and Maud were helping Asako in.

"We've got about sixty seconds," Mickey said. Darla torched Ali's cuffs until the plastic was soft enough for him to pull them apart.

"We have to move," Angelique said. "And we have to move *now*."

"You shouldn't have come for me," Asako said. "Now you'll be limited to moving through the gaming areas. You could have remained in the gaps."

"No man left behind," Wayne said.

"Asako," Scotty said. "It wasn't just the kindness of our hearts. You have equipment in your pod that might help us."

"How?"

"We don't know. We're making this up as we go along. Let's get going."

••• **27** •••

Outside

The mood in Kendra's nerve center had plummeted from bad to worse, but when Max Piering entered, she found herself feeling optimistic even before he gave her his news.

"We're pretty much shut out," he said. "I only see one real possibility."

"I'm almost afraid to ask."

"Well," the big man said, "all of the primary power was cut. They pretty much ran a perfect game there. But they missed something."

Was there actually some good news? "What?"

"Well . . . ," Piering said, and leaned toward her.

A precious hour had passed since Kendra Griffin had begun her spiel. In the interim, the mood in gaming control had shifted from glum to almost celebratory. Merry enough, in fact, that Kendra was not amused in the slightest.

Kendra watched Xavier prance between one workstation and another, improvising a happy little dance as he did.

Finally, she could restrain herself no longer. "Mr. Xavier, are you certain you understand the seriousness of this situation? You seem entirely too . . . entertained."

Xavier stopped his little leprechaun jig and peered up at her shrewdly. "Am I? I apologize. Sometimes I do forget where reality ends and fantasy begins. Do you think perhaps that's why I'm so *damned* good at what I do?"

Then he laughed, and turned back to his assistants.

Kendra turned to her own. "He knows more than he's telling us," she said.

"I do hope so. We have to let him do things his way," Max Piering said. "What choice do we really have?"

"Dammit!" She wanted to punch Xavier's lights out. "No time for someone else to learn the system. You're right."

The Asteroid Belt was its own society, so far from the rest of humankind that they coveted every Earth contact as if it would help them retain their humanity.

In one of the many small living modules, four men played cards, watching the lunar feed on a visual field that filled an entire wall. "Mitch—have you seen this? Is this for real or what?"

His partner laughed. "I say it's a hoax. A game within a game within a game, man."

"Yeah, well, put me down for twenty."

On Earth and around the solar system, the game was racking up unbelievable ratings, rapidly threatening to become the most watched event in human history.

All day Kendra had faced an office full of angry voices and floating faces, and by now she was near exhaustion. "I'm completely hamstrung!" She threw her hands into the air, frustrated. "There are so many overlapping jurisdictions that no one knows anything at all."

Chris Foxworthy's long face looked glum. "This is completely unprecedented."

Piering was just as large and solid as he had been four years before, when he had helped dig Scotty out of a deep, dark premature grave. But he seemed more brittle now, and at the moment very close to his edge. "We're paralyzed. Who in the hell has the authority to let me go forward? My men can't act if we don't know what to do."

Then . . . the message-balloon blossomed. A priority executive message, available only for corporate accounts at a very high level. Kendra's receptionist cleared her throat.

"Ms. Griffin? I have one here you might want to take."

"Which is?"

"An Adriana Vokker. She has information about your husband."

"Vokker? I don't know the name."

"She says she was one of your husband's clients."

Kendra shrugged and pushed the button. "This is Kendra Griffin. What can I do for you, Ms. Vokker?"

The woman appearing before her was very young, blond, pretty in a waifish way. She sat at a dark-stained wooden desk with still-life pencil sketches hanging on the wall behind her. She seemed very worried. "Do you know who I am?"

"I believe a few months ago you caused my husband considerable trouble."

The girl inclined her head. "I thought he was your *ex*-husband."

That took Kendra by surprise. Had she really been referring to Scotty as her husband all day? Fascinating. She wondered what a stress tech would make of that. "How can I help you?"

"The news is everywhere," Adriana Vokker said. "No one's talking about anything else."

"Ms. Vokker, time is at a premium. I need you to tell me what's on your mind."

"Yes, yes, yes." The girl folded her hands on the desktop. "When I heard what had happened, I thought that this might be a chance for me to make up for what happened in Switzerland."

Kendra sighed. Charming. Scotty had a groupie. This was a waste of time. "And how exactly did you hope to help?"

"Mrs. Griffin, I have access to all of my father's business interests. It's part of my education and legacy. And this morning, there were alerts from our cocoa plantations in Central Africa."

Kendra's eyes widened. "Central Africa?" This conversation had suddenly become ten times more interesting.

"Yes. The Republic of Kikaya. We buy a million pounds of their cocoa every month, so any internal unrest is a matter of great interest."

Kendra motioned to Piering to come join them. "And what exactly did you learn in this process?"

Adriana said, "There's been a news blackout from Kikaya, but through some of our sources we see that the capital is under attack. At the same time, the heir of the throne has been . . ."

"Kidnapped." Kendra turned to Foxworthy. "This is strong. If this is right, then we're talking about a kidnap operation that had to be coordinated months in advance. There will be money, resources . . . Who on our rolls has connections to Kikaya?"

"On it."

Kendra hunched forward toward Adriana's floating image. "What else do you know?"

"I know that Mbuto airport is only one hundred miles from the plantation. Modifications are being made and workers hired. The rumor is that preparations are for the arrival of a space vehicle."

And those words made Kendra's stomach clench.

Kendra and her assistants sat in the center, surrounded by technicians who seemed too stunned to speak.

"I think that we can make some guesses about this now," she said.

"We know their escape route," Foxworthy said.

"Yes," she replied. "There is a coup in Kikaya. The Prince is being kidnapped, and their plan is to get off the Moon—"

"Not as difficult as you might think. Nobody wants to touch this one."

Kendra ticked off possibilities on her fingers. "What are you thinking? That we'll be ordered to let them go. And they'll have a safe place to land, from which they will simply disappear."

"And?" Foxworthy asked.

"It's not going to happen. Kidnap, destruction of property, assault. Somebody died. One of their men died, and when people die in the commission of a crime, his coconspirators can be charged with murder. I can believe that wasn't a part of the plan. But it happened, and I'm not just rolling over."

"So . . . ?" Piering asked.

"So no direct actions. We follow those instructions. But we investigate."

"Good. Damned good," he said. "Coordination of communication, resources . . ."

"Such as?" Kendra asked.

"Weaponry. Personnel. Information. Money has changed hands, you can count on it."

"We backdoor this," Kendra said. "We don't use ordinary investigative channels. Too many politics, and too many potential conspirators. We trust no one except who's right here in this room."

Foxworthy hailed her attention. "Ms. Griffin? I have your call."

The worried face of Alex Griffin bobbled in the air. "Kendra! I'd been watching, but wanted to stay out of your way. Is there anything, anything at all I can do?"

Kendra gave a long exhalation, only at that moment realizing the depths of her shock and distress. Alex's smile, even one as worried and wan as this, was like a warm, fatherly hug.

"Dad, I need to brainstorm, and I can't think of anyone I'd rather talk to. You know about the kidnap situation. Hostages. But what we just learned is that there may be a connection between that, and the coup currently underway in the Republic of Kikaya."

"A coup?"

"You tell me," Kendra said. "There's been a news blackout on the lunar stream. Are you getting anything on your end?"

"I guess I'd seen a banner, but hadn't clicked through to read about it. Dammit, what was I thinking?"

"Don't beat yourself up . . . who could have known?"

"So Scotty's Prince has been snatched on Luna." A quarter-million miles away, Alex Griffin's brows furrowed. "This was to put pressure on the King?"

"We can only guess at this point, but it would make sense. The kidnappers may have been paid by the insurgents, or people sympathetic to their cause."

"That could answer their exit strategy. I'd wondered where they could get the nerve to think they'll get away with this. But they can only do that if there's a place to land, and if they can get off the Moon. Exactly who has jurisdiction?"

"The United Nations. Cowles Industries. Heinlein Explorations Limited. The lawyers are fighting over it, and as long as no one else is killed, we've been told to stand down."

Inside the dome, the gamers sat in a circle, struggling to understand what had happened to them, and what their options might be.

"We're not gettin' any help from outside. Bet on that," Darla said.

"None," Scotty agreed.

With one slender forefinger, Angelique drew a line in the layer of thin, fine lunar dust. "If we go back, we fall right into their hands. But we're boxed in here. To keep going, we'd have to knock a hole in the wall. No way that won't make noise. They'll see and hear, and catch us."

The others were quiet for a time, then Mickey cleared his throat. "Then we have to give up. If we can't go forward, the only thing that makes sense—"

"*No!*" Maud's face had reddened with anger. She looked as if she wanted to slap him. "What? Do you trust these people? Do you think they're just going to say 'righty-oh'? Not punish us for trying to get away? If you believe that, you're just an old fool."

"Maud!" Mickey chirped in protest.

She crossed her arms. "I'm not talking to you."

"People. People." Angelique as peacemaker. "Darla was about to say something, and I think it would be smart for us to listen."

"Look," Darla said. "If we can't get into the next bubble without noise, then we have to *make* some noise. Too much noise is as good as none at all."

"A distraction?"

"Got me an idea," Darla said. "While we were putting this dome together, we had an emergency alarm system set up in case of dome breach, release of toxic gases. Gremlins. Whatever. It's the most hellacious racket you ever heard. I heard one go off over at Tycho once, and it like to split my skull."

"Can we access it? Something like that might cause enough chaos."

"Not from the inside. They seem to have overridden most of the systems. But there's a parallel system on the exterior of the dome. With the right tools, one person could do it." She gnawed at her lower lip. "But I have an idea. It would take three people to pull it off. I know where we can find two suits, and we'll need another."

Wayne clucked. "Then what are we talking about? We can't. If there is no way, what difference does it make?"

"Once again, you forget that I am here." Asako's mechanical voice took them by surprise. "You talk as if I am not here. *I* am the reason you need to cross that breach. I am the reason that you cannot just disappear into the spaces between the bubbles—"

"Asako," Scotty said. "Even if we could, we can't just escape through the aquifer. You heard Kendra: It's sabotaged. Booby-trapped. Whatever. You want to blow us up?"

"At least we'd have options," her pod's speaker rasped. "This is what I am saying to you: You have to let me help."

"Help? How?"

"My pod is rated for vacuum. My treads should be able to lock on to the service ladders."

Only silence greeted her.

Then Darla broke it. "You saw mechs working on the outside of the dome. Standard utility tracks—your pod should work just fine. Fine. But Asako . . . it's just too risky."

The bubble-girl laughed. "Risk. You speak of risk? Darla, thank you for caring, but I have nothing in my life except this." Her frail hands gestured weakly. "No family save gamers. Have you any idea how my heart would break if I caused damage to my family? If you did not escape because you were trying to protect me? You must let me try to help."

The gamers glanced at each other. One at a time, they nodded grimly. Then Ali said, "I will go as well. None of you would be in danger, if it weren't for me—"

"No," Darla said. "Ali. Ain't no joy down that road, pumpkin. The only ones to blame are the pirates. They started this whole fandango. Listen, you got no training for this. Scotty and I do. Asako has the bubble, so we can't tell her no. But no one else has to take this risk."

"Can this actually work?" Scotty asked.

"Yes," Asako said. "It can."

The pirates of Neutral Moresnot had made their own plans and preparations.

"Shotz," Celeste said. "We have the pool sealed. We have their communication blocked. No one on the outside of this dome knows that they have gotten away from us."

Shotz ran his fingers absently through his long blond hair. "What are you saying?"

Celeste's hard face softened, became almost shy. "I'm saying that in a very real way, it doesn't matter. That conditions on the ground in Kikaya are dependent not on the reality of the situation, but its appearance. If the King abdicates, we still have our landing zone."

Shotz seemed to roll the idea around in his mind, as if savoring its taste. "Then . . . we need only have sufficient hostages to get to the shuttle . . ."

She nodded. "And once we're off the surface, it is a diplomatic matter. We were always in the hands of our employers there. Either we can trust them . . ."

"Or our emergency procedures go into effect," he said, finishing her thought for her.

She nodded. "Unless Motabu wants to spend the rest of a short life looking over his shoulder, he will ensure our passage to L5, and from there to Earth. We were satisfied that they had the leverage before. Perhaps we need not fear now."

Shotz scratched his scarred throat. "Excellent," he finally said. "We proceed."

The links between the bubbles were mostly structural, but partially practical for human entrance and egress. Sharmela and Wayne bustled Asako and her pod along the walkways between one bubble and another, being as quiet and cautious as possible. With great stealth, they made it to the northern external maintenance door.

Sharmela sighed. "If only we all had suits . . ."

"We could just walk away," Wayne said. "And if pigs had wings, we'd have flying barbecue. But they don't, and we don't, so don't drive yourself crazy."

Sharmela looked at the track used by the automated maintenance mechs. "Will the treads fit?"

Asako responded by locking her pod into position. She raised a stick-thin arm, made a "thumbs-up" sign and smiled.

It was the warmest smile Wayne had seen from her so far. "Why are you so damned happy about this?"

She sighed. "I've been sick longer than I ever remember being well. Imagination has been my only escape. I wanted to be an adventuress, to save kingdoms and right wrongs."

"You never wanted to be the one rescued?"

She managed a marginal shake of her head. "I've always been the victim. Always the rescuee. And now, for the very first time, I get to be the rescuer. Don't you dare even consider taking this away from me."

"All right. All right," Wayne said. "You've got it."

There were gear lockers and dressing rooms all over the dome, especially near the airlocks. Darla had promised two suits, and here they were, near the west-most dressing room on level C. The gear was not customized, and Darla's was a little too tight through the middle, while Scotty felt cramped all over. It would have to do.

She gave Scotty a once-over, and he did the same for her, soberly checking each other's equipment. "When you get outside, stick to the marked maintenance routes. Don't get fancy."

Scotty clucked. "Yes, Mommy."

He tried to sound cavalier, but his heart was thundering in his chest, and he was hyperventilating.

"Are you all right?"

"Yeah," Scotty said. "I'm fine. Let's do this."

It had been years since Scotty had stepped into vacuum. He'd never quite gotten used to it, never was able to totally forget that a half inch of pressure suit was all that kept his blood from boiling. Once, it had been exciting. Then it had become terrifying. What would it be now?

He looked out the lock's window at the naked stars. Immediately, they began to blur. He gulped air and lowered his head. "Breathe," he gasped. "Breathe, you bastard."

A third of the way around the dome, Darla had positioned herself, arm slung over a rung. She was waiting for the others to reach their own designated data entry spots.

"Little Dee on local area net. Sign in?"

A crackle on her radio. *"S-man."*

Another: *"B-girl."*

Darla nodded. "Good to go?"

"Good to go."

"Good to go."

Celeste sat at their main table in bubble 37-C, surrounded by the equipment the Frost brothers had stolen or borrowed and moved into the dome. "Sir," she said, "we have teams sweeping the bubbles. And the spaces between. It's hard, because we have to be certain they aren't slipping around behind us."

"To what end?" Shotz asked. "No. They will try to escape through the aquifer. We put men in the spaces there."

"Nonlethal force?" Celeste asked.

"For now."

Scotty kept his eyes focused on the concrete-white curve of the dome in front of him.

Darla's voice came to him clearly, almost as if she were right there with him. *"We have to assume that these Moresnot pirates have their fingers into the entire system. So what we have to do is put the sensors off-line so that they won't know the airlock doors are opening. There is the bare chance that they might real-ize what we're doing."*

"Pirates, huh?" He chuckled. "Close enough. I don't know how they would," he said. "You actually explained it to me, and I still don't understand."

"You will," Darla said. *"There is a biopad right level with your nose. To disable it, punch in the following sequence: XXA19836."*

He punched the combination in. "Light went yellow."

"I have yellow here," Asako said.

"All right. You're makin' Mama very happy," Darla said. *"Along the side of the box there are two slits. Insert a knife into the bottom slit on the right side, until you make contact. The light should turn red."*

Scotty did as he was instructed, and once again Darla was proven right. *Clever girl.*

"I have red," Asako said.

"Good." Scotty heard the engineer take a deep breath.

"Now. On the door itself, you just punch in a few little letters and numbers for Darla. XX563."

Scotty entered it, and the door began to buzz.

The door LCD displayed a message. *Warning. You have dis-armed safety shields on this pressure door. The outer door has been sealed, and cannot be opened until the safety mechanism has been reengaged.*

The message was repeated in Japanese, German and Spanish.

"All right," Darla said. *"Now, unscrew the top of the keypad. It isn't hard. When you have it unscrewed, you'll see two switches governing the emergency explosive bolts. You'll need to reverse the positions of those switches."*

"And then what?" Scotty asked.

"Get ready to rumble."

Scotty did as he was asked. "What do I do now? The digital timer is counting down."

"*Get in the opposite corner,*" she said.

Scotty hunched down in the farthest corner, breathing heavily.

Then—a moment of intense sound as the floor shook. Then . . . the curved door flew out into the lunar landscape.

"Here goes nothing," Scotty said, and climbed out.

Asako felt as if she sat on the threshold of infinity, the stars and crystalline rock and crater formations. She felt overwhelmed with wonder and joy.

Scotty's voice intruded. "*Asako. Are you all right?*"

"No," she said. "So much better than that."

"*Stay frosty. Let's do this.*"

"Aye-aye, Captain."

She rolled out into the blinding unfiltered sun. Her bubble's canopy polarized. The treads locked onto the maintenance tracks. And swung out onto the dome.

As Scotty moved out, he kept his eyes down, his breathing harsh and hard.

"*How are you doing there, big guy?*" Darla asked.

"Good to go," Scotty said. The words sounded flip, even to himself.

"*All right, handsome,*" Darla said. "*This part is easy. Just climb straight up.*"

Keeping his eyes down, Scotty began to climb up, listening to his breathing, struggling to remain calm. The side of the dome was stenciled with reference numbers. The numbers dropped as he climbed. Just to his left was the numeral 86.

"*Keep climbing until you get to the number 51. Do you see it?*"

"*My lower pod camera can see it,*" Asako said. "*My arms can reach it. We're still fine.*"

"*This is the only hard part. You have to move over to the secondary ladder. We don't have a tool to make your foothold. So you'll have to stretch out, grab hold and swing over. Can you do that? Asako, your pod can use the maintenance droid ladder. Type in 336-A, and it should move automatically.*"

Scotty looked over to the side. He could see stars. He breathed heavily. Looked down. Far below him, lunar soil. He stretched out his arm, and grabbed at the ladder, missed . . . and as he swung back he swung onto his back, so that he was staring straight up into space.

"Christ," he whispered. "The stars."

28

The Naked Sky

1327 hours

Heinlein base's nerve center was going berserk, their interlocking screens sectored into subimages as news agencies across the solar system descended upon them like locusts. In the midst of it all, Kendra fought to find an island of peace, from which she might think clearly.

"Kendra," Foxworthy said. "We have the biotelemetry on the suits, and we've hacked into Asako's bubble. Ah . . . your husband's vitals are through the roof."

"Oh, God. His agoraphobia. He's outside."

Was that a glint of perspiration on Xavier's bald head? "What is the problem?"

"Three and a half years ago, Scotty was trapped in a cave-in. His suit ruptured. He almost died. He was staring up into the sky the entire time, and it kind of burned in. This is no good."

"What can we do?"

She drummed her fingers on the desk. "Can you link us?"

"Outside the dome? We should be able to hit him with a line-of-sight. Get com on it now. I'll handle this personally."

"I think that's best," Kendra said. "These bastards didn't do this alone. Talk to no one you don't trust *personally*. Trust your instincts."

Heinlein base's Communications center was a confusion of voices and rushing bodies as Foxworthy ran in. He scanned the room. "Derek!"

"Yes, Chris?" the communications man answered.

"I need you to run a secure, scrambled line to the mining operation on Mare Australe," she said. "You've got a cousin out there, right?"

"Yes. What's this about?"

"I need you to run a maser line out there, highest priority," Foxworthy said. "Get it on the Cowles corporate code."

"When?"

"Five minutes ago," Foxworthy said.

Derek knew that tone, and didn't question. His fingers danced across the board.

At the mining operation, a call came through. A man there touched it into his PDA, and then ran down a pressurized hallway to another room.

He read the display. "We have a request for secure line-of-sight with Heinlein."

"Just a minute," their communications man said. "I have to retask the dish."

And with a few tweaks, a microwave dish turned toward Heinlein.

"This is Australe base, what's the sit?"

She leaned forward. "This is Kendra Griffin, Chief of Operations, Heinlein base. I need you to run secure line-of-sight to the gaming bubble. We have three walkers, and two of them should be visible to you."

A pause. Then: "I . . . yes, we have them. Can patch you in in three, two, one . . ."

A *crackle,* and for a moment the air in front of them seemed gray and patchy. Then it cleared again. *"We have a line."*

"Thank you! Scotty! Can you hear me?"

"Kendra?" His voice crackled with static. She felt weak with relief.

"Are you all right? We've patched into the Maintenance network. It should be shielded from the Earthers. What is the situation, sweetheart?"

He sighed. *"I shouldn't have come out here."*

Foxworthy turned back to her. "Kendra . . . his heartbeat is above one thirty. His respiration is spiking, and he could be hyperventilating."

He was definitely panting. *"I've got to get back inside. I have to . . ."*

"Scotty," Kendra said. "If you go back in there is no one to trigger that alarm. Which means that your people can't cut through the wall. They'll be trapped, recaptured."

"I can't," he said. It was heartbreaking to hear that tone in his voice. It was filled with defeat, and shame.

"Scotty . . ." She had a different idea. "Darla, are you there?"

"Here, Kendra." Darla's voice.

"How close are you? To Scotty?"

"A hundred meters, around the curve of the dome. I've bypassed the safety."

"Asako . . . where are you?"

"In position. My pod is linked into the surface computer system, and I can input the code as soon as Kendra gives it to me."

"Do you hear that, Scotty? Everyone's in place. But the codes have to be entered within sixty seconds of each other, so that no one or two people can possibly override. Do you hear me?"

Scotty's voice choked. *"I hear you. But I can't do it. If I open my eyes, it feels as if I'm falling. Falling."* Despair.

"Scotty," she said. "Listen to me. Why did you come back to the Moon?"

"I had a damned job, Kendra."

"No. That's not it, and you know it. You came back because you loved it here. You came back because you love me."

A deep intake of breath. *"Kendra . . ."*

Her focus had contracted to a point. They might have been alone in that room. "Scotty. We knew from the first weekend together. I knew."

"Don't do this. Not with . . ."

"What? Everyone listening? I'm not embarrassed. I love you, Scotty. I've missed you every night we weren't together in my—"

"Good Lord, woman!"

She managed a throaty chuckle. *Now* she had his attention. "What? How personal do you want me to be? Remember the last night before you left, when I finally let you take—"

"Dammit!" he yelped. But he was laughing and maybe crying now.

"Scotty," she said. "Open your heart to me. Lean on me, just a little, now. There are just a few things that you have to do, and it's over."

"But, what if I can't . . ."

Darla was moving into position atop the dome, climbing one ladder rung at a time, her voice rasping in her ears. She opened the control box.

Halfway through the process she stopped, gazing out at the lunar landscape, momentarily overwhelmed with its unweathered beauty. Then she returned to the work, moving clear chunks of plastic from one box to another. She used her tool to unscrew a box, and tapped in a series of codes.

"Here we go," she said.

Celeste found Shotz sitting among a pile of red cartons, gazing into a map. "The difficulty is in sealing off the bottom of the dome, and then searching every level in turn."

"The good thing in this situation . . ."

"I'm so happy to know that there is one. Please," Shotz said. "Enlighten me."

"The good thing is that we actually don't need to have the Prince in hand. As long as people outside the dome believe we do, we are safe."

"Yes . . . still, it does not serve our reputation. Not this instance, but for the next time."

"Shotz . . . you said that this was it. That if we could do this, everything we've ever dreamed would come true. Our own island. The nation of Neutral Moresnot, brought into reality by our will."

His eyes slid over her, slid away. Her heart sank. "Already, do you dream of a next time? There is no way to prevent our identities from becoming known. Our faces . . . but we're being paid enough to stop."

He chuckled. "We stop? I should stop? And what do you imagine I would do, Celeste?"

"Whatever you choose to do, it doesn't have to be alone."

For a moment, the air between them seemed to shimmer, and for that moment, a remarkably human smile softened Shotz' face.

He brushed his scarred knuckles down her cheek. "And what, Celeste? Did you imagine a picket fence? Bouncing babies? A rocking chair at sunset? How exactly did you imagine this playing out?" His voice was surprisingly gentle, not mocking at all. The machinelike character of his voice had relaxed into something approaching humanity.

She smiled. "Not a picket fence, Alexander." She almost never used his given name, even in moments of passion. His expression flickered surprise. "But General Motabu owes us an island, perhaps near Madagascar. Near the equator, where we could build a . . . what was it called?"

He smiled wanly, as if at a fond child. "A beanstalk," he said. "A space tether."

"Yes! This! We could be rich, and powerful." She grasped his hands. "When this is over," she said, "give me a chance. Give me a chance to make it good with you."

He was still pressed back against the wall, as if waiting for disaster. "All right. I owe you that much."

"We owe ourselves," she said. Her eyes and smile softened her face. "I could make you happy."

Her mood, her dream, was infectious. His thick forefinger traced her jaw. "If anyone could. Now." He balled his fist and tapped it against the wall. "Let's not begin the celebration just yet. We have game to flush. Gamers."

Wayne was poised at the wall of the next bubble, power saw poised and ready. "How long?"

"Soon," Angelique said. "Get ready."

Scotty leaned back against the curve of the dome, staring out and up, barely able to move. "Everything is so bright. So . . . loud. But . . ."

Kendra's voice in his ear. *"Don't look up. Don't even look at the dome. Just concentrate on the work. Can you do that?"*

"Are the others done?" he asked.

"All set and in position. We're just waiting for you."

"Then I guess . . . ," he said, turning over, "I'd better get to work."

One step at a time. He felt an almost irresistible urge to look up at the sky, as if it were a predator ready to strike. "Kendra?"

"Yes?" her blessed voice.

"Do you remember our honeymoon?"

A pause. *"On Vava'u? Vividly."*

"Me, too." He was struggling to get the lid off, his fingers clumsy.

"How are things going out there?"

"Pretty bad," Scotty said. "But I'll get it done. Helps me to talk. Do you remember the surf? Water was warm when we'd go down in the morning."

She laughed in his ear. A caress. *"It was like that when I was a girl. So warm. What I remember is warm sand between my toes."*

"I feel a little cold right now," he said. "I don't think my suit heater is working right. Tell me about how warm it was."

"Back when I was a girl?"

"No, when we were on our honeymoon."

Was that a touch of embarrassment now, on her side? *"Scotty . . . I'm not sure this is the time."*

"I can't think of a better one."

"It was warm at midnight, Scotty. Remember? I remember taking you to the cove where I used to go as a girl. I wanted so much to share my special places with you." She spun a string of musical Tongan polysyllables. *My sweetheart. My dearest love.*

"I remember the stars there, at night."

A sharp intake of breath on her part. *"Scotty. Are you sure you should be discussing stars?"*

"Maybe," he said. "Maybe this is the time, Kendra."

A pause. *"Maybe it is, at that."*

His fingers seemed to be thawing. "After this is all over. Do you think that maybe we could go back there? Sometimes I think I left the best part of myself there. And here, with you. What do you think, Kendra? Is it possible for people to go back, make things right, start over?"

"I hope so, Scotty. If we can't make up for the things we did . . . or said . . . I'm not sure there's any hope for any of us."

"Hah! It's open!" His fingers stung. He stared at the input plate. Would wonders never cease! "I think I have it. Give me the numbers."

"Security override XX5489223."

"Got it. Asako?"

"I've got that. And . . . entering it. My pod is shaking hands now . . . and . . . it's done."

Scotty exhaled hard enough to fog his faceplate, and rolled over. "The stars . . ."

"Scotty?" Are you all right?"

"It's . . . all right. They don't blink, or look away. They see me. I think maybe that's all right."

The alarm began to sound.

Inside the dome, Shotz' head whipped around as the alarm began to howl.

"What in the hell . . . ?"

Celeste was on the edge of panic. "I'm not getting the message. We overrode the computer, and it's taking me a minute to route the connection back to our board—"

The alarm grew louder.

"Here it is . . . it says 'emergency flush sequence.' What in the hell—"

Shotz' eyes narrowed. "Get the men back into the bubbles! Get them out of the gaps in this damned dome—"

"That's it! Drill!" Angelique screamed.

Wayne started up his power tool, an ear-shattering whine as it began to cut through the bubble's wall. The stench of burnt plastic choked them, and smoke filled the air as if they were in a hookah bar. The gamers retreated from the action, watching with wide, hopeful eyes.

Around the dome, the men of Neutral Moresnot were hustling themselves into the bubbles, slamming the doors behind them. Carlyle strained. "What's that sound?"

"The alarm, idiot!" Fujita replied. "Someone breached the dome."

"Not that. Another sound—"

"More! More!" The drill was loud enough to deafen them, and then suddenly Wayne was through the wall, into the interstitial space. Wayne continued cutting, the saw's burning blade whining as it sliced.

Then the chunk of wall fell away. Wayne stepped through onto the walkway. The second door opened easily. "We're in!" he screamed back.

"Hurry!" Angelique yelled. "Move. We've got to go, go, go!"

Scrambling, the gamers hustled through into the next bubble.

"Cut the damned power on the alarm!" Shotz howled.

"But—"

"Cut it, Celeste! This is a stratagem. There is no breach."

"But I hear the alarm!"

"Do you feel the air move? No. If there was a massive breach, there would be a drop in air pressure. Nothing. It's a fraud!"

Celeste spent a few moments on her computer, and the alarm died.

Scotty watched the alarm as it faded from the monitor. *"All right,"* Darla said. *"The bad guys killed it. Let's just hope our folks were able to get shed of that bubble. Let's hook up at door five. We'll be able to meet them. Is everything all right?"*

"Good to go," Scotty said.

"Good. Let's get down. We have to move. Asako . . . ?"

A pause. No reply. *"Asako?"*

When Asako spoke, her voice was very controlled and steady . . . but Scotty knew fear when he heard it. *"I'm afraid that I have bad news. It looks as if my pod's specifications may have been overly optimistic."*

"What in the hell does that mean?"

"It means," she said, *"that I am so very grateful for this opportunity to play with all of you. But I think this is as far as I go."*

"What?"

"I'm afraid that my pod has been losing . . . losing . . . atmosphere. Not much . . ."

"Asako, darlin'," Darla said. *"Can't you just get back* inside?"

"I'm . . . I'm not . . ."

Adrenaline fried his nerves. "Asako!" he screamed. "I'm coming!" Scotty began to crawl around the hand- and footholds, swinging.

"I'm coming, too, Scotty." Darla's voice. *"The two of us oughta be able to handle it."*

"Please . . . ," a whisper. *"Don't risk it on my account. Get back into the dome. Get our people away while we have the chance."*

"Will you shut up? We're all making it out of here together."

"I'm . . . afraid . . . not. Not this time . . . Scotty, I don't know what demons trouble you, but that woman, that good woman you were speaking to sounds as if she loves you."

He was almost in sight now.

"I love her, too."

"Don't let her go, Scotty. I haven't been touched in so long . . . so long . . ."

"Asako!"

It took six minutes to reach her, by which time she sat lax and pale, unconscious in her pod.

Darla was approaching from the other side. *"Pull. This way."*

The two of them began to leverage the pod up the side of the dome.

The eleven remaining members of Neutral Moresnot, plus Thomas Frost, had all collected in bubble 37-C. "Sensors say the dome has full integrity," Shotz said.

"Why would they pull an alarm like that?" Fujita asked.

"To distract us," Shotz said. "While they did something."

"Maybe . . . something noisy?"

"Possible. Probable." His mouth twisted, as if he were spitting out something toxic. "Dammit! Find them!"

Celeste clenched her fists. "I wish we could kill them," she said.

"That time may come."

He tapped fingers on the keyboard, and a display of the gaming dome appeared.

"There are a hundred and thirty-seven major bubbles in eight levels in the dome," Celeste said. "We've cleared the top twelve, and unless they sneak back and get behind us, they're still trapped below."

"Yes. And as you say . . . as long as they don't escape, we're still on track." Shotz yelled at his men. "Split into teams of two, and cover all the routes. Make your way down to the basement."

A thoughtful pause. "And be careful."

Huddled in bubble 45-D, the gamers jumped when the room reverberated with door-banging thuds.

"About time!" Wayne said. He looked through the plate, recognized Scotty, and released the emergency lock. The door cycled from red to yellow to green, and then opened.

Angelique threw her arms around Scotty. "You did it!"

"I can't believe it," Sharmela said. "This is fantastic. From bubble 45, we can get to . . ." Suddenly she looked around. "Hey! Where's Asako?"

The realization hit the others like a bomb. "She's . . . dead?"

Scotty nodded. "Her pod leaked. She didn't tell us until it was too late to save her."

"I can't . . ." Maud was shaking. "I can't do this." She looked up. "We need to quit. Now. Surrender. They won't hurt us."

Scotty looked at Angelique. "We can vote on it. Who wants to go on, and who wants to stay? I can promise you that Asako didn't die so that we could give up, but I won't try to make up your minds for you."

"I must go on," Ali said. "They want to use me as a weapon against my father."

"Mickey?"

The Brit shook his head. "If Maud stays behind, I have to stay with her," he said.

"I can't argue with that," Angelique said. "Maybe someone else can. But . . . I want to go on."

"Me, too," Wayne said. "It may be crazy, but I'm not sure that if we give up now, we'll be any better off than if they catch us later."

"Could that be true?" she asked Scotty.

"Only Ali is really safe," he said.

"And there's another thing," Wayne said

"And what is that?" Scotty asked.

"Let's just say that there are people with a lot riding on this game. And if we can finish it . . ."

"But the IFGS has to have canceled!" Maud squawked.

"Well . . . yes. But there's the IFGS, and then there is public opinion. If we finish it successfully, they will have to consider reinstating the points retroactively. It's happened before: Remember the second Aztec game?"

Angelique nodded. "Tony McWhirter broke his leg. The IFGS demanded he leave, and his team refused. They canceled the game, but Dream Park and the Game Master kept it going."

"I remember hearing about that," Scotty said. "There was a write-in campaign? Forced the IFGS to change its ruling?"

"Exactly. Now listen," Wayne said. "Do all of you realize that this is the greatest game ever? The only Dream Park game ever played for real? And we're right in the middle of it. We can give up later, sure. But the longer we can keep going, the—"

"The more pissed the pirates will be," Scotty said. "Look, I'm all for charging forward, but I'm not going to lie to you. Things will be better for all of you, if you're caught, if you're caught sooner rather than later. I'm betting on the whole enchilada. I think there's a chance we can actually get the hell out of here."

"Whatever!" Wayne said.

"I wish I could," Maud said, a touch of wistfulness in her voice. "I'm just so scared."

"Then use this!" Wayne said. "You're gamers. Just . . . just think of it as part of the game. Play your role. Focus on that."

"Maybe. Perhaps I can," she said. Mickey kissed her cheek.

"You people are crazy," Scotty said. "Sharmela?"

"Then I'm crazy, too. Listen. I won this trip, or I couldn't have afforded any of it. My wife and I had to think long and hard about how to use this opportunity to get out of a real financial hole we'd dug ourselves into." She gestured helplessly.

"And?"

"Fit/Fat. It was a miracle. We got in touch with the right person, and got corporate backing for my training, and the promise of a contract if I performed well. This means everything to us. It's worth the risk." She forced herself to smile. "So for a few more hours, I'll pretend that it's a game. Right? Everyone? We make that deal?"

Sharmela extended her hand. Ali slapped his down atop hers, followed by the others, except for Scotty.

"Scotty, please," Angelique said. "So we're a little nutty. That doesn't mean we don't understand the stakes."

"Scott," Ali said. "Either extend your hand, or you are terminated."

Scotty squinted at him. "You are the biggest ass I have ever worked for," Scotty said. "I think I'm starting to like you." And extended his hand.

While the others talked and built up each other's bravado, Scotty pulled Wayne aside. "A question."

"Yes?"

"You wouldn't, by any chance, have bet on yourself to win?"

Wayne's eyes opened wide. "Why would you think that?"

"Dunno. Just a wild question. Is there a law against gamers betting on games?"

"Frowned on, but not exactly illegal unless they bet to lose," he said. "That could be bad for the team."

"I'll just bet. I notice you didn't answer my question."

"Didn't I?"

"Uh-huh. Well. Face or gut?"

"What?" Wayne's expression of wounded innocence suddenly transformed into genuine confusion.

"If I find out you were betting, and that had anything to do with your little speech . . . well, I just wanted to be certain that I'd given you a choice."

Wayne searched Scotty's face, and found nothing in the cold smile to ease his mind.

"I . . . I'm not sure," he said finally.

"I'll flip a coin," Scotty said.

Back in Heinlein base, Kendra fought to keep her heart in the calm center of an emotional cyclone. "So we found the connection with the Republic of Kikaya. We have two men here in Heinlein who have relations there, is that right?"

"That's true," her assistant said. "That's true. It's in their personnel files—Thomas and Douglas Frost were orphaned in childhood. Their father was Kikayan, and the mother fled the continent and came to America."

"The heir to the Kikayan throne held captive. Revolt in Kikaya. Two Kikayan expats. That's not a pattern, it's motive, means and opportunity. Where are they now?"

The assistant chorded his keyboard. "They've both been on duty since the game began. Thomas in the farms, and Doug on a construction gig to the south."

"And now?" Kendra asked.

"I believe that . . . Doug is off duty, and Thomas is on. But again, they've both been on duty since . . ." Her assistant examined the screen more carefully.

"What is it?"

"This is odd. We have a data anomaly. I think that some of the coding has been . . . suppressed."

"What does that mean?"

"Well . . . ," Foxworthy said, "that was a level-three security facility, and the security has only been set at level two."

"How is that possible?"

"This is some kind of a short-term patch, but . . . hmm. I'll undo it, and run the data again."

"What do you think it's about?" She paused. "Let me get someone on Earth familiar with the science behind our security system."

In five minutes, they were linked to a fiftyish Brit woman with a sleepy expression and a tightly pursed mouth. *Dr. Phelps,* the name bar announced.

Phelps twisted her pert little mouth. "Well . . . based upon what you've told me, the retinal patterns might not have been analyzed properly."

"And what does that accomplish?"

Three seconds of delay, then:

"Perhaps," Phelps said, "one twin pretending to be both?"

"Excuse me?" Kendra said.

Another delay, while the doctor cleared her throat and assumed a professorial tone. "Identical—or monozygotic—twins form when a single fertilized egg splits in two after conception. Because they form from a single zygote, the two individuals will have the same genetic makeup. Their DNA is virtually indistinguishable. However, things like fingerprints and retinal patterns are not an entirely genetic characteristic. Scientists," she said, "love to use this topic as an example of the old 'nature versus nurture' debate. Retinal patterns, along with other physical characteristics, are an example of a phenotype—meaning that it is determined by the interaction of Thomas'—"

"Or Douglas'."

"—genes and the developmental environment." It had taken a few seconds for Kendra's interjection to travel a quarter-million miles to Earth, and for Phelps to realize she had been interrupted. "Yes, Ms. Griffin?"

"You're saying it's possible, depending on the sensitivity of our sensors, that one brother could pretend to be another."

"Why yes. But why?"

A pause. "Well, I can think of one reason," Kendra said. "So that one brother could be inside the game with no one on the outside realizing it. Dr. Phelps, thank you very much. I'll be in touch if there is anything else." She clicked the line off.

"Why?" Foxworthy asked. "Why would they go to all this trouble? We can't touch anyone in there. If the kidnappers have an escape figured, they can take the twins with them."

"Yes. So it's not just about escape. It's that there is something useful that the other brother can do outside that he can't do while inside the gaming dome."

Her assistant began to chord. "I'm putting a tracer on them. Actions and movements of both brothers for the last forty-eight hours."

"Wristlamps," Darla said, distributing bracelets with bulbed nodes at the center. "Found an emergency stash of 'em." Scotty slipped his on, flexed his wrist, and watched the bright beam splash against the wall. Nice. Darla knelt tracing a map in dust on the floor with her fingertip. "All right. We have to go through this dome to reach a hatch where we could get down a piece."

"And then?"

"Four levels down and we might be able to get straight to the underground pool. That's where all of this was supposed to end, you know."

Angelique managed a tired, wan smile. "Not sure you were supposed to tell us that."

"Xavier can sue me. Come on."

She tugged at the door. It opened, and they entered a triangular corridor, unadorned with gaming gear. They moved forward into it.

Sharmela seemed to test every footfall. "Doesn't look like this was a part of the game, does it?"

"No," Darla said. "But the next bubble is, so there may be some backup power on."

Angelique touched Scotty's shoulder, as if trying to siphon off a bit of his pain. "Where did you leave Asako?"

"In her pod. In an airlock. We'll have to get it later."

"If there is a later," Wayne said.

"There's always a 'later'—for someone," Scotty said. "Let's make sure it's us."

The next door opened. The gamers stepped in.

29

Fungus Fun

1350 hours

Clusters of mushroom shapes shadowed bubble 60-E. As they watched, lights glowed to life. The air crackled, and suddenly the walls and ceiling seemed to fly back, expand by a factor of three. The bubble expanded into a gigantic cavern, complete with staggered rows of stalagmites, and a hundred varieties of fungus.

Angelique was the first to speak. "Wow," was all she could manage.

In Heinlein, something new had happened in gaming central as a light popped up on the gaming map.

Wu Lin turned. "Xavier? We have a blip in the fungus farm. Someone has entered."

He spun heel-toe. "Have we got visual?"

"No. But I'm still trying."

"Auditory?"

Wu Lin shook her head. "Not yet."

"But you will continue to try, yes?"

"Yes," she said.

———

Scotty walked through the fungus farm slowly, his sense of disoriented wonderment growing with every new step. As he walked, it seemed to spring to life: Little caterpillar critters swarmed at his feet. Miniature mooncalves crawled hither and thither, munching at the fungus and ignoring the humans.

"What the hell?" he said, genuinely confused.

Darla sighed. "More battery backup. The IFGS insisted. Must be on a proximity trigger. It wasn't alive until we appeared."

"The world doesn't exist if we're not here," Maud sighed.

"Your solipsism is showing," Mickey said.

"There you go, spouting your methodological nonsense."

A mooncalf ran right up to them, squeaked, and ran away again.

"Metaphysical solipsism, not epistemological or method—"

"Oh!" Maud stamped her little foot. "You drive me crazy."

To Scotty's surprise, Angelique didn't just tell Maud to shut the hell up. "What's the difference?"

"Please," Maud said. "Don't get him started."

"Too late," Mickey said. "Metaphysical solipsism is a type of idealism. It says that the perceiver is the only real thing . . . and everyone else is just a part of that self, with no external reality."

"And in English?" Scotty asked.

"Like she said: Before I turned on the lights, the room wasn't there."

"Ah-hah."

Darla shushed them. "You go on like two chickens fightin' over half a worm. Squabble later. Help me find the exit hatch."

"Did they tell you where it is?" Scotty asked.

"I haven't the slightest clue . . . but I expect it will make itself known."

Without warning the air filled with a whirring sound, and an enormous section of ground began to shake. The gamers sprang back, as a mooncow the size of a city bus rose up from the ground, gazing at them with hugely faceted eyes.

There was a mechanism of some kind around its neck, like a gigantic golden pendant. The device clicked and popped at them.

Then it made a whining sound, and then a sound that resembled whale song.

"Hello?" Angelique said. "We're human."

Scotty frowned. "You're talking to a machine. Or a hologram, or something."

She radiated scorn. "It doesn't know that. Hello?"

"Hello," the mooncow said in English. "Who are you?"

It paused, and Scotty watched it cock its head as if waiting for outside guidance.

Angelique nudged him. "This is the fail-safe loop. In case of major power or communication outage, there is a small amount of on-site programming to keep things moving forward."

"Voice recognition?" Sharmela asked.

"Welcome, Earthlings. You are friends of Dr. Cavor?"

Wayne yelped with pleasure. "Yes! We're friends."

"That is good. It is good to have friends, and he is a nice human."

The mooncow emitted a lowing sound, and little calves the size of legless Great Danes wriggled in and out of the mushrooms. The cow's side fluttered, exposing a row of a thousand teats. Dozens of calves streaked in to suckle.

The mooncow seemed to smile. "Would you care for a snack?"

"Not now, thank you."

The creature's mouth seemed to pull down at the edges. Sadness?

"I think you hurt her feelings," Scotty said.

"Would you like to play a game?" The mooncow asked.

"What kind of game?" Wayne asked.

"Do you like riddles?"

Darla leaned toward Wayne, touching his arm intimately. "Say 'yes.' Whatever the next move is, the animatronics will have the information."

"Yes," Angelique said before Wayne could even begin to answer. "I love riddles."

"Oh, good," the mooncow said. "Professor Cavor taught me riddles. He was a nice man. Are you nice men?"

"Every one of us," Angelique said.

"That is so good. Because if you are nice, and I am nice, then we can be friends, and perhaps I can help you."

"We'd like that, too," Wayne said.

Again, a slight smile. "I'm sure you would. All right." The voice became slightly sing-song. "What's round, but not always around? It's light sometimes is dark sometimes. Everyone wants to walk all over me. What am I?"

Without hesitation, Sharmela snapped out an answer. "The Moon."

"That's right," the cow said. Then cocked her head quizzically. "But . . . are we really round? How odd. Well, another: The Moon is my father, the sea is my mother; I have a million brothers; I die when I reach land. What am I?" It blinked, then added, "I have to admit that I've never seen one of these, but they certainly sound interesting."

Wayne raised his hand. "Is there a penalty for an incorrect answer?"

"Oh no! In fact there is a reward! You get to stay here with me."

"I am just *so* delighted by that prospect. Waves?"

The mooncow reared up and clapped several of its tiny legs together. "Yes, waves! Congratulations."

"Can you tell us where the door is?" Sharmela asked.

"Soon. Now, listen very closely. It took me a long time to learn this one:

"Down below the shining moon
  Around the trees, a sacred gloom
  Running with the midnight sky
  Knowing the thing that makes you cry
  Night is full with my essence
  Eternal light betrays my presence
  Soaring through my endless task
  Shadows are my faithful mask."

The mooncow paused. "What am I?"

The gamers frowned and hemmed and hawed a bit. Then Angelique said to Mickey, "You've got a good ear."

"Not sure," he said. "Maud's been bending it of late."

"Hush."

Angelique frowned. "Did you notice anything odd about the inflection?"

Mickey closed his eyes for a moment. "Very careful. As if it was important for us to understand something beyond the words."

Angelique turned back to their inquisitor. "Would you please repeat what you said . . . ah, what's your name?"

"Dr. Cavor called me Maggie."

"Maggie the Mooncow," Wayne said. "Of course. Maggie, would you please repeat what you initially said?"

"Of course," she said, and did so.

"Down below the shining moon
Around the trees, a sacred gloom
Running with the midnight sky
Knowing the thing that makes you cry
Night is full with my essence
Eternal light betrays my presence
Soaring through my endless task
Shadows are my faithful mask."

Angelique was trembling a little now, like a hunting hound straining at the leash. "Did you hear it?"

"I did," Scotty said. "The stress on the first syllables." As he counted off on his fingers, Maud's eyes widened.

"Darkness!" she said. "The answer is darkness. It's the first letter of every line."

A pale holographic ghost of Maggie the Mooncow rose up, and began to dance.

"Dance with me!" Maggie said.

Angelique frowned. "Ah . . . do we have to?"

"Look at this," Wayne said. "There's some kind of an imitation loop running. Reasonable to assume that we have to imitate or respond to these motions, and that it is set up to trigger if we get it right."

"Like a dance instruction program?" Scotty asked.

Wayne nodded approval. "Just like that."

The mooncalves began to dance around the mother. The gamers, frustrated, began to dance.

Ali danced, but seemed none too happy about it. "Are we crazy? We are being hunted by assassins."

"Got a better idea?" Wayne asked.

A little mooncalf in front of Wayne rose up on its hind legs and turned in a circle. When Wayne responded, the larva glowed red.

"I've got it!" Wayne howled. "I've got it! Imitate the caterpillar until it glows!"

Sharmela first, then the rest of the gamers jumped, twirled, spiraled and capered in response to the little mooncalves. One at a time, the calves glowed red in their innards, until they all looked as if they'd swallowed emergency beacons.

The mommy rose up, her vast faceted eyes facing them.

"You honor my children. Here." The mooncow rolled over onto her left side, exposing a glistening length of pale flesh stippled with brown nipples.

Scotty stared, and then shrugged. "Ah . . . are we supposed to do something?"

"Please," Maggie said.

"I think," Wayne said, "that we're being welcomed to supper."

Angelique groaned. "Oh, jeez. That would make sense."

They crept up to the side of the mooncow. Its teats glistened. Wayne was the first to put his mouth on one of the nipples, and began to draw.

"Whoa," Wayne said. "Whoa. Tastes like . . . beer."

This announcement triggered a roar of pleasure, and the gamers rushed in. "I have milk here!" Maud said.

"I have . . . some kind of citrus juice."

"Beef broth."

The mooncow's eyes sparkled, and lights seemed to reflect from them, onto a nearby stand of mushrooms. Maud and Sharmela examined these more carefully.

Sharmela sniffed, and then smiled. "I think we have located lunch!"

"It figures. We don't have time for a picnic. Tear off chunks, and take them with us."

They did that, as the mooncow nodded approval. Then that "reflected" eye light focused on a pile of stones twenty yards away. "And when you are finished, my new children, you may exit to the deeper levels here."

Scotty and Ali ran over, arriving just as the light faded. They overturned the rocks, and revealed a hatch.

"I'm in love with a mooncow," Wayne said. "Let's get the hell out of here before I propose."

"If I'd known you were that easy," Darla said, "I would have fed you *loooong* ago."

30

Payback

1430 hours

From the safety of Heinlein base, Kendra watched the gamers climb down through the hatch.

"So . . . we can watch," she said, "but we can't communicate with them."

"No," Xavier said. "I haven't access to any of the lights. All are on automatic."

"And the dancing bugs," she said. "You had nothing to do with that."

Xavier sighed, as if trying to project infinite patience. "No. All of that was programmed before the kidnappers damaged the circuits."

Kendra glared at him. "And you *are* aware that their lives depend on their ability to navigate these passages?"

"Of course."

"Pardon me," Kendra said, "but it seems to me that you are enjoying all this just a little too much."

He smiled at her placidly, and she left.

Wu Lin drummed her fingers on the table. "Xavier," she said. "You have no control at all? The gamers *had* to perform that dance?"

"I wish I could say I had control," he said.

Wu Lin smiled at him. "It was very entertaining."

He interlaced his fingers behind his head, and leaned back in his command chair, drumming his feet like a happy child. "Wasn't it, though?"

Kendra was in the main communications center within ninety seconds of leaving Xavier. "What do we have?"

Foxworthy ran his finger along a column of recent notes floating in the air. "We have reason to believe that Thomas Frost has been talking to allies on Earth. We have communication with Cowles Industries on the conference channel."

"Mr. Walls?" Kendra said. A pleasant-looking, intense man appeared. There were several other heads floating in screens around him.

"Kendra," Walls said. "Let me begin by saying how sorry I am, how sorry we all are."

"I appreciate that."

"And I want to say that so far, you seem to have done everything a person could reasonably expect."

There was an anvil in that sentence, waiting to drop on an unwary head. "We have to do more," she said. "I've made queries about Thomas and Douglas Frost, and communications that they have made to Earth."

"I'm sorry that we were so long in getting this to you, but we have been backtracing their telemessages, and there is no doubt that they have been in touch with radical groups."

"What kind of radicals?"

"Expatriate Kikayans."

"Are you talking about people who might have wanted the Prince kidnapped?"

"Exactly. We located a snippet of a speech given by a Dr. Mubuto, speaking to the African community in America."

A second screen opened in the air.

"When was this taken?" Kendra asked.

Walls looked down and made a rustling sound in his lap. Notes. "Ah . . . two years ago."

Mubuto was a small, round-faced man who wore wire spectacles and shook his finger at the camera a lot. A line of translated text ran across the bottom of the screen. *"And there is no disgrace like that visited upon those who forget. Forget that we had a tyrant who controlled our lands, and threw him off. Followed by dictators, and we threw them off, and gave the reins of power to the one man who we could all agree upon. Who then threw aside our democratic ideals and made his title not President, or even President for Life, but King, and then passed that title on to his son."*

The crowd cheered.

"It is hard enough to toil under the weight of tyranny. Many of us could not bear the burden, and left our homeland to seek better lives, hoping that perhaps one day our children would enjoy the free homeland that we could not have." He paused. Kendra wished she could have understood the speech in its original Congolese.

"But now he wants to pass it to his child. And that child will doubtless wish to convey it to his own. And where will it end? When the rest of the world claws its way toward freedom, are we less? Will we stand by and let this injustice happen? We have friends! We have power! And one day we will find the way to end this travesty!"

The crowd cheered.

"I think we can assume," Walls said, "that they found their way."

Kendra sighed. "So the Frost twins have Kikayan sympathies. This Doctor Mubuto was the head of their parliament, and there was a powerful national movement to make him President and make the King a figurehead, but Kikaya fended it off. Some say illegally. Well, payback is a bitch."

"Our bitch, now. Mubuto and Frost must have been working together somehow. This operation took money. Lots of it. One thing we have to ask, though . . ."

He paused long enough for Kendra to volunteer a response. "Who helped them here?"

"Yes."

"Equipment. What equipment did the pirates have. What did

they bring, how did they bring it, and how did they acquire anything difficult to smuggle." She turned to her assistant. "I want you to get several of the NPCs who left the dome. I want them in here in five minutes. Room five."

Kendra strode to the front of a conference room crowded with former NPCs. Xavier sat at her side, watching everything carefully before speaking. "I am so sorry for what you have experienced. Most of you know me. And I assume that the rest of you know Xavier."

A few of them grumbled. "What's going on in that dome?" a bald man asked. "What are you doing to get them out?"

"The first thing we have to do is understand the game we're playing," Kendra said. "And the players."

The man shifted so that light reflected from his gleaming head. "It's easy. There are bad guys with guns, and they took over the dome. What's so complicated?"

"Complicated," Kendra said, considering. "You think that we should just sneak up on them?"

"Why the hell not?"

Kendra tried to keep the frustration from her voice. "And if someone tells them we're coming?"

"We can keep it secret . . ."

"We have no military," Kendra said. "No paramilitary, or SWAT. Barely any police or security. We're not set up for this."

"So you're doing *nada*?"

"Of course not. But I think we can keep this in the family. I need to ask you some questions: How were these men equipped? Did you really see guns?"

The gamers conferred with each other for a few moments, and then one smallish man raised his hand. "I saw a crossbow."

"Underwater breathing gear. I saw that, and air guns."

"What else? And please let me ask you a question: Unauthorized pistols or rifles aren't allowed down here. All luggage is scanned thoroughly."

The bald man squinted. "So . . . someone helped them beat a scan?"

"Is that what you think? Is that what you would do if you had the fix in?"

He frowned. "What do you mean?"

"Well," she said. "If you could smuggle any weapon past the screeners on Earth. And then the L5. And then here on the Moon. Would you choose an air gun?"

They stared at each other.

"The weapons were makeshift?"

"That seems the most reasonable conclusion. Yes," she said. "They were constructed here on the Moon. How many weapons? What resources would have been necessary? I'm going to go down that road. I would like everyone in this room to write down every resource they saw that would not have been allowed on the shuttle. Then . . ."

"Then what?" the bald man said.

Kendra felt herself snarling.

31

Rumors of War

1430 hours

Within the gaming dome, the gamers were making their way through a tunnel into bubble 61-E. Scotty was in the lead. He held up a hand. "Where are we? Darla: How's the map in your head?"

"One level up from bedrock. We can get down into the foundation layer if we make it through here."

They cautiously opened a door leading into the next bubble, and stepped in. It was a cavern filled with flowers with metallic petals. Their wristlamps stabbed into deep pockets of shadow.

"Look here," Sharmela said. "Somebody's home."

They gathered around to see a row of robotic Selenites lined up against the wall.

"My guess is that these were supposed to come to life. Some kind of display or attack. No power, no attack."

"Look," Wayne called. "Finally! An emergency communications node!" The glowing green triangle was obvious once you focused your eyes properly.

"Thank God!" Angelique said, and tapped at the flower indicated. "Xavier? Can you hear me?" She drew an earpiece from the middle of the flower. Scotty stood close, listening.

A pause, and then a thin ghost of Xavier's voice floated to them, from nowhere, from everywhere. *"I've been screaming at you, but I guess only the earpieces are working. No loudspeaker. Listen to me: We detect heat signatures moving in your direction."*

"What can you tell us about the search patterns?"

"There are two down on the pool level. They didn't even try to follow you, just assumed that they could cut you off if they got there first."

"Good thinking," Scotty said.

"Aside from that, they're doing a standard grid search, one level at a time. But the good news is that it looks as if they have one team searching from the top down, while another searches from the bottom up."

"Why is that . . . oh, I see. If they miss us, they'll go *up*. If we can fool them, we still have to get past the two at the pool."

"Yes, that's true. And we might be able to help. We're trying to route auxiliary power, but they scrambled us pretty damned well. You've got about three minutes. Find a place to hide."

"Where?"

"Here's a hint: You see stalagmites, but not stalactites? Nothing projects from the roof?"

". . . Funny," Wayne said.

"The stalagmites are hollow. We were going to ambush you."

Angelique stiffened. "What?"

"Well," Xavier said, *"if you look closely, those stalagmites aren't rock. They are actually piles of mooncow dung, calcified."*

"What? And what was going to attack us?"

Xavier chuckled. *"Let's just say that mooncows have worms. With teeth. I'd suggest that you hide."*

As he finished speaking, Scotty pulled another earpiece out of the flower. "What are these?"

"Just a local network. Probably only works inside this room. There are what, three sets in there?"

"Then let's use 'em," he said.

There had been no sound in the cavern that had proven to be a gigantic lavatory. The door on the far side vibrated, then foun-

tained sparks from a fist-sized hole. The door clanged open and
several members of Neutral Moresnot entered, fanning the room
with their flashlight beams.

"Attention!" the first one screamed into the silence. "If you
are in this room, we will find you. If you give yourselves up now,
there will be no repercussions. Any act of aggression against us
will be met with aggressive force."

There was no response, and Scotty wondered what they felt.
Anger? Anxiety? He could imagine that things had not been going their way, but the small brown lens in the plaster dung heap
didn't give him much of a view.

"All right." A woman's voice. "All right. Bai Long—go left.
Miller—right. Fan out. Report back in ten minutes." Celeste left
the chamber.

The men followed her orders, moving with care but no apparent wariness, like men hunting for rabbits.

Scotty spoke quietly, hoping that these guys weren't capable
of scanning multiple frequencies. "Darla. Are you there?"

"Here, Scotty. It should be safe to talk."

He peeked out through the lens. A guy with a flashlight lashed
to the underside of his crossbow walked past. As soon as he was
a dozen feet away, Scotty spoke again. "These guys are good, but
overconfident."

"Meaning . . . ?"

"Meaning that if the stalagmites were designed for ambush, I
think it would be a shame not to put them to use."

Scotty watched the two men Celeste had called Bai Long and
Miller work their way through the room, scanning carefully. It
was a nervous time: They seemed to be heading almost directly
toward him.

"What is this stuff?" the shorter one said. "It isn't rock." Scotty
labeled him Bai Long, engaging in a bit of racial stereotyping.

"Papier-mâché crap," the taller man—Miller?—said. "I've
seen better effects in Halloween spook houses. I don't know how
these guys got their reputation." A knowing laugh.

"Where do you think they are?"

"Hiding in a corner. Wait—what's *that*?"

The beam of light focused on a hollow Selenite head. Miller picked it up and examined it carefully.

"What's this?" Bai Long asked. "Think that someone's in here?"

"Might have been left behind."

Scotty cupped his earpiece. "Did someone leave that? *Crap.*"

Darla's voice answered him. *"I think it might have been left by a prop team. We were supposed to have time to get everything in place. You guys wouldn't have reached this level 'til tomorrow."*

They were heading right toward him. Had they heard him? Before sealing himself in, Scotty had tested the stalagmite's quick-release catch. He hoped to hell it would work properly.

"Scotty—?" Darla sounded as nervous as he felt.

"It feels as if, if I flip the one catch here, this thing should just open up. Is that right?"

"Yes, but . . ."

"Then get ready."

The men approached more closely, weapons at the ready. He held his breath as they paused . . . and then passed him. As soon as they passed Scotty, he flipped the release catch and leaped, smashing them both to the ground. A flurry of punches and kicks subdued Bai Long, but then Miller managed to scramble to his feet, swinging his weapon around.

Scotty looked up, directly into the pipe bore of an air gun, knowing that he was about to die.

Then . . . Sharmela broke out of her stalagmite, and hit Miller from behind. She was joined swiftly by the other gamers, bursting out of their petrified mooncow turds.

And after another flurry of blows and kicks, the two men were subdued.

As the others stood around panting and gasping for air, Scotty ripped off Miller's headset and tried it on. Then hefted the air gun. It was the size of a sawed-off shotgun, with a tube of compressed gas as thick as his wrist beneath a length of small-bore pipe anchored to a shoulder stock. It was fairly well balanced, not at all a bad weapon. He felt grudging admiration for its fabricator.

"Well, all right," Darla said, carefully hoisting an aluminum frame that must be a cocked crossbow. "So what do we do now?"

"Now, we talk."

He knelt down in front of the taller man. "I assume your name is Miller."

No response.

"Well, you look like a Miller. Miller, all we want to do is get out of here alive."

"Then you just made a very bad move," Miller said.

"Maybe," Scotty said. "What's your end game?"

The tall man's mouth revealed no emotion. "We recapture you—and we will. We complete our contract."

"Which is?"

Miller glared at Scotty as if he was a specimen on a slide. And remained silent.

Ali smacked his fist into his palm. "There are techniques. Palace children tell each other."

Scotty sighed. "What? You want to torture them? You have the time and inclination? Go ahead. But I say we keep moving."

Ali looked at him in disbelief. "They will tell others where we've gone! You want to fight them again?"

"Maybe," Scotty shrugged. "What are they going to say that Moresnot doesn't already know? Anyway, we can slow them down."

His eyes went from Tall to Short and back to Tall again. "I don't want to kill you, but I can't just leave you behind us. Sorry," he said, "but this is going to hurt."

"What are you going to do?" Bai Long asked.

"I watched both of you. You're both right-handed."

"I don't understand—"

And without further preamble, he broke first Miller's right thumb, and then Bai Long's.

Angelique looked pale. "I thought you said you didn't torture."

"Did I ask questions?" He hit Miller squarely on the point

of the jaw. Then Bai Long on the base of the skull. Both folded to their sides, unconscious.

Darla chirped in excitement. "All right! Here's the doorway to the next level!"

Scotty nodded. "Hoorah. Let's move. And keep it quiet, if we can. And conceal the opening."

Back at Heinlein, Kendra was growing aware that she hadn't eaten in eight hours. She ordered in sandwiches. Coffee alone was going to burn a sour hole through her stomach.

She looked over the data for a few moments, and then addressed her crew. "We have a list now. This is everything that our NPCs saw that the members of Neutral Moresnot could not reasonably have expected to move through our security, or things that clearly were fabricated here."

"Air guns, crossbows, aqualungs, communications apparatus . . . there is more," her assistant said.

"The Frost brothers," Kendra said. "We have tabs on Thomas right now—"

The air rippled, and a wire-frame map of Heinlein base appeared. It was filled with tiny red moving blips. "I'm filtering . . ." Kendra said. Dots disappeared until only one remained, near the ground level. "Thomas Frost," she said.

"You know," Foxworthy said, "the bad guys could have acquired the communications gear without complicity on the part of the supplier. But the air guns smack of Fabrication."

"Kendra!" one of the techs called. "We've got a link with your husband." And popped it through.

"Thank goodness," Kendra said. "Scotty?"

He appeared like a genie. "Kendra! We dropped down into some kind of monster fest. All holograms, and they're moving in loops."

She could see a little of what was going on behind Scotty. Creatures were battling, blocking an entrance highlighted in green.

"How are you doing this?" Kendra asked.

"It's some kind of a video link here, not on the main circuit.

Listen: I don't know how much time we have. Do you have any kind of thermal fix on the pirates?"

She was relieved that she actually had good news to offer. "Yes. If all of your people are currently with you, then Moresnot has six men working their way down from the top. Three more on the second level, two on the third. And . . . indistinct traces on the access stairs along C and E."

"They may be putting their wounded there."

"Wounded?"

"We used Xavier's little ambush against them."

She felt her breath catch in her throat. "What did you do?"

"Well, they won't be winning at 'thumb war' any time soon, and they'll wake up with the headaches of the year. Oh . . . and we have their weapons."

"You do? What?"

Scotty looked at his equipment. "Some kind of crossbow pistol. Very compact, very nasty. They almost tested it on us: drove a bolt through a quarter-inch steel plate. Uses a kind of hand-crank to cock the latch."

"Christ!"

The Kowsnofski woman appeared behind him. "And we have an air gun. Haven't tested it yet. Works on pressurized gas."

"Darla!" Kendra said. "You work in . . . Engineering, right?"

"Yes. Structural."

"That will do just fine. Look at those guns. If I told you they were constructed here on the Moon, who made them?"

Darla looked more carefully at the makeshift weapons. When she spoke again, her speech was more measured and clipped, with less trace of her Oakie accent. "I . . . hmm. That's interesting. I'd say that the energy efficiency on the crossbow suggests some kind of compound construction, maybe foamed steel stock . . . some kind of polymer. Falling Angels, maybe. But that's the raw stock."

"Construction?"

"Well," Darla said. "I can't get there with the crossbow. But the air gun? It's using the same gas cartridges used to drive the

Liquid Wall bubbles, but the size . . . these welds imply an arc. Most of the shops use laser welds, but this looks like plasma to me. More expensive, but higher temperatures and more precision."

"I need an opinion," Kendra said.

Now at last her speech patterns betrayed her childhood again. "Well . . . I'm not looking for a lawsuit or anything, Honey, but if I were you, I'd talk to Toby McCauley."

Kendra exhaled hard. "Thank you." She turned to her assistant. "Get me Piering." Then back to Scotty. "What can we do for you guys?"

"We need to stay ahead of Moresnot. Keep scanning us. Scan them. If we're in trouble, you tell us. We have their communications gear, and we're changing the frequency to . . . one point two three."

"Got it," Kendra said. "Good work. Get moving."

"What are you doing?"

"If Thomas Frost and Toby McCauley are implicit in this, then for the first time, we're ahead of the ball. And I want to stay ahead." A pause. "And another thing—"

"What?"

A hard smile. "You just won my election for me."

As the image faded, Kendra turned to see the hulking Piering squeeze through the door.

"Kendra?"

She nodded greeting. "I want to put out a hypothesis to you to see if there is anything I'm missing. But first I'm going to write a name on the other side of this paper." She did so.

Piering seemed puzzled. "What is this?"

"This is in reference to your experience. Someone is helping the kidnappers. We believe that the Frost twins are expatriate Kikayans with a grudge. They arranged this, but they had help."

"Help?"

"Help, yes. The kind of help that could get someone spaced. Weapons. Equipment."

Piering squinted, and frowned. "All right . . ."

"Now," Kendra said. "It could be money, but the Frost brothers don't have much. It could be that someone arranged payments to an account on Earth that we can't cover, so we'll look into that. But what I'm asking is: Did the Frost brothers ever touch on anything that might lead them to having leverage on someone connected with Fabrication or machining?"

Piering sat down, hard. "You know . . . back almost four years ago, your husband and I were looking into an information link."

Kendra winced. "Is this the same incident where he was injured?"

"Both of us were injured," Piering said. "Yes. Do you remember?"

"Data loss, connected with an He3 find if I recall."

"That's it." Piering nodded approval. "It was interesting because the Frost brothers vouched for someone. They said that he was with them at a time when a data terminal at his shop was being accessed."

"I remember. The lock on the shop was broken."

"And do you remember the name?" he asked. "It was Toby McCauley."

Kendra turned over the piece of paper. *TOBY McCAULEY,* was printed in block letters. "What a coincidence. Toby McCauley's shop has everything necessary to make the weapons used in the assault."

"Where does that leave us?" Piering asked.

"It leaves us setting a trap," she said, and then turned to her assistant. "Tell Toby I'd like a meeting with him in fifteen minutes. It's an emergency."

"If he asks what the emergency is?"

"He's not an idiot. He knows what it's about. Even if he's innocent, he knows what it's about."

The alien fungus farm looked like something out of Alice's Wonderland. As Shotz and Celeste entered, the overlapping shadows turned the entire room into a Halloween graveyard. Weapons at the ready, they searched the entire room. Not until Celeste heard a low groan from within one of the stalagmites did they find Miller. Bai Long was nearby, wrapped tight within a second spire.

Shotz shoved them awake as Celeste worked on the wire binding their wrists.

"What happened?"

The taller man groaned. "They . . . came out of the stalag-mites."

Shotz shone his lights around the room, feeling a grudging admiration for the trick the gamers had pulled. Their opponents were more capable than he had expected. "And now they have your weapons. I would kill you, but we've lost enough people."

Bai Long held up his hands. "They broke my thumb!"

"Then I don't need you, do I?" He grabbed a thumb and squeezed, just enough to produce a whimper.

"I . . . I can still search, or run communications!" he said.

Shotz patted Bai Long's head. "Don't make another mistake."

In bubble 80-F, the gamers huddled, conferring.

"Scotty. You need to get to the substation in bubble . . . 115-H."

"What then?" Scotty asked.

"We want to raid the dome, but the pirates have placed explosives. If they see us coming, they might detonate them."

"Yes. I saw one of the packages," Scotty said. "I don't know a lot about things like that, but I don't think they're bluffing."

"Scotty," Piering said. "I'll head up the team. What we need to do is send you a data feed. You save it on a PDA, and hand-inject it into the surveillance system. We have to believe they've compromised the security, turned it to their own use."

"Can't you kill the power?" Scotty said.

"We're also assuming that they have backup," Kendra said. "McCauley's shop could rig batteries pretty easily—"

"McCauley?" Scotty asked. "Toby? What's he got to do with this?"

"Well," Kendra said. "We believe that he's cooperating with the Frost brothers."

Ali's eyes widened. "The Kikayan? I've seen him."

"Jesus Christ," Scotty said. "We've got traitors inside, traitors outside—"

"We're going to deal with that," Kendra said. "But you need to get to 115-H. Can you?"

"We'll have to move through the interstits," Darla said. "If we can't find a way through the bubbles."

"We need to get going," Scotty said.

They generated a glowing, floating map of the dome. "Here we are. We have one more level to go, and I think we can get there within the protected pathways. We'll lose the advantage of knowing where the pirates are, but as of right now . . . we're clear."

"Then let's get moving," Angelique said.

"Ah . . . ," Maud said. "Can I find the potty first?"

"I think we all need to take five," Wayne said. "But just five. There's a restroom hidden right over there." He pointed. If you squinted just right, the rocks composed a familiar crescent moon. They broke off to take care of their needs. Scotty sat heavily, next to Ali.

"I am so sorry about all of this," Ali said. "It's my fault. Asako's death is my fault."

"No," Sharmela said. "She wanted to be a hero. She wanted a chance to die like a hero . . . instead of dying for nothing. If we honor her, we must also honor her choices."

When the third-level airlock door slid open, the Moresnot pirates discovered Asako's pod. "What the hell happened here?" Miller, the big bodybuilder demanded.

Carlyle speculated. "I reckon she must have tried to leave the dome. This contraption of hers didn't hold up."

"Hope the warranty's still good." Gallop tapped his communicator. "Shotz. We found the body of the Japanese woman."

"*In her environment pod?*" That damaged voice.

"Yes."

"*I want you to get the information from her radio. Pass the word to shift to alternate frequency Bravo in three minutes. I believe our quarry is communicating on a local network. If they make the mistake of using the same frequencies, we want to be able to capitalize on the error."*

In Heinlein base's nerve center, Kendra watched the dome map carefully, interrupted as her assistant turned to her. "Kendra . . . if this is a stalemate, they win. What's their endgame?"

"President for Life Kikaya abdicates," Kendra said. "And a new government is quickly recognized. Diplomatic and economic pressure is put on us to allow Moresnot to leave. Remember: Kikaya invested in this base. If he leaves, his successors control that investment."

Foxworthy blinked. "Could that happen? Could they just walk? The woman Asako *died*! They can't just . . ."

"They might," Kendra said. "We have to stop it, and the best way of doing that is to free the boy before his father steps down."

"What's happening in Kikaya?"

"Hard to say," Kendra said. "There isn't much news coming out. I just don't know."

Foxworthy cupped his ear. "Just heard that McCauley is on his way. What do you have in mind?"

A pause, then Kendra said: "Pain."

The gamers were making their way through a central corridor, looking out through the windows at the cross-hatching of ladders and walkways linking the bubbles.

"I'm just a little worried about the dome integrity. I wish you could see air." Scotty said.

Wayne snorted. "Ever been to London?"

"This is 102," Angelique said. "One-oh-three is one level down, and we should be able to get there."

"Was this a part of the game?" Scotty asked.

"The bubble, yes, but not this walkway. You'll notice that this hasn't been made up H. G. Wells style."

"What's on the other side?" Scotty asked.

Darla's smile was strained. "That would be telling, big guy."

Scotty shook his head. "You guys are frickin' crazy. All right. Let's go."

They cracked the door open, and then stared, agog.

The room was an impossibly vast junkyard. The walls seemed kilometers distant, the ceiling as high as the sky.

Scotty whistled. "What in the hell do we have here?"

The room was filled with technology, but the technology was alien. Martian war machines, walkers recognizable from plates in science fiction novels and theatrical films. And other odd equipment, of a strangely organic design.

Wayne matched Scotty's whistle. "This . . . looks like a museum."

"Yes. I think that the mythology was one of the entire Wells oeuvre."

"*War of the Worlds?*"

"Yes. Somehow, the Martians and the Lunies were at war, once upon a time."

They walked between the rows of giant machines, the ceiling impossibly high above them, brushing the stalactites of a major cave system.

Sharmela climbed up one of the walkers, waved her hands right through the metal. "Holograms. There's some power in this room."

Mickey frowned. "How many ways are there to get down to the aquifer?"

"Why?"

"I want to arrange a little surprise for our friends. Something to slow them down a bit."

Maud seemed to glow with pride. "Mickey. How you talk."

As Toby McCauley's shuttle pulled in, and he emerged, he was met by two security men.

"What's this all about?"

Piering smiled. "Just additional precautions, what with everything going on."

"Right," Toby said, sounding rather unconvinced.

They moved through a series of walkways and elevators to a low-ceilinged conference room. And there he was told to sit, and wait. He shifted uncomfortably. Getting nervous. Then the door opened, and Kendra and Max Piering entered.

"Toby."

"Sheila Monster. What's this all about?"

"I was hoping that you could help us, Toby. Remember three years back when Thomas Frost said you were with him when your computer was accessed?"

He tensed a bit. "Yes?"

"We were thinking that that was just a little too neat. Too coincidental."

"I don't understand," Toby said.

"You shall," Kendra said. "Piering?"

Piering stood up. His hands flew over a keyboard at the side of the room. "We began to wonder about the Frost brothers, after it became clear that this entire affair was connected to the Republic of Kikaya."

McCauley blinked. "How?"

"The target seems to have been Prince Ali, heir to the throne. The Brothers Frost . . ."

"Their parents were Kikayan, I think. I see." He seemed both nervous and attentive, as if on the edge of an admission, or perhaps seeking an escape route.

"We began to wonder how they funded the operation. We realized that if they had been responsible for the earlier industrial espionage, and perhaps others that went undiscovered, they could have amassed sufficient funds to mount this."

"Is there any proof?"

Piering gave a small nod. "We have reason to believe that while Thomas Frost was keeping you occupied, his brother was gaining access to your shop terminal."

"And further," Kendra said, "in the last year, there has been an acceleration of contacts between them and certain persons of interest to Interpol. They did a very good job of disguising the communications, but once we started looking for them, we found them." She turned to Piering. "I have to take care of something. Can you handle things here?"

"Absolutely."

After the door closed behind her, McCauley said, "This is incredible. What can I do to help?" He managed to ooze sincerity.

"We have reason to believe that they gained access to your shop again, more recently. Possibly other shops as well, and fabricated weapons and tools used in the assault."

McCauley leaped for the offered lifeline. "You're saying that if he has my codes, they might have others."

"Yes. There is no limit to how far into our security they may have penetrated. We need your help. Is there anything you can tell us, anything that might help?"

He stared at his fingers. For a moment it seemed he was about to speak. Then . . .

Thomas Frost sat quietly, staring at the beige walls of a nine-by-nine cell. Then, the door opened, and Kendra entered.

He managed to affect indignation. "What the hell is going on?"

"Where's your brother, Thomas? Where is Doug?"

He didn't flinch. "I don't know. We're not Siamese twins."

"No," Kendra admitted. "You're not. But we have reason to believe that he is currently in the gaming dome, and that he has been assisting the kidnappers. We have messages sent to persons of intense interest associated with radical groups in Kikaya, as well as expats. And we have evidence that the two of you colluded to practice industrial espionage against the interests of Cowles Industries."

He frowned. "What kind of evidence?"

"Piering?" she said. Her voice was clear and low and strong.

The security man pressed buttons on his PDA. Toby McCauley appeared on the wall monitor, face five times its normal size. Kendra appeared across the table from him.

"So . . . ," the onscreen Piering said. "Can you help us understand how the Frost brothers might have gained access to your security systems?"

"They had contacts," McCauley said. "Kikayan contacts. The

boy's father invested in the game, and some of the people negoti-
ating the deal had the chance to insinuate themselves."

"You have direct knowledge of this?"

"No," Toby said. Was that a tic at the corner of his mouth? A
bit of a squint? McCauley was nervous. "No, but we played
squash together, Thomas and I, and several times he implied that
the government of Kikaya was riddled with revolutionary forces,
and that some of them were close to the King."

"And?"

"They implied that Kikayan loyalists had fingers everywhere,
and knowledge that would one day be applied to the freeing of—"

Thomas slapped his hand on the table. "He is lying. I have no
such contacts. But Mr. McCauley has debts. It is known that, for
a price, his shop has made contraband items that have made
their way into Luna's black market."

Kendra pushed a piece of paper across to him.

"I want to know what you know, and from whom you learned
it. And I want to know *now*."

Thomas hesitated, and then began to write.

Piering met Kendra outside the cell. They walked together in
silence for a while, and then found an elevator.

"Did you get it?" Piering asked.

"Enough," Kendra said. "He was easier than McCauley. I
think he figured that the ball is in play now, and that after the
situation is resolved, he will have sufficient leverage to force us
to release him to Earth. While McCauley is making noises as if
he's still staying here, still running for election . . . but I think
that's bullshit. I think he's planning to take off with the others."

"Should we take a look at his residence? See if he's preparing
to leave?"

"Yes, send someone over to do that, I think," Kendra said.
"What the hell happened? The man used to have ambitions."

"Maybe he still does. Maybe someone made him a better offer."

They opened the next room, and Xavier greeted them. "Now,
that was fun. I was afraid that you wouldn't give me enough to
work with."

On the screens were wireframes of Frost and McCauley, partially filled in. "We are thinking that if they had more help outside, they wouldn't have sent one of the brothers in."

Wu Lin came closer. "Which means?"

"Which means that if we can control the visual feeds, and seal off the dome from outside communications, they might be blind." Kendra said.

"But," Xavier said, "they mustn't know that they are blind."

"No, they mustn't."

"It seems, Wu Lin, that we have a game after all. One with considerably higher stakes. Please, Ms. Griffin. Dazzle me."

Xavier and his people watched on a game monitor as the Moresnot men broke into the Mars room.

"We have no direct contact with the gamers, as you know. *Most* of the time. But we do have some system backup sensors. We received a notification that someone was attempting to hook several of them up in series."

"Why?" Kendra asked.

"I think they want to activate the animatics and preprogrammed holograms."

"Where are the pirates right now?" Kendra asked.

"Entering Mars," Xavier said after a glance at the screen.

"Would Scotty have known they were coming?"

"Very possible."

Kendra sighed. "Show me the thermals."

A gauzy map blossomed. A clutch of red silhouettes arrived through a connecting door. Their scans revealed two people hidden in the room.

Suddenly, Kendra understood. "Scotty's going for an ambush. We have to help him."

The little Game Master perked up. "What did you have in mind?"

"What exactly are your capabilities at this point?" she asked.

"In terms of communicating or controlling the illusions?"

Xavier closed his eyes and considered. Then he began ticking off points on his fingers. "I cannot control the illusions directly. I can't add data to the computers in the gaming dome. I cannot send outside power to any of the illusions, nor can I use the main camera feeds to observe."

"That's the bad news," Kendra said. "And . . . ?"

"And . . . our attackers were smart, but not brilliant. We can do a small amount of imaging, using a subsystem. We can route power from one part of the dome to another."

"How so?"

"The backups. In case of power failure, we wanted to be able to keep going until major power was restored. We have some backdoor controls there. Let's see . . . as you already know, in certain situations we can communicate with the gamers a bit, using Morse code."

"If Scotty is planning to ambush Moresnot," she said, "we want to help him. What can we do?"

A pause, then Wu Lin spoke. "There is little we can do directly. But there is one factor that must be taken into consideration."

"Which is?"

Wu Lin's eyes glittered. "Mr. Griffin is accustomed to our illusions. The kidnappers are not."

"True," Xavier said. "More to the point, the more complex and disorienting we make the situation, the greater advantage should accrue to the good guys, such as they are."

"What can you do?" Kendra asked.

"Well," Xavier said. "You have to understand that a game is controlled by both the technological constraints and the commercial considerations. That means that, as with any good story, there is a rhythm to the flow of the game. Smaller illusions give way to larger, more impressive ones until you reach the end, and use the most impressive ones of all."

Kendra nodded. "And so you suggest . . . ?"

"Taking off the gloves," the little man said.

The Moresnot pirates combed the Martian graveyard as best they could, when not gaping and gawking at the expanse of machines.

McCartney shone his flashlight up at the ceiling. "This dome . . . ," He shook his head. "Looks larger than it can possibly be."

Shotz made a harsh humorless sound. "That has to be the illusions."

"I thought we cut the power," Celeste said.

"Backup," Shotz said. "We cut main power, but some of the environmental systems have backup in case of emergency. I think the Dream Park have people tapped into those lines."

The shadows of the Martian machines loomed large above them.

"This is creepy. What are these things?"

"Some sort of robot," Shotz offered.

"It's hard to believe that people pay to . . . what? Be frightened? Have adventures?"

Shotz smiled, as if it required physical effort to hoist his cheeks into position. "You don't understand, because you are the kind of woman who makes her own adventures. People like this must have others make their adventures for them."

"How much does all of this *cost*?" Fujita asked. Despite his impressive mass, Fujita walked with great, almost incongruous delicacy and quiet.

"I think," McCartney said, "that I'm in the wrong bleedin' business."

"Quiet," Celeste said. "And split up. I say that they're in here, and frightened to death."

Shotz motioned two of his men this-away, two that-away.

Scotty and Wayne were hiding behind a tremendous tripod with a tiny dome on top. One outsized flat foot concealed them.

"What are they doing?" Wayne asked.

Scotty peeked out and then ducked back. "Splitting up. Trying to pincer us."

"Is that a problem?"

"Only if you want to stay alive. No, really . . . we have an advantage. There are only two of us, and they probably won't have time to search the entire room."

"Unless they have sensors."

Scotty made a clucking sound. "Now where would they get something like that?"

Almost as if she had been reading Scotty's mind, Celeste was operating a sensor pad covered with glowing green wireframes of everything in the room. Their nine men were marked in glowing orange. There were faint four-limbed orange glows marked on the far side of the room. "I think I might have something. I'm getting a signal."

"Good," Shotz said. He peered at her screen, and then motioned to his men.

Wayne snuck a peek, ducked back. "Listen. That looks like a rescue sensor the woman's holding. Used in the mines, but someone could modify it for other uses."

"You might be right," Scotty said, peeking out through the misshapen alien shadows.

"Then . . . why are they going in the wrong direction?"

Suddenly, and without any warning, the Martian war machines rose up, impossibly tall in the cramped space, their domes actually ghosting through the ceilings.

They roared, they lurched, and the Moresnot pirates fired at them with air guns and crossbows.

"Hold your fire!" Shotz said. "It's just a show. They can't—"

McCartney, the man next to him screamed as an arrow pierced his side. "Shit!" He crumpled over, clutching his side. "I'm hit!"

Shotz whipped around. "They're here, dammit!"

"Where?" Fujita's head snapped around.

A second arrow bolt flew through the air, hit a prop next to Shotz' head. "Down!"

The pirates hit the deck as the Martian war machines continued to rage, their heat rays sweeping across the floor. A brilliant ruby ray touched one of the Moresnot people, and his bones gleamed through his skin as if he were a cartoon ghost. He screamed.

"I have a visual!" Celeste screamed.

Shotz looked up and across the room, seeing a woman crouching behind a war machine.

"We don't need her—" Shotz said. "Kill her."

But when he fired, it was a *male* scream that answered.

"What the hell—" Shotz growled.

Scotty and Wayne had managed to stay out of the line of fire. "What the hell?" Scotty whispered. "What was that? They're shooting at each other—"

Wayne whispered in his ear. "Listen, Scotty—visual field manipulation isn't perfect from every angle. Doesn't need to be, as long as it's perfect from the angle of the target."

"What are you saying?"

"I think Xavier is helping us. He's creating illusions. Over there—Moresnot men. Over there, too."

Scotty blinked and looked more carefully. The ghost of an illusion around the Moresnot men, firing at each other and being lashed and confused by the illusion. One Asian woman had a handgun—

"Illusion," Wayne said. "That woman they're shooting at is Asako, before she got sick. Xavier at play."

"Let's get closer."

The two carefully crept from one lurching war machine to another. The machines targeted them with beams, but the pirates did not notice.

When Scotty and Wayne got close enough, they loosed bolts.

Fujita took a bolt in the fleshy left side of his back. Hardly fatal in a sumo-sized man, but he screamed. "I'm hit! I'm hit! They're behind us?"

Shotz wheeled around, scanning without result. "Dammit! Where—"

Celeste grabbed his arm. "I think we're making a mistake. They only took two weapons, but they're attacking as if they have more. I think we're fighting our own people."

Next to them Bai Ling screamed: "Look out!"

A crimson beam of light seared across the ground, smoke and

fire gushing up from the ground as it did. The air was filled with alien cries, screams, cries of dismay, curses.

And one very human "Dammit!" Rodriquez said that as the heat beam crawled across his body. He screamed . . . and then looked at himself in disbelief. "I'm alive!"

Then—an air gun bolt hit him in the throat. The Spaniard tumbled with the impact, dying as he fell.

Shotz bent to check the body—and perhaps to get out of the line of fire.

"Dammit. We have to knock out the power system in here. Celeste?"

She was too busy manipulating controls on her portable monitor. "Just a second. I'll have to take out the air system. I'll—there."

The upper sections of the war machines vanished. The din diminished. The Moresnot pirates got unsteadily to their feet.

"They're picking us off," she said. "That's one dead. Four wounded."

"Four," he breathed heavily. "All right: Playtime is over. From now on, shoot to kill."

The man pushing himself up off the ground was shaking, either with fear or rage. "There wasn't anything to shoot at! Where did they go, Shotz? Where did they go?"

"Celeste?" Shotz asked.

"There are three ground-level exits listed on the map. But there may be unmapped exits."

"We have to assume that they are heading to the caverns. Kill all the power, even basic life support. No more confusion. No more mistakes."

Scotty and Wayne had retreated to the spaces beneath the bubble. The tunnel was vertical, and they had to climb down a ladder until they reached a sealed door at the bottom.

"I hope the others had time," Scotty said.

Wayne seemed rattled. "Scotty. I think I might have killed that man. Have you ever . . . killed someone?"

"No," Scotty said. "But today sounds like a great time to start."

Wayne stopped to steady his breathing. "You aren't bad with that crossbow. If this was a game, I'm starting to think you'd be okay."

"Another time," Scotty said. "Another life." Scotty grinned. "And besides, this *is* just a game, remember?"

Scotty unscrewed the hatch. Below, another bubble. There was a ladder across the ceiling and down the inner curve of the dome, and they had to go hand-over-hand, brachiating in a way no one would try in Earth gravity. Their companions were down below, watching them.

The room was covered bottom to top with flat-screen monitors. The gamers gawked at them: The screens showed images from around the solar system, as well as some from a canal-riddled Mars. Locations within the nest itself, displaying a thriving insectile community.

Scotty dropped to the ground. "What is this place?"

"Some kind of communications nerve center," Angelique said. "Note that the images are stuck on a loop."

"So . . . we can't use them to try to keep tabs on Moresnot?" Scotty asked.

"No," Darla said. "But they may not find the maintenance hatch we took. Good Lord willing, we just got ourselves another couple minutes."

They took a moment to examine the screens.

Angelique spoke first. "So far . . . every major set-piece has come with clues, advantages, resources."

Wayne stood shoulder to shoulder with her, trying to see what she was seeing. "Could be the same here."

"Listen," Angelique said. "I think that Xavier is watching us, and believe it or not, he's helping us when he can. These puzzles are fail-safed, in terms of power. So we solve one, and get something in return. A door opens, a map appears . . . something."

"Don't all games work that way?" Scotty asked.

"Dream Park games do. So . . . ," the Lore Master said. "What's the point of this room?"

Scotty stared at the screens. What were they seeing?

"Martian walkers," Sharmela said.

Maud pointed. "What is that? Saturn? And . . . Europa?"

"This is the important one," Mickey said. On the screen, a titanic battle between Martian war machines and giant Moon creatures.

"Look," Angelique said, pointing. "Look. Notice that the Martians use machines, and the Moon people are fighting back with animal forms."

"What do you think?" Wayne asked. "A biologically based technology? As opposed to machines?"

"Maybe," Angelique said. "But it might just be that the Martians had to travel a long, long way to get here. Needed machines."

Sharmela nodded. "But it is possible that Martian technology, even war technology, is primarily mechanical. The Lunies, biological."

Finally, Scotty spoke. "Well . . . that would make some sense. The thrust of Wells' original story was that the Martians were weak, right? They needed technology to supplement their bodies?"

"While the Moon people supplemented theirs with creative breeding. So . . . they are stronger than the Martians. But not stronger than us."

"No," Scotty said. "Not stronger than us. But how does that help us?"

Angelique stamped her foot. "We've lost the thread of the game. Let's stop for a second. What is this game about? I mean, what was it *originally* about?"

"Rescuing Professor Cavor?" Scotty offered.

"Yes. Rescuing Professor Cavor. Professor Cavor is in this equation."

"Wait, wait wait," Wayne said. "Maybe we're looking at it backward. The lesson isn't that the Lunies are stronger. It's that their mechanical technology is weaker."

"*Was* weaker," Angelique said. "But then Professor Cavor arrived."

"Weaker?" Mickey said. "Remember the airlock door on the surface? Does that look like an inferior technology?"

"Maybe," Scotty said. "Or maybe it's a remnant."

Angelique seemed interested in that notion. "Regressed civilization?"

"Very popular theme in early science fiction," Wayne said. "Go ahead, Scotty."

He sighed. "Sorry. That's as far as I go."

"I might have an idea," Ali said.

"Go on."

"Consider. These two civilizations, Martian and lunar, have a certain parity. Mars had a mechanical technology, while the Moon has a biological technology."

"And?" Angelique said.

"This is only apparently a stalemate. The Martians attack, the Selenites fight them back. Can you all see the flaw in this?"

Sharmela snapped her fingers. "The Selenites can't attack the Martians."

"Right," Angelique said. "How do you go interplanetary with living weapons?"

"It would be reasonable," Ali said, "to think that a difficulty."

"What if that changed?" Maud asked.

"What would change it?" Wayne asked. Then suddenly, his face changed. "Oh, crap. Of course. Professor Cavor."

Mickey kissed Maud's cheek and she bubbled like a debutante. "Good one, Maud. Professor Cavor. He arrived here as one of Earth's greatest inventors in the Victorian age. Perfectly reasonable that the technology he shared with them might have had an effect on the war with the Martians."

"And how does this affect *us*?" Scotty asked.

"It might not."

"Sure it does," Wayne said. "No one is going to mount a room like this without a purpose."

"What I meant is that it might affect a coming clue rather than a previous one. If the Moon people got something that allowed them to attack Mars as Mars has been attacking Luna . . ."

"For instance," Maud said, "Cavorite."

"Yes," Angelique agreed. "Cavorite. Who knows what Xavier might have had in store for us."

Wayne shook his head. "That probably won't work now."

"I see it," Sharmela said. "I think I see it."

"What?" Wayne asked.

"A war. We landed in the middle of a war. A war that has been going on for centuries. Maybe millennia."

"Cavor's technology . . . ?"

"Look at these screens," the Indian girl said. "The design of the ships is kinda familiar, isn't it?"

"Moon ships," Wayne said. "Powered by Cavorite, attacking Mars. Crushing Martian cities."

"As Mars crushed human cities? We saw no evidence of that when we left Earth."

Angelique was getting excited. "So nobody spoke of it . . . directly. But the comments about 'the war' and 'the unpleasantness'—it was the War of the Worlds."

"Holy shit," Mickey said. "And Mars is pissed at the Moon. And their armada is on its way."

"I'd say that it's almost here. There's our time clock, people. If we were playing a game, we'd have to get out of here before the Martians blow us to hell."

Wayne cocked his head a bit sideways. "Wait a minute . . . that means that Xavier had to be prepared to simulate an all-out Martian assault. Darla?"

"Maybe," she said. "He'd have to shake the dome without damaging it. Sound, smell . . . big effects."

"Stage explosives," Scotty said. "If we can get to them, they might be very useful indeed. Good work. Damned good work. Let's get going."

··· 32 ···

Breach

1457 hours

Ten men and women had gathered beneath the harsh lights and sharp shadows of Heinlein's northern motor pool. The newcomers might have been confused by Piering's frantic calls, but all were committed to the task at hand. He recognized Gypsy from his own security team. Then there were Hazel and Lee, both tough women, a Communications tech and a Fabrication specialist. Then an ex-cop named Chambers, a guy from Food Services and an He3 miner.

"I'm sure you're wondering why we called you here," the big man said. "You are all either Security, or have police or military experience. All checked the little box on your contracts agreeing to serve in a Security capacity if needed. Well, you're needed."

"The dome?" the lanky miner asked. This was Jankins, probably the oldest man in the room. Tall, pale and looked like he was made of catgut wrapped around barbed wire.

"The dome," Piering agreed. "The Beehive, currently called the gaming dome, is now controlled by an aggressive threat calling themselves 'Neutral Moresnot,' professional kidnappers with allegiance to no nation or cause. We'll call them 'the pirates' for simplicity's sake."

"Fatalities?" the miner asked, his narrow face pinched.

"One that we know of."

Chambers scowled. "Who?"

"One of theirs, thank God. We think his name was Victor Sin-jin. British expat, mercenary, career criminal. In a few minutes, we hope that the gamers inside the Beehive will be able to blind the pirates, keep them from seeing what is happening outside the dome long enough for us to get there, get in, and take them out. There may be explosives planted in the dome, so our rescue team has to wear pressure suits in case of . . . accidents. The use of lethal force is authorized."

He paused, scanning their faces in challenge. If there was anyone who might object to killing, this was the time to speak. No one did. "Any questions?"

"Yes," asked Hazel, the short, round woman from Communications. "What are we facing in terms of weaponry, honey? And what exactly are our own resources?"

"Damned good question," Piering replied. "We believe that the opposition is armed with makeshift weapons. These include air guns and possibly crossbows of advanced design." He paused significantly. "Made here on Luna."

Her eyes narrowed. "Are you saying that somebody here *helped*?"

Concerned faces twisted into ugly masks. In an instant, the rescue party had transformed into a lynch mob. Piering raised his hand for silence. "We aren't sure what we're dealing with, and shouldn't leap to any conclusions. The point is not who might have turned against us. The point is that we have good people in bad hands, and need to do something about that—now."

He waved his thick hands above one of the workbenches, crowded with a hastily assembled array of weaponry. "Nail guns are lethal, but only at short range. No more than five meters. We've reworked a half dozen handheld welding lasers, but they aren't lethal at more than a dozen meters—but can blind up to a hundred. The most promising possibility?" He raised a bulky pistol-like device. "Used by engineering. Piton device. If it can throw a steel arrowhead into rock at fifty meters, it can kill a man."

He braced his meaty arms on the bench. "Here's what I ask. Everyone here has fired a weapon. I'm not asking you to stand down if you haven't fired a piton. But find the weapon that is *closest* to something you've already used. We have maybe an hour before we get the green light. Practice. And keep practicing. And then we'll take it from there."

"What's the entry plan?" Hazel asked.

"Two teams," Piering said. "One will enter at ground level, G. I'll take a team up the side to level C. That's where Asako Tabata's body is. I think the pirates might be a little spooked by that, and give us a clear shot."

Beneath the golden dome of Xavier's gaming complex, the mood was just as serious.

"Are you ready?" Kendra asked.

"Almost," Xavier said. He waved his little hands over a projection table, and a display of Heinlein base and its associated domes blossomed. "This image is ten hours old—just before the game began. It's been shadow-adjusted to be identical with what the pirates would expect to see right now. Unless I'm very mistaken, they should suffice."

"Good," Kendra said. She peered down more closely. A hundred-meter perimeter around the dome had been established, but there were holographic gawkers just beyond that limit. Controlling Lunies was like herding cats.

"Kendra," Xavier began, and then paused. "I assume I have permission to call you by your first name?"

"Knock yourself out."

"Once we've regained control of communications—"

"I wouldn't call it control. But we can get more than we have now."

"Fine," Xavier said. "Once we have *more* control, there are things we can do."

"What kind of things?"

"Let's just say that it isn't a good idea to attack a mad scientist in his own workshop," Xavier said.

"I like the sound of that." Kendra said. "What exactly did you have in mind?"

The flame of Darla's adrenaline had burnt down to a dim and dismal coal. Her stomach felt sore, her mouth tasted as if she'd drunk a cup of sour milk.

She had led the eight gamers to bubble 100-G. This was a small, partially furnished sphere strewn with communications and electronics gear. She thumped her palms against a foamed plastic plate and popped out a section of wall. In they crawled on all fours.

"Wish they'd make the access panels a little easier to access, dammit," the former mermaid said. "Come on, hurry up."

"This is a communications substation?" Scotty asked.

"Yes. And if I can change the protocols we should be able to communicate with the outside a bit. Enough, anyway. The voice and image feeds may be scrambled, but we've got some emergency hard lines in place. Just vanilla stuff, but I can get to them."

Darla walked around the dome, holding her wrist out in front of her as if she were dowsing for water. Reading the wiggles on the monitor imprinted on her cuff. An anxious pause and then she smiled. "We have a signal. Xavier is sending files."

"What kind of files?" Angelique asked.

"Visual files." Her smile broadened. "Kendra added a note: 'Sow confusion among the ungodly.'" Her expression grew sober again. "But I can't do it from here. Someone has to go out into the interstices and find a hard-line video input." She made a face. "I hate to say it, but I'm the only somebody who can do that."

"And?" Wayne said. "If the gaps are full of pirates?"

She patted his cheek. "Oh, sweetie. You're worried about me. I'll just have to figure something out."

Darla tapped at the floor until she found a section that thumped hollowly. She used her multitool's flat-headed wedge to pry up an edge, and slid down into darkness, up to her shoulders. "Seal this behind me," she said.

"Darla?" Sharmela asked. "How safe are these bubbles? What I mean to ask is, what would happen if the pirates depressurized the dome?"

Darla sighed. "Tell the truth, I'm not certain. By the time the Beehive was opened to the public in a couple months, everything would have been tested. The materials are up to standard . . . that's not the problem. The problem is that we're in kind of a transitional phase right now. May have been some shortcuts to speed things up for the game. I can tell you this: All of the doors are flanged so that air pressure will keep them sealed in the case of a pressure drop. You should be safe."

"Not you, though."

"I'll be right back. Scotty? Seal this door after me, would you?"

"You've got it," Scotty said.

Darla climbed downward. All around her was darkness and vague, hollow echoes.

She wiggled through tight spaces, breathing hard. She climbed up the side of one bubble, and stopped. Listened. *Machine sounds. Fluid in pipes. Humming of wires.* And distant human voices, fractured into echoes like water trickling over rocks.

She continued to climb, until she reached a stenciled number: 103-G. She pressed the side of her head hard against the wall, and held her breath. From within, a steady, thrumming sound . . . but no footsteps, and no human voices.

"Easy. Easy . . ."

She crawled up the side, lost her grip, and started to slide around the bubble's curved roof. She looked down. It seemed to Darla that the bubble structure went down forever, dissolving in shadows somewhere below in moonrock. She gripped at the walls with fingernail-shredding strength.

"Shit *fire!*" Pain shot down her fingers, and as soon as she stopped her slide, she sucked at her fingers, disgusted at the tears drooling from the corners of her eyes.

At a spot where the rim of one bubble's roof neared the floor of one just above, several cables ran out of the bubble's side, meeting in a knot before branching off again. She used her multitool to tap into a little juncture box, and attached her PDA. If the pirates had scrambled the com field, then they probably had the capacity to *un*scramble it to scan for intruders. With just a drop of luck, this might fool them.

Suddenly, muffled sounds from the bubble above her. Pirates?

Terrified but determined, she triggered the data transfer, keeping her breathing shallow until an *UPLOAD COMPLETE* message flashed.

She wiggled back through the spaces, until she reemerged at 100-G, the gamer bubble. She knocked three times, and the door lifted out.

She sealed the door behind her. "I did it." She rolled over on her back, gasping open-mouthed.

"Good girl," Scotty said.

The gasps turned into shivers. Darla rolled onto her side and clutched herself. "Give me a minute, hon? I think I'm gonna throw up."

Wayne's fingers brushed her cheek. "I'll buy you a gold-plated barf bag later. What's our next step?"

Darla swallowed air, forced herself to calm. "We have to let Heinlein know that it's done," she said. "Then it's up to them."

The Moresnot pirates had combed their way through the rubble of bubble 62-E without finding either gamers or evidence of their passage. In the last hours Thomas Frost had pinballed through a series of emotions: tension, joy, frustration, fear. Anger at Shotz and the mercenaries he had hired. And finally cautious optimism that they had behaved in a professional fashion, creating alternate plans when the old ones went south. They did not fall apart, and that gave Thomas hope.

"Celeste?" Shotz asked. "What do you have on the monitors?"

Thomas watched the big woman check a handheld monitor, switching rapidly from view to view around the dome. Viewing over her shoulder, the monitor displayed rocks, the curve of domes and spidery collisions of light and shadow. The line of her jaw was too strong, too masculine. He couldn't imagine being in bed with her, although he had the sense that she and the intimidating Shotz were lovers. Nothing said. Nothing in their body language. Just a sense. And that put a picture into his head that churned his stomach.

"Nothing," she said. "No changes. But no bad news, either."

"Small favors. Thomas?"

"Right here," Frost said, grateful that the image of a quarter ton of writhing beef was stricken from his mind.

"Contact your brother, ask if he has received any word."

Thomas tapped a code sequence into his sleeve's com link, and waited.

In Doug Frost's cell, a rusty voice began to sing "No High Ground." His wallet and its built-in communicator lay in a basket on the table, along with the other contents of his pockets. A star-shaped light glowed on and off and on again, in rhythm with the song.

"No high ground, no high ground, no high ground anymore . . ."

He looked up, but could do nothing.

"Kendra," the security guard barked into his communicator. "Mr. Frost is receiving a message from inside the dome. What should I do?"

"I'll be right there."

Doug looked up at her with no expression on his long dark face as Kendra entered, breathing hard from her half-kilometer sprint around the dome's rim.

"What does your brother want, Douglas?"

He peered up at her, expression unreadable. He gestured toward the wallet. "You would have to let me answer to find out."

She shook her head. "I'm sure you'd like that. Too risky." She turned to the guard. "Keep him isolated."

Thomas Frost punched a slender finger down at his PDA, ending its attempt to reach his brother. "I'm getting nothing," he said.

"What does that mean?" Shotz asked.

"They may have captured him."

Celeste nodded. "I agree that we should assume the worst.

That just makes it more important to catch the Prince." She turned to Stavros, their communications man. "I want you to open the emergency channel, see if we have any word. Perhaps we cannot speak, but we can still listen."

"At once," Stavros said, and hunkered in a corner of the room.

She turned back to Thomas. "We will capture the Prince. And once we do, we can force Heinlein base to free your brother."

He hadn't the slightest illusion that this gargoyle gave a damn about Douglas as a person, but it made good operational sense to pretend to. *Bitch.*

She turned and glanced at him, almost as if he had said that word aloud. Her face was neutral, but somehow he felt as if she was grinning inside. A death's head grin. God, this woman frightened him

"Nothing from the external feeds?" Shotz asked.

"Nothing," she replied. "I guess Douglas remained silent, after all."

Thomas stiffened. "Of course he did, but I could not expect mercenaries to understand such a thing. We are patriots."

Shotz smiled thinly. "Of course. She meant no harm."

Thomas hoisted his air gun. "Let's get them."

Thomas opened the bubble door, exiting to the next chamber. After he left, Shotz turned. "Stavros," he said. "What do you have for me?"

The Heinlein base motor pool was a flurry of activity as Piering's volunteer brigade checked their weapons, experimented firing pitons and lasers against makeshift targets. Some tinkered with their suits, trying to get a bit more flexibility and mobility out of the polyplastic joints.

"We have the go-ahead," he said. "Our people have cut into the communications lines, and right now these bastards are blind. Let's hit them."

"Yes, sir!" the brigade called. And if they didn't snap to attention as might a more practiced unit, enthusiasm compensated for group experience.

They piled into the Scorpion transport, and the pressure seals battened down. The Scorpion hissed and then levitated on the track, and slid forward into an airlock, which sealed behind them.

"This is Scorpion two three three," Piering said. "Awaiting permission for egress."

"This is control. You are cleared for egress through to maintenance track two-two. Good luck."

"Amen to that," Piering said.

The airlock lights cycled between red, yellow and green. The outer door opened, and the Scorpion slid forward. Eight men and two women looked out at the lunar landscape as the Scorpion progressed. It swung around the track and headed toward the dome. Ground level. Level G.

Although he did not need to, Shotz stood near Stavros. He stood straight, hands clasped behind his back, lecturing an unseen audience.

"Attention, Prince Ali," he said. "This message is being sent over all communications frequencies within the dome. Your father has requested that we convey the following message to you: 'Death does not sound a trumpet.'"

"What does this mean?" Stavros asked.

"A Congolese saying," Douglas replied. "And evidently a code phrase of some kind."

Crouched in their bubble, Angelique suddenly raised her hand. "I'm getting something," she said.

"Me, too," Mickey said. "It's coming over the gaming channels *and* the emergency com."

"What is it?" Scotty said.

Angelique frowned. "It sounds like 'Death does not sound a trumpet.'"

Scotty was baffled, but Prince Ali reacted violently, and at once. "My father!"

"What?"

He cradled his head in his hands. "It means that he has left

Kikaya. I am to do whatever I must to survive, and need not resist to save the crown."

He sobbed. "He did it for me. My father lost the crown . . . for me."

Scotty rubbed the Prince's shoulder. What in the world do you say to something like that?

"What happens to Kikaya now?"

"I don't know. It depends on who was responsible for the coup. There is a man named Motabu, a general quite popular with the people. My father would have removed him, or jailed him, but for that popularity. He might have the support to do such a thing."

"And what do you do now?"

"I surrender," Ali said. "There is no need for the rest of you to place your lives at risk protecting me any longer."

"You think we were doing it for you?" Wayne said. "Kid, you've got a lot to learn. The world doesn't revolve around your throne. We're running because we don't trust those murderous bastards."

"If they are hunting or fighting you, they will be more tense, more likely to overreact."

"They can sue me," Scotty said.

"I'm turning myself in."

"I don't work for you."

"My father abdicated!"

"He didn't cancel my contract, or was that part of the code words, too?"

Ali tried to puff himself out to be more threatening. "Yes, it was."

"Hands here?" Scotty asked. "Hands? Anyone believe that?"

"Please, help me," Ali said. "I want to turn myself in."

"They won't hurt you," Angelique said, gently now.

"But they might hurt you. And I couldn't stand that." His eyes widened. "I know. If we survive this, I will still be rich. Anyone who helps me turn myself in, I will give a hundred thousand New dollars."

Sharmela blinked. "Let me understand this. You want to bribe us to help you sacrifice yourself to save us. That is the craziest thing I've ever heard."

Prince Ali groaned, and sat, heavily. "You are all insane," he said.

Wayne ruffled Ali's tightly curled hair. "Yeah. Ain't it cool?"

"**Any answer**?" Shotz asked.

"Nothing, but . . ." Stavros frowned. "I'm getting a signal from the motor pool," he said, touching a finger to his ear. "A vehicle has been released from the northern bay."

Shotz froze, then turned his head almost as if it balanced on a pivot. "Is it heading toward us?"

"I can't see it, or track it." Stavros looked up. "I should see something, dammit. Either the monitor is malfunctioning, or . . ." His voice trailed off, brow furrowing.

Something was wrong. None of the Beehive's monitors indicated a problem, but Celeste was taking nothing for granted. She snatched the monitor from Stavros' hand. If he'd seen a Scorpion leave the northern bay, and then turn east or west, she might have relaxed. But instead she saw *nothing* on the monitor.

"Yes. The other hand is always possible. Alert alpha and bravo teams. And inform me if the situation changes."

The Scorpion had reached the Beehive's eastern edge, the dome's G level. The ten men and women fastened their own pressure suits, then checked each other's gear soberly. When the twelve-point survey was complete, each gave a "thumb's-up."

"We can't do this blind," Piering said into his microphone. "We need those deep-scans. Where are the hostiles?"

Kendra's voice was a welcome sound. "*Infrared shows them on E and F. Our people are on G.*"

"Couldn't be better. Is there any way to communicate with them?"

"*Not at the moment. But they've been told to hunker down.*"

"Then I think it's time." Piering clicked the com line off, and turned to his nine volunteers. "Let's move. Group A?"

The guy everyone called Gypsy stood first, five foot two of

pure flex-steel, and mean as a snake. The other five stood up after. Jankins, the miner, said "Good luck," and then joined Gypsy and the others in the airlock. Just before the door closed behind them, Piering said: "Take the Scorpion around to the next door. And . . . good luck."

Waiting for the lock to cycle to green felt like the longest minutes of his life. One of his compatriots, an ex-police officer named Chambers who had retired to Luna, spoke first.

"If the atmosphere is good . . . I mean if the dome still has integrity, do we shuck suits?"

"I don't think so," Piering said. "What if they depressurize the dome? It's their best threat. Remove that, and they might back down." He didn't like the unspoken possibility: That in the next minutes, every unsuited human being in that dome might die.

Kendra stood in the control center, examining the holographic model now shimmering on the stage.

"We've retasked the mining satellites," she said. "But I really didn't expect to have the images so quickly—or with such clarity."

"That," Xavier said, "is because you were not expecting me. Then again, how could you?" There was just enough self-mockery in his voice to take the edge off. A miniature gaming dome shimmered in the air before them like a floating crown. "I've created a map," Xavier said with a hint of real pride. "Mining deep-scans, some infrared information, reports from this Kowsnofski woman."

With a wave of his hand, the dome's outer skin peeled away. Tiny human figures in red and green were clustered in various bubbles. "Our best guess. We must accept that they've probably screwed with the inputs. I would. However, *if* the information is accurate, then our people are down *here*"—he indicated something near ground level—"and our antagonists are *here*." He indicated two levels up.

"That's good," Kendra said. "And that means that our best bet is to insert our people between . . . what did Angelique call them? Pirates? Fine. Pirates and gamers. At the very least, we slow them down. And maybe we stop them completely."

She took a closer look. The dome had seven public entrances and three service entrances. "We're assuming that they've mined some but not all of the entrances. Piering is going for door six."

Magique's fingers flurried with sign. Wu Lin watched, and then interpreted. "Why don't you think all of them were mined?"

"Because we know the pirates probably acquired their explosives here, and we've run inventory. About enough missing material to make four or five explosive devices. There is a very good chance that *here* on level C, where Asako Tabata's body was left, might still be clear. We can reach it up an access ladder from a service entrance on ground level G. We have no data suggesting that more entrances have been mined since the gamers broke free, and we have to assume that our gamers put a crimp in the pirates' plans. We'll split into two teams. One will go in at F, the other at C. And then we'll see what happens."

"We have *movement in the dome."* Kendra's voice in Piering's ear. *"Power surges."*

"Which doors?"

"Maintenance two and three."

"What about door seven?" Piering asked. He could smell the chicken sandwich he'd had for lunch, his own sour breath bouncing back at him from the faceplate. Nerves.

"Nothing so far. We picked up security camera blips, just after the attack went down. Look—they wouldn't be able to do everything at once, and when the gamers complicated things, it may have changed their focus."

"We'll find out in about sixty seconds," Piering said. "Let's get ready to move, people," he said, trying to shut the doubt out of his head. "We better have three 'esses' on our side: speed, silence and surprise."

"And serendipity," muttered Hazel Trout, the round woman from Communications.

"And shit-storm," Chambers said. "We'd better bring the pain."

The four heroes of group B opened the inner lock. The access ladder was only a meter away, and Piering grabbed a rung and began to climb.

It took about five minutes to crawl from ground level to C, and another minute to locate the correct maintenance doors. Piering punched in a code, and the door slid up. The first thing Piering saw in the lock was Asako Tabata's pod. It crowded the little room, so that they had to squeeze past, but none of the four rescuers could resist looking in through the polyglas lid. Her face was turned to the right side, pale and slightly bluish. He didn't know her, had never met her. But she seemed so small and vulnerable, so much like a sleeping child that his heart almost broke.

We'll get them for you, he thought. *Every one of the bastards.*

The airlock's inner door bore a single window, inch-thick composition plastic harder than glass and stronger than steel. And all he could see beyond it was an empty corridor.

"Unhook the door from the grid," he said, "and open it."

Chambers opened the inner panel, and slotted a handheld scanner into place. Piering watched as the guy manipulated glowing red and green lines, effectively isolating the door from the maintenance grid. If the pirates were monitoring, this might . . . *might* . . . bamboozle them.

He held his breath as the door slid open. No explosion.

Piering and his three partners stepped out onto a metal walkway. He motioned Hazel and Lee around to the right, while he and Chambers went left. The walkway curled around the inner wall, separating it from a maze of pipes, wiring and support struts. The microphone in his suit helmet picked up his own footfalls, and a mixture of small hollow machine sounds.

"Anything, Lee?"

Lee was a tall brunette from the tool and die workshops, a veteran of the Second Canadian War. *"Nothing so far. Hazel and I are on point. Can you find our gamers?"*

A map of the inner bubble layout played on his faceplate, a framework of intersecting green lines. The gamers' last known location was marked in red. Around the curve of the dome, and then in through a few rows of bubbles, then down a level. They just might make it. If they could find their targets, it might be possible to evacuate the gamers to the Scorpion, or at the least form a security wall between the innocent and the guilty . . . and then hang on for dear life until more help arrived.

His nail gun had an effective range of about a dozen meters. Beyond that they would tumble and act as dull projectiles, still capable of stinging but no longer lethal.

"Piering . . ." Lee whispered. *"I see something—"*

Red mist clouded Shotz' vision. He fought to keep it from swallowing logic, wished desperately to maintain perspective. He had known that Prince Ali Kikaya III could be grabbed. *Anyone* could be kidnapped or killed, given the appropriate resources and commitment. He had trusted that political pressure on Earth could control the security response. It had always been possible that the gamers might try to escape, but his soldiers had bottled them in the dome. Conceivably, even if their targets escaped, but remained within the dome, the political situation in Central Africa would not be negatively affected.

And now, in defiance of her own superiors, the Griffin woman was striking against them. Though it was invisible to their monitors, Douglas Frost had finally done something useful and spotted the Scorpion transport through one of the dome's few external windows. Shotz had positioned his people to protect the unmined doors. Pure strategy: Give your opponent an apparent entry point, bottle them there and set up a kill zone.

And then: Demonstrate the price of disobedience.

Two of his men were positioned at the dome's base level, with complementary fields of fire directed at different doors and maintenance ladders in the southern section of the dome. Others were positioned on levels C and E.

When he first glimpsed his adversaries, he cursed silently. *Damn!* They were wearing pressure suits. Well, of course they were, but frankly he hadn't factored that in when designing their assault and defensive gear back on Earth.

Celeste might be right: There was no way to deal with these problems if their highest priority was zero casualties. Celeste was often right.

That was one of the reasons he cared for her. He wouldn't call it love, exactly. Wasn't entirely certain he could actually feel that emotion. He considered it, and infatuation, and even sexual attraction to be snares. As he had used it to snare that silly little chocolate heiress in Switzerland—

There! A head popped back up for a moment. Someone was climbing the ladder. Shotz counted three and then pressed the wireless detonator. A sharp explosion and a shower of sparks from the ladder. A scream, and the climber tumbled down out of sight.

Shotz was scanning for their communications frequency, but so far had picked up nothing. Communications along a private, hidden frequency? Possibly.

He shifted position until he could see the shattered ladder and the three men clustered at the bottom, one still apparently stunned.

This was the moment. He raised his hand, motioning for Frost and Fujita to follow his lead. He aimed the air gun carefully, and pulled the trigger.

Piering heard the scream as the first explosion rocked the dome over around to his left, and a second howl of dismay a moment later, elongated as someone plunged a long distance, to a solid impact. Then . . . his external mike picked up a short, sharp explosion, and another scream.

Damn! Lee and Hazel had been discovered. "Get back," he screamed. They would try from the second ladder! If he failed, there were still his A team down on level F . . . if any of them had survived that first explosion. If he could even keep these bastards busy, that might be enough to give his compatriots a chance. The makeshift weapons put everyone on a more equal footing. These men were experts. Perhaps trained killers, but certainly willing to use violence. In comparison his own people, however well intended, were mere amateurs.

Moving farther left around the catwalk, he and Chambers reached a second ladder. Helmet infrared showed no one lurking around the edges, and visual failed to detect anything dangerous. Still, his heart thundered as he began to climb.

Piering got halfway up, then motioned the ex-cop to follow.

He reached the next level and crouched as much as the suit would allow him, cradling his nail gun, scanning the shadows. Nothing. Perhaps he could circle back around and help Lee and her people. "Lee?" he asked into the helmet. "What's happening over there?"

"*Hazel is down,*" she said. "*An arrow stuck in the suit, didn't rupture, thank God. But the explosion knocked out her visuals, damaged her faceplate.*"

"Stay where you are," he said. "But make noise. Make them think you're still an active threat."

He duck-walked into a shadow, pressed himself against the bulk of a compressor, peering around the corner trying to pierce the shadows.

Then . . . the second ladder exploded. A wall of light and air, followed a moment later by a high-pitched scream from Chambers. He knew what had happened: Their enemies had outthought them, split their forces rather than simply destroy access to the next level. Now he was stranded on C level, with the wounded Chambers isolated on F. Smart.

"Chambers. Are you all right?"

"*Damn! My faceplate cracked, and the sealant is clouding my vision. The explosion screwed up my suit balance somehow. I'm having trouble getting up.*"

He was being watched, and somehow the watchers had avoided his scans. With a *ping!* something struck his air cylinders, and swung him around. Damn! If those cylinders were damaged, he was completely—

A quick check of his indicators suggested that no such disaster had taken place. The pencil-thin red beam of a laser lanced through the murk.

"*Damn it!*" Chambers swore. "*Bastards!*"

"What?"

"*Ah, fall like that should have killed me. Tweaked my knee, too.*"

"Stay where you are. Snipe if you get the chance. Let's see—"

Another explosion, short and viciously sharp, and his suit doppler fixed it at a hundred meters distant. That would be his first team. "Gypsy!" he called. "What's the situation?"

"*We have snipers. Boss, we didn't blind 'em. They knew what we were doing. What do we do?*"

"Can you see any of them?"

"*May have blinded one. Not sure.*"

"All right. That's something. All right. I think that time is on our side. Take it easy—we'll have reinforcements, I hope. And meanwhile, our guests are safe."

Safe, perhaps, but not secure. The eight gamers were clustered in a bubble on G level. The ugly *thrum-thrum* of dual detonations echoed through the bubble's floor.

"What's happening?" Maud asked, clutching Mickey's hand. She seemed very frail.

"That's the cavalry," Mickey said.

"He might be right," Scotty said. "Assuming that Kendra took action—"

"Who is Kendra?" Sharmela asked.

"Chief of Operations of Heinlein. And . . . my ex."

Wayne cocked an eyebrow. "Family that plays together."

There was another sharp explosive *thrum*. Angelique sidled up to him. "Scotty. Where did our rescuers enter the dome?"

He shrugged. "Darla?"

"One of the ground-level entrances, I reckon."

"Could they have brought a vehicle with them? Is there any chance at all that we can exit the way they came in?"

"Maybe. If we had pressure suits we could just walk home. Unless the entrances are covered."

"What do you mean?"

"These people. The Moresnot pirates. They ain't even partial stupid. They'll have entrances covered."

"Can they cover all of them? They don't have enough people."

"Not all. But maybe enough."

"What can we do? Isn't there some way we can help?" Wayne asked.

"Stay out of their way," Scotty said, his voice brimming with a confidence he did not feel. "And let the professionals work."

We're the professionals, Shotz snarled to himself, ducking back as a bolt from some kind of air gun splattered against the wall next to him. It was off target, and even if it had hit, the wall was barely chipped by the impact. While it was certainly true that the pressure suits acted as elementary armor, his opponents weren't in a much better position.

There was a potential upside to the situation, which even now could hardly be considered a standoff. The positive possibility was that the gamers, in a misguided attempt to aid their rescuers or even escape, would reveal themselves. If the assaulting team were in contact with their prey (and he had a very real instinct that they were), then they might have entered the dome at their quarry's level, or above. Below? Perhaps, but Shotz and his people had searched levels A through F thoroughly, and found nothing. He was going to make a bet: their quarry was somewhere on G, planning to make their way down to the pool for an exit. Well, there was no exit there, and so long as he kept these incompetent fools bottled up, or sent them packing, all was well.

"Shotz!" a voice barked in his ear. It was Carlyle, covering the dome's northeast side. "We have action here. The ladder is down, but they managed to hit Bai Long with a laser, I think. Half-blinded him, dammit!"

"Pull him back. Don't expose yourself if you don't have to, and—"

And then, there was another explosion. Deeper this time, shaking the very flooring below him, followed by the frenzied shriek of an alarm. He had heard that alarm before, but this time, he didn't think it was a bluff.

"Piering?" Klaus Gruber whispered. Gruber was in Food Handling, but in a former life had been a sergeant in the European Union. Piering knew him a little. Once, Gruber and Lee had gotten into a friendly karaoke duel about "49th," the notorious ballad about the Second Canadian War. The thing about "49th" wasn't that it was particularly obscene. No worse than "Eskimo Nell," in all probability. But there were two entirely different sets of lyrics, one from each side of the border. And it was always dicey whether such duels would stay friendly or end with someone getting peeled off the ceiling.

That night there had been children at the club, and Gruber had held to the family-friendly lyrics, even in the part about Americans retreating in disgrace:

We kicked their butts in Montreal
It really was a sight
To see the G.I. Joes and Janes
Run naked through the night—

The referenced original incident had been a successful assault of what should have been a secured American base. The Canadians had been too busy laughing to bother rounding up the dozen soldiers who'd been showering when they attacked. Lee had been out-sung, but let Klaus buy her a beer after they were done.

"*We've got the southeast door disarmed.*"

"I told you," Piering said. "If the door is mined, don't mess with it."

"Yes," Gruber whispered. "*I know, I know. But we've really got a chance to get behind them, I think. I figured it out. They expect us to avoid the traps, and go through the open door. If we let them—*"

"Klaus, this isn't a game!"

"*We're so close,*" Klaus said. "*I've almost got—*"

And then there was a blast of static, so loud that Piering winced, staggered back against the wall in shock. The entire structure hummed with that blast. Then the alarm began to ring.

"*Inner wall breach,*" the automated voice screamed. "*Alert. Inner wall breach. Immediately seek shelter. The outer door of lock Northeast-G has been damaged. The seals will erode in approximately thirty seconds. Alert. Seek shelter immediately—*"

"Good God," Max Piering whispered, stunned. "We're screwed."

"**What the** hell?" Angelique said. Panic tightened her voice.

Scotty and Darla glanced at each other. "Alarm," she said. "And I'm betting that's the real thing."

"All right," Wayne said. "But what does it mean?"

"That there's been a breach," Scotty said. "And that the sensors are detecting an outer hull damage as well." He paused. "And that," he said, "is very bad news." He slapped his hand against the bubble wall, not at all comforted by the solid thump. "They say these things will hold a full atmosphere against vacuum. We're about to find out."

• • • **33** • • •

Love Lost

1527 hours

The air pressure at Earth sea level is approximately 14.7 pounds of pressure per square inch. The air in the gaming dome was held at a pressure closer to 10 pounds per square inch, still dense enough for easy breathing, close to the cabin pressure of a jetliner. The dome, roughly the diameter of a football field, held a volume of about 175,000 cubic meters of oxygen, imported nitrogen and helium left over from He3 mining.

When members of Piering's A team tried to avoid the ambush by exiting and reentering the dome through another lock, the air pressure had been stable. When Gruber's unfortunate mistake with the explosive device shattered the inner door and damaged the outer, it was as if the air was a living thing, seeking a path of exit, testing and pushing against the outer door as emergency blasts of Liquid Wall sought to heal the breaches before they became fatal.

But (and there is no way to put this delicately) there had been human beings in that airlock. When the inner door exploded, what remained of Gruber and Enroy was spread around the lock like a layer of lumpy raspberry jam and shredded pressure suit fabric. Nozzles that should have spread Liquid Wall evenly and swiftly were twisted by the blast, and jammed with human debris. Damage to the outer door became the weak point attracting every pressurized molecule of the oxygen-nitrogen-helium mix.

The crack deepened, and split, and the outer wall breached. Instantly, the airflow pushed against the opening, deepening, widening, and then ripping the door from the inside out.

The gaming dome became a screaming hell.

The warning klaxon was drowned out by the howl of air, and for the first time in her memory, Celeste panicked. Their men scrambled toward the open bubble above them, and Celeste screamed, her hands slipping on the ladder as she tried to climb in. Already, in mere seconds, the air was so thin that her lungs felt as if they were going to explode. Within moments, even if they made it into the bubble, it too would contain an atmosphere so thin that their lungs would hemorrhage no matter what they did.

She slid down the ladder, knocking Shotz back, furious at herself for losing focus. She fought to keep her head, vision swimming as she pulled herself up and into the bubble.

"Alexander!" she screamed. No one used Shotz' given name, ever. She had barely used it even in their intimate moments. But some part of her, looking back through the hatch where he was six rungs below her, knew that there was a last time for everything.

She couldn't breathe. She saw him struggling to lift himself, one agonizing rung at a time. She watched him stretch out his arm, hoping, and yet knowing hope was lost.

He grabbed the door, designed to close from inside so that air pressure would keep it sealed . . . and swung it closed on himself.

Celeste rolled over. She saw Thomas Frost reach the far door linking them to the next bubble, and turn the manual wheel to open it. When it opened, air from the next bubble blasted in like a bomb burst and sent him rolling.

The three of them flopped onto their backs, gasping like beached trout. She cursed her weakness, cursed the fear that coursed her veins like waves of lava. Cursed the shame she felt. Decades ago she had sworn that she would never allow herself to feel shame. She had been a child in war-torn Montreal, bereft of mother or father and forced to steal, and worse, just to survive. All gentleness had died within her then . . .

Until a man harder than the hate that sustained her had recruited her to a quixotic dream called Neutral Moresnot, a fantasy of creating their own nation. Somehow, this wild man had awakened a heart she had thought long dead.

She crawled up onto all fours, and staggered against the doorway, trying to peer down into the depths of the dome. Just machinery. She couldn't see the ladder, but knew that Shotz' strong hands no longer clutched at its rungs. Knew that somewhere far below them, he lay dead, blood foaming his nose and mouth. His hands, his loving hands would never again hold her. Touch her.

Celeste screamed, and screamed, until Fujita touched her shoulder, perhaps intending comfort. She wheeled, smashing him with a backhand. The sumo-sized Asian fell back, eyes wide, staring up at her as if viewing his own death.

She felt disconnected from herself, floating above her own head in some odd way. *Shock,* she recognized dimly, struggling for clarity. *I am in shock.*

She should have begun breathing deeply, slowing herself. Begun normalizing the systems now pumping overtime. But didn't. She embraced this floating sensation, and dreaded its retreat. Dreaded what would happen when she plunged back down into grief.

She heard her own voice: "Can we . . . get his body?"

Fujita shook his head, eyes still focused on her face. "No. We have no pressure suits. We can't open the door," he said. "I think it's over. The gamers could all be dead, Celeste. We need to—"

Shrieking, she lifted Fujita and slammed him into the wall. On Luna, the explosive uncoiling of her leashed rage and grief was almost enough to break bones.

She pushed her forearm against his neck, and Fujita struggled, barely able to breathe but afraid to fight back. He knew what would happen if he did.

"Shotz is dead," he whispered in graveled tones. "Everything is blown to hell. We don't know what to do—"

"Yes, he's dead," she said, the words ashes on her lips. "But I am alive. I am in charge now. This is all you need to know."

His eyes locked with hers. The entire world achieved an eerie clarity: She saw every vein, every imperfection in his irises. She knew his mind, knew that he wondered if she was still entirely sane.

She didn't know either. And frankly, she didn't much care.

*"**Jeee-zus,**"* Scotty whispered. Darla's eyes were wide as walls, arms folded tightly together. The other gamers were confused, startled, but none of them understood the enormity of what had just happened. No one who had spent time on Luna, or outside the protective envelope of Earth's atmosphere, who had ever been near a pressure seal failure, let alone an explosive decompression, could feel anything but terror at the sound of that klaxon.

He had seen the fleshy results of mine accidents, construction failures and ignorant tourists. It wasn't pretty: The human body is 60 percent water, and in vacuum, water boils.

"What happened?" Angelique asked.

"I'm not sure. Let's make a guess: The pirates mined the doors, and our rescuers triggered a mine." Scotty said.

"Damn," Wayne said. "That means—"

"That people died out there. Probably our people. We need to move. The Pirates might be shaken enough to slow them down."

"What if they aren't?"

Scotty thought about that for a moment. "Then I really, seriously doubt that they're in a good mood. We need to move. But only bubble to bubble now. No more moving in the in-betweens. There's no air out there anymore."

Fortunately, their path through the G-level bubbles down to H allowed them to move from one sealed environment to another. These were all unfurnished and unpainted Liquid Wall bubbles, none modified for gaming, most of them empty or crammed with crates. Every time Scotty opened a door, they tensed.

"Scotty?" Ali asked. "If the dome is breached, what then?"

"It depends on the size of the opening," Scotty said. They stood on a sealed catwalk, a bubble used primarily to connect two other bubbles. Here there were no windows, and the walls dampened sound. "If it's the size of your fist, the dome can heal itself. Some kind of threaded epoxy resin, I think. Larger than that, and if the mechs are operating, they will automatically try to fix it. Then there are work crews from Heinlein. I don't know what's going to happen here. We better assume we're on our own, though."

When they reached the next door, Scotty turned the manual wheel. It opened with a slight *hisss* that suggested the pressure level between bubbles wasn't equalized. The sound made his skin creep, and he was happy when his crew was all in, and they could seal the door behind them.

"This is 100-G," Darla said, dropping to her knees. "There should be an exit port to H level. From there . . . well, hold on to your butts, but Mama thinks we can take a shortcut to the end of the game."

"What was *supposed* to happen?" Wayne asked.

She narrowed her eyes. "That would be telling . . ." Then the absurdity of her reply struck her, and she sighed. "Oh, fudge it. There was loads of running and jumping and fighting and climbing. And you would have rescued Professor Cavor from the caves, and then struggled to reach the sphere. You know, the spaceship. And from there . . . Game over."

"So what do we face between here and the bottom?"

"I don't know everything . . ." Her fingers scratched at the floor, and then she made an *ah-hah* sound, opened her multitool and pried harder. A popping sound, and the white tile slid up, exposing a steel-plated maintenance door. "But keep your eyes open," she said. Her fingers found a ring and tugged, and the plate came up. Looking down she said: "Here we go!" and dropped down.

One at a time, they followed.

34

The Da Vinci Machines

1623 hours

The very first thing Scotty noticed was the moist, cool air against his cheeks. He realized that he had missed that over the last hours: The atmosphere throughout most of the dome and its bubbles had been fairly dry. This was different, and his pulse raced: There was open water nearby, perhaps within a few hundred meters. As Maud brought up the rear Scotty closed the door behind him, glaring at its insufficient lock. The inner side had been retrofitted with a turn-wheel that might have seemed at home on Captain Nemo's submarine. That, he thought, must have amused the engineers tremendously.

He twisted it back and forth, testing the mechanical works. Yes: The wheel was fully operative. Turning it engaged both bolts and bars. Fantastic, but he wanted more. He looked around for something to brace it with. The door opened onto a grilled metal pathway suspended across a suspiciously vast cavern. Most of the cavern was the sort of fused-wall lava bubble he'd seen and explored so often during his lunar tenure. But a hundred meters farther out the smooth surfaces were disrupted with jagged cone-shaped stalactites and stalagmites. More Dream Park magic, no doubt.

Discarded bits of equipment and material were strewn about. This chamber was meant to be some kind of a workshop. Scotty clawed through the conveniently tumbled debris until his fingers curled around a slender steel bar. He slid the bar into the wheel and tried to bend it. Failed.

Wayne, Angelique and Mickey stepped up to help. Angelique wrapped some of her shirt's beige fabric around her slender fingers to protect them. The others just grabbed and began to heave. With a slow groan, the bar bent until it was jammed in the spokes. When he tried to revolve the wheel, the bar thumped against part of the rock wall. And there it stuck.

Scotty rubbed his hands together, immensely satisfied. "Great." He turned to Mickey. "Find something heavy to prop against the door. In fact, just pile up everything you can drag. Should slow the pirates down."

Maud looked skeptical. "They'll just blow it open."

Scotty's answering laugh was ugly. "Considering their recent experience with vacuum, I'm hoping they might be a bit more . . . mindful."

Leaving Mickey to work on the door, Wayne and Angelique led the gamers across a narrow steel bridge through a labyrinth of unweathered rock, into a glittering cavern. The walls curled away into mist. A low fog hugged the ground and wreathed the walls.

Wayne looked up at the ceiling, whistled. "What is this? Stalactites? This looks strange." He squinted. "Why does this look strange?"

"That's because there aren't any stalactites or stalagmites on the Moon," Scotty said.

"Why?" Sharmela asked. "There are caves . . ."

"Beside the point, darlin'," Darla said. "Scotty's right. The caves are mostly volcanic. Sure as sugar weren't made by flowin' water."

Scotty nodded. "In all likelihood, there never *was* liquid water on the Moon. Ice crystals, yes. But this kind of natural formation is only caused by mineral-rich water dripping from the ceiling."

"Which means," Angelique agreed, "that this is more of Xavier's con. This is Wells' world. Everything operating as if the Moon had an atmosphere and flowing water. Living creatures."

The chamber glittered in the mist like a field of diamonds. They wandered through a forest of mushrooms, and a few caterpillar creatures that sat, unanimated, observing. Their faceted eyes witnessed without judgment or reaction. What would this chamber have been if the power was running, if all control lights were green? Would it have swarmed with life? Here and there a few critters shuffled in slow circles, trapped in an endless loop.

The pathway ended in a chasm at least thirty meters across. Scotty peeked down. A glowing river of red and black liquid rock oozed below, wafting sulfurous steam. Heat prickled his face. He laughed uncomfortably. "Are we sure that's just an effect?"

"Your lips to God's ears," Angelique said.

Maud peered down, her shoulders slumped. "And here . . . it ends. We end. We're finished." Shaking her head, she knelt down. "What are we supposed to do? Climb down? And then climb up again? I can't do that. How can they expect me to do this? Did they expect poor *Asako* to do that?" Scotty was sorry to see her this way: Maud seemed like a confused old woman. He preferred the old Maud, acid tongue and all.

"I'm not sure," Sharmela put as much comfort into her voice as possible. "But we'll work something out."

"There's *always* a way," Wayne said, and pointed across the divide. "Look: Notice that the far edge is lower than this one. I think that's a clue."

"Clues are good," Angelique said.

"I think that we need to pay attention to this."

Scotty knelt down, compared the levels. "It does raise some possibilities. If we could get a line across . . ."

"Look!" Ali screamed. "Over here!"

The boy was crouched over at the right side, near another collection of alien tools. At a flat area to the side, they found the carcasses of winged beetles, husks curled on their sides, the size of small children. Scotty looked more closely: Their membranous brown "wings" seemed suspiciously well preserved.

Next to the wings were strewn additional heaps of tools and

materials. This misty cave was a workshop of some kind, a place where busy (alien?) hands had constructed a pair of rickety-looking, skeletal man-shaped pallets with foot pedals and space for a prone human rider.

"Flying machines?" Scotty asked.

"Similar to Leonardo's designs. Reasonable that Cavor would have been familiar with them, and tried to replicate them here."

Scotty raised an eyebrow. "Here?"

Ali gave a wan smile. "Not real here. Game 'here.' You know."

Scotty swatted his head, tickled, and glad to feel a trace of amusement. "And that answers that. We're supposed to use these to cross the chasm."

"Without practice?" Maud whined, incredulous. "This is absurd! How could Xavier expect us to do this?"

Wayne crouched down and ran his hands over the device, checking the lines and pedals. "I'm going with Maud on this one. This is insane. How the hell are we supposed to figure this out? How much time were we supposed to have?"

"More than we've got, that's for sure." Angelique raised her hands. "All right. All right. We have to figure the IFGS signed off on this. You've never used one of these?"

"No," Wayne said. "I mean, the Da Vinci in Vegas has a tourist setup, virtual simulation of how unpowered human flight might feel."

"And you tried it?"

"Yeah, a couple of times," Wayne admitted. "But . . . naw, you've gotta be kidding me."

"That's all it might have taken for Xavier to get it past the board. Who else?"

Sharmela raised a plump brown hand. She looked uncomfortable. "I have glider experience. And have simulated flight hours." Her expression, momentarily brightened, dimmed once again. "The 2080 World's Fair in Ceylon had a winged gliding chamber, but I never went."

"That answers it then," Angelique said. "For what it's worth, I suspect we would have been able to contest this . . . if it was a game."

"Big if. I think we have bigger fish to fry," Scotty said.

"I have." A quiet, embarrassed voice. Ali's voice.

"You what?" Angelique asked.

"I have flown. Ceylon in eighty. Simulators. Wingsuits. It was a hobby for a while."

No one said a word until Wayne cleared his throat. "You again? You just happen to have *another* skill none of the rest of us possess?"

Ali's protest was weak. "I and Sharmela."

Angelique was having none of it. "Sharmela is a happenstance. You, on the other hand, are a pattern. I heard a line once: 'Once is happenstance. Twice is coincidence. The third time, it's enemy action.' I've overlooked this before, but you are leaning on my last nerve. What in the *hell* is going on?"

He stammered and stuttered. "I . . ."

Scotty took the boy's shoulders. Hard. "Ali. I don't know what other gamers' houses or rooms are like, but yours I've seen. The walls were covered in images, gear, games . . . and some of those images popped up in this little adventure. Now why is that?"

Ali tried to rebut. "We are being pursued! The bad people will be here soon. We do not have time for this!"

"Yes," Scotty said. "We have time." And he meant it, too. When it came to ferreting out the truth, they had all the time in the world.

"Ali. Your father invested heavily in the Heinlein dome. It looks very much as if the game was modified to make it easier for you. If that's true, if you were cheating . . . I don't know quite how to put it, but if there is anything you can tell me . . ."

Tears sparkled in the boy's eyes. "I should confess to cheating? It would end me!"

Scotty was incredulous. "End you? End *us*! This is real, Ali. People are dying. You're afraid of the IFGS? Screw the IFGS! You'd better be afraid of those killers following us!"

Angelique looked as if she wanted to murder him. "To hell with them, too. You'd better be afraid of *me*."

"Maybe it's more than that," Maud said. "*His* life was never at risk. They don't want to kill Ali, they want to ransom him. So to him, this whole thing is still just a game."

"That's not true!" he yelped.

Scotty shot him a warning glance. *Let her finish.*

"To us, it's life and death. Can you understand that?"

Ali paused, looking at the faces around him, tried to bluster, and then folded with a sigh. "I . . . have no direct knowledge. But in the months leading up to the game, my father's advisers took special notice of my hobbies. I noticed that they examined my drawings most carefully. Asked many questions about things that had previously held no interest to them."

Maud seemed to have calmed down a bit, assuming an almost grandmotherly air. "And then what happened, Ali?"

"Then I arrived here, and when the game began I saw many things that felt . . . familiar."

Angelique slapped his face, hard. "Just 'familiar'?"

"All right! All right," Ali said, collapsing into surrender. His eyes glittered, but more with tears than anger. "These Moon creatures, they're derived from my artwork. I didn't know what to do, what to think. I thought you would throw me out of the game."

Sharmela shook her head, dark curls jiggling. "And you didn't think to say anything once our lives were at risk?"

Moisture glittered at the corner of Ali's eye. "I've had no time to think. And when I did, I did not think it would make a difference."

They looked at him, skeptically.

"It is the truth!" Ali said. "I did not know, was not certain. You . . . you all came back for me. I trust you."

"But can we trust *you*? How was it done?" Angelique asked. "Are we supposed to believe that Xavier was bribed? Because frankly, I don't."

"Tricked," said Wayne. "Never mind, it's not important." He grinned. "Except to Xavier. He's not going to like this at all. Somehow, Ali's father gamed the Game Master. What did he think, Ali? Let you win the biggest game in history, you'd get bored and decide to grow up?"

Learn to run a kingdom, Scotty thought. But Ali was in torment. "Darla?" Scotty asked. "What do you know about these things? About flying."

"A scosh. Read some of the specs." She closed her eyes, as if reading the inside of her lids. "I know that the most important thing in any flight is control. What is it . . . ? Pitch, roll and yaw axis? You have to have all three in hand from the time you launch until you land."

"Stability augmentation system," Scotty said from memory, and she nodded enthusiastic agreement. "The thing has to be statically and dynamically stable around all three axes."

"So . . . ," Wayne said, seeming to grow fascinated despite himself. "We don't have a lot of thrust, but we do have an elevated surface."

"Look," Darla said. "We got to figure that they did all the calculations, and we have a pretty serious margin of error for sustained flight. In this place, muscles will produce power at greater than what they call 'minimum sink rate.' "

"I like the sound of that," Scotty said. "That lava might even give us a thermal!"

"Hell yes!" Angelique grinned, then sobered. "Wait a minute. That's not real lava." A pause. "At least, I don't think it is."

"Damn. I forgot," Scotty said. "Nix on the thermal."

"What about a safe landing?" Wayne asked.

Darla closed her eyes and concentrated. "We need a controlled energy loss. If there's a short runway you might use some kind of netting for absorption—"

"Like an aircraft carrier?" Scotty asked.

"Exactly like that. If you were going for some kind of sustained flight you'd want some redundancy built into the system, but this was supposed to be short and sweet." She ran her hands over the wiring, inspected the pulleys. At any distance it all looked jerry-rigged, but up close this was clearly the work of talented, sober artisans.

"It looks rickety for the camera, but trust me: This is first-class equipment. We can do this."

Scotty tried to visualize it. A flying machine with beetle

wings . . . the pilot would lie on a surface of leather over "wood," with his feet stretched behind him on pedals . . .

Yes, it could work. It damned well better. And there were two of the wooden cradles. Xavier expected the first flyer to crash.

"How are we going to do this?" Scotty asked.

Angelique squatted, drawing in the dust with her fingertip. "We have to assume that Xavier knew that Ali and Sharmela had flown before, and that that was how the IFGS approved this." On hands and knees, she looked down over the edge of the chasm into the flaming horror. "That smoke smells scary real."

"Too bad the effects are off here. I'd like to know what that bloody munchkin had in mind."

"Long way down," Scotty said.

"Probably not as deep as it looks," Angelique said. "A few of the holos are still working."

"What exactly do you think we're really dealing with?"

"Safety nets, masked with effects. No safety lines, I think . . . Foam stalactites on the ceilings . . . there may have been some kind of maglev device to take the sting off a fall."

Wayne nodded. "Remember that we're on the Moon. Falling just doesn't have as much energy, so safety isn't as stringent, I'd bet. I have no idea what Xavier must have said to Cowles, but I think he got his way. As usual."

"All right, Scotty," Angelique said. "What do you think?"

"That we have to go for it," he said. "Mickey, you and I will keep an eye on the door?"

"What about me?" Darla asked. "I'm not just a pretty face."

"Stay here. An engineer's mind will come in useful."

"Do what I can."

Mickey clasped her shoulder. "Keep an eye on Maud, will you? She seems a little shaky." Then to Scotty: "Let's go."

Ali and Sharmela were crawling over the flying machines, inspecting them inch by inch.

"So . . . ," Wayne said. "What do we have here?"

"Look," Darla said. "We've had limited human flight at Heinlein, and some of the larger domes." She glanced at Scotty.

"I think your lady Ms. Griffin was big into it. Mostly, though, it's just a little playtime in half-furnished domes. You know, before the liquid wall bubbles go in. The locals would gin up some hang-glider wings, and go at it. There've been a few flappers, but again, we just haven't had open areas large enough to really take advantage."

"Talked about it, though," Scotty remembered.

"Absolutely," Darla said. "I'm guessin' they were planning to follow up this game with some kind of tourist flight package."

"Should I feel comforted?" Ali asked.

Wayne donned an expression that he probably hoped would be comforting, but was actually a little creepy. "They wouldn't want a disaster first time out."

Sharmela ran her fingertips over the flying rig, judging. "So the foot pedals operate the wings," she said. "The arms guide them. The material looks pretty flimsy."

"Yeah," Darla said. "But try to tear it. Look a little closer. That's Falling Angels, the zero-gee facility. Nanothreaded graphene. Pure carbon. Spider silk is maybe twice as strong as steel. This stuff is about a hundred times stronger than that."

Angelique was examining the cave. Anything, anything in the environment might be usable. The walls were festooned with vines.

Ali stood up, walked along their side of the divide, judging. "Look at this. We have a long flat runway, and a glide path right across. *Practice room.*"

Wayne brightened. "Well, God bless the IFGS. Let's get this in position."

"I don't know about this," Maud said. "Even if they work, I can't do this."

"Can't what?" Wayne asked.

"I can't fly one of these."

He shrugged. "There are only two. They couldn't possibly expect us all to fly across."

"You're right," Angelique said.

"*Here* we are," Ali said, pulling "vines" down from the walls. "We have line." Rope, damned fine rope, and plenty of it.

They fussed over the rope while Sharmela stretched like a tabby cat.

Angelique nodded approval. Flexibility was going to be important. "Three of us have had some experience with winged flight. Two were purely virtual. Factor in fear of heights, perhaps, and it's really only reasonable for one of us to fly across this chasm."

"Then . . . why are there two sets?" Sharmela asked, looking up from an impressive downward dog. Fit/Fat for sure. She was bulky, but as flexible as a seal.

"Back up," Angelique said. "I'm not sure. But the others were supposed to create some kind of rope bridge."

"That could be done," Wayne said. "So . . . attach the rope to the end of a set of wings. Maybe the flyer's ankles. Someone flies across, anchors it to the far side, and then we're in business."

Maud shrank back. "I can't do that. I can't."

"Let's just wait," Wayne replied, "until we have things set up before we decide what we can or can't do, okay?"

The next five minutes were practice time. With two gamers providing each flyer initial momentum, Ali and Sharmela took their wings up and down the slope, as the rest watched the flapping and gliding. Sharmela had wonderful coordination, her foot pedaling and arms working perfectly in unison. But what they had to admit was that Ali, cheater or not, was simply better at this. His prior experience might well save their lives.

"All right," Angelique said. "Ali? We're going to give you the chance. Are you ready?"

"Yes," Ali replied.

"First time I've ever been happy to have a cheat on board. Anything else to tell us?"

"I have no idea what else my father's advisers had in mind," Ali said stiffly.

"Not the answer I was hoping for," Scotty said. "Too bad."

"Horses."

"You ride a horse?"

"I have won awards," Ali sniffed. "There should be horses in the game. We'll find them."

"Oh, we may have gone around them already." Scotty shrugged. "Let's do this."

"You'll need to fasten a line on the far end," Angelique said. "Show me your best knot."

Ali took a vine and looped it around and tightened it. A decent hitch knot. Angelique examined it, and handed it back. "Try this," she said, demonstrating. "Right over left, left over right, makes a reef knot both tidy and tight."

He obeyed.

"Again," she said.

Again he did as requested, and this time they passed the result around for comment. "Looks good," Wayne admitted.

"We need to glide this until he gets his momentum," Angelique said. "You and me, Sharmela."

The Sri Lankhan stepped up instantly. She gave Angelique an appreciative once-over. "Your legs are longer than mine. We will have to match paces."

As they practiced, Mickey jogged over, looking a bit weary. "I've piled about a half ton of junk against that door," he said. "If that doesn't work, I don't know what to do. Barricaded and barred . . . they'll need to blow it open."

"And probably have the explosives to do just that," Wayne said. "Get back over there and keep us posted."

Mickey glared at Wayne, but jogged back, bouncing as he went.

"What's happening here?" Scotty said.

Even under the circumstances, Wayne's smile was blissful. "Man's oldest dream."

Ali lay down in the frame again, and Scotty tied a vine rope to his left ankle. Ali worked the pedals and then his hand controls a few times. *Squeak, squeak . . .* When he wiggled, they did as well.

"Well," Scotty said, kneeling down beside him. "Some game, huh?"

Ali tried to smile. "I'm afraid you did not know what you were signing up for."

"I never do. Did any of us?" Scotty squeezed his shoulder.

"You want to be a hero, kid? This is your chance. Probably the best you'll ever have."

Ali nodded. At that moment, the boy looked so young and vulnerable Scotty's heart ached.

"This is your moment, then. Take it." They shook hands. "See you on the other side," Scotty said.

The women hoisted the contraption onto their shoulders, and braced. Angelique counted to three, and they sprinted down the slope, Sharmela's short legs taking three steps to every two of Angelique's, carrying Ali high . . . and then the winged craft was aloft.

Kendra spoke without turning from the screen. "Horses?"

"Horses. They're in there, too," Xavier said, and silently dared her to speak.

She didn't.

"Terrance Ivanovich Ladd," Xavier said. "Every book a best-seller."

"Sorry, I was watching the gamers," Kendra said. "Ali is about to fly. What about Ladd? I read his books, of course."

"Of course. Twenty years ago, he was the most celebrated English-language writer in the world. He wanted into my world. He wanted to write the Moon Maze Game with me. I'd have given up my smaller testicle, which is the right one. He was in love with an artist, January Prince. I couldn't contact this January Prince. Reclusive. Nobody's ever seen him, or her. I based my Moon folk on his sketches just to get Ladd."

"Prince, hmm?"

"I am such a fucking idiot," Xavier said. "I'd heard about Ladd's money problems, but never thought someone might be able to buy him. I just didn't think."

"He's launched!" Wu Lin called. "The Prince has launched!"

Ali was *flying*. On the Moon. For a moment, all thoughts of threat and risk were simply . . . gone. He soared and swooped between the stalactites, lips stretched in an endless grin, eyes bright with joy.

Below him, the lava boiled. A stench of sulfur clogged his nose. *One chance to do this. Get it right.* As he left the edge the flying machine hit a thermal, jumped up a hair, and he had to correct, skewing sideways. Ali pumped his feet madly, working his arms to stabilize again.

A moment of panic, and then he flexed his arms hard to regain control.

Flying. By all his ancestors, he was flying! He stretched his arms out, extending the wings, and embraced the wind. Then . . .

No! He had misjudged the distance. His left wing tip brushed a stalactite. The stalactite sprayed fragments, more like cork than rock. The flying machine skewed sideways, stabilizing just too late to make a safe landing. He crashed onto the edge of the far cliff, and teetered, beginning to slide back into the abyss. Ali clawed his way free, clinging as he slid down. The line tied to his left ankle flagged behind.

He didn't know what was real, and what was not. Whether the lava below him was mere effect, or actual boiling rock. Whether the stench of sulfur in his nose was genuine or fantastic. Nor did he think of cameras that might be streaming his struggle to Earth and beyond. All he knew was that he would not fall, would not tumble down into the glowing crevasse.

Would not.

A foot at a time, he clawed his way up. Gasping and panting, he found hand holds, pulled himself to safety even as the flying machine tumbled down and out of sight. And when he was secure, Ali rolled onto his back, face split by an absurdly silly grin. He had never imagined that air could smell so sweet. On the other side of the canyon, the gamers howled in joy.

Ali forced himself up and began to search, finally finding an anchor point for the rope vine. It wasn't hard. One of the stalagmites was tinged slightly silver, just enough to catch his attention. It was concrete, and anchored into rock. Strong enough. He fastened it, chanting his mnemonic to himself. "*Right over left, left over right, makes a reef knot both tidy and tight.*" His hands were shaking so hard that he tucked them into his armpits to calm them.

Tested the line again, and was satisfied. He walked back to the edge of the chasm, and waved.

"Well, all right!" Scotty said.

Wayne rigged a safety line around his waist, attached the loop to the rope, and grinned at Darla. "Give us a kiss, love."

She did so, pressing her hips against him as she did. Then Wayne winked at Angelique, jumped up and began to climb hand-over-hand across the divide.

Angelique smiled wanly, and the shorter, rounder woman winked at her.

Mickey came running up, wide-eyed. "Scotty. I heard something from the other side. I think the pirates are rattling the door."

"Not surprising," Scotty said. "They wouldn't flounder around forever. This rope is graded for a thousand kilograms. It'll hold us all at the same time. Get your asses up there."

Darla jumped up and began to shimmy across. Scotty, Mickey and Maud were last. "All right, beautiful. It's you and me now," Scotty said.

Maud shrank away. "I can't. I just can't."

"I'll go with you. We can do this. I swear."

"Maud," Mickey said. "You have to. I won't leave you here."

She could not be consoled. "I can't! I thought I could, but . . . it's just too much. There's just nothing left. I'm tired," she protested. "Let me stay here. They won't hurt me." She paused. "I'm just an old woman."

"Scotty," Mickey said. "Thank you for your offer. I think this is something I have to do myself."

"Are you absolutely sure?" Scotty asked.

"I'm absolutely sure."

"All right." Scotty left them to their devices, and stomped on the second machine's wings. The fabric would not tear, the glue did not give way, but finally the struts themselves bent until the device was useless. "Just in case," he said.

Scotty jumped up on the line, and began to haul himself across, hand-over-hand, a safety line on the rope. In lunar gravity, it was relatively easy. A moment of panic as his feet slipped on the far edge, and then he was across.

He looked back. Mickey and Maud were fastening themselves onto the line. "I can't look down!" Maud screamed.

"Then don't," Mickey said. Mickey roped himself together with Maud, and a safety line over the top. "Up we go, moppet."

Maud managed a smile. "Moppet," she whispered. "You haven't called me that in years."

"We're not done yet, love," he said, and kissed her. Maud threw her arms around his neck, and he began to hoist them both across. One pull at a time, grunting and groaning with every heroic effort.

Behind them: A sudden chuffing sound, followed by a dull *thung* as the barricaded door flew open and slammed back into the rock wall.

Maud screamed and lost her grip. Suddenly she dangled from Mickey supported only by her safety rope. He strained to cross as three men and a tall, broad blond woman burst through the door—the pirates arrived.

"Kill them!" Celeste's severe face distorted with rage.

Lying on his stomach, Scotty aimed back through gusts of lava stench, firing a bolt back across at the pirates. Some ineffective firing back and forth followed as Mickey and Maud struggled to cross the remaining distance.

Screaming, Maud climbed up the rope, holding on to Mickey's pants, which slid down so that he had to crook his knees to keep her from falling off.

Finally they made it to the far side, and climbed up, to the applause of gamers who pulled them behind fiberglass stalactites, and away.

Scotty pulled the line free of its mount as Frost began to climb across. A moment later, and the pirate might have plummeted into the crevasse. Instead, Frost thumped howling down onto rock. *Damn,* he thought, hoping that the traitor had at least separated a shoulder. Celeste watched him, radiating hatred. He just couldn't help it: Scotty gave her a little bow, then turned and fled.

Celeste balanced at the lip of the gorge, her eyes blazing, fists clenched.

"How do we get across?" Frost asked, rubbing his wounded shoulder.

With a palpable effort of will she tore her eyes from the far side, investigating the walls, the ceiling, the gap. "Was this part of the game?" she asked. "How much of this is real?"

"Look at the weird equipment," he said. "The big insects. Yes, I'd say game. Most of it."

"Have you seen flowing lava?" She snarled it, tense as an angry mandrill.

"No, but . . ." He finally understood her body language, the tone of her voice and her expression.

"Yes," she said. "'Oh.' Get me a rope. I'm going down there."

Fujita and Miller glanced at each other. The huge man scratched his bald head, nervously. "With all the illusions," Fujita said, "we must be careful. Once we begin to disregard what we see and hear . . . we become vulnerable to ambush."

If there had been real lava in the chasm, her expression would have frozen it. "If you have no use for your balls," she said, "I'll just take them now."

The big man broke eye contact, muttered something inaudible and stepped aside.

35

Little Wars

1646 hours

Mickey crouched, hugging his knee, moaning and muttering as he rocked. Scotty said, "You don't kick a door down on the Moon. We build 'em strong."

"I felt it give, just a little." Mickey looked up, suddenly hopeful. "Maybe both of us?"

What the hell. But there was only room for two. "Rest the knee. I've got this." Scotty motioned to Wayne. The two men braced themselves and charged the portal, and rammed through, spilling onto their bellies in close-mown grass that didn't smell like grass, or anything else.

A shadowed mansion loomed above them, edged by blue sky. Rows of meticulously manicured hedges, enhanced by life-sized statues of animals, nymphs and men in heroic poses. An English countryside estate?

Angelique caught herself mugging astonishment, audience always in mind. The others were more sensible, or quicker. They fanned out and took cover behind solid-looking concrete sculptures. Scotty's hand whacked a Chinese dolphin experimentally: foam plastic. "Not good cover," he barked. "We need to get inside. I'll lead."

Nobody said, *"It could be a trap."* Scotty bent low and ran for the huge front door—which stood open, very trap-like. He slid in on his belly, rolled right, and looked.

High ceiling, high enough to make him feel like a child. Floor made of . . . cork? No clear targets.

Light glowed only in this nearer region. They had entered a vast playroom, dotted with chairs and card tables and bureaus pulled against the walls under a facing pair of big, ornately framed mirrors. Wooden blocks had been shaped into miniature castles, public buildings, row houses. Dowels for chimneys. Cardboard had become walls and bridges. A waterfall drawn in blue chalk plunged down one wall and became a river, growing wide, until it was a rapids running in blue-and-white stream lines around pale rocks. Clumps of leaves and twigs were arrayed into a miniature forest. Nothing moved.

Beyond the play area blackness loomed.

"It's some kind of kid's game. I don't see a threat," Scotty called.

Angelique eeled in and rolled left. Then Ali, Wayne, Sharmela, Darla. Maud followed, leaning on Mickey. Wayne was trying to work a "detect danger," but there weren't any signals from the Game Master's control suite. "We're on our own," he said, "but there's power—"

"Look at this," Ali said. He was on the floor some distance in, playing with a toy cannon a foot long. He triggered something. A light foam projectile flew from the cannon to impact a foot-high toy soldier, which rolled away.

No. *Crawled* away. In the shadows, Scotty had assumed the soldier shapes were carved wood, or ivory. Now he saw that they were grubs, infant versions of the mooncows, balanced absurdly on their tails and waiting for instruction. Their tiny limbs twitched. Their eyes rolled in endless loops.

"What in the world is this?" Angelique asked.

"At first I thought it was lawn chess, with living pawns and pieces," Ali replied. "But now I don't think so. This is part of Wells' world. It's from a pair of pamphlets called 'Little Wars' and 'Floor Games.'" He lined up another target. The projectiles were little wooden cylinders; the gun was spring-loaded. There were several scattered about the floor, clustered like opposing artillery. He fired into a rank of frozen grubs and when the soft projectile struck they skittered away in different directions, then regrouped and looked at the gamers, their faceted eyes some-how . . . hopeful.

Alien children playing toy soldiers.

"'Floor Games'?" Wayne asked. "What in the world is *that*?"

"H. G. Wells," Maud gasped. "Tracts on gaming. Little-known, but legitimate canon."

Ali rolled over and spoke rapidly. "I'm sorry to admit this may be more of my father's doing. I have played a version of 'Little Wars' on many occasions." He sighed.

"Regrets later," Scotty said. "Right now, Daddy's perfidy might save our butts. Give it up."

"H. G. Wells invented tabletop war gaming with tin soldiers and spring cannons. He laid out systems of rules that were used for a good century. Blocks to make toy buildings. Coin flips, at first, to win hand to hand conflicts—"

"Ali! Lose the history lesson and tell us how we use this."

"Well . . ." The grubs were lined up in three armies, like three different sides of a triangle. While all were the infantile insectoid forms they had seen previously, those directly in front of them were gussied up in little British uniforms. Those across the way were relatively uncostumed, and those to the right, amid toy tri-pod Martian walkers, had a vaguely Lovecraftian appearance.

The Selenite soldiers carried slender insects with wasplike hindquarters. In place of artillery stood rows of potato bug–looking critters, their butts turned up in the air. Coils of glowing intestines within transparent bodies, they resembled fancy little Christmas tree ornaments. Living energy weapons, perhaps? Surely, in the game Xavier had planned for them, all this would have been explained by now.

How to make it all go? The grubs mewled and crawled in little circles, then returned to their original positions. Awaiting instruc-tion.

Wayne's eyes lit up. "All right. This is the same biological tech we've seen all over the hive. Living chess pieces, and a nice plush chair here. I'm thinking Cavor sat *here*."

"And how did he control the game?"

Wayne shrugged. "Charisma. Language skills. I don't know. And it doesn't matter. We have psychics. If this game module is programmed for independent action, I would bet that . . ." He turned and looked Maud dead in the eye. "We have someone just about perfect for this adventure."

"M-me?" Maud asked. She struggled not to stutter. "Maybe Mickey—" She grasped at his arm as if holding on for dear life.

Politely but firmly, he peeled her hands away. "I don't know 'Little Wars,' love," he said. "I think you really are the expert this time."

"I don't have time to learn," she said, eyes gleaming with fear . . . but something else, too. Eagerness? "We'd have to play it first," Maud said. "Think there is an instructional program built into this?"

"Meanwhile," Sharmela said tartly, "we're being hunted by armed killers. Madame Deceased Guide, is there an easy way through here? Or around? The real game is to get down to the aquifer."

Darla frowned. "I haven't seen this place. The lights are on, so we've got power. No communication. It'll be on automatic. Between the bubble rooms it's still vacuum until we get down into the aquifer. We're going to have to game our way through."

Angelique said, "We would have had a meal and rest break here, I think. Fat chance of that now."

Scotty said, "The pirates can't fly. They couldn't have trained on the Moon, and I broke their wings. I'd say we have an hour, maybe a little more. We can do this, people. Look—this was almost the end of the overall game, wasn't it?"

Angelique nodded. "Probably."

"And do things accelerate toward the end? Or do they slow down?"

"Accelerate. More betting, more monsters, usually bigger special effects."

"And this is relatively sedate." He waved at the lawn, the mansion, the statuary.

Wayne seemed to catch his meaning. "This is a pause, a breather before Xavier hits us with whatever he's got at the very end. It'll be pretty straightforward. Actual play, usually combat, as opposed to running in circles trying to figure things out. That would be frustrating for the viewers as well as us. So assuming that we have the right resources, we should be able to just . . . play the damned game."

He crouched down. "Look. We're not going to have to read some friggin' book. Wouldn't *that* be exciting to watch? I'd say that game time would be no longer than we've got right now in 'real' time."

"So . . . ," Ali said thoughtfully. "We're supposed to be able to figure it out pretty quickly."

"Right. So look. What is this game? What is it that all war games do?"

"Simulate wars," Angelique said.

"That's right. Whether you're talking football, or chess, or RPGs, there is"—he started ticking off points on his fingers— "territory to be taken, people to be captured or killed, perhaps a King or Queen to be neutralized. Tactics and strategy. Individual and group action. Defenses to be degraded, and weaponry to be destroyed or taken. The rules are just to simulate the structure or chaos of a military campaign, and allow a conclusion within some agreed-upon framework of time and location, you see?"

A thread of excitement was worming through the group, but Scotty couldn't let himself get swept up in it. "Listen: Moresnot may be an hour crossing that gap, but we still need to set a guard. That's me, I think." He waited for a nod from Angelique, then slithered out the front door.

Mickey said, "Maud and I'll take the Earth army. The Brits."

"I'm not sure there's another choice," Angelique said. The chair on the Lunar side held a grub that looked annoyingly like the caterpillar from *Alice in Wonderland*.

The Martian chair was filled with another young Selenite,

wearing some kind of partial facemask with antennae and pincers more mollusk than insectile.

"I'm betting that this is straightforward: Our psychic sits, and the game begins. Shall we give it a try?"

Maud sat. Instantly, a gigantic head and shoulders appeared above the field. It was human, white, male, bearded. And spoke in thunder.

"I am Dr. Claud Eustuce Cavor. I have been on the Moon for twenty years. The Selenite Queen has entrusted me with some of the guidance of her children, over two hundred of them. I designed this place at her command."

Scotty was studying the floating head carefully. "I know him," he whispered. "Another Lunie, name of Piering. So he was supposed to be Professor Cavor? Geez, he must be pissed."

"Shhh!" Angelique said, waving her hand angrily.

"I have never seen an attack by Martians, but I am assured that such has happened, and that the weaponry we have given them in this game accurately represents reality. So do the Selenites' weapons and various troops, of course, and I've imitated our own cannon and transport and other devices as best I can.

"I ask you to be gentle with our young grubs, and to remember that the nurturance of tomorrow's leaders is today's greatest responsibility."

Maud wiggled to find a more comfortable position in the chair, wincing as the helmet embraced her head. An instant later, the grubs "playing" game pieces commenced moving with purpose and apparent consciousness, shaking themselves and stretching as if from a prolonged slumber.

"How shall we begin our attack?" she asked. Her hands twisted in air, as if seeking control levers.

"Let's try shelling the village," Wayne said. "Soften them up a little."

And she set herself to it.

"All right. Ah . . . burn down those villages."

A thin current of moist air wafted through the room, but nothing else happened.

"It's broken?" Scotty asked.

Wayne snapped his fingers. "The autopilot thinks you aren't gaming hard enough. Rhyme it, Maud."

She looked at Wayne as if he must be mad, but then laughed. With a level of theatricality she had not displayed in hours, Maud touched the tips of her fingers to her temples, and fluttered her eyelids closed.

"Children of Luna," she whispered, "fulfill my desire. Use your strength and rain down fire!"

Their team's little grubs mouthed the trigger strings controlling the cannons. The cannons roared, arcs of fire blazed above the field, and cannonballs the approximate size and heft of marshmallows sailed into the complex of buildings representing Luna.

With a fiery *whoof* they splintered or collapsed. Cannons on the lunar side popped, and some of the Earther buildings exploded.

Then the Martians weighed in, sending fire at either side, and the war was on.

Scotty set himself behind a foam pillar, wishing he had a better weapon than the crossbow. What he heard from inside the mansion drifted to him in bits of talk, incomprehensible.

The bubble wasn't as big as it looked. The far landscape was hologram wallpaper, slick to the touch. Scotty prowled, looking for other doors. Nothing. Any exits must be within the mockup mansion—which wasn't all there either.

Someone had to guard . . . but could Moresnot come through inside the mansion? The gamers would be shredded. Shouldn't he be guarding Ali directly?

Twenty minutes had passed . . . and there was Wayne, taking too little care for cover while he looked for enemies. Scotty whistled from behind a tall brick-like chimney.

Wayne looked up. "How did you get up there?"

Scotty gestured around and up and over. "It's not all that steep."

"I relieve you," Wayne said. "I took my shot. Earth lost. Mars and the Moon are still fighting."

Sharmela was examining the game environs, perhaps measuring lines of sight.

"I think I see what the problem is," she said finally. Her brown curls bounced as she nodded to herself. "We wasted shells hitting these buildings, but we've already seen that the Selenites are primarily an underground society. So there isn't anything really valuable here."

"So . . . ?"

"So the Martians have been dealing with the Selenites a lot longer than we have. I think they're strong enough to kick lunar butt, and the Selenites know it. So . . . they win against Luna, then invade us and die from germs?"

The plan seemed reasonable. Earth declined to engage as Mars attacked Luna, waiting until much of the destruction was already complete. Then and only then they joined the attack. The "floor" beneath the game seemed to open up, and smoke poured out: The Selenite society was destroyed.

But instead of the Martians sending walkers to invade Earth, they launched their assault from a distance, until the buildings were knocked apart, the grubs had retreated to safety, and all the little pieces scattered.

Maud groaned and said: "So to save us grief and pain, I beg you to begin again!" The battlefield shimmered and was whole: all holograms.

Just in case they had accidentally done the right thing, Maud looked around, hoping a door might open . . .

Nothing.

"Damn!" Mickey said, and slunk away, defeated. "I'll take guard."

Ali advised Maud next, and his attempt at a pincer assault came to no better a conclusion.

Scotty came in to find the boy in depression. "The Selenites split their army. I thought it was a mistake, but they ran a pincer on us. Chewed us up. When we got our cavalry as far as the left wall, the rest of the room lit up." Ali gestured into a cratered moonscape. "Now we're trying to figure this next part. We still have three sides, don't we?"

"Martians *there*. Wells' Martian tripod walkers and some big brained wrinkled critters. Selenites *there,* including a few we haven't seen before. And those soldiers with us are human. Cavor himself must have played those."

It was a roughly triangular distribution of troops. Three "front lines," with a "no-man's-land" in the middle, and battles along adjoining sides.

"I wish we had more time," Wayne said.

Angelique said, "Yeah. And while you're at it, butter brickle ice cream. Scotty, any suggestions?"

"Double cappuccino, one sugar. There *must* be a way . . ."

"No," Darla said. "There doesn't. This game could be dead. It might not know what to do, and we're just burnin' time. We could play this and never win. Or win, and it won't make a lick of difference—we're just waiting for the pirates to catch up with us."

After watching the others flail about, Angelique had decided to try her hand.

East, by Angelique's ornate compass, was the front door. And East was several ranks of grubs balanced elegantly on thick tails, dressed as British soldiers equipped with rifles and cannon, wagons, a railroad, and a steamship docked on the river.

South: Martian war tripods and other machines, and four spacecraft each built like a diseased potato with a hatch open at the nose. As the Martians marched onto the field, more emerged from the hatches.

North: A variety of creatures, all of the basic lunar insectoid design. They moved onto the field with various gaits.

West was unoccupied.

East: Maud got some soldiers moving in blocks, Angelique advising from the sides.

This time, they detected a weakness in the Martian war formation, a hesitation to engage they were able to exploit. Toy cannon roared, knocking down toy machines. When the hullabaloo was over . . . no door opened.

"Back to square one," Angelique said in disgust.

Ali's turn.

South: The Martian war machines were on the move. North: Four Lunie insectoids of varying shapes put their heads together and babbled in high-pitched gibberish, then set some much bigger creatures moving. Under Maud's control, the humans declined engagement. The alien armies converged, fought, swarmed, died. Then all suddenly froze, and—

Reset.

Again and again the armies clashed, with Earth getting the worst of it until, by careful observation, flaws in the defense of Martian and Selenite became clearer.

Slowly, the Martians were driven back, Angelique directing their forces via the mystical Maud. Driving them back opened no door, but grubs toted new, shiny toys out of the darkness, and placed them among the ranks of Earth's defenders.

"What is that?" Sharmela asked, pointing.

"I think we won something," Wayne said. "This is different. We must have done something right."

"Maybe . . . ," Darla offered, "we captured Martian war machines, took 'em apart and learned their stuff?"

"That would be something Cavor might think of, yes. A lesson for the Selenites."

And now they were in the right position: Thundering pellets at both Mars and Moon, until their enemies were a smoking ruin. They heard a low, thrumming sound, like some ancient machinery stirring slowly to life . . .

And then nothing.

"Dammit!" Angelique shrieked. "We won, dammit! We won! What in the hell are we supposed to do?"

Mickey came in. "I've been hearing sounds. I think that the pirates are working at the blocked door. What do we do?"

"Stay here," Scotty said.

"He screwed us!" Wayne snarled. "Xavier snuck something past the IFGS, and we are frickin' dead. We're going to die, because he's pissed at me."

"Ah . . . why is he especially upset with you?" Scotty asked. "Anything we should know about?"

"He thinks I narked on him a long time ago."

"And did you?"

"I'm not going to dignify that," Wayne said.

"And you didn't bet on the game, either, right?" No answer.

Scotty hopped down, looked at the game. It all seemed like a confusion of cast-iron pieces to him. Even though some of the pieces curled and crawled in aimless circles, seeking direction, they had run out of ideas. Earth had lost. Earth had pulled a draw. Earth had beaten Mars and stalemated Luna. Earth had beaten both Mars and Luna.

And no door had opened.

Frustration and fear were wrestling for control of his stomach. Could this really be it? If the pirates got through that door . . . and they would . . . the gamers were trapped here, and in a straight-up fight, they hadn't a prayer.

But a last stand was better than no stand at all.

"Drag that topiary over next to the front door," he shouted.

"The stuff is just foam. It won't stop them."

"If they blow the door, it might cushion the explosion. Listen," he said. "They want Ali. The rest of you were just following my orders."

"And why would I follow your orders?" Angelique snapped.

Scotty drew close, and said in a quiet voice: "Tell them that I swore I'd beat the shit out of you if you didn't. They'll believe you."

Her eyes narrowed. "Is that a—"

"I'm trying to save your life, lady. Let it go."

Her mouth worked a few times without producing words. Then she broke eye contact.

Ali clutched at him. The boy's eyes were frantic. "No!" he said, voice husky with fear. "I don't want you to—"

"I'm in charge," Scotty said.

"You . . ." Ali looked down. "The woman Celeste is insane. They will kill you."

Scotty took Ali's small hands in his own rough ones. "That's the job," he said, forcing his voice into a calm that he did not feel.

"You . . ." Ali's eyes misted. "You . . ." Words failed him.

But Maud had found her voice. "Listen up," she said, a spark of new excitement in her voice. "I may have figured something out."

"What?" Angelique asked.

"I'm starting with the assumption that there is a solution to this, one that makes sense in context." She sounded like a British schoolmarm. "The IFGS simply wouldn't have let that dreadful Xavier back us into a corner without a way out."

"All right . . ."

"Follow me. We went about this all wrong. This is a teaching game . . . for Selenites. That means that the lesson to be learned is for *them*. We can't win by beating them, you see? We tried that."

"What else is there?"

"Join them. The point of the game was of desperate importance to Cavor. Remember what he said? 'Teach the young generation the rules they will need to thrive.' *New* rules. For a new time—a time of human-Selenite cooperation."

She paused, hands spread a little, eyes wide and mouth open in a smile, as if waiting for them to catch up with her.

And then, Angelique said it: "Truce?" She blinked. "Maud, you are either brilliant, or an idiot."

"May I offer an opinion?" Mickey asked.

"When pigs fly," Maud said. "Come on. Let's be idiots, shall we?"

It looked as absurd as it felt. After requesting "reset" again, scouts from the army of Earth approached the Selenites with little white flags attached to their muskets, around the left side of no-man's-land, as far from the Martians as possible.

They stood there, at Maud's direction. There was nothing to be done but wait: Only the Earth forces moved at human command.

But at last, something happened: A caterpillar humped out

from the lunar side, a white flag attached to one of its drooping antennae. Xavier's idea of a joke, no doubt. Human and insectoid confabbed for a few seconds, and then the worm humped back to its own ranks.

"What?" Ali asked. "What is happening?"

Maud's expression was serene, for the first time in the entire game, she seemed to be in control. "Watch," she said.

She concentrated, waving her hands in arcane patterns, and the Earth forces turned toward the Martians, attacking with all force, and exposing their flank to the Selenites.

The Selenites did not betray them. Instead, they attacked the Martian forces it had lured into a ground assault, obliterating them, trusting Earth to protect them from the longe-range Martian response.

But the war machines had their mechanical hands full. Upgraded human defenses hammered at them, and grubs wearing little spaceship hats humped across the no-man's-land and struck at the Martian home base.

The Martians broke, and Earth forces harried them home, inflicting terrible casualties.

The gamers were transfixed, panting as if they'd hiked a hill. The small war game was motionless . . . and then . . .

"We won. Where's the door? Dammit!" cried Angelique.

"There," Scotty said. He jogged back to the entrance. One of the mirrors was ajar. He swung it wide open. He knelt, as gamers crowded around him. "It's a ramp. Steep." He put his hand flat on a darkly shining surface. "Slippery. In fact . . . frictionless. We're in for a ride."

Angelique said, "Wayne, take point. Scotty, you go last, and facing backward. You get the crossbow. Everybody, hang on to your weapons! They could be right behind us. Ready?"

Wayne slid smoothly into the dark opening, air gun in hand. Angelique followed, and the rest, in haste.

36

The Moon Pool

1821 hours

Wayne dropped, cradling his crossbow in his arms, alert as if something very real and dangerous might be waiting for them. The tilted, twisted floor was very slick, but friction heat was still building up under his butt and shoulderblades.

He hit the water hard, and sank deep. Kicked away and leftward as Angelique dropped in behind him. The water was tepid. Not salty, but something . . . spent gunpowder? A taste of moondust.

His head broke the surface and he scooped water off his eyes and mouth, and looked around him quick.

The pool was a circle of Olympic size . . . a hemisphere, in fact, very deep in the center. A ledge ran all the way round under a tremendous volume of rock cave. The slide had dropped them near the middle of the pool.

"Get to the edge!" he cried. "If we're standing and they're floating, we can shoot them like sitting ducks!" He started swimming like mad.

Angelique popped up behind him. Others were following.

How much was real? This stone ledge, at least. It seemed to run all the way around, making a perfect swimming pool. Wayne heaved himself out. Water came with him, a sheath that drained slowly in lunar gravity.

The cavern was bathed in blue, a restless wave of azure light washing across the floors and ceiling. The entire room was gray unweathered rock. He was stunned by the size . . . until Wayne realized that it simply *couldn't* be this large. It was larger than the largest caverns on Earth, with stalactites the size of Moon missiles depending from a ceiling high enough to shelter clouds. To the sides . . . well, there were no limits to the sides, so far as he could see. The room's light dwindled away to shadows long before it revealed walls. Just . . . rock. Spars of rock like jagged teeth, broken jaws grinning and gaping at them in all directions.

How much was illusion?

"Nervous?" Angelique heaved herself clear. Her crooked little smile had never seemed so endearing to him. She had watched him with Darla. Angelique had set the rules, from the very beginning. Had she come to regret them?

He turned to her. The others were still far enough behind that they had a moment of privacy. "Angelique," he said. "Look. Whatever happens now . . . whatever happens in there, I just wanted to say . . . thank you."

She seemed genuinely startled by this. "For what?"

"For the best game anyone ever played," he said.

Their eyes held each other for a long time, and then she cupped his cheek in her hand. "Let's play this out, partner. Time for good-byes later."

"Not always," he said.

A narrow rock path led up into gloom. The pirates of Neutral Moresnot must have exited the pool and entered the dome from here.

"Wow," Ali said, rising from the water, Scotty Griffin close behind.

The pool shimmered with a deep and lovely blue light radiating up from the depths. Echoes sent wavelet sounds from every direction.

"I see something," Maud said. And made a magical gesture

with her hand. Her face blossomed into a bright, wide smile such as she had not displayed for at least twenty horrific hours. "The magic is working!"

"Holy shit!" Scotty said. Then paused. "That's good, right?"

"When the gods are awake, please refrain from blaspheming," Margie said piously.

Mickey waved them over to the left side, where, hidden in a tumble of rocks, they found strange-looking tumbles of steel cylinders and leather straps. It looked like a cross between traditional rebreather gear and a conch shell. And it was ruined, smashed and bent.

"What is this?" Wayne said, lifting one so that he could examine it more closely.

Scotty pulled it from his hands and examined it himself. "Well, under the plastic I think we have a local version of standard Euro Union search-and-rescue gear. The pirates found it before us, and trashed it." He looked up. "Nobody's using this."

"All right . . . but what does that mean?"

"It means," Angelique said, frowning, "that the way out of here is down through the pool. This gear was supposed to get us out of here. That's why they made sure we were all certified with rebreathers." She paused, pinched face reflecting a painful thought. "And why Asako's pod was airtight."

"What now?"

"Now . . ." Angelique pushed the red button on her belt, twice. The air above them rippled, and a visual field tried to focus. They breathed a collective sigh of relief. They seemed to have come out of a long, long shadow.

Xavier's pinched face appeared on the field in front and above them. And for the first time that Wayne remembered, the little guy actually seemed rattled and relieved. "Angelique!" he said. "I . . . I wasn't at all sure this would work."

"What exactly is going on?" she said. "What do we do?"

"Look," Xavier said. "Neutral Moresnot—"

"The pirates."

"The pirates scrambled our communications, as you know.

And they knocked out most of the control mechanisms. But the aquifer's on a different grid from the rest of the dome, and they weren't able to kill it."

"That might come in useful," Wayne said. "We've got full effects?"

"I've run all the diagnostics I can from here, but you'll need to tell me what you think."

"There's no time for that right now. How do we get out of here?"

"There's only one way—down through the pool."

"Under water? Are you mad?" Maud asked.

"Opinions differ. But you can't even do that. According to Kendra, the door is mined."

"Mined?" Maud again. To her credit, she wasn't whining.

"Makes sense," Scotty said. "They've thought of everything. And it gets worse, Xavier—"

Scotty's expression reminded Wayne of something from a cheesy version of the *Ten Commandments,* Moses staring up into a talking cloud rather than down into a burning bush.

"They've destroyed the rebreather gear. Even if the door was unlocked—"

"Despite any personal antipathy, we would have come to get you," Xavier said. "Listen. We have rescue on the other side of that door. If you can find a way to defuse a booby-trap, we can open it. Wait—"

There followed a momentary pause, while the visual field blanked out. Then another face appeared. Dark hair, strong cheekbones, Polynesian eyes. A far prettier face, far more welcome.

"Kendra!" Scotty said, and Wayne could hear the naked relief in the big man's voice.

"Scotty." Whatever their history might have been, the affection in her voice was clear. Dammit, he wanted that for himself. If there was nothing else this adventure had taught Wayne, it was that he wanted someone to care like *that.*

Darla?

She was close behind him, and her hand stole into his. He pressed it.

"Scotty," Kendra continued. "Piering and a rescue team are down in the tunnel, on the far side of the airlock. If you can disarm the bomb, they can get in. What do you think?" Her smile looked just a little desperate and sick. "Could bomb disposal be part of that wild, wide, wonderful training of yours?"

"Ah . . ." Scotty looked a little scared, and Wayne saw that the answer was no.

Darla raised her hand. "Listen. If this bomb is like everything else, it was jerry-rigged. Can't be terribly sophisticated."

"If it was made here, then . . ." Kendra's eyes closed for a moment. "Maybe I have someone who can tell us what we need. Give me ten minutes, will you?"

"If we can."

"I'll get right back."

The air in Toby McCauley's holding room was stifling, almost as if it had gelled thick with fear. When Kendra entered, he was staring at his fingers.

Very slowly, he turned to look at her. That mischievous, cocky light in his eye was dead and gone. "What do you want now? I already told you everything I have to say."

"I'm thinking that you might want to say a little more," Kendra said. "There seems to be an explosive device attached to the airlock leading from the aquifer into the maintenance room."

"I wouldn't know anything about that," McCauley said, his long face had taken on a greenish pallor, but managed to stay neutral at the moment.

"I know, I know," Kendra said. "But there's something you need to know. So far, no one outside my staff knows what you have done."

"What I'm *suspected* of doing," he corrected, without much enthusiasm.

"Not to us. But here's the thing. My husband is down there.

And he is going to try to dismantle that bomb. And if he dies . . ." Kendra stopped herself, surprised at the lump that had materialized in her throat. "If Scotty dies, I swear that all and any evidence needed to convict you in the court of public opinion will materialize, and be mysteriously leaked far and wide. I further promise you that you will be moved, in a low-security vehicle, to a holding cell in the mining district. And there will be no pressure suit or emergency supplies in that vehicle." She leaned closer. "I promise you that that vehicle will never make it. It will break down . . . or be hijacked . . . or spring a mysterious leak. Look at me, Toby. *Look at me.*"

He forced himself to face her. Stared into her eyes, and blinked.

"We've played poker for years. I usually lose. You know me, Toby. I'm not a good bluffer. Am I bluffing now?"

Toby blinked again, and looked away. "What if I did have something to say?" The words came slowly, like pulling teeth. "What happens then?"

"I swear to you that if you can help us, you will be allowed to leave Luna. Health reasons. You'll have your career, and your reputation. I will have no reason to want you prosecuted . . . so long as you leave."

Toby said, "They brought their own detonator. It looked like an old wristwatch."

"Which door is mined?" Scotty asked, when Kendra was back on the line.

"Big Figjam said just the inner door. Our side. You should be able to enter the chamber, from your side." She ran down the rest of what she had learned from McCauley, while Scotty listened intently.

"What's the length of the tunnel?" he asked.

"Fifty meters. Why . . ." Then sudden comprehension. "Oh, right. Your breathing equipment is broken."

"We'll manage it, Kendra. I'll make contact when we're in."

"You be safe," she said.

He nodded, giving her a cocky smile. Then when she clicked

off he turned to Darla. "Can you hold your breath that long?" Scotty was already peeling off his pants.

"Hey, cowboy. I'm a mermaid, remember?"

Together, the two of them stripped until Darla was pink plumpness in panties and bra, and Scotty buff in briefs. "Fifty meters," Scotty said. "That's Special Forces stuff."

Darla poked a finger at his gut. "Ow. Smuggling drywall there? Good swimmer?"

"Yeah." He could hear the voice in his head clearly: But are you *that* good?

She nodded. "All right. Hyperventilate to get your lungs full. The trick will be to stay relaxed. Don't panic, and we might just get through this. We have to swim it, get into the chamber, and trigger the cycle. Can you do that?"

"Easy," he lied.

"Not to be a wet blanket," Mickey said. "But what if they've sealed the door? Or you can't open it?"

"Then we'll have to swim back," Darla said.

Her smile didn't mask the fear in her eyes. And suddenly, Wayne's heart broke.

Standing there in her underwear, shivering in the cold, Darla seemed so brave, so strong, so very beautiful to him. He went to her and held her. "When this is over. If we're still—"

"When this is over," she said. "I'm coming back."

"Right," he said. "Right." Wayne scratched his head, sighing. "Look. I don't know if it would make more sense for me to invite you down, or you to invite me to stay up here for a while. But I think . . . I think I'd like to find out what there is between us."

She laid the softness of her palm along his cheek, a fond gesture. "Sex," she said. "And right now, I could use a lot more of that. We'll work out the details later."

He sighed, deeply. "You've got it," he said.

And kissed her. And no kiss of his life had ever been sweeter, or more sincere.

For three minutes Scotty had been breathing deep and exhaling shallow. He gulped air, exhaled half of it, took another and then another until he felt full almost to bursting, and light-headed. Let it out. Then inhaled deeply again.

He and Darla nodded to each other, waved to their companions, and then dove.

The water was chilly but not freezing. If the power had been off here, the cold might have given him muscle-lock. The aquifer was intended for recreation. They must have sealed off part, and warmed it with induction coils.

He followed Darla's lead, diving deep into the pool, strong smooth strokes taking them down. His ears didn't hurt. Lunar gravity made for less pressure. The blue lights were mounted at the bottom, down through a forest of what simply had to be fake coral.

A startling sight: Seahorse-type creatures as big as real horses, anchored deep, motionless, waiting to play.

Ali's horses. Briefly he wondered: What was supposed to have happened here? How would the game have gone, barring pirates?

No time. He swam on: Darla was an eel, thank God, and seemed to know just where she was going, down into a tunnel halfway to the bottom. *Fifty meters.* All right . . .

He clamped his mind down on doubt and swam on.

Angelique clapped her hands together. "All right, everyone! We can't just wait for help. We need to prepare, in case the pirates arrive before the marines."

She looked up into the Game Master's cloud. "Xavier—what do we have in terms of control?"

"Just about everything," he said. "Including a few things that you would have picked up along the way."

"Good," she said. "I need all the help you can give us. We want to make the next few minutes absolute hell for the pirates, and hope that that's enough. It should be easy. When they drop into the water they'll be dead meat."

"Hold up a minute, love. I can't see them in the 'Little Wars' scenario. They may have used the other mirror."

"Other mirror?"

Something alive and frantic kicked in Scotty's chest, struggling to win freedom. Not pain. Not yet. But pain was on its way. And soon after pain, panic. Then blackness, and death.

Hewn from bedrock, the underwater tunnel seemed to go on forever, little rows of blinking yellow lights lining the sides like reflective speedbumps on an endless desert road. Fifty meters? Seemed more like five hundred. The more they swam, the farther away that door seemed. Had to be an oxygen-debt hallucination, but still he wondered: Could Kendra have been wrong? Was it possible she had misread the specs, sending him and Darla to their deaths?

Then he saw the end of the tunnel, blessedly close at hand.

Darla scanned it briefly, then punched in a code.

Every disastrous scenario imaginable flashed through his mind in those seconds. She had the wrong code. The pirates had sabotaged the door, McCauley had lied about their intentions. He would drown here in this tunnel, his lungs exploding as he—

The door slid open. They entered, and the door slid shut behind them. The world spun, darkness and blood pounding at his vision. When the water began to drain from the chamber he braced his arms and legs against the walls, lifted his head up above the level of the water, sucked, spat, and gulped air.

Damn, that tasted good. If he'd been the first man to drown on the Moon, Saint Peter might have laughed him out of heaven.

As the water was pumped out through the floor grill, Darla was already crouched at the inner door, studying a package composed of a bundle of red clay–like bricks bound with wire and anchored to the door with some kind of clear, hard resinous substance. A dial the size and appearance of a wristwatch was set into it, anchored with wires and covered with more of that clear resin. Darla's expression was glum indeed.

"Well?" Scotty asked.

"With the right tools . . . maybe. But I'm not sure at all. This isn't makeshift, like I'd hoped. McCauley said they'd smuggled up some kind of fancy timer, and he'd spliced it into a bundle of mining explosive." Darla had spoken with McCauley for almost a minute, and one tense, terse conversation it had been. "Someone knew exactly what they were planning to do, and smuggled a piece of equipment up from Earth. This"—she pointed at the watch—"started life as a wristwatch. The display is wonky. It's been seriously reprogrammed. They turned it into a movement sensor. I'm guessing that it's also sensitive to a range of other stimuli. Pure pro."

"Can you beat it?"

"Maybe," she said. She felt around her belt pod, extracted her multitool. "I'm not sure. Judging from this readout . . . I'd say it's not very forgiving."

"What can I do?" Scotty asked. "Is there anything I can do?" He was feeling useless, and there was no worse feeling in a crisis.

"Yes. Get the hell out of here," she said.

Scotty pressed his face against the fist-sized viewport. Through inches of composition plastic, he waved at the room on the other side.

A flurry of movement, and Max Piering appeared on the window's far side. Despite the tension, Scotty smiled, recognizing Professor Cavor's face shorn of facial hair. Piering motioned down to the communications link on the inner door.

Scotty felt nervous about triggering it. "Darla?"

"Go for it. I think McCauley told the truth about this whole setup."

He turned it on.

"How are you doing in there?" Piering asked. Scotty hadn't seen the man in years, not since shortly after the accident that had stolen his Moon legs.

"Not bad. Could be a lot better."

"Can you see the device?"

Darla nodded. "Looks like it's synched into the door. Mechanics, electronics—try anything, and it will go off. Boom."

"Can you deactivate it?"

"Same question, same answer. Maybe. With the right tools. All I have is my multi. I'm really not sure. But I'll try."

"What can we do out here?"

"Get back. Way back," she said. "In case I'm wrong." She

turned and looked at Scotty. "You, too, cowboy. I think they have more use for you up top."

Scotty nodded. He would have backed away from her, but the chamber was too small for any effective backing. "If you're sure."

"I don't think I'm sending you to a picnic, mister. Go on."

Scotty extended his hand, and Darla shook it, hard. Was she saying good-bye? "Good gaming with you," he said.

"Good gaming with you, too," she replied. "Take a deep breath."

37

Final Gambit

1841 hours

Scotty emerged from the pool, water thick as syrup sliding slowly from his face. The cool air bristled with magic. Angelique danced five feet above the ground, levitated by a pillar of light flowing from Sharmela's palms. He had to look very closely indeed to detect the tiny blur of the "real" Angelique, concealed in radiance.

Ali held both hands in front of him, projecting a wall of shimmering crystal. "I speak to the Gods of my fathers," he said, "who peopled the Earth in the First Days. Children of Air and Water and Earth. I call upon *Zarabanda,* God of iron, God of my fathers long ago, to give me strength! I throw off the colonial shackles, and step into my true power as a warrior of my people!" He held his arms up, waiting . . .

And waiting . . .

Nothing.

Scotty shivered, wiping himself dry with his shirt, and then slipping his pants back on. Soggy. "What . . . was that?"

Ali shrugged. "If this is to be my last stand," he said, "I want to die as a hero of my people, not just another African soldier loyal to one European crown or another."

"A little late to get political, isn't it? And . . . this isn't a game, Ali—"

The boy laughed at him, but the tone was bitter. "Oh, it's a game. This entire thing is a game designed to trap my father. He escaped their grasp, but I have been caught. You have been caught. All of you—"

The gamers ceased their practice to listen. Ali seemed to have grown somehow, easily commanding their attention. "All of you!" he said. "Whatever happens here today, know that Prince Ali knows what you have done for him. Know that I will not forget, and that I will not forget you, any of you."

Sharmela slapped his shoulder, hard. "Nor I you, young mage. You may have concealed secrets, but you have carried yourself with honor."

She extended her hand to him, and he took it. Wayne placed his hand atop hers. "All of us. We all came from distant lands, at the call of our Queen. And the adventure we have shared went beyond our dreams."

Scotty still couldn't quite believe what he was seeing. This wasn't a game! It was . . .

Oh, what the hell. Some games are played for very high stakes. This time they were betting every marble they had. If there was a right more sacred than the ability to choose the manner of one's own death, he didn't know what it could be. He watched as, one at a time, they clapped their hands down one upon the other in a vow of fealty. "We stand together," Mickey said, and put his hands down. Followed by Maud. And Angelique. They were a clan of a kind, making the very best of the very worst. Something dark and magical glittered in their eyes. For the first time he thought he grasped the logic of it all.

Angelique turned and extended her hand to Scotty. "Come on, big guy. Get in here."

Scotty hesitated, and then felt the voice inside him say: *Oh, why not.*

And he put his hand onto the pile. Win, lose or draw, this had been one hell of a game.

"And I," he said, impressed by the timbre of his voice. "A

mere thief, pledge my all in this mortal combat. We stand together!"

The others nodded, a circle of power, well pleased with what
they had wrought.

Xavier, a floating bald god, smiled down upon them. "I will
help where I can," he said. His expression grew more serious.
"And get ready. Griffin and Gibson, you are both thieves. Your
power is stealth. You would have found something right out of
Wells, given the right path—" Xavier jerked. "I hear them. Take
your places. The pirates are coming."

Celeste moved slowly, unwilling to take even the slightest
chance that some hidden trap or concealed antechamber hewn
into the lunar rock or constructed by Cowles engineers might
provide comfort and safety to her prey.

They were her prey now, especially that smug bastard Griffin.
Nothing else mattered. She would see them all dead, all but Ali . . .
if that was possible.

Kill them all.

Shotz, darling dead Alexander, would not have had that. He
would say that she had obligations to her men, to those who had
followed him in the name of a country that would never be. An
artificial island that might have been their home.

Madness.

She fought the sound of a giggle, a tickle in the back of her
throat that triggered the urge to laugh aloud. That would be insane, wouldn't it?

The five men remaining to her followed behind as they combed
the stage, this strange setting decorated like an English manor,
seeking signs of life. A game of some kind had been played here,
one for which the rules were uncertain. Cannons, strange toy
tripods and inanimate costumed grubs were strewn about, as if
awaiting commands for a new awakening.

"What is all of this?" Fujita said, crossbow cradled in his
huge hands like a child's toy. The wound in the big man's side
had been bandaged, but it seeped red. Still, he was more than a
match for three of these play-acting morons.

"More nonsense," she said. "I am tired of this fantasy. We will finish this, and go home."

No one dared disagree aloud, but she could read their expressions. None of them seriously believed that they were going home, regardless of what happened here.

They circled the room and returned to near the big entrance door. Standing between barber's mirrors, she saw two infinite lines of her own images . . . skewed. One mirror was ajar, just by a crack. "Here," she said.

Slow and steady. Their prey were bottled. There was nowhere to go. They could afford to be . . . careful. Thorough.

Just as Shotz had taught her, long ago. *Take care of the small things, and the large ones will take care of themselves.*

She looked through the open mirror and into a ramp. A water slide minus the water.

This was not the path they had followed coming up from the pool. There had been more than one route. Shotz had booby-trapped the other door, and this one had been concealed on both ends. So long as her prey was trapped, it did not matter if the last act of this strange story was played out in an English manor, or in the subterranean lunar pool.

But they were going to come out like bullets, into . . . what?

"Wait, Celeste," Fujita said, wrestling with the other mirror.

Gallop grew impatient, swung the butt of a crossbow. The mirror shattered. A stairway was concealed beyond.

"Go," Celeste said, and followed.

The stairway was so narrow that her broad shoulders brushed both sides. Fujita had to twist and turn and push to squeeze himself through. It dropped and twisted, and expanded before a door of what seemed gray stone.

The six pirates spilled through and fanned out fast.

Angelique crouched behind her stalagmite, watching. She blinked. Her contact lenses, useless for most of the game, flared to life so that a huge blue arrow danced above the heads of each of her enemies. Each arrow was indexed with weapon indicators:

crossbow, air gun. The woman Celeste was labeled *Leader* in fluorescent green—high score for anyone who could take her out.

The pirates fanned into the chamber, very alert, and spread out, maintaining an effective field of fire. Angelique looked around: Each of her team were also labeled clearly with an arrow. Pity that the pirates couldn't see it. She muffled a giggle, but allowed herself a nasty grin.

There was something else they couldn't see, and as they passed a man-sized stalactite they learned what.

The big Asian guy to the right of Celeste suddenly buckled. Angelique saw only a hint, a flash of light, but suddenly the guy was down, groaning.

And that was the signal! Suddenly, from all sides, bolts driven by crossbow and air pressure whizzed through the air. Only one of them found a target, the shoulder of a short, wide man to Celeste's right.

Celeste turned—a blur! Dear heaven that woman was fast! And fired even though she could see nothing. The air gun bolt disappeared, but they heard a yelp. Scotty's yelp.

Xavier, bless his black heart, had given them an invisible thief.

Scotty yelped as the dart hit his calf, the tip lancing through muscle and into bone. Swallowing a groan, he faded back. Xavier's magic had enhanced his thieving abilities, the capacity to hide in plain sight, but had been no protection against Celeste's dart.

He had taken out the big woman's wingman, but this wound put him out of the action until he could remove the dart and staunch the flow of blood.

Scotty leaned back against the stalagmite, gritted his teeth and pulled the dart out. He tore his moist shirt into strips, and bound his calf. If he focused his eyes carefully, he could find the shimmer in the air where Xavier's magic bent the light. Could Celeste see him? Had that been a lucky shot? The big woman peered in his direction, body tense, but without specific focus. So . . . some combination of luck and feral instinct.

The waters of the pool glowed in bands of light like a field of new snow reflecting an aurora borealis.

The pirates were goggle-eyed for a moment as the chamber expanded, became even vaster, until it seemed like the pool was an infinite ocean, the dry land merely an insignificant speck upon it.

And what an ocean! Its waves rose up and rolled toward them like a tsunami, and Miller screamed in terror.

"It is just an illusion!" Celeste barked, but the dart that blossomed in Miller's stomach was real enough.

Fujita whirled and fired blindly, once, twice . . . and got a satisfying scream in return. They had made someone pay. Not so dearly as they shortly would, but these . . . amateurs, who had ruined the plans of a lifetime, would pay more. There would be more screams. Oh, yes there would.

Two down. She knew she had hurt another one, the pain-filled squeal made it clear. And that left . . . five. Five to go.

"Damn!" Wayne squawked. "I'm hit!" His breath in her ear. Direction? Angelique peeked up over the plastic stalagmite, and saw Wayne's blue arrow shade to red.

"He's bleeding!" Maud's voice. Whatever calm they had been able to impose upon her was gone now—the panic was breaking through like a whale through ice.

Angelique heard a *z-zing!* sound and something flew past her eyes, lodging in the rock behind her. She threw herself flat, wondering how the pirates had seen her, knowing that Xavier's illusions were up against technology no gamer would ever have possessed. Their final gambit might be more final than any of them had anticipated. Certainly than they had hoped.

Then . . . *something* was crawling out of the water. It was *huge,* and oceans dripped out of its spiky fur. It looked like a mutated mooncow. Angelique realized she was looking at a male version of that creature, with giant jaws and claws.

It levered itself up, shook itself—damn, that was real water spraying around! She felt it!

The titanic beast headed straight for two pirates crouched

behind stalagmites. Its teeth tore and short cilia-like tentacles around its mouth grasped. The pirates screamed as they were hurled in all directions, bodies broken on the walls, impaled on stalactites.

And above the din, they heard a voice: *"Hold fast! It's a trick!"*

Celeste, damn her!

"We're about out of ammo," Angelique said.

Xavier's voice whispered in their ears. "I can force everyone into the water. Shall I? Angelique? *Everyone?*"

"Do it."

Darla was stumped. She had examined the bomb top to bottom, probed carefully, and knew that she was looking at death. The tamper switch was totally beyond her. If she tried to disconnect the wires, or remove the explosives from its anchoring epoxy blob, the damned thing would trigger. There was just no way, no way to stop it from . . .

And then she had an inspiration.

The former mermaid triggered the communication link. On the other side of the window, Max Piering picked it up.

"Got an idea," she said. "This thing is designed to trigger if you jostle it. And they did a damned fine job. What they didn't consider is that someone might want to set it off on purpose."

"What?"

"The timer. They concentrated on the motion sensor, but the timer can be engaged. I can set it for . . . four minutes. Get your people out of there. Up the stairs, at least thirty feet away, and above the water level."

He frowned. "What are you thinking of, girl?"

She managed a smile. "Mischief," she said.

Piering cleared out his men, and she extended the tip of her multitool's probe, and very carefully tapped out a two, a four, and a zero. Two hundred and forty seconds. This had to work. She didn't know what was going on up top, but it couldn't be good.

She gulped air, exhaled, gulped again, and again. She'd held her breath for almost three minutes on the way down here. In three minutes she'd be breathing air again. No need to worry about the bends, not in lunar gravity.

Darla took a last deep breath, and then let the water back into the chamber. It splashed around her, and rose to her shoulder.

At the moment the pressure was equalized, she triggered the bomb and dove back out the door. With all her strength she swam toward the Moon pool's distant blue light.

The walls of the pool chamber erupted beasts from a madman's dream, nightmares of tentacle and fang, furred and scaled and glistening pink wetness. Celeste held her ground, but three of the other five pirates flinched away. For the last minutes, the pool had expanded to enormous dimensions, and with the sensation of solid ground beneath their feet, the pirates had grown too confident.

Too much pool was exactly the same as seeing no pool at all. They misjudged their distance, and fell in, yelling obscenities—briefly. Then their cries were swallowed by water.

The pirates were infinitely better prepared for combat upon the land. Even in water, they outclassed gamers by a wide margin. But the combination of visual and auditory effects and strange water behavior confused them just for a moment.

And then it got worse. Robotic seahorses rose up from the water, gliding straight for the bewildered pirates. Nosed up against them in what should have been a friendly fashion, but the pirates reacted by shooting and stabbing, losing focus . . . and the gamers attacked them from behind.

Driven to extremes and knowing that this was their very last chance, even Maud jumped howling from the edge of the pool, holding a damaged air tank in her hands, bringing it down hard on Gallop's head.

He glimpsed the blow a moment before it landed, and managed to roll so that the metal cylinder scraped down his ear and glanced from his shoulder.

Then he had his hands on her. Maud screamed, as if suddenly remembering that this wasn't merely a game at all, that she may have made a critical mistake . . .

And Sharmela raised her arms, screaming: "Ouroboros! Serpent of light! Hear my call and join the fight!" A glowing band of light grew out of the water, coiling around the pirate's face, obscuring his eyes and vision. He panicked, thrashing, and released Maud.

"I'll 'ave you, asshole!" Mickey screamed, suddenly grabbing the man's throat from behind.

Another pirate grabbed Mickey from behind, and it turned into a four-way tussle, the special effects blinking as the computer tried to keep up with the constantly shifting holo-targets.

To call the results "chaotic" would have been a massive understatement. Pirates dove to get away from the grinning, attacking seahorses, and came up with water sliding in slow sheets from their faces, choking them. And right into the swinging fists of gamers who, while hardly professional, were certainly enthusiastic.

In water, there is little balance, and no traction to push against. Much of a professional punch or chop is a matter of gripping the ground or twisting the hips, and all of that was taken away from them, their aquatic environment more of a leveler than they might have thought.

Not enough, though. Mickey's nose was broken almost immediately, and he barely evaded choking by biting a slippery wet arm seeking his throat.

Darla burst half out of the pool, sweeping water from her face so she could gasp. Fair enough. Now get to shore before—

All about her were gamers and pirates locked in mortal combat. She had to reach shore before—but the blond demon was still on land, aiming a crossbow directly at her face. Darla let the water pull her under.

Elsewhere in the pool, Wayne struggled with a pirate who seemed half eel. Only the fact that robotic seahorses kept slamming into him from the sides kept the contest even vaguely even. Then Wayne screamed as the pirate's knife slashed his side, and he kicked away, trying to put distance between them.

The pirate, grinning, outswam him, and retracted his arm to strike—

And suddenly the world exploded.

In the history of the universe, there may never have been an explosion quite like this: industrial blasting–putty funneled through a fifty-meter tunnel into a natural aquifer in a low-gravity environment.

Under ordinary circumstances the shock wave would have been harsh. In this very special world it felt as if half the water rose out of the pool in a savage pulse. Water, gamers, pirates and robot seahorses all fountained into the air. Friends and foes alike, confused and confounded, screamed like frightened children as they flew toward the ceiling.

Up until the last moments before the explosion, the pirates had been swinging the tide of battle their way. Angelique had not taken to the water, preferring to remain on the land, waiting to make use of her last bolt. And then, perhaps, sell her life dearly.

Rivers of fire, assaults of monsters, wind and lightning . . . even an invisible man had merely slowed them down.

Now Angelique heard another scream, and it was her own. A blow to her head from behind, and she realized, sickened, that one of the Moresnot bastards had snuck up behind her. One of the pirates stood over her, drawing a bead with his air gun. Double vision told her that the ringing in her head was concussion.

Then the man grunted and went down sideways, knocked back by a flying dark body whose limbs were a cat-quick blur of action.

Ali to the rescue! The man rolled, punched, and Ali's head snapped back, blood rushing from his nose.

Angelique dove forward, and managed to grab one of the pirate's limbs, before his booted heel caught Ali under the chin, driving him back and up into the air, landing with a *woof*!

Then the pirate tied her into a knot. "Quiet, bitch, if you know what's good for you—"

Scotty saw his opportunity, and dove at Celeste. If he could stop *her*, it might put an end to all of this. But the instant he hit her she collapsed beneath his weight, went down with reflexes so fast it was like bouncing a ball off a wall. And his entire world was full of crazy woman.

She was strong, almost as strong as him, and to his alarm, quicker and more skilled, in some art he had never before encountered. It wasn't a blind brawl: Rather some kind of grappling art that was all head-butts and knees driving for his groin at the same time she was seeking crippling locks on his wrists and fingers. It was like being dropped into a sack with a rabid weasel.

Damn!

She tried to bite his right eye! Scotty jerked his head sideways, realizing to his dismay that she was winning. In combination with his wounds and fatigue, Celeste was just too much for him to handle. The world was spinning.

And then . . . the Moon pool exploded.

Water shot up in the air like a waterspout, a thunderclap that smashed against the ceiling and showered back down with a Moon-shaking *ker-whoom!* The shock wave forced Celeste to slacken her grip on him, as her eyes widened in surprise. Perhaps she'd thought it was just another special effect!

The heart went out of him. He knew what that explosion meant. It meant that Darla had failed, that she was blown to jelly, and it was over.

Something went black and red behind his eyes. *No matter what happens to me, this bitch is dead!*

He got two hands full of hair, and even as she sank her teeth in his forearm, rolled Celeste over and into the pool.

Scotty managed to drive his fist into her gut the moment before she hit, so that the air gushed out of her mouth even as he gulped a breath. In the water she panicked, struck out for the surface, but with all the strength remaining to him he rolled her under. Wiggled around her and clamped his legs around her waist as she pried at him, struggled . . . and then finally, blessedly, went limp.

Gasping, Scotty hauled her back up, in time to look directly into another gas-powered dart gun as the pirate triggered the bolt—

The shock wave lifted Darla out of the pool and into the air, almost gently, like an avalanche of foam. The combination of fatigue, oxygen debt and shock made the entire experience surreal. She watched men, women and molded plastic automatons flying through the air with the greatest of ease, saw it all in a kind of slow-motion tumble, rising, rising . . .

The water pushed her firmly into a wall, stunned but not really dazed. She held onto a rock projection that had missed her head by inches. Beneath her, a big Japanese man was about to step on Ali's neck. She dropped down, landing on him, and while he was twice her size, tumbled him back into the Moon pool.

Ali dragged himself to the edge of the pool and jumped in with her, and the three struggled and wheeled through the water, alternately gulping air as their heads broke the surface, and thrashing each other with fists and feet.

Finally, improbably, they both ended up on top, their feet pushing against the big man's shoulders. She felt his hands on her leg, saw the flash of a blade and realized he had had time to clear his mind and draw a knife, knew that she had made a terrible mistake and then . . .

He was *gone*.

Scotty gritted his teeth and prepared for the greatest pain of his life. Then before the pirate could loose a bolt, both of his feet were off the ground, and he was flying backward.

What the . . . ?

A stun bolt had hit the pirate in the middle of the chest. A non-lethal riot round fired by a big broad man rising from the pool. *Piering*.

More men and women rose, in rebreather gear, carrying riot guns. One dragged a half-drowned Japanese man from the water.

Help had arrived at last.

The siege . . . the *game* . . . was over.

··· **38** ···

Aftermath

2341 hours

Eventually the reporters were asked to leave the gamers alone. The survivors had been debriefed; the pirates were still being questioned. Now, finally, the gamers staggered, exhausted, into the makeshift gaming lounge. For a time they just sat in their chairs, wounded and pale and tired. Medics moved among them. They stared at each other, bandaged and bruised, and then grinned.

"Now *that*," Wayne said, "was a game."

"It would be just about perfect," Angelique said. "Except for Asako."

"Asako," Wayne said. "Shit. I'd almost managed to forget. Hey. Let's dedicate the game to her. I mean, for what it's worth, let's make her the biggest gaming heroine in history."

Sharmela managed a tired smile. "I think she would have liked that."

"I'll second that," Scotty said. "Woman was die-hard."

At his side, Darla wearily agreed. She and Wayne were draped around each other, touching, kissing and whispering as if there was no one in the room. She had almost drowned, almost been blasted apart, almost been knifed . . . almost drowned again. It was a wounded Wayne who had spotted and rescued her.

And to the rescuer went the spoils.

Scotty thought that there was something strong there, something that might last.

And that was fine with him.

Xavier swept into the lounge, followed by Wu Lin and Magique. "The IFGS has, for the first time in almost a decade, called this game a draw. We have an invitation to mount it again, in six months."

"Oh, no." Angelique rolled her eyes. "You have *got* to be kidding. That's not happening. I can't even afford, let alone—"

Xavier grinned. "Can't *afford*? Have you checked your bank balance? Do you realize that this game had the highest ratings in history?"

She looked at him dubiously. "Were we broadcasting?"

"Every minute. Everyone in this room is rich. And a couple of us are just absurdly rich. Numbers will be forthcoming, but think six or seven zeros."

"I'm already drowning in zeros," Sharmela said, sagged back into her chair, almost delirious with contentment. "Carnation Fit/Fat came through. I didn't know anyone really got that much money. For *anything*."

The gamers dissolved into talk. Scotty noticed that Xavier and Angelique leaned very close together, while Magique and Wu Lin looked on in approval.

Wayne approached. "Hey, Xavier . . ."

"Yes?" the little man said, looking up.

"You, uh . . . you came through for us. I owe you."

Xavier narrowed his eyes. "All right. Let's see just how grateful you are. How about the truth. Did you turn me in back at UCLA?"

"Did you take money to put Ali's drawings in the game?"

The two men stared at each other. "No," Xavier said. "I was stupid. My favorite writer wanted to collaborate with me, right out of the blue. But Ladd had a favorite artist, and he turned out to be a pseudonym for a Kikayan prince. I'm disgraced. I may never completely recover my reputation from that. Is that honest enough for you?"

Wayne paused. Then he nodded.

"Yes it is enough, or yes, you betrayed me?"

"Just . . . yes," Wayne said. He chewed at his lower lip. "It was the worst thing I've ever done. And I'm sorry. And thank you for saving our lives."

Xavier gazed at him, his own alien thoughts swarming behind the blue eyes. A silver serving-bot slid past them, with brandy snifters filled with champagne. Xavier plucked up two of them. "So, Mr. Gibson . . . shall we work together, and become even more ridiculously wealthy?" He held one of the snifters out to Wayne.

"You . . . would trust me again?"

"I trust no one," Xavier said. "I trust myself to know what a man considers to be in his best interest. I believe I understand you now."

Wayne accepted the offered glass. There was a tremor; his champagne foamed. Xavier tilted his in a toast, his arm around Angelique's waist. "Good game," he said.

Scotty tiptoed out of the room. No one would miss him, and he had things to do.

He found Ali in a com room, chatting excitedly with his father. The three-second delay seemed to have no effect on their enthusiasm. Ali saw Scotty, smiled warmly but turned back to his father and spoke in rapid-fire Congolese. The room had standard translation software, and Scotty slid on a pair of headphones, clicked his throat and said, "English."

"*Father! You gave up your throne for me!*" Computer generated speech, but it maintained the Prince's high register.

"*You are my son,*" the king replied. "*What else was I to do?*" He looked as if he had not slept in days. How long had it been since the game started? Sixteen hours? It seemed like months. "*And you made me proud.*"

"*Me?*"

"*I saw you fly! I saw you stand and declare yourself one with the Ancestors. I saw you at war. And I am not the only one. I believe millions of our people saw you, or will see you in the coming months.*" His father gave a sly smile. "*A father and son have much to speak of. Remember that democracy is coming to the republic. And in a decade, perhaps, a son returning home to lead his people, a great hero? Perhaps the republic no longer needs a king. But a president . . . ?*" The King finally seemed to notice Scotty's presence behind his son. "Mr. Griffin?" he said in English. "Come in."

"Am I interrupting?"

"Not at all. I must thank you for my son's life."

"I return him almost undamaged."

Ali laughed and fingered his nose, which looked like a squashed plum. The retired King's image said, "Perhaps even better than you found him. Your bill will be honored. I suggest you add lavish expenses."

"Did you come away with money?"

"Oh my, yes. Of course the new proprietors have a kingdom to pillage."

"They won't have as much as they thought," Scotty said. "I spoke to Foxworthy. Whatever you invested in the Moon has been confiscated to pay for the damage to the dome, medical expenses for gamers, fines, quite a lot of lost water . . ."

"Ah," Kikiya II's image said. "Is there anything that a deposed, but very wealthy king can do for the man who saved his son?"

"I . . . will think about that. It is always good to have friends."

"Indeed it is, Mr. Griffin. And you have most certainly made a new one."

It seemed a good time to leave.

Kendra awaited Scotty in her office, welcomed him in and closed the door. He noted the plaques and statuettes already boxed, and raised an eyebrow. Instead of an answer she gave him a kiss long and deep enough to make him forget his myriad wounds and bruises.

"Thank God," she said, crushing the lush length of her body against him. "I thought I'd lost you."

"I'm not that easy to get rid of," he said, and then winced as she squeezed him. "Careful there, careful! Watch it. That witch broke a rib, I'm sure. Where is she, anyway?"

"She and three of her little pigs are in lockup, under guard. Five more are in the infirmary, under guard. Three are in the morgue." She shook her head. "Wow. Don't mess with gamers, I guess."

"The infirmary. Is that enough security?"

"Not like there's really anywhere for them to go. The big Asian's in a coma. It might take a month just to work out jurisdiction. Some of our people just want to send them for a naked stroll in the sunlight. We won't let that happen, of course."

"What about the Frost boys?"

Her expression soured. "They . . . are a different matter. Traitors are worse than mercenaries. If they're lucky they'll spend a year on hazardous duty in the mines. Might make them work their way home."

"And what about Toby?"

"McCauley? On his way back to Earth. He helped us here, but he's lost all his holdings and is lucky not to be breathing vacuum."

"And you?"

She sighed. "Well, you can see I'm packing my office up. Fired." Kendra brightened. "But not leaving. Not yet." She looked at him suddenly. "Not unless you want me to."

"Me?"

"I'd go anywhere to be with you, Scotty."

"Well, then . . . let's just stay here for a while."

Her face brightened immediately. "I love the sound of that. I may have lost my job, but I'm still running for office, and with McCauley out of the picture, I'm a shoo-in. Cowles International might regret firing me. It's independence, all the way."

They kissed again. "So . . . let's say we decided to stick around. Think I could find a way to earn my keep around here?"

"I'm sure Piering can find work for a hero."

"Hero?"

"My hero," she said. And kissed him again. "Your parents will be here in a week. I'd really like something good to tell them."

"Good? Like what?"

"What do you think they'd like to hear?

"Ummm . . . maybe that we're working on some grandkids."

She grinned. "You call that work?"

"Lock your door," he said. "And we'll see."